The Catch

(Summer Nights Series book 1)

LAUREN H. MAE

To The Chat.

"The time will come when winter will ask you what you were doing all summer."

—Henry Clay

One

"**W**HAT DO I WIN?" CATIA Roday shouted over the screaming guitar of a cover band. Her best friend Dani was so close that their sweaty arms kept sliding off of each other, but the volume still made conversation cumbersome.

Dani tapped a manicured nail on her drink and pursed her red lips in thought. "I'll buy your breakfast tomorrow," she offered.

Cat considered the terms as she bent to gather her thick, heavy hair off of her neck, tying it in a knot on top of her head. Unfortunately, a man in a neon-green *Virginia is for Lovers* tank top took that as an invitation to stare down her shirt. She shot him a look to let him know he'd been caught, then spun away from him. When she righted herself, though, his eyes just slid to her ass.

Okay. She officially hated this place.

It was a long overdue vacation—a road trip down the coast to Virginia Beach to celebrate their friend Emma's upcoming wedding—but the club Dani had dragged them all to, with thumping dance music and skimpy outfits might as well have been Narnia.

"How is that even a fair bet?" Cat asked, gesturing to Dani's cleavage, barely contained in her dress. "Who wouldn't buy you a drink?"

Dani tossed her bouncy platinum curls over her shoulder. She didn't look at all as out of place as Cat felt. "Not a drink. *All* my drinks. Bet is I can drink all night without spending a dime."

Cat weighed the wager. For a potential free meal at their swanky hotel, why not? It was Dani's bet to lose. "Fine," she said. "Every time we get another round, you get a guy to buy yours, or breakfast is on you."

"Deal. Let's go." Dani spun on her heel, clutching Cat's wrist and tugging.

"Wait. What?" Cat sputtered. She planted her feet, but her flat-bottomed sandals were like ice skates on the sweat and beer-soaked floor. "This was your idea. I'm not playing."

"Stop being a wuss! You're the only other single one on this trip, and I need a wingman."

"Forget it. You can buy your own drinks, Dani. I'm not here to get hit on, especially not at this place. Look around you. Every guy here is trouble." She pointed to a circle of men openly ogling the bartender as an example.

Dani let go of Cat's arm and set her hands on her hips. "It's not about getting hit on. Think of it as beating these guys at their own game.

They're going to look anyway, might as well get a drink for it. It's like... feminist or whatever."

"It definitely is not." Her argument was cut short when the same man who'd been staring down her shirt approached them in a scent cloud of drugstore body spray and fake tanner.

"Ladies," he said, perusing them each from head to toe. He gave Cat a smarmy smile over his bottle of Michelob Ultra and hooked a muscled arm around Dani's shoulders. Now that he was close up, her first thought after *that shirt is ridiculous* was *wow, he's really short.* Being only five-foot-two herself, that was saying a lot.

Dani took one look at him and winked at Cat. She could not be serious.

"How are you two beautiful ladies doing tonight?"

"We're just fine," Dani purred. "How about yourself?"

"I sure am better now."

Gag! Cat kicked Dani's shin to show her displeasure, but she didn't react. Instead, she flipped her hair again. "We were just about to get a drink."

"Why don't you let me do that for you?" the guy said, his eyes squarely on Dani's ample chest. He gestured for her to join him against the bar. "I'm Brad."

"Nice to meet you, Brad. I'm Dani, and this is Cat." Dani spit Cat's name out through clenched teeth, attempting to get her to play along, but Cat had already checked out.

This was so typical Dani. They were supposed to be celebrating Emma. Couldn't they have a girls' night without bringing men into it? Yeah, she and Dani were the two single ones on this trip, but single for Dani meant something entirely different than it did for Cat. Cat was single on purpose because men—at the risk of making a sweeping generalization—sucked. And lied. Oh, and also ruined everything. At least the one she'd met, fallen in love with, and almost married.

Sure, he was one guy. She'd heard that argument before, but that's all it took to throw her entire life off course. Why bother spinning that Wheel of Fortune again?

Her chest did that familiar achy-angry thing it did whenever she thought of Micah, and she gulped her sickly-sweet cocktail to push it away. The thick, syrupy flavor only made her cough.

She felt an elbow connect with her ribs as Dani tried again to draw her into the conversation she was forcing with Brad. "So, Cat was just saying what a fun place this was," Dani said. *She definitely was not.* "Do you come here often?"

"I like to be wherever the pretty girls are," Brad said. "Looks like I picked the right place tonight."

This guy was something else. And, not for nothing, the way he was leering was setting off all sorts of alarm bells inside her head. She was used to the standard bullshit spinning that men do, where they tell you exactly what they think you want to hear in hopes you'll act against your better judgment. This guy, though, he was standing way too close and staring way too hard. He had "watch your drinks, girls" written all over him.

Cat looked around the bar, spotting the rest of their friends on the dance floor. Maybe she could use the Bon Jovi song blaring from the speakers to entice Dani to join them. Who could resist "Living On A Prayer"?

She tugged Dani's arm and pointed to the rest of the group, but Dani shook her head.

"What's with the shirt?" Dani asked Brad. "You look like you're ready to party."

Brad beamed with pride as if he thought that was a compliment. "And you look like you're ready to join me," he said, inching closer.

It was going to be a long night.

This wasn't his type of place.

Josh Rideout stood squished against the sticky bar, catching stray elbows into his back every time one of the frat boys behind him did another shot. He'd already had a beer and something pink spilled on his shirt while waiting for

Dylan, his best friend and purveyor of poor decisions, to order another round.

He scanned the club through flashes from the DJ booth and raised beer bottles—loud music, ten-dollar cocktails served in tiny plastic cups, girls who looked way too young to be wearing what they were wearing and dancing how they were dancing. Yeah, this was Dylan's type of place. That's how he and their friend Shawn had ended up at this dive that Dylan swore was the hottest place on the beach. Frankly, all of them being in their early thirties, Josh thought they were a little old for it.

This was the type of place where everyone was looking for something, and whatever it was that Josh was looking for these days, he was pretty sure he wouldn't find it here.

Dylan handed Josh an overpriced rum and Coke, then a beer to Shawn, and threw some bills down, stepping aside so the eager mob could take his place at the bar.

"Shit, man," Dylan said. He ran a hand over his dark, perfectly-gelled hair and whistled through his teeth. "You see that girl I was talking to? I think I'm in love."

"Yeah, we saw," Josh said, pushing away from the crowded bar to find a clear spot on the deck. "What about the girl from the last bar, Casanova?"

Dylan hated the nickname, which made it all the more fun. But seriously, they were at a bar that mixed drinks in plastic cups, and Dylan was dressed in trousers with the top buttons of his dress shirt undone like a model from a men's cologne ad. Who was he kidding?

Dylan smiled over his cup. "You know, you could stand to loosen up a little bit, Joshua. You're on vacation, remember?"

"Damn straight!" Shawn agreed.

Josh raised an eyebrow at the advice from his happily married friend, but Shawn only shrugged.

"I remember," he assured them both, taking a large swig of his drink.

They managed to hold on to the more comfortable spot as the crowd ebbed and flowed before them. Throngs of people pushed onto the deck when the music slowed, pulling back like the tide once the beat picked up again. At that moment, the bass from the speakers was vibrating through the floorboards, so they had plenty of elbow room.

Josh leaned against the railing and watched intoxication wash over the space. The clientele at this place was at least more entertaining than the shitty cover band if he had to find a bright side. There was a woman in cowboy boots and a miniskirt attempting to climb her way onto the stage, a bunch of rowdy twenty-somethings cheering her on. To his right, a couple was having a slurred argument over whether or not this was a "classic song."

It wasn't, but the guy was making some interesting points.

Past the couple, he noticed a pair of women having a conversation with a man who seemed to be enjoying it more than they were, considering the look on the dark-haired woman's face. They didn't know the guy—Josh could tell. Reading body language was one of the things he considered himself particularly good at. He'd spent a lot of time as a kid silently observing adults who were choosing not to say something outright, and this guy's unspoken intention was to continue this conversation with one or both of these women until well after last call.

The woman with bleached blonde hair seemed to be egging him on for her own amusement. Her friend, with the big dark eyes and light-brown skin, looked like she was trying to decide whether to be polite or deck the guy. He was on the smaller side—she could probably take him if he got out of line.

Dylan and Shawn started in on their typical armchair analysis of the upcoming Virginia Tech football season. Unlike him, the two were born and bred Virginians, so they tended to be more fanatical. Besides, he was a baseball guy. He sipped his drink while he half-listened to Shawn opine about their alma mater's defensive line until an awkward hollow laugh came from over his shoulder.

He turned back to where he'd been watching

the two women, noticing the blonde scanning the crowd behind her. She was searching for an exit. The man was invading her personal space now, and she was beginning to look uncomfortable. Her pretty friend was starting to look pissed.

Josh stood up straighter. He sized the guy up again, confident he could end the situation pretty easily if he needed to. At six feet tall, he would tower over this little snake of a guy. It would probably only take a stern look to send him on his way.

As he contemplated whether or not he should get involved, the blonde woman suddenly flashed her eyes in his direction. To his—and her friend's—surprise, she pointed a finger at him and waved. His back was against the railing, but he still turned over his shoulder, half expecting her to be gesturing to someone behind him.

She plastered on a wide grin, and walked the few steps over to where Josh was standing, hooking her arm through his. "There you are, babe," she cooed, dragging him to their circle. "I've been waiting for you to come back." She turned toward Snake Guy and smiled. "This is my boyfriend."

Okay. He was happy to help, but he wasn't expecting that.

Blondie squeezed his bicep, and her friend's scowl relaxed a fraction as she blinked at him curiously. He froze for a moment, watching those thick, black lashes flutter until Blondie nudged him.

Josh cleared his throat. "Sorry, sweetheart," he said, with his best boyfriendy smile. "There was a long wait at the bar."

The man they were trying to escape looked him up and down, his eyes narrowed. Seeing that she was unconvincing, Blondie ran her fingers over the stubble on Josh's cheek, giving him a look like she was contemplating kissing him right then and there to sell her story. He quickly wrapped his fingers around her wrist to stop her stroke, planting a chaste kiss on her forehead instead while he stole another glance at her friend.

She was even more striking up close. Her dark hair was pinned up in that way girls do it so that it looks intentionally messy, and she had a handful of freckles in the same color splashed on her face, like an artist with a paintbrush had flicked them there. He drank her in discreetly while she and Blondie argued with their eyes.

"It's okay, babe," Blondie said to him, leaning into his chest and wrapping him in an aggressive hug. "You're here now. I guess we should get going. Nice to meet you, Brad." She waved to the man and reached for her friend's arm. "Come on, Cat."

Cat.

Josh rolled the name around in his head while he allowed his new girlfriend to pull him away from the poor guy who was still standing there with his mouth hanging open. He'd never met a Cat before. It fit her soft, pretty face and dangerous eyes. Like an adorable kitten that you wouldn't be able to resist picking up and cuddling, even though you knew she might leave you a bloody mess.

She pushed ahead of them, her hips swaying beneath the sarong-style skirt she wore. He was staring so hard she could probably feel his eyes on her, so he forced himself to refocus his gaze past her shoulder at nothing in particular.

When they had sufficiently blended in with the crowd, Blondie released him. "Thanks," she said, using her palms to smooth his shirt over his chest. "You're a doll."

"No problem." He looked over her shoulder at Cat. She was smiling now, causing two little dimples to poke at her cheeks.

"I'm Dani. Let me buy you a drink for playing along."

"Josh—and it was no trouble. Besides, I already have one." He held up his cup of rum and melted ice, tapping it against hers.

"Let her," Cat said, surprising him with the way she met his gaze and held it hostage. "She owes you. Dani, get the man a drink."

He swallowed hard, his muscles feeling a little watery at the sound of her voice, bubbly and sweet with just a hint of a Spanish accent. She pulled her lip between her teeth, gazing up at him, and his heart thumped.

Dani looked back and forth between them. He didn't say anything. He really didn't want Dani to buy him a drink, but it occurred to him that he might be left alone with Cat for a few minutes if Dani took off for the bar. He was weighing the options when a hard slap landed on his back.

"Thought we lost you, man." Dylan slung an arm around Josh's shoulder, forcing him to break away from the staring contest he'd started with Cat.

"You found me," he said, his jaw tight. Dylan's ability to appear where he wasn't wanted should be on his resume. Josh was going to add this untimely arrival to the list of brotherly betrayals he liked to keep at the ready.

"You make some friends, Josh?" Shawn squeezed in beside Dylan, closing them all into a circle. "How's it going, ladies?"

"Excellent, thank you." Dani placed her hand on her hip and smiled.

The Shawn effect was undeniable. Big and burly with a crinkly-eyed grin, Shawn had a teddy-bear innocence that instantly put people at ease. Both women were already beaming at him in a way Snake Guy could only dream of.

Dylan, however, already had his prowling eyes on. Josh shrugged out of his embrace, taking a step back as they said their 'hellos'. He pretended to scratch his forehead, peeking from under his hand to watch his best friend introduce himself to Cat. He didn't usually engage in this kind of competition with Dylan, but something told him Cat might just be the exception to that rule.

He was pleasantly surprised, though, to find she didn't seem all that impressed with Dylan, even though he was giving her his most charming smile, his green eyes shining with sexual confidence. Cat smiled politely at Dylan and Shawn, then flicked her eyes back to his. He knew he should stop staring, but she wasn't looking away either.

He'd forgotten anyone else was there until Dani spoke again. "This is Emma and Sonya," she said.

He tore his eyes away from Cat to politely introduce himself to two women who had just pushed into the circle: Emma, a tall wispy brunette, and Sonya, who was equally thin, but in a strong, lean muscle sort of way. Both of them seemed to have caught the way he was looking at Cat, and they smiled knowingly as he shook their hands.

"Nice to meet you," he said. "Josh Rideout."

"It's Emma's bachelorette party," Dani said, bouncing her eyebrows.

Emma's pale cheeks turned pink under the light from the bar. "It's a pre-wedding girls trip. Bachelorette parties are silly."

"Right," Sonya said. She tossed her ponytail of dark braids over her shoulder and gave them an exaggerated wink. "And your fiancé is having a barbeque at his buddy's house."

"He is having a barbeque!" Emma exclaimed as if she'd heard this accusation before. "What about y'all? Celebrating something?"

"Celebrating being alive, ladies," Shawn said, tipping his chin to the starry night sky and taking in a deep pull of salty air.

"Dylan and I were here for work," Josh said. "We decided to make a vacation of it. Shawn decided to join us."

"I don't miss a party. Even if I have to invite myself."

Cat laughed along with the others at Shawn's joke, but she still hadn't said much. She sipped the remains of a cocktail with a paper umbrella floating in the top, studying the cast of characters that had followed him into their evening. Josh wished they would all find somewhere else to be and leave him to Cat, but it didn't look likely.

He tipped back his cup and swallowed the last of his drink, catching her gaze again over the conversation that had sprung up around them. Feeling emboldened by the rum burning in his chest, and her apparent immunity to Dylan, he stepped around Dani and Emma and pressed a finger to the back of Cat's arm.

"Cat," he said, trying her name out on his tongue.

She turned to face him, her chest just inches from his, and her chin tipped upward. "Hey."

"Would you let me buy you a drink?"

Cat brought her cup to her lips, draining it, then gave him a cautious smile. She was trying to get a read on him, he figured, after the situation with Snake Guy, and he wanted nothing more than to be a book that she could browse all night long.

"We still owe you," she said. "You should let me buy."

"You don't owe me anything." In fact, if Cat was going to give him her time, he might owe Dani drinks for life. "Please?"

"Okay, sure. You can buy me a drink."

Josh gestured for her to lead the way, letting his hand graze the small of her back as they wove through the crowd. She stood on her toes, leaning over the bar, and the bartender made a beeline for her. "Rum punch, please."

Josh held up two fingers and handed the bartender his card.

When their drinks arrived, Cat tipped her cup to his and smiled. "Thank you."

"You're welcome."

"That was kind of you," she said. "Helping us out with that guy."

"It was no big deal."

"Do you always go around rescuing girls at bars?"

"First time, actually. And you don't look like you need rescuing that often."

"Maybe not."

He took in the square of her shoulders, and her chin held high. He could already tell she was the type of woman who could make you melt or kick your ass, depending on how much she liked you. "I bet you could have handled that guy," he said.

"Probably, but I really didn't want to." She sighed wearily as a guy in a trucker hat elbowed his way into the space beside her and raked his eyes down her front.

Josh shot him a possessive look that he had no business doling out, considering he'd known Cat for about ten minutes. As insane as it sounded, though, he already felt some way about her.

Crazy or not, no one was going to look at her like that while she was talking to him. He angled himself between her and the crowd, and Cat settled into the little space he'd made for her. "This place is like a meat market," he said.

"Right? That's what I told Dani."

"That's what I told Dylan."

"So how'd you end up here?"

He groaned. "I was outvoted. You?"

"Pretty much the same." She smiled up at him mischievously, leaning into his arm. "Given how my night has gone so far, I guess I'll just have to take your word for it that you're the one guy in here who's not a total creep."

16

Josh laughed, narrowly avoiding spitting his drink out. She was adorable. "Come on now. Would Dani have dated me for these last few minutes if I was a creep?"

"Oh, you don't know Dani," she shot back, joining in his laughter. She turned her shoulders toward him and held her cup up to her neck, letting the condensation drip down her skin. *Jesus.* "So, what do you do, Josh? You said you were here for work."

"I'm an architect. We were down here for a training on windows and tropical wind ratings."

"Fascinating."

"It is when there's a hurricane."

"Mmm. Touché."

"What about you?"

"I work for a victim's advocacy organization." She paused to chew on her straw. "And I just finished law school."

Interesting. She was definitely a few years younger than him, but not young enough to still be in school. The way she said it indicated there was a story there. He added it to the list of things he found intriguing about her. Like the way her eyes had a fire to them, even though her fingers were twisting nervously in the fabric of her skirt. He imagined it would be a cold day in hell before Cat admitted any weak spots.

"I bet you'll make a good lawyer," he hedged.

"Oh yeah? Why do you say that?"

"You have this whole take no prisoners thing

going on." He shrugged. "I don't know. I can just see it."

Pink crept up her neck, and she dipped her head. "I've heard that before. Not as a compliment."

"I meant it as one."

"I know you did."

The crowd around them grew thicker with more people vying for the bartender's attention, and Josh noticed the music had had a change in mood. A familiar guitar riff, something he recognized from high school dances and romantic scenes on television, filled the air. The strobe lights tapered off into a warm glow. The ambiance seemed to shift to accommodate the moment, and he wasn't going to waste it. "Do you think my girlfriend would mind if I asked you to dance, Cat?"

She smiled and leaned into his ear, making his blood rush. "I hate to be the one to tell you this, Josh," she said. "But I think you're about to break up."

Josh followed her gaze and saw Dylan's arm wrapped around Dani. He wasn't surprised in the least. "Is that a yes?"

"Okay. Yes."

They waded through a wall of sweat and hot breath to an open spot on the floor, and he pulled her into his arms, letting his fingers splay over the soft curve of her hip, his other hand holding hers against his chest. With her waist tucked in the crook of his arm, she felt smaller than before. Her head barely brushed his chin, and he imagined the way he'd have to duck down to kiss her, how she'd push to her toes to meet him. The way her eyes kept darting to his mouth made him think that maybe she was picturing it too.

"So, where would you be if you weren't outvoted?" he asked. "What's a Cat type of place?"

"A Cat type of place is my couch with a glass of wine."

"Sounds exclusive. What's the dress code?"

She laughed. "Pajamas, of course."

"Do they serve food?"

"There's a drawer full of takeout menus. Open all night." The scent of coconut and sun-kissed skin drifted from her, and he leaned closer, chasing it. "I'm making myself sound like a hermit," she said. "I'm not."

"No. I get it. That sounds like a good place." He squeezed her hand and tipped his head to the couple beside them. The man's hand had disappeared under the woman's skirt while they danced and slobbered all over each other. "Though, not as romantic as this."

"Oh my God. Gross."

He laughed at the way her face twisted. "Don't judge. We might be watching a true love connection here."

"Or the beginning of a very bad decision. Oh, no." Cat clutched his shirt nervously as they watched the man attempt to dip the woman. Miraculously, he pulled it off without dropping her, but it only made him more confident. His next move was way too advanced, and his dance partner lost her footing and stumbled on her wedge sandals. Her cup sloshed toward them.

Josh twisted Cat out of the way, but his shirt caught most of the woman's drink.

"I'm so sorry," the woman slurred.

"It's fine," he said, waving her off. He looked at Cat. "Are you okay?"

"Yeah. I'm fine. Your shirt..." She was trying to look concerned, but he could tell she was holding in a laugh.

He shrugged. "That's the third drink that's been spilled on me tonight. I could probably sell this shirt with a straw at this point."

She brushed her fingers over the wet spot on his stomach, and his skin prickled with electricity. "Does anything upset you?" she asked.

"What do you mean?"

"You just seem very chill. Look at you." She ran a finger over his brow. "You don't even have any frown lines."

He laughed, then captured the hand she'd just touched him with and held it. He'd learned not to sweat the small stuff a long time ago, but he couldn't imagine getting upset about anything while he had her in his arms. "Well," he said, pulling her closer. "My shirt aside, I'd say all in all, I'm having a pretty good night."

She grinned, her nose scrunching adorably,

her tongue pressed into the back of her teeth. When she rested her cheek on his shoulder, he was sure she could feel his heart beating. A pang of disappointment lodged in his chest. This beautiful girl had his pulse racing, but he was on vacation, hours away from where his real life took place.

"How long are you here?" he asked, bracing himself for the answer.

"We leave the day after tomorrow."

"And then where?"

Cat let out a regretful sigh, as she blew out her answer. "D.C."

"Really?" He stopped swaying for a moment to squint at the top of her head.

"Yeah. You?"

"Ferry Island. About an hour east of the city."

Cat looked at him with the same cocked eyebrow she'd given Snake Guy, except with far less malice. "That's not a Maryland accent."

"It's not, but that's where I live."

"So we both traveled two-hundred miles to end up at the same sweaty bar on the same little stretch of sand? How?"

He shook his head and huffed out a laugh. A lifetime's worth of good fortune was the only explanation he could come up with.

Cat still looked floored. "Where are you staying?"

"Comfort Suites... Dylan picked it."

"We're two hotels down; The Tidal Inn. Tall one with the white balconies."

"I saw it from the beach this morning," he said, as the song came to an end. He prayed for another ballad, but the beat picked up, and the crowd filled in around them. Sonya appeared on the floor, pulling Emma behind her, and the two started dancing beside them. Emma playfully bumped into Cat with her hip, forcing Josh to loosen his hold.

Cat gave him a wistful look, and the air in his lungs started to thin. His heart took off in a sprint. "Can I see you tomorrow?" he shouted over the music.

"I assumed you were going to ask me to go home with you tonight." She flashed a sexy smile that broke his forehead into a sweat, and his mouth dropped open, his words stuck like cotton on his tongue. "I would have said no," she amended with a laugh.

"Right." He nodded humbly and laughed with her. "Glad I went with my plan then." Her two friends worked to surround her and take back her company, but he held tight to her hand until he had his answer. He wasn't letting her disappear.

Cat looked him up and down, and her smile straightened like a spell breaking. "Like I said, we're on the same little stretch of sand. If you want to see me tomorrow, you will." With that, she allowed Emma to pull her into an intoxicated dance embrace, gifting him one more smile over her shoulder before turning away.

Josh felt a hand on his elbow, tugging him in the opposite direction of the hole that Cat had left in her wake, and he turned to see Dylan nodding his head towards the door. He reluctantly followed his friends, the three of them pouring out onto the concrete pathway that connected the bars and hotels on the water's edge.

"Thought you were gonna get yourself some tonight, Josh," Dylan said as they set off in the direction of their three-star hotel. Shawn snickered beside them, having had too many drinks to inject his usual wit into the conversation. "You had that intense look you get when you ain't fucking around. I thought for sure Shawn and I would be getting ourselves some earplugs from the concierge and sleeping on the living room floor."

"I'll see her again," Josh answered, not wishing to go where Dylan was headed with this conversation.

"All right, bro. Just remember what I told you. Vacation!" He simulated a sexual act with his hands and hips, laughing at his own humor.

"I got it," Josh answered, glancing up as they passed Cat's hotel on their walk.

Two more days.

Two

RINKING PINK COCKTAILS WITH LITTLE umbrellas was never a good idea. Cat knew this. She was a gin and tonic girl—simple, sophisticated, suitable for all seasons. The drink had never let her down. Last night, however, she'd been coerced into a more vacation-worthy concoction that left her head pounding and her mouth tasting like it was covered in soap scum.

It also left her with the memory of someone slow dancing with a stranger, swooning over his charming banter like a schoolgirl, all the while calling herself Catia Roday. But Cat didn't drink fruity drinks, and Cat certainly didn't swoon.

She had, though.

Josh Rideout. He was almost too handsome to look at with his insanely blue eyes that practically glowed in the dark club, and that adorably out of place Northern accent that turned her knees to jelly. Swooning was an understatement. It was more like all of the oxygen in the room had deserted her, and she'd gone temporarily insane. She couldn't stop staring at him, mouth agape, like a lunatic. He was so pretty, and there was something about the way he laughed that felt like Christmas morning, and chocolate cake, and the summer breeze all rolled into one. People should pay money to hear that laugh. That laugh could solve world hunger.

But heart-stopping laughs considered, her behavior had been entirely un-Catlike. What the hell was she thinking? Okay, she knew what she was thinking. *Jesus Christ, those eyes.* But what was she doing? She was at a sketchy beach bar, not Junior Prom for God's sake. Holding hands and leaning her head on his chest—yup, girly drinks were the devil.

She knew better. She'd given Dani the same speech minutes before she met him. Men like Josh, with their perfect faces and sweet words, were nothing but trouble and heartbreak. Not to mention the fact that he only lived an hour from her. She hadn't even given that little coinkydink her proper Cat freak-out yet. The low hum of her hangover started to surge into full-blown nausea. If there was one thing she did not need in her life right now, it was Josh Rideout.

Luckily, morning had come, and she'd come back to her senses. She would just put the whole thing out of her head and—

"Cat!" Sonya shouted, interrupting Cat's self-flagellation. She was pacing around the living room of their two-bedroom suite with a clipboard, looking like a cruise director, while the rest of them were barely functioning.

"Sorry. I'm listening."

"Good. On the agenda today is breakfast, the beach, lunch, more beach, then dinner and dancing."

"You needed to print that out?" Dani asked. Her feet were slung over the arm of the loveseat, and her head was in Cat's lap. Cat snickered quietly, careful not to disturb her own aching brain.

Sonya was taking her maid of honor duties seriously like she did everything else. She was a nurse manager, youngest in her office, and the helm of the ship was the natural place for her, but she had a tendency to take things too far. The clipboard was exhibit A.

Sonya flipped her braids over her shoulder, unfazed by Dani's attitude. "I printed a list of restaurants to choose from, and tonight's entertainment schedule for all the clubs around here. We are not missing a minute of fun googling places to go." She turned her attention to Emma, who was leaning on her elbows, sipping water through a straw. "Right, Em?"

Emma groaned.

"I think that's about all any of us have in us today, anyway," Cat said, giving the bride-to-be a sympathetic look. A quiet day on the beach, no pink cocktails, no stunning blue eyes.

"Perfect. Everyone up and at 'em. We're meeting in one hour for breakfast." Sonya glanced at her phone for the time, then scratched a line off her paper. "Make that brunch."

Once they had all showered, changed, and forced food into their vengeful stomachs, Cat was starting to feel like she could actually make it through the day. The temperature hadn't given up since the night before, continuing its climb toward unbearable, and the water and the sea breeze were calling her name.

The four of them made the short trek from the lobby to the beach, and Cat glanced down the sand at the hotel where Josh was staying. She pushed in front of Sonya, leading them in the opposite direction of the Comfort Suites, and kept walking until she could barely see it, before picking a spot.

"So, this is the plan until further notice right, Sonya?" Emma lowered herself onto the towel she had laid out and pulled her thick, black Wayfarer sunglasses over her eyes.

Sonya made an excited little shimmy with her shoulders. "Until the sun goes down and the night heats up, girls."

Emma groaned at the mere mention of another night out, and Dani plopped down beside her, burying her blonde head in the crook of her arm.

"I'm feeling good," Sonya said, crossing her long brown legs out in front of her. "You feeling good, Cat?"

"I'm feeling like a million bucks." A greasy breakfast and a couple of Tylenol, and she was back to her old self. Of course, even with the fruity drinks, she did tend to pace herself a little better than Dani, and Emma was always letting their wilder friend influence her.

"I mean, I'm not jogging on the beach in the scorching heat good," Sonya said, nodding down the sand with her chin. "But then again, I never was."

Cat tipped her aviators up to see who Sonya was gesturing to, and her whole body flushed with recognition. Josh and Dylan were out for a late morning run and headed straight for her.

Josh spotted her almost immediately, his stride faltering as their eyes met. He grabbed Dylan by the elbow, forcing him to stop, and pivoted in the direction of their row of towels. Dylan was shirtless, but Josh wore a tight white t-shirt, soaked through with sweat. The moisture spread across his broad chest, tapering into the shape of a V on his abs, like an arrow drawing her eyes downward against her will.

"Hi, Cat," he said.

"Hey," she said. "What a coincidence."

He was out of breath from his exercise but still managed a blinding smile. "I guess it was meant to be."

"You mean you weren't out here combing the beach for me?"

"It's still early," he said. "I wanted to give myself a chance to win without having to cheat … but I would have."

And just like that, her insides were mush again. What the hell was wrong with her? She tried her mental switch again—on and off, on and off, like testing a burnt out bulb—but it was no use. Her body kept reacting to him. She could actually feel her cheeks stretching from smiling so hard.

She dropped her sunglasses back on her nose, hiding behind the mirrored lenses. "This is pretty impressive," she said, waving a hand between Josh and Dylan. "As you can see, we aren't faring as well this morning."

"Shawn is still passed out on the floor beside the couch," Josh said. "So you're doing better than him."

Dylan was pretty quiet at the moment, and Cat had to guess they were probably doing better than him too.

"Do you have any big plans for the day?" Josh asked. He eyed Emma and Dani, still prone and motionless.

"This is pretty much it."

"We're renting some jet skis after lunch." He pointed to a row of brightly-colored tents at the end of the pier where all kinds of water sports equipment were on display. "You guys should come with us."

Dani's head popped up from the sand. "That sounds like a great idea."

The sweat that had been gathering on Cat's brow started to turn cold. Running into Josh again was beyond her control, but setting up a date was out of the question. She'd made the decision to put him out of her mind, and she meant it. Though, she sure was having a hard time getting her mouth to say the words.

She turned to Sonya, figuring she could consult the clipboard and explain their strict schedule, but her wonderfully conspicuous friend just stared back with a tight-lipped grin and wide eyes, looking as eager as Josh was to hear her answer.

"Um," Cat stuttered. "This is sort of a bridesmaid thing, so... Sonya planned it."

Her ambiguous reply flickered across Josh's face, and Cat felt an elbow hit her ribs. "You know what?" Sonya said, her eyes dancing with amusement. "I think we have plenty of time to fit that in."

Josh's mouth shot up into a delighted grin that sent Cat's tummy into a series of flips and handsprings she remembered from the night before. She gave Sonya her most murderous look. "All right," she said, still stabbing Sonya with her gaze. "That sounds fun."

"Great. Our reservation is at one." He pointed

again, and the muscles in his forearm flexed deliciously. "Red tent. We'll see you there."

"See you there." She swallowed hard. This was a terrible idea.

Once Josh and Dylan had taken off for their hotel, Sonya drove her fist into Cat's arm and cackled annoyingly. "Look at you!"

Cat grabbed a book from her bag and attempted to slide down next to Emma, but Sonya wasn't about to let her off the hook. She yanked the paperback out of her hands, tossing it behind her.

"Hey!"

"Start talking," Dani said, as Sonya blocked Cat's attempts to retrieve her book. Now Emma was up too. They were all staring at her.

"Talking about what?" Cat leaned back onto her towel and adjusted her bathing suit top, telling herself her stomach gymnastics were the result of her determined hangover, not seeing Josh again.

"About you and Hottie From The Bar," Sonya said.

Dani peered at her over the sunglasses perched on her button nose. "You were flirting with him. You two hit it off with that slow dance last night, Kit Cat?"

Traitor. Dani was supposed to take her side. It was the roommate rule: in a group, whomever you've lived with previously gets shotgun in your car, gets dibs on any of your clothing or accessories, and automatically has your back in these types of gang-ups. Cat and Dani shared a dorm for three years and an apartment for two more, but her memory of the rules seemed to be failing her.

"It was fine," Cat answered coolly. She threw an arm over her eyes, content to doze in the sun if she couldn't have her book.

Sonya was less content. "You're very smiley for just fine."

"We're on vacation, lounging on the beach with a beautiful view. What's not to smile about?"

Sonya crossed her arms over her chest and raised an eyebrow. "And it has nothing to do with your new friend?"

"Like I said, just enjoying the view."

"Bet you twenty bucks I end up bunking with you two tonight," Dani said, gesturing to Emma and Sonya.

Sonya laughed. "This is Cat we're talking about. You're gonna lose twenty bucks."

"Stop it, Dani," Cat said. "I have no intention of pulling a *you* on this trip and hooking up with some random guy."

"You could stand to take a page out of my book, Cat. What's it been? A year, maybe more? Like you said, you're on vacation. Have some fun."

"I am having fun," she insisted. Why were they always accusing her of not having fun?

Dani flicked a t-shirt at her. "Well, have some more!"

The last thing Cat needed was to be more like Dani. She could say that because Dani was like a sister. She was closer to Dani in most ways than she was her real sisters, given that they were ten and eight years older than her. That devil-may-care attitude was a front. Dani had had her heart broken too because that's what happened with things like this, whether you admit it or not. People always want something different than what they say, and that's why this game with Josh wasn't going any further than a quick ride on the back of a jet ski with a cute guy. *A cute guy who she hadn't stopped thinking about since the night before.*

"I told him I'd see him later," Cat said, closing her eyes. "And I will."

Three

"Y'ALL EVER RIDDEN ONE OF these before?" Dylan ran his hand along the nose of a neon green Kawasaki, tipping his sunglasses to inspect it. He'd perked up since they last spoke, and he'd obviously showered and spackled his hair with product.

Josh stood knee-deep in the water beside him, looking effortlessly handsome like he might roll out of bed that way every morning. Cat allowed herself to explore that image for a minute while she watched Dylan stroke the big machine.

Josh's other friend Shawn was up the beach, sprawled out in a folding chair that looked miniature under his frame. He'd looked as though he'd been forced from the room against his will, though it would probably take a team of horses to drag a guy his size anywhere.

Emma had spotted him first and saw her opportunity. Without a word, she'd set her towel down beside him and bowed out of the adventure portion of the day. Now the two of them were sharing a package of water crackers, and a Bud Light that Shawn had sworn was a secret hangover remedy. "Hair of the dog, honey," he'd said, making a get on with it gesture with his hand. "Can't have you missing your own party 'cause of a little over-indulgence." He was retired Navy, he'd told them proudly, so he had some experience.

"I've been on one," Dani said. Dylan tossed her one of the life vests he had hanging off his arm, then threw one to Sonya.

"The real question is: have you ever driven one?" Sonya said, snapping her vest in place. "I don't need to die in paradise because you're wing-manning for your buddy over here." She waved in Josh's direction, and Dani and Dylan both laughed.

Cat did not.

"Sonya, you're a nurse," Dani said. "We'll be fine."

"That doesn't mean I can save a drowning victim."

"I was a lifeguard through college," Josh said. He'd been quiet since they arrived, standing there with his big arms crossed over his chest, listening to Dylan crow. Cat got the feeling it was a familiar dynamic. "I guarded at the campus pool and taught surf lessons in the summer."

She'd known him for all of twelve hours, but the anecdote snapped into the image Cat had been drawing of him with a perfect click. "I knew you were the white knight type," she said.

He gave her a long, crooked smile, then waded further into the water to pick up the two vests that were sitting on what was presumably his ride for the day. It was a much less flashy, but striking, navy blue. Fitting.

Instead of tossing the vest the way Dylan had, Josh held it open, tilting his head to beckon her over. It was silent, simple, and goosebumps swept over her whole body when he did it.

She slipped her arms through the vest, and Josh reached around her from behind, snapping the straps into place. Then he spun her around and tugged on the shoulders, testing the fit.

Cat's knees went wobbly. What exactly was it about him that was causing the invasion of butterflies swarming her insides like the eighth plague?

Josh shrugged on his own vest, and she pretended to be straightening her bathing suit while she secretly peeked at him from behind her aviators. Between their height difference and the darkness of the club, she'd only been able to study him from the shoulders up the night before. By the time she'd caught a glimpse of his face, practically doing a double-take at his perfectly arranged features, she'd been too close to do a full inspection without getting caught.

He was in good shape. Not surprising, since she'd witnessed his morning workout. A light sprinkle of chest hair shaded his toned pecs, and a darker trail led from his belly button down into his shorts. He wasn't a Greek God type, but he was cut in all the right places, and the way his arm muscles bulged as he adjusted the tie on his suit made her taste buds flood. He looked like somebody's really hot husband, or a picture a co-worker might have on their desk of their exceptionally handsome son—someone real.

"You wanna hop on?" he asked.

Cat hesitated. A couple nearby was getting situated on their own jet ski, and it suddenly occurred to her how close she was going to have to sit to Josh while they shared a ride on this thing.

Dani was already on the other jet ski, though, while Sonya walked around it, inspecting it like it was one of her patients. There was no going back.

"You need a hand?" Josh asked Cat as she attempted to step on by grabbing the throttle and lifting her foot.

"Nope."

The jet ski bobbed and tilted as she hoisted herself up. Josh stepped closer, but to his credit, he didn't insist on helping.

Once she'd climbed somewhat awkwardly onto it, she scooched to the back and watched Josh jump up in one athletic motion, swinging his leg over the seat in front of her. The back of his life vest pressed the front of hers, and even though there were four inches of foam between them, it felt way more intimate than their dance the night before.

He pressed the ignition, and the jet ski hummed, vibrating beneath her seat.

Sonya was still in the water.

"Dylan will be careful," Josh said. When she still didn't move, he said, "You want to ride with us?"

Cat pasted on a *get your ass on this jet ski* smile, but Sonya's desire to challenge Cat was stronger than her fear of Dylan's driving.

"Thank you, but I can't leave Dani alone with the sharks."

"There are no sharks out here," Dylan said, watching Dani's ass as she bent to give her hand to Sonya.

Sonya skewered him with her eyes. "Mm-hmm."

"Let's go out to the sandbar," Dylan said to Josh, pointing to a blurry blob way in the distance.

Josh nodded and revved the gas making the jet ski lurch in place. Cat reflexively gripped the sides of his vest to keep herself upright.

Dylan took off first, Dani with her arms wrapped around him, and Sonya clutching the back of her seat.

"You ready?" Josh asked over his shoulder, raising his voice to speak over the engine and the splashing waves.

"I guess."

"I promise no tricks." He placed his hands

over hers and moved them higher up on his vest. "We'll just take it slow."

"Slow is good," she said. Sonya was getting way more than murder eyes when they got back to dry land.

The sandbar was empty, peaceful compared to the main beach, and Cat allowed herself to relax just a fraction as she sank her toes into the rippled sand and watched the surf form little tide pools all around them.

The ride over had actually been kind of fun. Josh had kept his promise—no tricks—and the noise of the water and the motor kept her from having to say anything coherent. Now, though, they were walking alone on the far end of the oval-shaped bar. Dani, Sonya, and Dylan were just offshore, taking turns diving off of the jet ski.

Josh pushed his sunglasses into his hair and wiped a bead of sweat from the back of his neck.

"Sure is hot today," Cat said, inwardly groaning at her lacking conversational skills. She was much better at this with a few drinks in her. Not that she cared. She wasn't flirting.

Josh replied with a wide grin, though, as if she were. "Perfect day to be on the water. We might be able to see dolphins from here."

"Really?" Her excitement got the better of her,

and she sounded way too giddy. "I've just never seen one."

Josh stopped walking and turned her toward the water, pointing over her shoulder. "Keep your eye on the horizon," he said. "Watch for them jumping."

She did what he said, but she found herself stealing glances at him instead, his hands on his hips, looking out at the sea with a peaceful look on his face. The clouds had turned into thin wisps, unable to accomplish the task of offering any shade, and the light reflecting off the water made his nut-brown hair look lighter than it had the previous night. It gave his appearance a certain easiness, like a lazy Sunday morning. An image popped into her head of him lounging half-naked in bed, that thick wavy hair of his a mess from a night of being tugged on by greedy fingers.

Woah. Okay, Cat. That's enough of that.

"So, you surf?" she asked, casting her eyes back out to dolphin hunting.

"Since I was a kid. I was teaching lessons by the time I was eighteen."

"Wow. You must be good."

"Pretty good." He gave her a smile that said that was a modest assessment. "What's Cat short for?"

"Catia."

"Catia." He repeated her. Sort of. His accent made it sound more like *catcher* without the R.

It was absolutely adorable. She considered officially changing the pronunciation right then and there.

"It's Ca-tee-ah," she corrected him, rolling her tongue in a way she knew he couldn't replicate.

"That's not what I said?"

"Try again."

"*Catia.*"

She shook her head, laughing. "It's hopeless."

Josh laughed now, too, shrugging. "Nah. I just need to keep saying it. Over and over and over."

He looked down at her with this soft smile and something in her shoulders loosened. Something she hadn't even realized was permanently wrenched tight. She could definitely listen to him say her name a few more times.

It was Dylan's voice she heard next, though, calling to them from offshore.

"Hey, lovebirds," he yelled. Josh gave Cat a long-suffering look, then waved at his friend. "Enough sunbathing. Let's see what these things can do."

"Where do you want to go now?" Josh asked when they'd rejoined the group.

Dylan pointed. "Let's race to the buoys."

Cat held a hand above her eyes and squinted at the finish line. She could barely make it out.

"I'll wait here," Sonya said.

Dani hoisted herself up onto Dylan's jet ski, her blonde ponytail dripping. "Sonya, what are you going to do? Bob like a seagull until he comes back?"

Dylan winked. "If I come back."

"No one is getting left," Josh said, grabbing their vests from the sand where he'd dropped them. Cat took hers and followed him, this time letting him offer her a hand up onto the jet ski.

Sonya finally relented, climbing up behind Dani, and Dylan taxied his jet ski until they were side by side, gearing up like a racehorse bucking the gate.

"Count of three," Dylan said, then he nudged Dani and grabbed the throttle.

Dani held three fingers up like one of those ring girls in a boxing match. She made a chopping motion with her arm as she counted. "Three. Two..."

Josh leaned into Cat's chest and tipped his head back, so his mouth brushed her ear. "You trust me?"

"Not even a little bit."

Josh laughed, his chest shaking beneath her fingers where she held onto his vest. As much as she wanted that to be true, it wasn't. She suspected he knew that.

"One!" Dani yelled. The nose of their jet ski lifted as Josh gunned the gas. Cat held on tight, pressing her forehead into Josh's back, and clenched her eyes shut. Wind kicked up the surf as Josh accelerated, and the spray stung her cheeks. They hit a large wave, her tailbone smashing into the seat, then another that made the nose of the jet ski dive as they landed, pushing her even closer to him. If that were possible.

The engine whined, then Josh shifted, and they bounced again. She had to squeeze her thighs around him to keep from being thrown into the ocean, and her body couldn't decide if she was turned on or terrified. Now that she couldn't see him, and he wasn't doing that thing where he looked at her like they had lifetimes between them, she was reminded that she didn't even know him. Here she was putting her life in his hands. It would serve her right to die out here.

But just as Cat was devising a plan to come back from the dead and haunt Sonya and Dani, the engine throttled down, and the painful spray of water petered out. She dared to open her eyes and saw Dylan still riding away at top speed, his middle finger raised high above his head, while Josh curved them in a gentle arc away from the wake to where the surface was smooth and glassy.

He cut the engine and let the machine bob in the water.

Cat blinked at him, wiping wet strands of hair from her forehead. "You didn't want to win?"

"I wasn't done sunbathing. Why? Did you want to win?"

Dylan's jet ski was heavier with three riders.

There wasn't much chance of them losing. But she certainly didn't want to die trying.

"Losing is safer," she decided. She plucked her sunglasses off her face and attempted to dry them on one of the little ties of her bikini bottoms. "And staying with the lifeguard."

Josh took the glasses from her and used the hem of his shorts instead, puffing a breath on each lens, then polishing. "You think Dani and Sonya are okay? I can tell Dylan to take it easy."

Cat could hear Sonya's squeals as Dylan jumped over a large wake, but really, she deserved it for making them do this. "As long as you think he can handle that thing."

"He's fine." Josh handed her back her sunglasses, then unbuckled his vest, laying it over the handlebar. Again with zero danger of slipping or falling overboard, he stepped capably onto the running board and dove off the side. He disappeared under the water, and Cat twisted in her seat to watch him resurface.

"Come in with me," he said, running a hand through his hair. It curled like crazy in the salty water.

She looked down at herself, still perched on the jet ski, fingers clutching the straps on her vest as if those little strips of quilted nylon would keep her from doing anything stupid.

She threw her leg over the seat so she was sitting side-saddle and let herself slip toward the water, her butt hitting the running board before she splashed in and her vest jerked her back up.

Okay. This was fine. She could float here with him and enjoy the bright blue water, that sly little curve to his lip that screamed heartbreak. Like the sun, she just wouldn't look too long.

"Can you swim?"

She nodded, and he helped her take off her vest, tossing it on the seat of the jet ski next to his.

"Much better." He cupped his hands and splashed water onto his forehead, leaving little droplets of water beading like diamonds in his luxuriously long lashes. When he ran his hand over his face, though, something else caught her eye, making her forget all about watching his biceps contract. On his left hand, rubbing at the stubble on his jaw, was an unmistakable white band of skin around his ring finger.

Cat's heart sank. There it was, the proverbial other shoe drop. Even though she'd seen it coming a mile away, she felt a little sick. Like someone was squeezing her stomach in a vise. *See!* she wanted to scream at Sonya, at Dani, at herself. *You've already gotten close enough to be disappointed!* She knew there would be a catch, but apparently, Josh was a top-tier asshole. And thanks to Dani and Sonya, now she was stuck in the middle of the ocean with him until he felt like taking her back to shore.

"So," she said, her disappointment turning to

an eagerness to tell him exactly what he could do with that smile. "Are you one of those guys who goes on vacation and takes off their wedding ring so they can have a little fun for a few days?" She pointed to his hand, and confusion pushed down the corners of his mouth.

He brought his hand up and stared at it while she waited for some sort of stuttered out lie. But her well-practiced *screw you* scowl evaporated when his full, pink lips formed a sort of melancholy smile instead.

"First summer it's seen the sun," he said. He looked like he was explaining to himself why he was still forced to wear a reminder of what was obviously an unpleasant memory. "It was last fall when I took it off."

Something sharp tapped her sternum as she realized her mistake. "I'm sorry," she said, recoiling from her own insensitivity. "It was shitty of me to assume that."

"It's okay. I'm sure women have to put up with that kinda thing all the time. I'm divorced, though." He swallowed hard and shrugged. "Guess it took eight years to make that mark, it's gonna take more than a little time for it to fade."

"Eight years is a long time." She studied his face, guessing he had a handful of years on her at the most.

He must have read her mind.

"We were really young," he said. "Things look

a lot different in your twenties than they do in your thirties."

That was for sure. She'd had the exact same thoughts as her twenties dwindled, leaving a lot of hard lessons behind.

"Anyway, she decided she'd be happier with someone else, and she left to start over with him."

"Wow," she whispered. "I feel really bad for bringing it up."

"Don't. She figured it out first, but she was right."

"That's awfully magnanimous of you." Of course, she didn't know the whole story. People were always telling her there were two sides to everything. Still, she found herself angry on his behalf that he should just be expected to let it go because all's well that ends well.

Josh looked out past her shoulder. His mouth twitched into a half-smile, but he couldn't maintain it.

"I might sound a little more magnanimous than I feel," he admitted.

"They say forgiveness brings you peace," she said. "I don't buy it."

"You sound like you're speaking from experience."

"Everyone has a story."

"Well, now that I've passed the *not a creep test* and the *not married test*, maybe you can tell me some of yours."

Cat's throat burned as a bitter memory swirled in her belly. "It's not all that different, really. Someone promised me something once, and they didn't mean it."

"An ex?"

"Yup." She almost laughed at how simple she could make it sound, her whole life screeching to a halt, but it was enough detail for this conversation.

The ocean swell rocked into them, and Josh clasped her elbow, keeping them tethered. "How about we talk about something lighter?" he said.

This time his smile made it all the way to his eyes, and the tension the conversation had brought to her neck released. Lighter was good. Talking about anything but Micah was good.

"What do you want to—oh my god!" Something slippery brushed against her calf, and she kicked her feet and screamed, launching herself at Josh.

He grabbed ahold of the running board, and caught her with his free hand, searching her face. "What is it?"

"Fish! Or... I don't know." She hooked her legs around his waist, so whatever it was wouldn't mistake her feet for lunch.

Josh fought off a laugh, and her cheeks started to burn. She looked down at the way she was clinging to him, suddenly wishing she still had that vest on. Her heart was still racing from the conversation about Micah—the intimacy she'd let build between them—and now her chest was pressed against his, sans foam barrier, and she could barely pull in enough air.

"Is it gone?" he asked.

She slowly stretched out her legs, and when she didn't feel anything swimming around down there, she breathed out. "I think so."

He didn't let go, though, and since she was there and already looking foolish, she slid her hands down the slope of his arms, stealing a touch. Her fingertips glided over the drops of water beading on his sun-warmed skin, exploring the curve of his biceps, the tight cording of his forearms.

Josh tilted his head, his smile straightening, and his eyes dropped to her mouth. He was going to kiss her, and her whole body was betraying her—her fingers squeezing his arms, her chin tipping without her permission. She just wanted to see how those full lips felt on hers, that dark stubble on her cheek. Just one taste.

Josh raised an eyebrow—a silent ask—but just when she'd resigned herself to bad vacation choices and things she could blame on sunstroke, a hum that she'd been vaguely aware of while she was hypnotized turned to a roar.

Then a wall of water rained down on them.

"Time's up!" Dylan called over his shoulder as they sped by.

Josh let her go, wiping the water from his face while she rung out her ponytail and forced her heart from her throat. He took her hand again, holding it beneath the water. "What's your plan tonight, Cat? Can I see you again?"

She stuttered. Whatever spell she'd been under had been broken by their impromptu shower, and now she only wanted to get back to shore and forget how she'd almost just kissed a stranger in the middle of the ocean. "Like I said, Sonya has us on a schedule," she said, deflecting. "But it's a small area, maybe I'll see you around." Her words were breathy, her pulse pounding. She was not pulling this off.

Josh's eyes flashed with amusement. "You're going to make me search the whole strip for you?"

"It's not that big." She grabbed his wrist, checking the face of his expensive-looking diver's watch. "Dylan's right. Time's almost up."

"Yeah," he said, his smile fading. "Okay."

Four

"**Y**OU GONNA CALL HER?" DYLAN asked as he ran a hand through his hair for the umpteenth time, preening for the mirror.

Josh grabbed a slice of pizza from the delivery box on the coffee table, stretching out as much as he could on the hotel room's half-sized couch. After they'd dropped Cat and her friends back at the beach, they'd wasted the rest of the afternoon nursing mild sunburns, and watching baseball and drinking beer in the air conditioning. Now they were waiting for Shawn to get back with a bottle of scotch he'd promised them after inviting himself to stay on their couch for the weekend.

"I will if I don't run into her first," he said. "It's not a big place." Though he hadn't agreed when Cat had given him that line. She'd been flirting, giggling even, and he was sure that in that brief moment when she was trying to escape a fish, and he'd gotten to press her body against his chest, she was going to let him kiss her.

But the minute he'd asked to see her again, she'd shut down.

When he'd asked if he could at least have her number, he wasn't sure she would have said yes if Sonya hadn't have been standing there, fixing her with a very loaded stare.

Dylan grabbed his wristwatch off of the bathroom counter, having finally settled on an outfit, and came to sit in the chair across from Josh. "This doesn't really feel like a Josh thing to do," he said.

"What's that?"

"Chasing a girl. It was always the other way around in college." Dylan transformed his voice into a feminine lilt and pursed his lips into one of those duck faces girls make. "Who's your friend *Josh*?" he sang. "The one who barely looked in my direction all night. I think I'm *madly* in love with him."

"You're just jealous."

"Damn right, I'm jealous. I'm out here working for it, man."

Josh laughed. Dylan was always working for it, and to his chagrin, Josh's lack of effort tended to attract the opposite sex just as easily. A girl he'd dated in college once told him he was classically handsome with the kind of bone structure that women were programmed to seek out in a mate. She was an anthropology major, and he'd frankly found the comment creepy as hell, but he couldn't deny he gave Dylan and his meticulously groomed good looks and smooth talking a run for his money just by standing there. It was fine by him, though, because unlike Dylan, he'd never been one for the thrill of the chase. Seemed to him, having to chase someone's affection from the get-go only meant that you needed them more than they needed you. That was a feeling he knew all too well.

Cat, though. There was something about her that he couldn't leave alone. She'd seemed hesitant today, standoffish even, and that would normally be enough to make him cut his losses, but the wall she had up was full of little cracks where they kept connecting—moments where she looked at him like she felt the same undeniable pull between them. Like last night on the dancefloor, when she'd let her head rest on his shoulder with a vulnerability that was at complete odds with her previous toughness. Or earlier, when they were walking along the sandbar, and she'd watched him, studied everything he did, openly checked him out. Those sunglasses weren't keeping her secrets like she thought they were.

He might not have noticed it, the way she was struggling with herself, if he hadn't seen her ready to skewer that guy Dani had them caught up with, or how she so quickly dismissed Dylan's well-rehearsed charm. She'd hinted at something in the water too. *Someone promised her something*, she'd said. That could mean a million things, but he got the feeling it was bigger than she let on, and that it was directly related to her skittishness around him.

She hadn't dismissed him, though, and it was enough to make him want to prove to her he was worth her time. He'd been shaken the minute he saw her, with her dark hair and eyes that he wanted to swim in, and when she'd said they lived an hour apart, it was like the universe was finally settling its tab with him. Maybe he was chasing this girl, but he wanted her, even if it meant breaking some of his own rules.

"I've just never seen you make the effort," Dylan continued. "Definitely not since Sarah. I was beginning to wonder if you still had a pulse."

Josh pictured Cat's face blushing pink and smiling at him, her legs wrapped around him in the ocean, and he felt his blood quicken. "I guess things change."

"You look like you need a drink, sweetheart."

Cat felt a warm body press against her back and her teeth ground together. She and Emma had been standing near the stage, listening to a band warm up for maybe ten minutes while they waited for Dani and Sonya to get back from the bar, and this was the third guy who'd found it appropriate to touch her. The big rock on Emma's left hand was like a forcefield that they all bounced off of, landing in front of Cat instead.

She turned over her shoulder to see a fairly handsome face looking down at her. Straight teeth, tan complexion. *Not wearing a tank top.* This place was a little classier than the club the night before, but that just meant the bad lines came in more expensive packages.

"My friend is getting me one, actually," she said, waving him off.

"Male or female?"

"What?"

"Your friend? Is it a boyfriend?"

She thought of the guy from the night before, finally getting the hint after Josh's pretend boyfriend act. "Yup," she said. "Boyfriend. We're practically married. I should probably go find him."

She tugged Emma's arm through a set of doors to an outdoor deck. The music was much softer outside, the metallic notes of an island melody dancing with the flickering light of the tall torches in each corner of the space. The back of the club ran along the shoreline, and below them, there was a large swath of beach roped off with a few picnic tables set around in various spots. High-top tables dotted the balcony where tiny white lights were strung in rows above them.

"He was cute," Emma said, looking back over her shoulder at Mr. Perfect Teeth.

"He'll find someone else to spend his money on." Cat's eyes did another involuntary sweep of the faces around them. She'd been doing it all night as if Josh might appear if she thought about him one more time. Like some really hot Beetlejuice.

Emma polished off her drink and set the glass on an empty table, giving Cat a smile that could only be described as a mixture of pity and thinning patience. "Okay, listen," she said. "I know everyone was joking around down at the beach, but I think you should give this Josh guy a chance."

Cat blinked. Did Emma acquire mind-reading powers? She actually wouldn't be surprised. "What brought that on?" she asked innocently.

"You're looking for him."

"I most certainly am not," she lied. "And I spent the whole day on a jet ski with him. I'd say I'm giving him a chance."

"So why didn't you agree to see him tonight?"

Emma's tone was conversational, but Cat knew when Emma gulped the last of her wine, she was about to get a famous Emma Dawson couch session. Sure, Emma had her masters in psychology and worked as a family therapist, but didn't her actual patients give her enough work? Did she really need to psych-judge her friends in her free time?

"Emma. Don't."

"I know you, Cat. You're trying to find some-thing wrong with him."

Actually, she *had* been doing that, and she'd come up empty, which maybe annoyed her more than if he'd just been a jerk from the start. Figuring out what lurked behind Josh's nice-guy act was exhausting. Way too exhausting for vacation. "If I find something wrong with him, it will be because there is something wrong with him. Not all guys are like Adam."

"Not all guys are like Micah, either," Emma said, her voice melodic, as if she were explaining away the existence of the boogeyman to a frightened child.

Emma's placation and the mention of Cat's ex had her glancing at the railing and wondering if she could survive the jump. She did not want to talk about Micah again.

"Adam's not perfect," Emma continued. "He can't keep a secret to save his life, he likes playing video games, despite being a grown adult man, and he would probably order pizza every meal if I didn't cook, but I saw the way Josh looked at you. That's the way Adam looks at me. That's why I'm marrying him. You can't go wrong with being looked at like that for the rest of your life."

"Now we're talking about the rest of my life?" Cat laughed, genuinely amused. This was why Emma couldn't be trusted for advice. Emma met Adam at freshman orientation and they'd been naming their future children together ever since. Her life was an all-you-can-eat buffet for the ravenous little romantic parasites that lived in her brain. When she'd told Emma where Josh lived, her eyes went all doughy, as if fate and a birthday wish had conceived a child and placed its little cherub body gently into her arms. That was ridiculous, though, as Emma often was when it came to these things.

Sure, finding out Josh lived an hour from her seemed like a bit of a mind blow when they were sharing a dance in some faraway bar, but that was fairytale stuff. Kissing him in the middle of the ocean was fairytale stuff. The real world was full of dirty little details that the fairytale leaves out. Promises get broken. Compromises turn to resentment. She knew what havoc love could wreak on your life. Anyway, the serendipity of it all was even more evidence to support Cat's skepticism. Things that seem too good to be true always are. There's always a catch.

"I didn't come here to meet a guy, Em. It's literally the last thing I want to do. We're here to celebrate your wedding; to celebrate you. "

"Nope," Emma said. "You're not doing that. I wasn't kidding when I said I didn't want a bachelorette party. This is just as much your vacation as mine. I'm not going to be your excuse." She sighed. "Cat, I know you're scared of going down that road again, but you can't be alone forever. Take a chance. Have a little fun. Who knows? Maybe it will turn into something else."

"I don't want it to!" Cat felt her cheeks burn. Emma didn't get it. None of them did. Taking a chance on Josh meant setting herself up to be disappointed and embarrassed when she put her trust in him and he eventually broke it. What was *fun* about that? She'd already done that with Micah, and she'd lost a lot more than just her pride.

So what was she doing? Why had she been scanning every place they went, looking for Josh? And why had she been picturing that lopsided grin of his while she was getting ready to come out tonight? It needed to stop. She was so close to putting her life back together. She couldn't get pulled into another mistake.

"Don't you remember what I gave up the last time I took a chance on *something else,* Em?" she asked. "You have your own practice, Sonya just got promoted, Dani's on her way to making partner at her firm. Me? I'm still clawing my way back from the mess Micah left. I'm twenty-seven, and I just finished school. I'm studying for the bar exam while working fifty hours a week because *something else* ruined my life. I'm done with men, and that goes double for ones I meet in a bar."

Emma's face fell. "Okay, Cat," she said defeatedly. "I just don't want to see you waste an opportunity to find happiness again. It won't always be this way for you. You'll catch up, and I'd hate to see you find yourself alone when you do."

Dani and Sonya finally found them, crossing the deck with a round of drinks and matching secret smiles.

"I can handle alone," Cat said to Emma before the other two could hear. "And I'm done talking about it."

"Hey, Catia," Sonya said. She handed Cat a cocktail, her eyes sparkling. "Don't look now, but your man just walked in."

Cat looked over Sonya's shoulder, and there he was, his hand in the pockets of his shorts, an easy grin on his lips as he laughed with Dylan. After all of her protests and denials, her whole body sighed in relief.

Josh spotted her as soon as they walked outside, and he nearly pumped his fist in relief. It had only taken him two bars and one god-awful jazz club before he finally found her on the balcony, leaning her elbows on a high top table. Her fuchsia shorts glowed like the sunset against her warm brown skin, and she had a black silk blouse tucked into them, the sleeves rolled up to her elbows, and the buttons open low. The somewhat conservative top hung off of her curves so perfectly, it might as well have been a piece of lingerie. He licked his lips involuntarily, trying his hardest to be gentlemanly while undoing her remaining buttons with his imagination.

Emma, Sonya, and Dani were with her, and they all turned in his direction.

"Ladies, we meet again," Shawn said, crossing the deck and throwing a friendly arm around Emma. Josh cringed as Shawn made himself comfortable, but Emma didn't seem to mind.

Josh wasn't interested in them, though. "Hey, Cat," he said, touching her elbow.

"Josh." She stepped toward him immediately, and her thick black eyelashes fluttered. He bet if the lighting were better, he'd be able to see her blushing again. "I guess it is a small place," she said.

"Nah, this time I really was looking for you." Her lips parted in surprise at his boldness, but if he was going to chase a girl, he might as well do it. "No paper umbrellas tonight?" he asked, pointing with his beer at the clear cocktail in her hand.

"That might have been a mistake."

"They usually are."

"Well, where were you when Dani was ordering them for us?"

"Probably talking Dylan out of the same thing." She dipped her head to hide the girlish grin that spread across her face. He was going to get another one of those if it took him all night, but he really wanted to do it alone. "Can we talk?" he asked. There was a clear spot on the railing at the other end of the balcony, and he tipped his head to it.

Cat glanced at her friends, but they were all laughing at something Shawn was saying, paying them no mind. Josh could have kissed him.

She nodded and followed him. When they got to the railing, she leaned over and breathed the strong salty air through her nose.

"This is better," he said, letting his hand fall next to hers on the railing. He fingered her bracelet while he spoke, turning the little beads with his thumb. "How was the rest of your afternoon?"

"Relaxing." She reached up, brushing her fingers across his face. "You got a little sun."

"I did. I was rushing to get to you, and I forgot to put sunscreen on."

Cat shook her head at him, and the pinkish-gold shimmer on her eyelids sparked. "Are you always like this?"

"Like what?"

"It's like you're feeding me these perfect lines, but I get the feeling you're just telling the truth."

He leaned his elbows on the railing beside hers, letting their shoulders graze and their body heat mix. "I don't have any lines. Dylan's the smooth-talker, and Shawn is the funny one. I just say what I mean. There's less confusion that way."

"Being able to trust what someone says is worth a lot more than a suave delivery," she simpered.

He got the feeling she was testing him with that, and he wished they could find a quieter place so he could whisper every truth he knew into her ear.

"You know, this is my first vacation in five years. If it wasn't for Emma getting married, it might be another five." He watched the ends of her ponytail flit on the breeze, her chest rise as she took another deep breath.

"Well, I'll have to thank her then, for getting married and putting us on this same patch of sand."

"You should. She also told me to give you a chance. Said you seemed like a nice guy."

"And Dani introduced us. You've got good friends."

Cat laughed with him at the group effort that was keeping them circling each other, but as if she'd caught herself spilling a secret, her smile quickly disappeared. "Really, though," she continued, "I work a lot, and studying for the bar takes all of my focus. Doesn't leave much time for other things. Vacations... dating."

"I work a lot too," he said, ignoring her obvious attempt at an excuse. She wouldn't be out there with him if she wasn't at least a little curious about the chemistry they seemed to have. "Owning a business is a 'round the clock job."

"So, you get it."

"Sure. I just never found that work kept me from doing what I really want to. Truth is, I haven't wanted much else lately... until now." Now he was spilling his own secrets, but he couldn't seem to stop. Not while she was looking at him like there was a chance she could be convinced. "I wasn't going to stay this weekend," he said. "After the conference. Dylan made me, called me a pain in the ass. He said he was tired of me being afraid to enjoy life a little."

"I'm not afraid," she shot back, firmly enough that he could tell he'd hit a nerve. She took a sip, then pointed her glass toward him. "You know, sometimes that little voice inside your head telling you not to do something is experience, or... or intuition. Sometimes you should listen to it before you listen to Emma—" She paused at her slip, her eyes going wide. "I mean Dylan."

"Sure," he said, wondering what exactly Emma had said that had her riled up. "Sometimes, though, it's just... I don't know. Comfortability. Stasis." He shrugged. "In my case, anyway. I'm only talking about me."

A little line formed on her brow, and she pulled her bottom lip between her teeth. She was considering something, and he'd give anything to know what it was.

"Vacation and the real world aren't the same," she said quietly.

He brushed his thumb over her cheek and felt her temperature rise beneath his fingertips. "This feels pretty real to me, Cat."

She covered his hand with hers, holding his palm to her cheek, and for all his confidence when he'd called her over here, he wasn't ready for it. He stood there, letting her appraise him, her eyes narrowed and bouncing around his face while he tried to look earnest and worthy. When she tipped her chin ever so slightly, temptation stampeded through his veins. He wasn't going to kiss her at this bar, though, to the soundtrack of club music blaring from inside, surrounded by a bunch of people getting sloshed and trying to get laid. He wasn't a pro, but he had a little more game than that.

He forced himself to let her go, taking a sip of his drink to occupy his mouth.

Maybe he could convince her to go somewhere else, a walk on the boardwalk, or even just a quieter bar. He was trying to think of a way to ask without sounding like he was trying to take her home when Shawn's voice sounded from behind him, booming across the balcony.

"Look who I found!" Shawn said, addressing the rest of the group following behind him, their foreheads all slick with sweat from time spent on the dance floor.

"Emma is going back to the room," Dani announced.

"Why?" Cat turned to her friend, her brow pinched in concern.

Emma sipped from a cup of water, her face looking even more pale than usual. "I tried to make it, but I'm still paying for last night. Besides, we have a full morning, and I'm not going to be any good for it if I don't get some sleep."

"You know you're getting old when your hangover lasts into the night, Em," Dani said.

Emma yawned and waved her off. "Y'all stay out. I'm serious, I don't want to see you back at that hotel room before you're ready, but I have to sleep."

"You can't walk back by yourself," Shawn said sternly. Captain O'Toole was already counting the four women as part of his ranks.

"It's not far."

"Josh and I will walk you," Cat offered, surprising them all. No one more than him.

Sonya narrowed her eyes, sizing him up as if she was deciding whether or not to grant her permission.

"I'll bring her right back," he said, pushing aside his shock. "I promise."

"Or don't," Dani said. "She has no curfew tonight."

"Thank you, Cat," Emma said, setting her empty cup on the table and hip-checking Dani as she walked by.

Sonya poked a finger into Cat's shoulder. "You call me if you aren't coming right back. I mean it."

Josh offered his hand to Cat, and she took it. "Of course, Sonya. I promise."

Emma pulled her phone out to call her fiancé as soon as they stepped onto the street, still bustling with the late-night activities of people on respite from their real lives. The glow of replica gas lamps and the fluorescent glare from the trinket shops lit the night sky, and notes from every genre of music danced out of the clubs giving the air its own pulse.

The change in the atmosphere seemed to massage Cat's shoulders loose, and her lips turned upward into an easy smile. "Are you having fun?" Josh asked, using the crowd as an excuse to pull her closer to him. He still wasn't sure why she'd suddenly decided to steal off with him, but he was going with it.

"I am. I don't think I want to go back to the bar after we drop Emma off, though."

His cheeks shot up in a grin. Even better. "Where do you want to go?"

"Let's go swimming."

He tipped his head down to look at her, one problem nagging his brain. "Sonya looked like she would hunt me down if I didn't return you."

"I'll call her. Come on, let's go."

"Where are you going?" Emma tucked her phone in her purse and joined them. They arrived in front of the lobby of Cat's expensive hotel, and the scent of the saltwater found them again, bolstering her idea.

"Josh is going to take me swimming." Emma gave her a curious look, but Cat kept her eyes on his. "Go get changed and meet me back here, okay?"

He looked over his shoulder at his hotel

two buildings away, then back at Cat. She had grabbed Emma's hand, already starting in toward the door.

"I'll meet you in the lobby," he called after her. "Don't go anywhere by yourself."

"I promise."

"I'll be back in ten." He took off in a half jog toward his hotel.

Five

CAT HAD ALWAYS PRIDED HERSELF on her will-power. Well, not always, but ever since she'd learned her lesson. She didn't get caught up in romantic moments. She didn't do things just because they felt good. But when Josh had touched her face and looked down at her mouth with those gorgeous blue eyes and then pulled away, a thought that had first nudged her brain in the ocean that day begged to be heard again: It had been entirely too long since she'd been kissed. A lot longer than that since she'd rounded any of the other bases. Staring at Josh all day, letting him stand that close and touch her like that, had been a frank reminder that that wasn't sustainable.

She wasn't trying to fall in love like Emma suggested—the thought of that made her feel dizzy and a little nauseous—but maybe she was selling herself short by not taking advantage of a different opportunity. She'd sworn off love a long time ago, but with that decision, she'd inad-vertently sworn off sex. Josh was gorgeous. Like really, unfairly good looking, and he made no attempt to hide his interest in her. When he'd been the third person that day to tell her she didn't know how to have a good time, another thought had materialized. Maybe she *could* do the no-strings-attached thing.

Sure, she'd seen Dani's hidden disappointment after these encounters, but that was because deep down Dani always had higher hopes. Cat didn't blame her. People weren't made to have sex with no emotional attachment, at least not for the long term, but Cat wasn't getting her hopes up over anyone anymore, and there was no long term about it—she was leaving the next day. So what was the harm in using Josh before he used her? She'd have messy, sandy vacation sex with this gorgeous man, and then he'd never call her again, but that would be okay because that was what she wanted. She was completely in control. She'd check "have more fun" off her list of accomplishments and never, ever, see Josh Rideout again.

She pulled all of her bathing suits out of her suitcase, deciding on a white halter-style bikini, then covered it with a t-shirt and wrapped her ponytail into a bun.

"I don't understand," Emma said. She was lying on Dani's bed, sipping a ginger-ale she'd snagged from the vending machine in the lobby. Emma was confused by Cat's sudden eagerness to spend time with Josh, but a little spark of romantic hopefulness still flickered behind her concern.

"What's to understand? I want to go swimming."

"What happened to your whole speech about how meeting a guy is the last thing you want, etcetera, etcetera?"

"All of that still stands." Cat buzzed around the room, tossing her phone and a towel into a bag. "I just decided that maybe you guys were right. A vacation fling might be exactly what I need."

"Catia," Emma groaned, "that's not exactly what I said."

"You said I should have fun."

"I said give him a chance, not chalk him up to a bucket list item."

"It's not like that," she said, rolling her eyes. She was letting herself enjoy this, wasn't that what they had been begging her to do? "Look, Em, he's cute and fun, and we're enjoying each other's company, but I'm not looking for 'something else' right now, or ever."

Emma narrowed her eyes and looked Cat up and down. "We'll see," she said in that tone she took when she was comparing your life choices to her textbooks. Cat ignored it. "Just don't do anything you'll regret."

"I don't plan on it."

"And be careful. Stay in well-lit areas."

"You do remember who you are talking to, right? What I do for a living?"

"Yes, of course. I just feel like a friend should say these things."

"Well, thanks. I'll see you later. Don't wait up."

Cat caught the elevator, leaning against the back wall as she rode the many floors down to the lobby with Emma's rolling eyes imprinted on her brain.

She stepped into the lobby and didn't spot Josh yet, so she used the time to send Sonya a quick text letting her know where she would be. She immediately received an inappropriate emoji in response, and a reminder about the episode of *Law and Order SVU* they'd watched together that had started eerily similar to this. She also confessed that Emma had already texted her.

Cat could only imagine how that conversation went. Emma was probably writing "Cat & Josh" in little hearts on the hotel stationery as she spoke. At least Sonya was being realistic about this, more worried that Josh was going to murder her on the dark beach than his potential boyfriend specs.

The revolving door spun, and a rush of warm air charged against the air-conditioned room. Josh pushed in behind it, wearing a sweatshirt unzipped and the same bright bathing suit as earlier that day. She tossed her phone in her bag and regarded his bare chest and strong legs, this time letting the flutter in her belly spread.

"Were you waiting long?" He looked as if he might have run there.

"Nope. Right on time." She hooked her arm through his again, his bicep round and firm under her hand, and they headed outside and around the building, arriving on the sand almost immediately.

The beach wasn't deserted, but the few people who roamed it at this hour were enjoying the waves from afar. A flash of light lit up the distant horizon, flickering wildly across the clouds and startling her. She hesitated. She'd been playing in the ocean all day, but now it had magically evolved into a dark and brooding force in the dark. She was suddenly nervous about exploring it. "Maybe this wasn't such a good idea."

"It's just heat lightning," Josh said. "It's still far away." He had a confidence in his estimation that she assumed came from living on the coast, under undiluted night skies and open air where people could really feel nature. It fit him to know that.

She accepted his assurance, and they continued down to the edge of the water, dropping their things on the sand along the way. The lazy advance of the tide began to reach her toes and she turned to him, anticipation skittering through her veins. "Ready?"

"I am if you are," he replied.

She wondered if they were still talking about swimming.

Making the decision that she was ready, whatever the proposition, she grabbed his hand and waded in, letting the water splash the front of her thighs. She could feel his eyes on her, and she let their fingers fall apart, continuing until she was waist-deep. Leaning back into the water, arms outstretched to keep afloat, she smiled brightly at her own bravery. This wasn't so hard.

"It's warm," she said.

Josh followed in after her, recapturing her hand and pulling her up against his chest in one smooth motion. The courage she'd been riding on quickly deflated, making way for a feeling akin to leaning over the railing on a rooftop balcony and letting yourself imagine the fall.

"Cat?" His voice was a low rumble, and he tipped her chin up with his fingertips. "Would it be okay if I kissed you? I've been trying all day."

Well, that didn't take long. But she supposed that's why they were there. Her heart thudded as she settled against him, studying the restraint on his face. He was giving her control, and she desperately wanted to take it, to flirt and make him dangle in uncertainty for a few more moments. Her attempts at a smart answer were defeated, though, by the way the moonlight was cast across his strong jaw and glowing eyes. All she could do was nod.

It was enough. Josh took her face in his

74

hands again, the way he'd done at the bar, but this time there was no way he was pulling back. She squeezed her fingers around his arms, and his eyes rolled shut for a long blink. When they opened again, his fully bloomed pupils had turned his blue eyes almost black, the way the night had darkened the sea. She was equally as intimidated by the change as if at any moment she might be swallowed up by either one.

Josh's hands remained innocuously on her hips as he pulled her closer and slowly leaned down. By the time he finally pressed his full bottom lip between hers, she thought she might faint from holding her breath.

His mouth curled into a smile against hers. He pressed again, parting her lips and letting their tongues gently touch. The kiss was sweet, respectful—everything she would have wagered against in such a charged moment, and her whole body melted like butter in his hands.

Josh's grip on her tightened as she let him in further, and his hands began to explore the planes of her bare back between the two islands of her bikini. She fought the urge, initially afraid of the intimacy of the gesture, but she finally pushed her fingers into his thick, dark hair, gently tugging. He seemed to like that. He grunted against her mouth, lifting her onto her toes.

Cliché, she tried to tell herself, as she stood there, tasting mint and alcohol on his tongue, letting him hold her like she was something precious to him. She would have rolled her eyes at herself if they weren't squeezed shut in reverence to the moment.

Finally, he pulled away with a sweet smile that dropped straight into that empty cavern behind her rib cage and began unpacking its bags. He set her back down on the sandy bottom, and clasped his hands behind the small of her back, holding her up. Thankfully, or she might have just floated away after that kiss, never to be heard from again.

"Now that that's out of the way," Josh said, still grinning.

"Right."

Another flash exploded from behind the clouds. "Let's sit," she said, desperate for some solid ground to cling to. She led him to the spot where they had carelessly tossed their things and put her t-shirt back on over her wet bathing suit while he laid out the blanket she'd packed.

Josh sat down first, setting his bent knees wide enough for her to settle between his legs, and she took the spot without letting herself think too much about it. His chest came flush with her back, and a low rumbling, almost imperceptible behind the splash of the water meeting the sand, coincided with another flash. "There's the thunder," he said.

She giggled, feeling some of her nerves calm at the sound of his accent. To a girl accustomed to the syrupy Southern drawl, it sounded clipped and rough. She found it highly amusing and un-believably adorable.

"What's so funny?" he asked, his words un-mistakably framed by a grin.

"Nothing. I just like the way you talk." She tried to imitate the inflection but failed.

Josh's chest shook with a laugh. "You like making fun of my accent, huh, *Catia*?" He play-fully poked her in the side then wrapped his arms tighter around her waist. "Home and away are sort of the same for me," he confessed.

"You couldn't deny that if you tried. Where'd that accent come from?"

"Cape Cod. I moved down to Ferry Island to live with my grandfather when I was twelve. He was a Navy man; spent a lot of time in foreign countries, so he never developed much of a drawl to influence me with. Guess that's how come it stuck."

"That's a big move. Especially for a kid."

Instead of elaborating, he only shrugged.

She tipped her head back onto his shoulder and studied the planes of his face. His cheeks were sucked in, and his eyes were less expres-sive than usual. Like he'd turned them off.

"Hmm. Well, now I'm going to ask you about this," Cat said, changing the subject. She reached up and brushed her thumb against a thin white line that ran from his nose to his up-per lip. She'd noticed it during their slow dance, the way it tugged at one side of his smile, giving him the illusion of a constant mischievous smirk. Now, with the white moonlight making it glow against his dark stubble, she was even more curious.

"Got hit with a baseball when I was twelve," he said. "Chipped my tooth. Took a few stitches." Josh reached up to touch it himself. Something flashed over his expression as he traced the line, but then his eyes dropped to her own mouth.

Cat shifted in his arms, enough for him to dip his chin and capture her lips again.

Like the first time, there was a sweetness to it. Something soft and full of raw affection. It was part of what made him feel so safe. Safe enough for her to do what she did next. She'd come down here for a reason and now was as good a time as any.

She pulled up to her knees, breaking the lock of his arms around her, and spun around so they were face to face. Josh looked at her curiously, but she ignored it, taking his face between her hands. Forgetting all of the permissions and pauses of before, she nudged his lips apart and kissed him deeply, like she'd done it a hundred times before.

He welcomed her tongue back with the fervor he'd been holding back before, gripping her hips and lifting them so their legs could trade positions, and she could sink down closer, straddling his lap. The warmth of his chest spread through her body as she wrapped her arms around his neck and let her fingers back into his hair as they kissed.

Josh was being gentle, so gentle she started to worry that maybe he wasn't planning on taking this where she was. Eventually, though, his hands moved to the swell of her ass, and his grip began to flirt over the polite line he'd drawn. He strummed the edge of her suit with his thumbs, and when they finally dipped beneath the fabric, Cat sucked in a sharp breath.

This was what she'd planned all along when she'd suggested they not go back to the group, but even so, the feel of him between her legs, hard and ready for wherever she decided this was going, threatened her fearlessness.

Josh pulled away, his eyes flickering over hers, his lips bee-stung. He looked like he was holding back a speeding freight train with his willpower alone. "You okay?"

Why was he asking? Was she shaking? She felt like she might be shaking. *Be normal, Cat. Act like you know what you're doing.*

"Yes. I'm good."

She glanced around the sand, taking in their relative seclusion from the handful of people left on the beach, then summoned the type of vampish expression confident women make in movies. Slowly, seductively (she hoped), she lifted the hem of her t-shirt, pulling it over her head.

"So pretty," Josh breathed. Before she'd even tossed her shirt aside, his mouth found her bare stomach, teeth and tongue latching onto the supple flesh there, and a shudder swept from her head to her toes.

Josh seemed satisfied that they were on the same page now, and his touch became greedier. Working his way back up her body, he landed beneath her ear, alternating between drawing her soft flesh between his teeth and pressing his lips along the rigid line of her jaw. The opposing sensations, rough then tender, had her imagining all of the ways she could possibly have him.

Maybe once won't be enough. The thought materialized before she could stop it, and she squeezed his biceps, keeping her mind on the physical gratification—his hard body pressed against hers, his warm, wet tongue on her neck.

Josh hugged her to his chest, collapsing back onto the sand. He let her rest on top of him for a fleeting moment before he rolled her onto her back and hovered above her. "Still good?" he asked.

It was sweet of him to keep checking, and she appreciated his vigilance, but at the moment, she didn't want to be reminded that she was doing something out of character and maybe a little dangerous.

"Josh." She slipped her hand between them, tugging the drawstring on his bathing suit. "I'm good."

He made a low growling noise as the knot gave way and kissed his way to the valley of her breasts. His tongue stroked and dipped into the crease there in a display of talent that had her mind racing at the implications. Still lower, he bounced around her stomach and sides, marking her with a trail of hot breath. He was almost to her hip when the sand started to feel cooler around her, and new moisture mixed with the wet marks he was leaving on her skin. She pushed it out of her mind when his fingers began toying with the waistband of her suit.

He pushed past the fabric, traveling the line of her hip bone with his thumb, and she drew in a hopeful breath, waiting for what came next, but Josh froze as if startled by something. She almost whined at the interruption until she felt it too: big wet splashes on her shoulders, then her forehead.

Both his hands stopped what they were doing, and he lifted his face to the sky. "Shit," he cursed, looking utterly torn.

There was another flash, this time shedding unwanted light on their hidden corner of the beach. Josh looked back at her with palpable exasperation, his lips swollen, his neck flushed. The rain pelted his back now, the drops coming quick and hard, and he sat back on his knees, pulling her up with him.

He used the hand he'd just been about to pleasure her with to wipe a drop from her forehead. "Looks like the storm caught up with us," he said as the thunder returned, sharper than a rumble.

She looked upward too, praying it was a passing sprinkle, but the sky had opened, dropping tiny wet bombs of disappointment onto them.

Cat's heart was still racing as Josh tucked her head under his chin and held his hands over her hair in a futile attempt at shielding her from the rain. "Let's go to your room," she whispered against his neck.

He tilted his head in response, searching her eyes. "Are you sure?"

"Yes. I'm getting soaked." She kissed him again, feeling the precipitation pool on his swollen upper lip.

He pulled back, still looking for any sign that he shouldn't take her up on the offer. She'd already crossed this line in her mind, though; she didn't want to bail now.

"Josh. Take me to your room."

He didn't need any more convincing. He found his sweatshirt, left crumpled in a pile on the sand, and draped it over her shoulders, then quickly gathered the rest of their things. "Come on, then."

Six

THE ELEVATOR RIDE WAS PURE torture. Cat was smooshed up against him to accommodate a group of drunken guests who, despite the late hour, were traveling between floors and trying to make conversation. Luckily, her position was hiding the outward signs of how turned on he was, but being pressed into her ass made it all the more difficult to contain.

They finally made it to his floor, and Cat barely waited for the elevator door to close before wrapping her arms around his neck, pulling him into another heated kiss. He hadn't had any expectations when she'd asked him to take her swimming instead of going back to the group. He'd really just intended on kissing her on the beach, and hopefully charming her enough that she'd agree to a date when they got back home. This took him by surprise. A good surprise, like winning the lottery or finding out you were the only heir to a rich uncle that you didn't know you had.

He forced his feet to move, stumbling down

the deserted hallway, their mouths glued together, and their hands roaming each other greedily. When they reached his door, after bouncing off of the wall a few times, he pressed her against it, pinning her there with one hand above her head. He reached blindly into the pocket of the sweatshirt he'd lent her to find his wallet. Finally thumbing the key card, he broke away briefly, letting his eyes travel the length of her as he envisioned what he wanted to do when he got her out of that wet bathing suit. The thought brought to mind his earlier conversation with Dylan, and he paused for a moment, contemplating if he should slow things down. He liked Cat. A lot. The last thing he wanted was to treat her like some vacation hookup, but the amount of strength it took to turn down a girl like her was quite possibly more than he possessed.

"I don't do this," he said, running the card through the slot until he heard the quick little beep and click of it unlocking. He kept his eyes on hers while he pushed the door open. "I mean, this isn't a habit for me."

"That's for damn sure."

Josh jumped at the sound of Dylan's voice, grabbing Cat's arm and pulling her behind him.

Dylan appeared from behind the door, holding a freshly poured drink. His face split into a shit-eating grin, and his eyes danced with pure, unadulterated amusement.

"Do you two know what time it is?" Shawn

called from the living room, shaking his head like a disapproving dad.

"Not last call yet," Josh ground out. He was trying to mask his irritation at his friends' unexpected appearance, but he was failing miserably. "Not like you guys to call it an early night."

"Sorry, bro." Dylan chuckled. "The girls wanted to go home, and Shawn offered us up as escorts. It was closer to just come back here and drink our booze." He gestured to the bottle of scotch on the coffee table, surrounded by rows of cards that looked like they belonged to a game.

"You want us to deal you two in?" Shawn asked behind a poorly hidden laugh.

Josh ground his teeth, running a hand over his mouth to contain the words that were bubbling on his tongue. *Of all the times for these two to be responsible.*

Cat pulled away from his grip, tossing him a look that said, *it's okay* and *be nice,* and ran a soothing hand along his stomach as she passed to enter the room.

"What are you playing?" she asked. She took a seat across from Shawn, her polite smile in direct opposition to the scowl Josh was aiming at Dylan, who shrugged an apology. It might have felt more sincere without the smirk on his face.

"I'm going to change," Josh said to Cat. "You wanna borrow some clothes?" The air conditioning and his wet bathing suit had him shivering. She was wearing a lot less.

"Sure. Thank you."

When he returned a few moments later, having swapped his bathing suit for a pair of jeans and a t-shirt, Cat was sitting cross-legged on the edge of the couch, dealing out a round of cards. He handed her a pair of cotton pajama pants that he hoped she would be able to roll into a comfortable fit and took the seat next to her, where she'd been collecting a hand for him.

The smile on her face proved she was taking this turn of events in stride, and he decided to be thankful that it looked like she was going to stay and let him spend a little more time with her, even if the agenda had changed.

When she was finished dealing, Dylan pointed to the bathroom. As she shut the door, he broke into a laugh. He stood from his chair and grabbed ahold of Josh's shoulders, giving them a hard shake. "Man, I did not think you had it in you. I'm being serious here. When you two didn't come back, I figured you were off getting ice cream cones and holding hands or some other benign shit. But you were about to lay it on that girl."

"Knock it off, Dylan," Josh warned, his previous ire coming back in full force. "I'm not kidding around. Watch your mouth around her."

Dylan held up his hands in mock surrender, still laughing as he fell back into his chair. "All right, look, I'm sorry. I really am. If we had known, we would have found another place to be. Right, Shawn?"

"Absolutely. Cock-blocking was not part of our plan, buddy."

"It's fine. Just don't be an asshole." Josh's warning was cut short when Cat appeared from the bathroom. His pants were rolled low on her hips, the legs cuffed to her shins. She had her bikini bottoms in her hand, and the thought of that thin fabric being the only thing that separated him from where he was supposed to be right now had him squirming in his seat. It was a test of his resolve not to kick his friends outside in the rain and carry her back to his bed.

Cat tossed her suit in the bag she'd brought and sauntered back to him, sitting close enough that her arm brushed his. "Tell me the rules," she said to Shawn as they all took hold of their cards.

Josh listened half-heartedly to the instructions, having played this game before. Instead, he brooded into the drink he'd accepted from Dylan and stole glances at Cat. She still wore the top to her bathing suit, and his sweatshirt hung oversized and unzipped on her, leaving her tight stomach exposed. Despite the lecture that he'd just given Dylan, he couldn't help but allow his eyes an impolite jaunt across her body, conjuring the taste of her skin on his tongue as he roamed.

He came back to the moment at hand when

he noticed Shawn pouring her a double shot of scotch.

"I can get you something else to play the game with," he offered. "We have beer."

"No, this is fine." She gave him a confident smile that made him believe she could probably handle it as well as the rest of them. "Besides, I don't want to give you any excuses when I kick your ass."

"Competitive little thing," Shawn said, laughing. "I like it."

He liked it too. Christ, she was being cool. As much as he wanted to finish what they'd started, watching her play cards in his pajamas, hanging out with his friends, was maybe turning him on more than touching her on the beach.

He could picture her beside him on all sorts of nights like this—sitting beside the campfire on Shawn's annual birthday camping trip, lounging around on weekends watching baseball. She didn't seem to have any trouble dealing with Dylan, and when she leaned her head onto his shoulder and laughed at one of Shawn's Dad Jokes, he wanted to keep her more than ever.

He wrapped his arm around her, pulling her closer.

"I know you're not trying to look at my cards, Josh." She folded her hand on her lap and gave him a teasing scowl. He wanted to kiss it off her face.

"I told you I don't cheat."

"Actually, you said you would if you had to."

She tipped her chin up at him, and her face was free of the conflict he usually saw there. It was a pure, unrestrained smile, and he felt himself falling as he imagined what it would be like to have that smile belong to him.

Dylan snickered into his beer, and Josh realized he'd been staring at her for more than a beat. It was his turn.

He cleared his throat and quickly threw a card onto the pile.

They played a few more hands of Shawn's game, Josh's lack of focus evident as he was knocked out almost immediately each time. Cat really was putting all of them to shame, but even with her winning streak, the scotch was getting to her. Her eyelids were heavy, and she sank further into his side.

"Joshua, you've earned the couch tonight," Shawn said, throwing down his cards after his final loss. "Thanks for bringing your girl over here to hustle us." He tossed a throw pillow at Josh's head, stumbling his way into the bedroom to take the bed opposite where Dylan had already disappeared to after the last round.

"I should walk you home before your friends worry," Josh said once they were alone. He regretted it as soon as he said it. He didn't want her to leave.

"Wait until the storm lets up a little." She looked out the sliding glass door at the rain. It was still coming down in sheets onto the balcony, and she sank down beside him, swiping the pillow that Shawn had thrown and pulling it beneath her head in his lap.

Josh wasn't about to argue with that. He brushed at her hair with his fingers and watched her eyes close. "I'm sorry about how this turned out."

"It's okay." She yawned. "It was fun."

He adjusted his position, leaning into the corner of the couch, and let his hand curl over her belly. Her body went lax almost immediately. "Cat," he whispered, shaking her gently. "You should call Sonya, let her know you're staying here."

She didn't stir, and he considered just shutting off the light and falling asleep beside her, but the thought of getting on Sonya's bad side didn't appeal to him. He reached over her, plucking her phone from the coffee table, and scrolled through her contacts until he found Sonya's number to send her a text.

Josh: Hey, it's Josh. Cat is safe. She just fell asleep here. I'll walk her back in the morning.

Barely a moment went by before a response came through from her vigilant friend.

Sonya: Send me a picture so I know she's safe.

Josh chuckled at the request, but quickly found the camera on Cat's phone and did as she asked. He adjusted the sweatshirt to cover her bare midriff for good measure then held out his hand to snap a photo of her sleeping peacefully in his lap.

Josh: Don't get me in trouble for sending this.

Sonya: This is going straight onto Instagram... just kidding, thanks for taking care of her.

Josh: You're welcome.

Seven

THE EARLY MORNING LIGHT POURED unfiltered through the balcony door, slowly rousing Cat from the few hours of sleep she'd managed. She was curled into a ball against Josh, his hand resting casually on her hip and the warm wall of his stomach greeting her as her eyes blinked open. She watched it rise and fall with short breaths, corresponding puffs of air falling from his lips while he slept.

The pillow she'd been using had fallen to the floor, and she realized she was resting her face directly on Josh's crotch. She groaned, trying to decipher the mixed messages the universe was trying to send her. First, the night had forced an end to her attempt to have him, and now she was waking up conveniently face to face with exactly what she'd been denied.

She rubbed at her temples, feeling vindicated in the fact that her plan for the evening had been a complete bust. Although it did end up being a lot of fun. Josh was a lot of fun, even though she could tell he was again being more magnanimous than he felt. She pictured the look on his face when he'd seen Dylan and bit her lip to keep from laughing. It was cute how he'd struggled with his politeness at that moment. She probably should have just left, but the idea of watching him in his natural habitat was too compelling. She'd had a secret hope to hear that laugh come back, maybe be the reason for it.

She slowly lifted her head, praying she didn't have an imprint from the fly of Josh's jeans plastered across her cheek and tried to wiggle out of his embrace without waking him. His eyes fluttered open, though, and a lazy grin spread across his face, reminding her of the sexy, morning-after fantasy she'd come up with the day before. His hair wasn't quite as disheveled as she'd decided it would be, and he was wearing more clothes, but other than that, she'd imagined it well.

"Morning," he whispered, rubbing at his back. It couldn't have been comfortable sleeping like that, and Cat felt a little twinge of guilt for using him as a pillow. "Where are you going?"

"Bathroom. I'll be right back."

She tiptoed across the room, hoping to avoid the attention of his two friends, and shut the bathroom door behind her. She could hear Josh walking around in the kitchenette on the opposite wall, opening and closing the refrigerator, and she went to work wiping away the makeup that had shifted out of place on her face and splashing some water on her tired eyes. She looked ragged, and she could only imagine the looks on her friends' faces when she showed back up at her hotel room. Was it still technically a walk of shame if she hadn't actually done any of the shameful stuff she'd tried to do? Or if she wasn't particularly ashamed? She wasn't sure.

Before she dealt with her friends, though, she still had to go back out and face Josh. She hadn't intended to stay the night, even if they had gotten to the sex part. She was going to do that thing that guys did where they say they have an early morning and slip out into the night. That plan had been tossed to hell by a double shot of liquor and her competitive side when it came to card games—and maybe a little bit by how enticing it had been to cuddle up with him on the couch, wearing his sweatshirt and listening to the rainfall outside.

There was a small travel case on the shelf above the sink, and she took a quick peek inside, pumping her fist in the air and mouthing a silent *yes* when she saw a bottle of mouthwash. She quickly swished it around in her mouth, spitting and rinsing as quietly as she could, then pulled out the bun she'd slept in, letting her long hair fall around her face. Josh's sweatshirt was still hanging off of her shoulders, and she played with the zipper, trying to decide exactly how much skin she wanted to be showing when she walked back out. Settling for zipped to just below her breasts, she took one more deep breath and crept back out to where he was.

Josh was leaning casually against the counter when she emerged, holding bottled water and a box of the same crackers Shawn had given Emma on the beach. The sight of him, all puffy-eyes and wrinkled clothes, settled her nerves. He wasn't acting awkward at all.

"We don't have much for food," he said, handing her the water. "Unless you want a beer or some pizza that's been sitting out all night."

"You guys are living like a bunch of frat boys over here," she joked, snatching the cracker box from him and stealing a few to ward off any repercussions from their late-night drinking game.

"I suppose you girls wake up to mimosas and croissants every morning." He gave her a playful smile and watched her as she went back for more crackers.

"Of course we have croissants," she said with a wink. "What are we? Heathens?"

Josh took a cautious step toward her, his hand finding the same spot on her hip where it had rested all night. Her skin tingled as she prepared herself for one of his soul-shaking kisses, but instead, he gave her a chaste peck on the cheek that was dripping with self-restraint. Even as Cat recovered from her disappointment, she couldn't help but smile at his impeccable manners. It was obvious he was unsure if the liberties she'd granted him the previous night stood up in the daytime, but she was leaving this place in a few hours, and she was pretty thankful he'd looked after her, so he deserved a proper good morning. She covered his hand with hers, moving it around to her backside, and grasped his face, pulling him back in for a more intimate greeting.

When she pulled away, she spied relief behind his intense gaze and felt him relax in the loose hold she had on him.

"Let's go then," he said. "I'll get you a fancy breakfast somewhere with all the croissants you want."

Cat dropped her eyes down her front. "I'm wearing your pajamas and a bikini top. I'm not dressed for a fancy breakfast."

"Then, I'll get you a bagel and some shitty coffee on the beach." He brushed her hair out of her face, and she leaned into his fingers.

A breakfast date certainly wasn't part of her plan the night before either, but the way he was looking at her made a bagel on the beach sound like the spaghetti scene from *Lady and the Tramp*. Maybe she had time for coffee. She wondered what he drank. Probably something strong and reliable. Dark roast. Cream. No sugar.

Stop. She didn't have time, and it didn't matter how Josh drank his coffee. She felt her eyes turning into little hearts, and she knew it was time to retreat. Mission Vacation Hookup was a failure. Regardless of what did or didn't happen last night, this was the part where she never saw Josh Rideout again. Right?

A bubble of disappointment pushed against her ribs, but she did her best to pop it. She needed to go before she did something stupid. "I can't," she said. "I'm already going to be in big trouble for not coming back last night. They all know I would kick their ass if any of them did that."

Josh let go of her, giving her room to drink the water she was still holding. "I texted Sonya last night when you fell asleep. I hope you don't mind. I just didn't want them to worry."

"You did?" Her voice turned girlish against her will, and she cleared her throat. "I guess I should have known since there doesn't seem to be an APB out for me right now."

"She asked for a picture," he confessed. "I guess she wanted to make sure I wasn't lying about you being safe. Sorry. It's a nice one. You looked good."

Cat groaned, finding her phone and pulling up the picture in her text log. "She is a piece of work," she said as she read through their exchange. "But she's right, thanks for letting me stay and, you know, not being a murderer."

"You're welcome." He laughed, unoffended.

She turned her phone over in her hand, absently gazing around the living room where they'd slept. She was suddenly acutely aware of the feel of the empty air between them. She wanted to go back to where Josh was standing, feel his body heat against her skin again, but she couldn't think of a nonchalant way to pull it off. Nothing about the way she was procrastinating was nonchalant.

"I guess I really do have to go." She tossed her phone in her bag, sitting on the breakfast bar where she'd dropped it the night before. "I wish I didn't, but we have a full schedule before we leave this afternoon. Sonya didn't want to waste a minute of this trip relaxing."

He nodded, giving her a tight smile. She got the impression he thought she was blowing him off, and even though that was sort of classic Cat Modus Operandi, she actually hated for him to think it.

"Give me a minute to try to get my shoes without waking these guys up," he said. "I'll walk you back."

Josh crept through the door to the bedroom where his friends were asleep, and she poked around the room, looking for her flip flops. When he came back, he was wearing a pair of sneakers, and one of those mesh-backed ball caps with the brim pointed backward. He looked entirely more adorable than she'd anticipated, and a montage of abs and biceps and dimples flickered before her eyes. She could feel herself staring and had half a mind to check her chin for drool. Did he have to be so freaking cute on top of sexy and sweet and great at kissing and—

"Ready?"

That bubble from before inflated another puff, and her shoulders fell. "Yeah. I'm ready."

The street was deserted, leaving a peaceful quiet where all the revelry had happened a few hours before. The air outside had a chill to it from the pressure change that the rain had carried in, and Cat was glad for Josh's warmth when he linked their fingers.

"Where are you headed this morning?" he asked, eyeing the horizon through the breaks between the buildings. The sunrise was a ball of fire with magenta streaks slashing across a grey sky, and the familiar scent of the approaching tide hung on the droplets of moisture still lingering in the air. "Looks like it may not be a great day."

Smiling at his second weather prediction based on the sky, Cat looked out to the water to see the warning clouds gathering around the pink and red. "We're taking a harbor cruise. Seafood, drinks, sightseeing."

Josh slowed to a stop as they reached the glass lobby of her hotel. He tugged her hand until they were standing chest to chest. "I don't want to be greedy with your time," he said. "I know you said you have a full morning, and I know you're here to celebrate with Emma, but if there's any chance of seeing you before you leave this afternoon, just tell me, and I'll be there."

Cat glanced over her shoulder at the door, then back at his face—blue eyes flashing, crooked grin. God, she wanted to keep looking at him, even though her brain was telling her to turn around, book it up to her room, and hide under her duvet until it was time to leave.

"Um..." She started to sputter, and Josh dropped his eyes to the ground, running his thumb over that jagged little scar on his lip. For the span of one breath, he was a wounded little canary, and she was the proverbial cat. The scenario shocked her into an unlikely response.

"I still have your pajamas." The thought occurred to her like a shove to her shoulders, and she glanced down her front. Josh's eyes followed. "I'll text you when we get back from the cruise. You can come by and get them."

Just like that, he was back, all square shoulders and panty-dropping smiles.

"I'll be there," he said, stepping closer to rest his palm on her pulse point. He tipped her chin and pressed his lips against hers, whisper-soft. It was the kind of kiss that made you want to chase it and damn it if she wasn't falling for it. She pushed to her toes, taking just a little bit more before he finally let her go with one last peck on her forehead.

"I'll see you later," she said with a silly little wave.

Her brain whispered *you're an idiot, Cat,* as she pulled Josh's sweatshirt tighter around her body. But inside her chest, her heart was sighing.

She waited just until her back was turned to roll her eyes at herself.

Eight

JOSH THOUGHT HE FELT A raindrop or two as he hurried down the strip of beachfront hotels. The fog hadn't budged all day, the grey clouds still lingering close enough to touch.

When Cat had texted him to say she was back from the cruise, he'd jumped off the stool at the sports bar where he and Dylan and Shawn had been wasting the dreary day, and booked it through the rain to the Tidal Inn. He'd been looking forward to seeing her again all day, but now he was fighting off the creeping concern that this could be the last time. She was headed home now, and even though he wasn't far behind her, she was right: Vacation and the real world were two different things. He still had to convince her they could have both.

He chose the stairs to get his blood circulating, and by the time he got to Cat's floor, his heavy breaths were helping him get some oxygen back to his brain where it had been lacking. He leaned an arm casually on the wall and rapped his knuckles on the door to Cat's suite.

Dani answered, giving him a devilish smile that forced his shoulders straight.

"Well, look who it is," she said. "My ex, coming to see my best friend. How could you, Josh?"

"Sorry, Dani," he said. "You know I never meant for you to get hurt. Can we still be friends?"

"I'll think about it."

Emma shoved Dani aside with her hip and welcomed him in. He stepped into the impressive suite—two bedrooms and a large sitting area complete with a mini-bar—and began to think he was right about the croissants and champagne in the morning.

There were suitcases piled on the couch, and both women wore yoga pants and tank tops, a stark contrast to the heels and club-wear they'd all had on the night before. That nagging fear that this was all an illusion echoed in his elevated pulse until Cat came out of the bedroom on the right and gave him a shy smile. "Josh."

"Hey, Cat." He crossed the room to greet her, and it took everything he had not to kiss her hello. He wasn't sure if she would want him to in front of Emma and Dani. Instead, he shoved his hands in his pockets and drank her in with his eyes. She was also dressed in athletic wear— tight black pants, cropped mid-calf, and a white t-shirt with the hem knotted and *The Future Is Female* printed across the front. Her cocoa-colored hair was wet and tied up in a wild knot on top of her head. She didn't have any makeup on, but her cheeks still blushed pink against the brown of her skin.

Sonya emerged from the opposite room, hauling a rolling bag behind her, and glanced pointedly back and forth between the two of them. "Josh," she said with an ill-contained smirk. "I heard you ratted yourself out about the sleeping picture you took of Cat. Too bad. I was going to keep that secret for you, dude."

Josh laughed. "Compulsive honesty has always been a problem of mine," he said.

"Mm-hmm. Bodes well for you." She turned to Emma and Dani, who were both standing there, staring at Cat, and she tipped her head to the couch. "Let's take the bags down. Give Kit Cat a minute."

The other two women snapped to attention, nodding and hurrying to fill their arms with luggage. "Cat, we'll see you at the car in a few?" Emma asked, giving Josh a wink that said *you're welcome.* He didn't know if it was a good thing or a bad thing that her friends seemed to be pushing so hard. He didn't mind the assist, but he was kind of hoping that after last night, he might be able to sink this one on his own.

"Yeah. I'm right behind you," Cat said, glancing at him out of the corner of her eye.

She looked nervous.

Sonya waved a hand behind her. "Take your time."

Dani winked, and Emma giggled, and then they were gone.

"So, um, I have your clothes," Cat stuttered. Finding herself alone with Josh in an instant, she struggled with the way the tension in the room seemed to balloon. She started toward her bedroom to retrieve his pants, and Josh followed, lingering in the doorway while she walked the rest of the way to the bed where she had placed them.

"Thanks. It will be nice not to sleep in my jeans again tonight."

"Yeah. I'm sorry about that."

The corners of his eyes crinkled. "I'm kidding. I was really glad to wake up to you this morning."

"Me too." She wanted to say she enjoyed it way more than she should have and had been thinking about it all morning when she was supposed to be enjoying a very expensive cruise, but instead she asked, "Is it raining yet?"

Josh shifted his weight, swallowing. "It's starting. Be careful driving home. It's supposed to be downpours all afternoon."

"We will." His intense stare was making her jittery, so she brushed past him and back into the living room, offering him a seat on the couch.

"What are you going to do on your last night here?"

"Same as the last couple nights, probably."

"Bring a girl down to the beach and fool around?" She gave him a cool smirk, but the thought made her stomach knot.

"No." He smiled. "Not that."

Josh shifted, turning his shoulders in her direction. Maybe the couch wasn't such a good idea. He was so close she could smell the rain on his t-shirt. *Damn it, Sonya.* It would have been much easier to say goodbye with them all standing there. Why were her friends always testing her? Couldn't they just let her be a coward in peace?

"So I guess this is it," she said.

"Not as far as I'm concerned."

"I mean this place. This trip. I wish we could stay here longer."

"Me too. But nights like you and I had on this beach, in this place, we can have more anytime you want." He reached out to touch the mess of hair on top of her head, watching his fingers like he'd tried to stop himself but couldn't. "I want to keep seeing you, Cat. Can I call you tomorrow night? When we're both home?"

Cat opened her mouth to answer, but she hadn't quite figured out what her reply would be yet. She admitted that it didn't feel like she'd never see him again, but she thought she'd have time to go home and dissect this encounter—analyze every word, touch, and look they'd shared in true Catia fashion before she would have to decide what to do about it.

Josh leaned in closer, his eyes doing that little shimmy across her face that she was beginning to find familiar. It was an offer; his lips lingered just out of reach, his nose brushed hers, and the pull was too strong to resist. She closed the distance, and his hand came to the back of her neck, holding them together. This time there was no teasing to the pressure. It wasn't the heady tongue-battle they'd engaged in on the beach, but there was no denying the intent. If her friends weren't waiting for her downstairs to drive her away from this little dreamworld, they both knew what would happen next.

"This is crazy," she whispered when he released her lips with a shaky breath.

His brow pinched, and the corner of his mouth twitched amusedly. "Why?"

"It's just... I feel like I know you in ways I shouldn't after only two days."

There. She admitted it. Let her pride begin its death march.

Josh pulled in a deep breath, blowing it upward. "Yeah," he said. "I feel like that too, and that part might be crazy, but if anything, it's a sign we should spend more time together, figure out what it means."

"It's going to be hard to make that work. With the distance, our jobs, real-world stuff."

"Everything's harder than being on vacation," he said, "but we do it anyway. I'm not afraid of a little work, Catia." His fingers slid down her arm, lacing with hers.

"Ca-tee-ah," she chided him playfully.

"And I wanna keep working on that name. Next weekend?"

She sighed, taking in his puppy dog eyes that she was sure he'd wielded successfully in the past. How did she go from *leave it alone, Cat*, to this moment here? Her memory splashed her back into the water with him, running her fingers through his hair while he held her so carefully, kissed her so gently. "You're very convincing," she said. It wasn't exactly a yes. She needed more time. Some distance from this place to think.

"Good," he said. "I was trying to be. Come on." He stood from the couch with his pajamas still tucked under his arm, then grabbed her hand and pulled her up with him. "I'll walk you to your car."

Cat gathered her keys and her bag from the table, and something caught her eye. "Wait!" His sweatshirt was still hanging on the back of the bathroom door. She hurried to get it, handing it over.

Josh took it and placed it over her shoulders. "Bring it to me next time."

Nine

AT GAZED OUT THE PASSENGER side window of Sonya's Pathfinder, the raindrops bringing a secret smile to her face. She hadn't been thrilled about the storm the night before, but looking back it was sort of romantic getting caught on the beach in the rain—the electricity of the storm, and the way Josh had tried to cover her head with his hands as if he could keep her from getting wet. Okay, he was pretty cute, but the fact that she was wearing his sweatshirt right now and blaming it on Sonya's affinity for air conditioning was just embarrassing. She'd been telling herself this whole time that they would part ways at the end of this trip, and he would be a fun memory. The way she was feeling right now was not part of the plan.

"Somebody is happy today," Sonya said, sharing a look in the rearview mirror with Dani and Emma that was clearly at Cat's expense.

"Come on, Kit Cat," Dani whined from the back seat. "We've got a five-hour drive and we need to talk about something, so entertain us. Tell us what you were doing all night."

"You know what I was doing. I told you the truth this morning. I fell asleep there. That's it."

"You conveniently left a few things out," she said. "How did you end up there, and why were you wearing his clothes?"

Cat leaned back in her seat and shrugged her shoulders, but she couldn't help the grin that was threatening to betray her as she replayed the answers to Dani's questions in her head.

"You've got it bad!" Sonya exclaimed, slapping a hand to her thigh and doing a little jump in her seat. "Look at your face right now. Y'all see her face right now?"

"Mm-hmm," Emma agreed. "I see it."

"Eyes on the road, Sonya," Cat said.

"You totally slept with him," Dani yelled, kicking the back of her seat like a pouting toddler. "You're a liar. Tell us right now!"

"I did not!" Cat exclaimed, but she knew her defense lacked luster since she was omitting the very important fact that she'd intended to do just that. "Look, I don't know what would have happened if we were alone, but we went back to his room because of the storm, and Dylan and Shawn were already there. We just played cards."

"I bet Josh was pissed to see them," Dani said with an evil chuckle.

"He was fine. It was fine."

Sonya glanced in her direction, her eyes narrowed. "So, you didn't want to sleep with him?"

"I didn't say that." Three pairs of eyes stared at her impatiently. "Fine. I had every intention of screwing him on the beach and then leaving, but it didn't happen that way."

Sonya pulled in a sharp gasp. "Catia!"

"What? You said I should have a little fun. He's hot, he wanted me, but clearly, I can't even pull off vacation sex." She buried her face in her hands and the scent of Josh's sweatshirt filled her nostrils, adding insult to injury. "I suck, you guys."

"Maybe it's a sign," Emma said. "Your little plan was thwarted because you're supposed to take this more seriously."

"It was thwarted because of a rainstorm and his two friends."

Dani leaned forward and flicked Cat's ponytail. "I think you're just scared."

"Why does everyone keep saying that?"

"Because it's true," Dani said. "Miss All Men Suck met a real-life Prince Charming, and she *likes him.*" It was a sing-songy taunt, and if they were still kids, she would have shoved Dani down and kicked dirt on her dress.

"I didn't say I liked him."

Emma groaned. "Please. Is that his sweatshirt clutched in your hand like a teddy bear?"

Cat looked down at the tight hold she had on her little memento, then let it fall from her fingers. "Fine," she said, rubbing her temples, "but I don't know what I'm doing. One minute we're talking about the thunder, the next minute I'm asking Josh to take me to his room. I mean, he seems incredibly sweet and he's really, really good looking..." She sighed as her friends nodded and chimed in their agreement. "But this is silly. Men like that don't exist, and you don't meet them at a bar. It's just this place. It made me forget about how things work when you're not sipping cocktails on the beach, when you're back in the real world. A guy like Josh? That's just asking for trouble. His pretty blue eyes making me all flustered... then I end up looking like an idiot when he turns out to be some kind of a jerk. I'm not falling for that. I told you all I would have a good time, and I did, but I certainly don't have it bad for anyone."

Exhausted from her soliloquy, Cat looked around the car to see all three of them staring at her; Dani rolled her eyes, Sonya shook her head, and Emma gave her that pitying look she'd come to know all too well.

"Cat, do you hear yourself right now?" Sonya asked. "Liking a guy doesn't make you silly. And not every man is going to turn out to be a dick just because Micah did."

"He seems like a good guy, Cat," Emma added. "You're making a mistake if you don't see where this goes. You two have an energy between you. We all saw it."

Dani laughed. "I thought they'd both lost the ability to speak when they first met." She let her mouth fall open, and her eyes bug out, apparently in imitation.

"Exactly," Emma said.

An energy. That's what she'd confessed to Josh before she said goodbye. There was some weird thing that overtook her senses and made her go all soft when he was around. She leaned her head against the window, closing her eyes to her friends' pity, and remembered how she felt standing on that beach, wrapped up in Josh's arms, like she'd found something that was about to shake her world. But the best thing you can do when your world is about to be shaken is to find somewhere safe and hold on tight. Shelter in place and wait for it to blow over. Or even better, defend yourself.

"Okay, Em," she said, wrenching herself back to reality. "I'll make you a little wager. Josh said he wants to see me again after we leave here. I'll do it. I'll go out with him, but I bet you all it takes is a little time on dry land for this Prince to lose his Charm."

Emma shook her head. "I'm not betting that, Cat. I'd never gamble on your happiness."

"Why not, if you're so sure? You think I make up my problems with men, but you'll see. Strip away the vacation goggles and he'll be just like the rest."

"I'll take that bet," Dani chimed in.

"Me too," Sonya said. Emma groaned theatrically. "What, Emma? I like this Josh guy. I think he's gonna turn our little kitty cat around."

"Okay," Cat said, feeling her sails billow with the reminder of all the reasons and responses she'd been carrying around before Josh had made her temporarily forget them. "The terms are this: I go out with Josh, Prince Charming from the dive bar, and as soon as the castle comes crumbling down, you two pay up."

"Pay what?" Dani asked.

"Starbucks every day for a year."

"Or," Sonya said, "you fall madly in love with him and have to spend the rest of your days thanking us publically on every relationship milestone you hit until death do you part."

"So dramatic," Cat said, rolling her eyes.

"I'd like to go on record as saying I don't like this one bit," Emma said. "You're mocking fate."

"Duly noted," Cat said. She turned to Dani and Sonya. "You've got a deal."

Ten

REE COFFEE FOR A YEAR was no joke, and Cat had no intention of wasting any more time than necessary winning that prize. She just had to see Josh a few more times and wait for reality to come crashing down.

She'd been working on her rational response to him during their phone calls and texts leading up to this date. She even made a mental list of all of the reasons Josh wasn't as perfect as he'd seemed.

> 1. He texted in full sentences with proper punctuation, which felt a little judgy.

> 2. He called to the exact minute of the time he said he was going to. Only a psycho or someone who was totally anal-retentive would do that.

That was all she had so far, but she was sure there was more.

In the six days since they'd left the beach, she'd built a nice little wall of composure to wrap around herself Saturday afternoon as she walked down the street from her office building to the park where she'd agreed to meet him.

Josh had suggested the daytime date. She'd found it a bit conservative, considering he'd already had his hands inside her bathing suit, but she also really appreciated the sentiment. He was good at the gentleman thing.

In the same vein, he'd also insisted on coming to the city instead of her traveling to him. She'd already gone through all of the possibilities there. Maybe his place was a pigsty. Or worse yet, a shrine to his previous marriage. Maybe he had a girlfriend in town and didn't want the neighbors talking!

Or maybe he was just being considerate. She really couldn't decide.

Emma and Sonya had read her the riot act for that list of maybes and what-ifs. Emma, with her calm therapist voice, had started in again on her self-help book speech about being open to opportunity and not letting past mistakes dictate her future. Sonya, a flurry of flying hands and curse words, had shamed her for being "emotionally stunted" and accused her of trying to sabotage herself. Dani had kept quiet during the exchange, silently smirking the word *coward* in her direction.

After taking into account her friends' unsolicited advice, as well as the annoying, persistent butterfly feeling in her belly, she'd set aside her worry and decided the only way she could win was to play. So that morning, she strapped on some sparkly (but flat) sandals, a pale peach-colored romper with flowing bell sleeves, and just enough makeup to avoid being accused of not trying, and here she was.

And there he was looking perfect.

She spotted him across the street, leaning casually against what she assumed was his gunmetal-grey Jeep Wrangler, wearing a pair of dark jeans that clearly knew his body intimately given the fading on the seams and pockets. A dark blue, v-neck t-shirt hugged his chest and biceps, showing off the tan he'd taken home with him from the beach.

"Cat!" Josh's pale blue eyes sparked as he flagged her down, greeting her with a grin that belonged on the front page of a magazine. She crossed the street to meet him, and he gathered her against his chest in a hug as soon as she was in his space. He kissed her cheek, but his eyes traveled further, taking her in. "You look gorgeous," he said, causing a wave of those butterflies to be released.

"Thank you. You look nice yourself." With the thick crowd of pedestrians lining the sidewalk and pushing them together, he was standing almost as close as their slow dance, and her view was filled by his handsome face—clean-shaven and stuck in a perma-grin.

"I hope you didn't have to walk too far," he

said, looking past her in the direction she'd come from. "I wish you would have let me pick you up." She could tell it was a big concession on his part to forgo that chivalry, but she wasn't quite ready to invite him into her space yet. She was trying to think of him as a leftover loose end from her vacation, like luggage that still needed to be unpacked. She wasn't keeping this souvenir.

"My office is right down the road," she said. "With the streets closed off for the festival, this was easier."

Josh had suggested a local beer and wine festival that he'd seen a sign for, and Cat jumped at the chance of having hundreds of other people join them for their first real date. Dating was torture even when you weren't trying to win a bet, and alcohol and distraction sounded like exactly what she needed. Between the music—loud enough that she could already hear it from a block away—and the eating and drinking, there wouldn't be too much deep conversation. The kind they'd so easily fallen into in the ocean and on the moonlit beach. She could observe him, try to figure out exactly how he was going to disappoint her before it snuck up on her.

"Do you always work on Saturday?" Josh's hand settled on her lower back, steering them into the crowd of people filing down the street. He pulled her close, and she noted the scent of sunscreen and salt he'd worn a week ago was replaced by a hint of clean, masculine-smelling cologne.

A couple of guys, over-dressed for a day in the park, and wearing Dylan-esque grins, passed by on her right, and Josh moved his hand to her waist, his fingers splaying across her hip. It was a possessive gesture, one that she should have found irritating on a first date, but she supposed they were working with a different set of rules after their little beach tryst. And besides, she sort of liked it.

"No. I just had so much to catch up on since I took that vacation." Feeling as though she'd just admitted to something, she backtracked. "But I do work a lot of late nights during the week. Sometimes past dinner."

"You mentioned that." They approached the entrance to the festival area, a big white tent with long tables underneath, and Josh held up his phone so the staff could scan it.

"You already got the tickets?"

From behind the table, a lady wearing a purple t-shirt with a picture of a beer bottle and wine glass clinking together handed Josh a couple of lanyards with laminated passes.

"Yup. All set." Josh slipped her pass over her head, pulling her long ponytail through the strap, then he donned his own.

"You didn't have to do that. Let me buy lunch."

He scrunched his nose as if she'd said something distasteful.

"Josh…"

"Cat, just let me take you out. It's the only way I know how to do things. Please?"

She nodded, feeling a little fondness for that politeness she remembered. Maybe they could both make concessions. "Thank you."

"You're welcome. How about a drink, and then we can decide what to eat?"

"Sure." He gestured for her to go ahead, and they stepped through the gate and onto a grassy pavilion filled with people and more tents. The sun was high in the afternoon sky, reflecting off of the white canvas and the vinyl pennant flags strung between the booths. A fine sheen of sweat dampened her hairline, but just like at the beach, Josh looked unbothered by the heat, by the crowd, by… anything.

"Beer or wine?" he asked.

Vendors lined either side of the grass. To the left was a crowd of college-aged kids tipping back clear cups of amber liquid and forming little islands of laughter and general rowdiness. To the right, couples meandered through the tables of reds and whites, holding hands and looking at each other lovingly.

She pointed at the line of barrels and kegs, and Josh nodded, letting her lead the way. "Do you come into the city often?" she asked when they each had a cup of a locally made IPA.

"I do a lot of work here." He took a sip, licking the moisture off of his bottom lip. "You ever come out to the islands?"

The island where Josh lived was more like a peninsula. You didn't have to take a boat to get there, but it still had that isolated feel. It was a well-known vacation spot, so it was kind of funny that he'd been vacationing elsewhere when they met. Fatefully funny, according to Emma.

"I've only been once," she said. "It's beautiful there."

"Maybe I can get you to come a second time."

Cat snorted a juvenile laugh at his inadvertent double entendre, and his ears pinked adorably. "For a visit," he clarified. "But I'm not ruling that out."

She laughed again, genuinely. He was good at this too—banter, flirting in a way that made her feel safe instead of like she owed him something for playing along. She started to get that cartwheel feeling in her belly again. She was making this way too easy for him, purring at every little thing he said. Time for some hardball.

"So, Josh," she said, "you said that night in your hotel room that it wasn't a habit for you to pick up women at bars and take them home. How do you usually pick up women?"

Josh's lips parted in surprise, the corners of his eyes crinkling in amusement. He licked his bottom lip and shrugged. "Well, now that I think about it, I guess it sort of is a habit."

A scowl pinched Cat's face, her teeth grinding. She should have known. "I don't do this sort of thing"—what a line. She squeezed the plastic cup in her hand, contemplating tossing it at him before remembering that she was the one who practically demanded that he take her to his room in the first place. All to prove a point to herself. *This* was why she didn't do stuff like that.

In the midst of her internal rant, she noticed he was smiling down at her, his eyes dancing with mischief. "I'm kidding, Cat. You're the first woman I've *picked up* since my divorce." He used his fingers and satire in his voice to quote her somewhat churlish choice of words.

Oh. She'd forgotten how recently he'd been divorced. Less than a year and most people would require a little time before they got back out there. Maybe he really hadn't been out prowling when they met. She started to feel guilty for once again judging him so quickly until another thought flashed in her head like a neon sign: Rebound. If she was the first, then she was destined to be the rebound to a marriage that lasted the better part of a decade. It all made sense now. Great. Just what she needed.

"So you haven't dated at all since, you know?" she made a rolling motion with her hand in lieu of saying the word *divorce.*

"I went on a few dates with one woman. I didn't pick her up, though," he said, nudging her elbow with his. "Dylan set it up. She was friends with his girlfriend at the time. It didn't go anywhere. I should have known it wouldn't but..."

"But what?"

He blew out a long breath and led her around another couple that was blocking the path. "It was a few months after my ex-wife left," he said. "She just... she reminded me of her in a way. It wasn't that I was pining away over Sarah. We were like polite roommates by the time we finally signed the papers. I just thought I wanted that familiarity. To go back to what I knew. But then I'm sitting there, staring across the table at this woman, and all I'm seeing is Sarah, hearing her voice in everything she was saying, and it hit me that this was a story I already knew the end to. Like I'd heard this song before, you know?"

"I do know," she whispered, a little flustered by his mature response. Maybe he *had* worked through some of this already. Maybe he even had her beat on that front. That was exactly how she felt the last time she saw Micah again, years after they had broken up—thinking she wanted that familiarity, that comfort. She quickly realized, however, that she'd been broken and put back together in a completely new way and they just didn't fit anymore. She imagined it was like that for Josh, trying to fit into a box you had outgrown. Only he seemed to have a better handle on what kind of box would fit the new him. She was still unsure if one existed.

"Anyway," he said, summoning back a lighter moment. "Are you hungry?"

"Always."

Josh laughed from his belly, proving he'd forgiven her for being a jerk. "See," he said, his grin back in full force. "We already have so much in common."

Cat chose tacos from one of the food trucks lining the festival—Baja fish and avocado. Josh ordered something fried and smothered in a cream sauce, and he did insist on paying. Even if he turned up no other faults, he was clearly going to be a horrible influence on her diet. She'd eaten half of his chips dipped in that cream by the time they found a clear spot to sit and people watch.

The festival was in one of her favorite neighborhoods; rows and rows of brownstones strung together by brick sidewalks and old-fashioned lamp posts. It was a historic district, protected by the city, and it oozed charm and nineteenth-century romance. They walked to the edge of the festival area and found a patch of grass in the shade. The scent of cilantro from their lunch mingled with the sun-soaked earth and grass. The combination felt exotic, like they'd transported to a place where dining al fresco to the sound of steel drums was a normal occurrence. Like they were still on vacation. If she wasn't there with him, she'd probably be eating a prepackaged salad in her office with the blinds closed to stop the glare on her laptop.

Josh laid out all of their food and two full cups of summer ale onto the grass. He sat criss-cross and offered her his hand while she climbed down beside him.

Cat crossed her legs, laying her napkin over her lap. "Tell me more about yourself, Josh," she said, stealing another taco chip. "I feel like you and I started with all of the heavy stuff, but I don't know very many basic Josh facts."

"What do you want to know?"

"What do you do for fun?"

"Pick up pretty girls at bars."

She nudged his knee and laughed girlishly. Apparently, her impervious wall of composure was made of paper, and Josh was a strong breeze.

Josh unwrapped his fried taco and pulled out the tomatoes, dropping them into the cardboard serving box. "I play poker once a month, surf, watch baseball, run."

A vision of him running toward her on the beach popped into her head; sweaty and testing the limits of his t-shirt, definitely burning off fried food and cream sauces. Another memory of him waist-deep in the water quickly followed, his wet trunks clinging to his thighs. Her cheeks flushed and she took a sip of beer. "Running isn't fun," she said.

"I guess you're right. How about you? Give me some ideas."

"I..." She scanned her brain, expecting to easily supply him with a hobby or activity she enjoyed, but nothing came to mind. "I study and work," she said with a frown.

"Sounds like you need to take up running. Have a little more fun in your life."

She laughed, meeting his eyes again. "What about your family? Big? Small?"

Josh flicked his eyes away before answering, and she didn't miss the gesture. It was the same break in connection that he'd made when she'd asked him about moving there as a kid.

"You've met them," he said. He ran his thumb absentmindedly over the scar on his lip as he answered. It was the same thing he'd done when he'd asked her to see him before she left the beach. She wondered if he knew he did that or if it was more of a nervous tic. "Dylan and Shawn are my family. I've known them both since freshman year in college, and they're like brothers to me."

"But you don't have any real siblings?"

"No. I was an only child. My parents died when I was twelve."

She watched the statement travel across his face, but like a stray cloud on a sunny day, it disappeared just as quickly. "I'm sorry, Josh."

God, she was good at this. Between the ex-wife talk, and now this, she should get a prize for most wounds pressed on a first date.

He kissed the top of her head, absolving her. "It was a long time ago."

"Is that why you moved here?"

"My grandfather took me in. He was in his seventies. He did his best, but he had no business raising a kid. I just tried to be as helpful as I could and not cause him any trouble. In return, he put a roof over my head and used his Navy pension to pay for my first year of college. What about you?"

"I have a huge family." She started counting cousins in her head as she prepared to shock him with the reach of the Roday family tree branches. "My grandmother was Catholic—the kind that puts her faith over her sanity. I think she was pregnant half of her life."

Josh snorted a little laugh, sipping his beer and waiting for the rest of the story with a wistful look in his eye. Maybe it was insensitive to tell an orphan about your eight aunts and uncles and the seventeen children between them. She couldn't help but think that if anything had happened to her parents, she and her sisters would have had an army to care for them.

"Do you see them often?" he prodded, noticing her sudden reticence.

It was too late to stop now. He could probably see her heart dancing in her eyes from the minute he asked. "My parents live in the city and I see them frequently. My two sisters are married with kids, so I see them less—I'm the youngest. Holidays are... big." She smiled at the thought, and so did he. She wondered what holidays looked like for Josh.

He took another bite of his lunch, letting the subject drop. "I've done some work in this area," he said when he finished chewing.

"Yeah?"

"The theater two streets over. It was a historic renovation. I did the plans."

"I've been there," she said excitedly. "Before and after. You did nice work."

"Thanks. The new tower of condos a few blocks up was mine too. There's a lot of regulation in this part of town, making sure it maintains its atmosphere. But it's nice to work on something more interesting than a box with windows."

Cat nodded, imagining him hunched over a drafting table, drawing some of the buildings she passed by every day. "What's your favorite project you've done in the city?"

She watched his face react to what she assumed was a mental catalog of options. "I think it's The Abbott Building," he said. "We're working on it now. It's an old convent turned senior living."

"I know it, actually," she said. "My abuela—my grandmother—used to live there." Josh's face flashed with confusion, and she smiled. This story was one of her favorites. "She was a nun for a few years before she met my grandfather. He was a congressman."

"Wow."

"Yeah, it was scandalous. They worked together helping a local immigrant from Mexico who was trying to get his wife and family citizenship. The family was reunited, and my grandparents fell madly in love. She left the convent and became a politician's wife."

"That's quite the story."

"It is. She was a rebel in her younger days."

"I'll say."

"I always wanted to go see the building when the historical society used to give tours. I never made the time, and then they sold it."

Josh held his cup between his teeth and pulled out his phone. "Hold on," he said. Cat eyed him curiously, and a moment later, he shoved the phone back into his pocket and grinned. "You still want to see it?"

"How?"

"You want to walk or drive?"

Eleven

*T*HE MASSIVE BLOND-BRICKED BUILDING WAS surrounded by a construction fence and 'no trespassing' signs, but to Cat it was like walking into one of her abuela's stories. She'd passed by the old relic a hundred times, always on her way somewhere that wouldn't allow her to stop and take it in the way she wished. Now she was standing there, looking up at the stained-glass windows and the arched entry, and it was breathtaking.

"These are why it's my favorite," Josh said, gesturing to the bright purple doors. The heavy oak groaned obnoxiously as he pushed them open, and he smiled at the quirk. "I like to think about a bunch of stuffy old clergymen silently bucking the system by painting the doors purple."

Cat laughed. "My grandmother used to talk about these doors. How she couldn't help but smile when she came home to them, no matter how bad a day she'd had. Maybe you're right. Maybe they did it on purpose."

A stout man, his hair receding beneath his hard hat, came trotting over from one of the construction trailers. "Hey, man," he greeted, shaking Josh's hand. "You working the weekend?"

"No, this is a social stop. This is Catia. Cat, this is Jim Booth. He's the general contractor."

She shook his hand. "Nice to meet you."

"You take all your dates to construction sites, Josh?" Jim chuckled.

"Only the special ones."

"Well, go ahead and take your own tour. You know the place. I'll be in the trailer if you need me."

"Thanks," Josh said, taking her hand again. "I won't."

Josh led them into the grand foyer, and she spun around, taking in the vaulted ceilings and intricate stonework that served as molding throughout.

"Where do you want to start?"

Straight ahead of them was a wooden staircase with rich mahogany railings and treads, and she pulled him toward it. The whole place still smelled of incense and that musty, yet comforting scent of mothballs and grandparents. She ran her fingers along the polished railing as Josh trailed behind her. "What made you want to be an architect?" she asked as she climbed.

"I guess I like the responsibility of it."

"That's an odd way to put it. I figured you

would say you played with a lot of Legos as a kid."

"That too. But I like the idea that I can design something that will last forever, or in this case, preserve it. Places are important to people."

"This place is important to me."

"Then, it's important to me too."

When they reached the landing, a gold carpet unfurled on either side of them, stretching before rows of doors. Old, interesting sculptures hung on the walls between the dorms. A thought occurred to her, and she wandered down the hallway. "There was an angel carved out of wood hanging outside of my grandmother's room," she said. "She talked about it a few times."

Josh followed behind her, checking all of the statues carved into little nooks on the wall every few feet. She found it first, stopping to study it. Painted white and about a foot tall with its wings spread, it looked like the one she'd heard about.

"Maybe this was her room," Josh said, nodding across the hall at one of the closed doors.

"Can we look?"

"The rooms have already been stripped to the studs. I'm sorry."

"It's okay," she said, reaching up to touch the little statue.

Josh kept walking, leading her through a much simpler door to another steep stairwell, plain and full of cobwebs. He brushed a few of them down with his hand and gestured for her to duck her head. "This is the best part."

She could feel the open air before she saw it. Josh stepped to the landing, ducking under a beam to let her pass, and she knew exactly where they were. "Oh my God!" she said, squeezing between him and the metal bell that was taller than her.

"Careful." He reached for her elbow, helping her step on the old planked floor. They were surrounded by open window frames where only some weather-beaten chicken wire kept them from the outside. Josh had one hand braced on the wall, and he wrapped the other around her waist as she took in the panoramic view of the city.

"This is unbelievable!" She leaned as far as Josh's firm hold on her would allow and searched the landscape for her favorite places. She could see her office building, and the park dotted with the white canvas tents of the wine festival they'd just left. She spotted the domed roof of the theater they were just discussing and rows and rows of cherry trees.

"They didn't take people up here on the tour," he said, looking pleased by her reaction.

"I wonder if my grandmother ever snuck up here."

"Wouldn't you?"

"Absolutely." A gust of wind whipped around them, lifting her hair, and Josh's arm contracted until she was pressed against his side. "This might be the best date I've ever been on," she admitted, feeling a little starry-eyed despite herself.

"Good," he said. "When can we do it again?"

Cat tipped her chin to look at him, her blood rushing dangerously. He was looking at her the way he had on the beach that night when the lightning had flashed across his face. He was going to kiss her, and she was going to like it way too much. Then he'd smile again and say something sweet, and she'd be done for. She was supposed to be finding something wrong with him, not making out in a bell tower.

Before she could attempt to slow herself down, find that composure she thought she'd packed, he reached a hand out, his thumb brushing against her dangly earring as he cupped her jaw.

"I like you, Cat," he said, stepping closer and pulling her into his warmth. "Can we do this again?"

He kissed her then, lightly enough for her to answer his question against his mouth. She didn't, though, and he did it again, this time letting his teeth graze her bottom lip. Her hands wound around his neck, and when she still didn't answer, he deepened the kiss, taking advantage of her parted lips to let their tongues touch.

Before she could stop herself, a dreamy sigh slipped from her lungs and into his mouth, curling his lips into a grin.

Josh pulled away, waiting while she struggled

to gather air. Her lack of response didn't seem to trouble him—she'd just tipped her entire hand with that one audible expression of pleasure. Sonya was right; she had it so, so bad. The realization pulled a cold sweat from her pores. She watched him smile down at her, and she could almost feel the future pain she'd feel when looking at his face. Even this place would be ruined by it now.

"How does this go wrong, Josh?" she whispered.

"What do you mean?"

"You're going to break my heart. I just can't figure out how."

His smile shattered.

He dropped his hands to the side, and the breeze suddenly felt cold where his touch had been. "I have no intention of doing that, Catia," he said. She couldn't read his expression, but she had to figure he was trying to discern what kind of mental defect she had. She was sure he was going to rescind the offer, make up some plans he'd forgotten about and tell her he'd call her some time—meaning the day after never. Disappointment jabbed at her, and she rushed to close the distance he'd put between them, touching the soft cotton of his shirt.

"I'm sorry," she said. "I don't know why I said that. Actually, I have a thing next weekend. For work. Maybe you could come with me."

To her surprise, Josh rearranged his shocked

expression into a forgiving smile, but her accusation still hung on the slight downturn of his
cheeks. "Sure. What kind of thing is it?"

"It's a cocktail party—my boss is retiring. It's
in the West End."

"Sounds fancy."

"Not too bad."

"I'd love to go with you."

"Yeah?"

"Yeah."

"Good," she said. "It's a date."

"It's a date."

"Thank you for bringing me here."

"You're welcome."

It was an ungodly hour for a Sunday morning,
and only fourteen hours after her date with Josh
had ended (most of which were spent sleeping),
when Cat's phone buzzed across her kitchen
counter. She looked at the caller ID and nearly
hit the ignore button before she realized Emma's
early morning wake up could only mean she was
headed to yoga class, which happened to be right
around the corner from Cat's condo. If she didn't
answer, she would surely hear a knock on her
door in about ninety minutes.

As she swiped the little vibrating phone icon
to accept the call, her brain started scrambling
for an answer to the obvious question: how to

unpack her first date with Josh without it sounding like a major failure. Of her bet, that was. The date itself had been practically storybook. Prince Charming had taken her to a fairytale castle, one that just happened to be home to one of the most romantic stories she'd ever heard. She was still walking on air. Emma was going to love this one.

"Hey, Em. What's up?"

"What's up with you?" Emma didn't even have the decency to hide the giggle in her voice.

"Spill it," Sonya yelled in the background.

"Oh, good. Two for one." Cat padded over to her couch and fell backward onto the cushion dramatically, even though no one was there to witness. "What would you like to know? Be specific because I don't have time to go over the whole thing right now."

"It's Sunday morning. You're lying on the couch in your pajamas, wishing you had remembered to set the timer on your coffee maker. You have time."

"If you know me so well..."

"Just tell us how the date was!"

"It was very nice." *It was dreamy. Did people still say dreamy?* She shook her head. "He was charming and sweet, but we knew that."

"We did. Where did he take you?"

"To a wine festival."

"Did he pay?"

"Yes."

"What did he do when you reached for your wallet?"

Cat's cheeks warmed, and her mouth turned upward into a slow grin, remembering. "He said, 'Cat, please let me take you out. It's the only way I know how to do this.' Then he tipped the food truck guy really well."

A duet of affected *awwws* rang over the line. They were so easy. Maybe she was too.

"Then what?" Emma asked.

"Did he come back to your place?" Sonya shouted.

"No. It was late by the time we left."

"The festival?"

Here we go. "No, we went for a walk around the city."

"Romantic. Where'd you go?"

"A few places," Cat said, off-handedly. Unfortunately, she never could pull off off-handed. "The Abbott Building."

"You didn't make him go on that tour with you… "

"Of a convent?" Sonya asked. "Was that like a subliminal message?"

"I think my coffee is done…"

"No, tell us!"

She sighed and let all the lurid details spill. "They don't give tours anymore. They're turning it into senior living. I told Josh my grandmother used to live there and that I'd always wanted to see it. Turns out, he's the architect on the project, so he took me there."

Silence.

"Hello?"

Something way too close to a sniffle.

"Are you crying?"

"She is," Sonya shouted.

"Oh. My. God."

Emma's voice cracked. "That is the sweetest thing I have ever heard. You're going to tell this story to your grandkids, Cat."

"Why is she like this?" Cat called to Sonya.

"I don't know, dude." There was a brief shuffle and some whispering, and then Sonya had the phone. "Okay, so it sounds like it went well?"

"Yes, it was a very nice date."

"And the next one?"

"Next weekend."

"Hey, Cat?"

"What?"

"What do Dani and I win again?"

"Ugh."

Twelve

I T WAS FRIDAY WHEN JOSH returned to the Abbott Building site again, messenger bag slung over his shoulder and coffee cup in hand. The air was hot and dry, and the dirt from the construction lot dusted around his shoes. He hated parking there. He usually tried to find a spot on the street ever since Dylan's Audi had taken an errant two-by-four to the windshield one afternoon when one of the trucks had parked too close. Their business insurance hadn't covered it, so they were more careful now. He was rushing today, though, so it had to do.

He made his way to the trailer to find Jim and Dylan already huddled over a folding table, sharing a pizza while they poured over job packets.

"Just the man we needed," Dylan said, gesturing for him to take a seat. He held up a paper plate for him, but Josh declined.

"What's going on? Why the last-minute meeting?"

"Just a little snafu with the clients over the price point on some of the salvage work."

"They don't have a lot of wiggle room. The city says what we have to keep."

"That's what I told them," Jim said, around a bite of his lunch. "But they want you to go back over the details again, see what you can reasonably cut."

"Fine." Josh dug his laptop out of his bag and pushed some trash around the table to make room for it.

Jim finished his slice and pushed his folding chair away from the table. "I'll let you two at it, then," he said.

As soon as the door slammed behind Jim, Dylan started in. "How'd it go with Cat last weekend?"

"It went well."

"That all you're gonna give me?"

"For the moment."

"Jim said you brought her over here." Josh looked up from his screen to see Dylan leaning back in his chair and smiling at what he must have deemed secret information. "If you need some help planning a date, man, I'd be glad to give you a few pointers."

Josh forced himself to keep his face neutral, even as he recalled Cat's expression when she'd climbed the grand staircase to the dormitories, and how she smiled like a kid on Christmas when she took in the view from the bell tower. He had half a mind to give Dylan a few pointers.

"You know, I would have thought a construction site would have less office gossip," he said.

Dylan shrugged. "You seeing her again?"

"Tonight."

"Look, I get the whole don't kiss and tell thing, but you gotta give me something."

Josh pushed his laptop away and stretched back in his chair. "No locker room bullshit."

"Promise." Dylan crossed himself reverently before circling his hand to indicate his waning patience.

"I like her, man. She's got this way about her." He thought about stopping there, keeping it vague, but he felt like a balloon ready to burst. Though he'd take Shawn over Dylan for this confession any day, he couldn't shut up. "She makes me work for every smile I get out of her, but when I get one, it's like I can't breathe. All I can think about is getting the next one and the next one."

Jesus. He sounded lovesick. To his surprise, though, Dylan didn't have anything smart to say. He didn't have anything to say at all, actually; he just nodded with the kind of smile that said none of this was new information. And he supposed it shouldn't be. To Dylan's credit, he'd sort of called it from day one. Cat was different.

It was like he'd been sleepwalking since Sarah left. Dylan had been gently reminding him of that for almost a year now, but Cat was a shot of adrenaline straight to his vein. He was hooked on the jittery feeling he had when she was around. One slow dance with Catia left him wanting things he'd long since given up on. He daydreamed about waking up beside her, tangling his hands in her hair, making breakfast together. Hell, even watching TV with her on a Wednesday night. Anything to have her beside him.

It wasn't smart. He knew that. Letting himself get taken by someone who was so clearly reluctant to be taken by him rubbed at a particular sore spot he liked to ignore. But why couldn't he be the one to take that fear out of Cat's eyes? Why couldn't she finally be the one who needed exactly what he had to offer? She could be sure of him, and he could be good to her. Didn't they both deserve that?

"I think it's good, man," Dylan finally said. "She seems like a nice girl, and though I can't condone this foolishness," he waved his hand at Josh's face, gesturing to the stupid smile he was wearing, "it's good to see you happy."

It was good to be happy. Smart or not, he wanted to enjoy it.

Josh pushed the little glowing button beside Cat's apartment number and waited. They'd both cut out of work early so she could get ready, and so he could pick her up this time. He'd made it through the city rush hour traffic and arrived at ten minutes to seven. Just on time.

"Come up," her voice called through the intercom. "Top of the stairs, door on the right."

Catia lived in an old row house that had been turned into condos. What used to be the home's stately staircase, was now the main walk up for the upper units. He'd done the plans for a few of these types of renovations before the city started trying to limit them, and the zoning considerations became more hassle than the profit was worth. This particular building maintained most of its original charm, despite the modern conversion. It was quirkier than the massive apartment complexes that littered other parts of the city. It was charming and colorful and had a vibe to it that was hip, but classy at the same time—just like her.

When he got to the top of the stairs, the door was already ajar, and her scent swirled around him immediately. It was salty, fresh, like a lime mixed with the spindrift at the top of a wave. He pressed his palm to the heavy door, and it swung silently, giving him a moment to take in the candid view.

Cat stood back to him, her delicious hips swaying to the music she had playing as she worked what looked like a corkscrew. She had on a fitted black dress with sequins on the skirt that danced along with her. The top scooped low in the back, exposing the blades of her shoulders as she twisted and turned the bottle in her hands. Her dark hair cascaded over her shoulders in sleek, elegant curls. She was wearing heels, and red nail polish, and... he was staring. "Hey," he said, forcing himself to blink and tuck his tongue back in his mouth before she turned.

She smiled with her whole face when she saw him, wrinkling her nose adorably, and the air left his lungs. "Hey."

"Nice place."

She crossed the small open room to greet him, waving her arm to usher him in. "Thanks. It's cozy, but you don't get much more than cozy in this city on my budget. I'd give you the tour, but this is pretty much it. Bathroom and bedroom are down there." She pointed down a narrow hallway with shining hardwood floors and thick crown molding. "And the rest, well, what you see is what you get."

He spun his gaze around, trying to get a feel for the place where Catia spent her time. The narrow living room was painted a vibrant shade of aqua. It was grounded by an oversized ivory couch that took up nearly the entire room and overflowed with colorful mixed and matched pillows. He pictured lots of Netflix and wine being consumed there. Her big-for-a-girl television was flanked by what looked like original built-in shelving, crowded with books and a colorful menagerie of photographs and mementos. It was small, but she'd fit a ton of personality into the space.

"I like it," he said. "It suits you."

She smiled, her eyes flicking to his hands, and he remembered he was still holding the flowers he'd picked up on the way over. "Right," he said. "These are for you."

"I was hoping they weren't for my boss." They both laughed, and Josh's shoulders relaxed. He handed her the peonies, and her grin doubled, her perfect white teeth gleaming as she brought them to her nose. "Thank you."

"You're welcome."

She headed back to the kitchen, beckoning him to follow with a tilt of her head, and he allowed himself the indulgence of watching her ass as she swayed on those spiky heels.

She pulled out a vase and arranged the flowers in some water before setting them on the island.

"You want a drink before we go? We have a few minutes."

"Sure. Whatever you're having." He watched her waltz around the kitchen, choosing a couple of glasses from what looked like an eclectic collection. He could kick himself for not kissing her immediately upon arrival, and he wondered how he was going to reclaim that opportunity while she poured from the bottle she'd just opened.

"Do you work from home?" he asked, pointing to her kitchen table which had been set up like a desk. Her laptop was plugged in and open, stacks of manila folders set neatly beside it.

"Sometimes. I like the office atmosphere, so I make the trek in most of the time, but I can really work from anywhere. Unless I have to be in court."

"That's convenient with the traffic around here." He stepped toward a floor-to-ceiling window that looked out over the city, watching the cars in a tight line below. The summer sun was low in the sky, and it glinted off the metal and glass of the cityscape.

Cat came up behind him with his wine, and he stepped closer, reaching for the glass. She pulled her lip between her teeth, her thick black lashes fluttering as their fingers brushed. He could feel her nerves humming, something between trepidation and sexual tension brewing behind those big brown doe eyes. Whichever it was, he wanted to alleviate it. He set the glass down on the table beside him and took her face in his hands, gently. Her heels made her taller than usual, and her bright red lips were right there for him to take.

Cat sighed, kissing him back. He kept his touch light, letting her guide them as he studied her reaction. He wanted to learn her tells, something unique that he could memorize and use to please her whenever she let him have the chance.

She wrapped her arms around his back, still

holding her wine, and he dared to go a little further, moving one hand from her cheek to the back of her neck. Her soft hair threaded between his fingers, and she shifted in his arms. So did the tenor of her embrace, from cautious to indulgent. Her lips parted, and he matched her need with a swipe of his tongue, then a full-on exploration.

Cat set down her glass then too, and her hands settled on his hips, tugging until he was flush against her. *Fuck.* There was no hiding behind his manners now. Every dirty thing he wanted to do with her was pressed like lead into her tummy. When she moved her hands up his back, clutching the cotton of his shirt beneath his jacket, he had to concentrate on not grinding against the front of her dress like a teenager.

God, she felt good. The muscles in her back rolled and stretched under his arms as she stood on her toes to meet his kiss. Her hair was like silk, swishing back and forth over his hands as her head slanted to accommodate his eager tongue. She seemed to vibrate with an energy that was larger than her petite frame could contain—like a hurricane kept in a jar—and he wanted to find the button that would release it.

Cat pulled away, her palm firm on his chest. For a moment, he thought she'd come to her senses and was about to insist he mind his manners, but instead, she tossed a glance behind her and gave him a look that set his whole body on fire.

"Couch," she whispered, before crashing back into his mouth.

Josh walked them backward without breaking their kiss until the hardwood floor turned into soft carpet beneath his shoes. He opened his eyes just long enough to maneuver in front of the couch, then he fell backward into the cushions, pulling her with him. Her dress stretched around her thighs as she climbed onto his lap, straddling him. He pushed the taut material up her legs until it didn't look in danger of tearing, then he let his fingers squeeze and caress their way around to her ass.

"Christ, Catia," he said, as she rolled her hips forward and dug her fingertips into his hair. He wasn't prepared for her to touch him like this. She'd been rationing out her affection since that night when they'd almost had sex on that beach. She'd pulled them back to the starting line, and he completely understood. If this was going to be something real, which he hoped it was, then he was prepared to earn that. But this starting and stopping was more than he could take. He loosened his greedy grip, whispering into the skin below her ear. "Tell me what you want. I don't want to get this wrong."

Cat pulled back, meeting his gaze with a little flicker of confusion. "I don't know," she said. "I'm sorry. I'm bad at this."

He chuckled at her choice of words. Given his physical state at the moment, she was anything but bad at this. But the last thing he wanted to do was to take advantage of her confusion. He moved his hands to a safer place on her waist and his lips back to her mouth. "This is good," he said, kissing her softly. "We can stay here."

She nodded. She let go of his hair, and her hands fell chastely onto his shoulders.

They did stay there for what seemed like forever, kissing and talking and completely ignoring their wine until the evening sunlight that lit the room had turned the color of fire.

"We're going to be late," he said, glancing at his watch behind her head.

"I don't care."

Her teeth were on the shell of his ear, and he had two handfuls of sequined goodness—at that particular moment, he didn't care either. But, she'd said this was important. "Are you sure?"

Her warm breath prickled his skin as she sighed out her response. "Fine." She sat up, adjusting her dress. "I guess we had better get to this date then," she said, her eyes telling him she wanted to stay just as much as he did.

He finally let her go with a parting squeeze. "Guess so."

"I just need to fix this." She waved a hand in front of her face. "Then we'll go."

Thirteen

THE DOWNTOWN RESTAURANT WAS BUSTLING by eight-thirty on a Friday night, and despite the air conditioning, the air was dewy with the humidity that shamelessly hitched a ride in on each new guest. After Cat had fixed her makeup and called an Uber, they'd arrived still punctual enough not to draw any undue notice.

The lounge area was a circular room with windows on one half and a twenty-foot long bar on the opposite end. Candlelight flickered from a sea of tall tables and bounced around the groups of well-dressed people enjoying the buzz of the end of the workweek. It would have been a romantic night out on the town if they weren't surrounded by a dozen of her co-workers.

Josh was engaged in polite conversation with Bill Cranshaw, the middle-aged IT guy, whom Cat never actually spoke to except for at these types of things. Cat had always felt sort of bad for Bill. He was socially awkward, to put it kindly, and he couldn't seem to help himself from making every painful conversation worse by launching into the intricacies of cybersecurity and firewalls. Josh, though, had a way of fixing his expression to one of complete and genuine interest, whether you were talking about the appetizer selection or world peace. Bill was practically basking in the attention.

Cat listened only half-heartedly while she replayed the earlier scene on her couch. She didn't know what had come over her. She'd only intended to have a glass of wine then get them to this safe public place as fast as she could. But damn, he looked good in that suit that matched his eyes, and that five o'clock shadow that she just had to get her hands on. Then he'd done that thing where he rested his palm on her neck and twirled her hair around his thumb. She liked that thing.

Ugh. He was Cat Kryptonite. Just when she started to feel like a normal human being around him, he touched her just so or said something adorable, and that drunk-on-Josh feeling swooped in and shoved her off her guard.

Maybe it was the way he always seemed so in control. They'd been going at it like a couple of teenagers on her couch, and even though she could see his physical reaction—flushed neck, dilated pupils... other things—his hands were steady. If he was nervous at all, he didn't show it. He was so sure, so comfortable, in every touch or look they shared that her constant confusion felt utterly sophomoric in comparison. Like when he'd asked her to tell him what she wanted and instead of purring out some sexy reply, her cheeks had burned red and she'd admitted to being a complete amateur in the arena of adult relationships.

Josh laughed at something Bill said and tightened his fingers on her hip. Probably to remind her that she should participate in the conversation. She had to get it together. She couldn't cheat at the bet by acting like a total weirdo. Dani and Sonya would accuse her of sabotage if Josh dumped her because she could only seem to go mute or babble incoherently whenever she was in his presence.

Speaking of the bet, clearly she couldn't just keep going on these dates with Josh, waiting for him to make a misstep on his own. Date number one was already a point on his board, and she didn't have weeks to invest. She was already getting used to having him around and spoiled by his torturously slow hands and knack for using his teeth in all the right places.

Now she was feeling more than dewy. She was practically overheating. *Enough of this bewitching.* Fantasizing about what would have happened if they had just ditched the party and stayed on that couch wasn't helping her stay unattached. She needed a way to push things along. She stepped away from the circle the three of them had made, feeling terrible about sacrificing Josh to Cranshaw, but she needed a splash of cold water and to think.

"I'm going to run to the ladies' room," she said, with a squeeze to his fingers. "I'll be right back."

The hallway to the restroom was well-lit, and Cat squinted against the fluorescent bulbs as she left the dim lounge area. When she pushed open the door, she spotted one of her agency's interns leaning against the bank of sinks, scrolling through her phone with one hand, her drink in the other. An idea hit her like the flash from the girl's phone as she took a selfie.

"Hey! Kasey. I'm glad you're here."

"That makes one of us," she said, taking a long pull from her wine glass. Kasey was a senior at UVA, and Cat had immediately bonded with her when she found out they not only shared an alma mater but had both lived in the same dormitory as freshman. Kasey was also hot as hell with auburn hair and flawless skin. Not to mention a rack that stopped men mid-sentence as she passed. She would be perfect.

"You're not here with a date, are you?" Cat asked, formulating the best way to phrase what she was about to ask.

"No, but thanks for reminding me."

"I need a favor."

Kasey nudged a clump of mascara away from her eyelash with her pinky finger, then pouted in front of her phone for another shot. "What do you need?"

"Come here." She hooked her arm in Kasey's and dragged her out of the bathroom and into the corner of the restaurant, pointing. "See that guy over there? Blue jacket, talking to Bill?"

"Um, yeah. Wow." Kasey took another gulp of wine, looking as though she were undressing Josh with her eyes.

"He's my date."

"Oh!" Kasey said, straightening her shoulders. "Sorry for staring."

"It's okay. I need you to hit on him."

Kasey's head whipped around, her long ponytail nearly smacking her in the face. "What the—?"

"Hear me out. I just want you to flirt with him a little, maybe slip him your number. Then let me know how he reacts."

"That sounds bizarre, and yet not entirely unlike you," Kasey said with a judgy little sip of her wine. Maybe Cat was spending a little too much time with the interns. "Why exactly are you trying to give that one up?"

"I'm not. I'm testing a theory."

"Like a social experiment?"

"Yes!" *Exactly Kasey, you little soc major, you!*

Kasey peeled her eyes away from Josh and settled them on Cat's with a filthy expression. "Do I get to fuck him if he calls me? Are we gonna compare notes?"

Kasey's words fell over her like an emerald-colored veil. Cat's hands tightened into fists, and her teeth began to grind. *What in the literal hell, Kasey?*

"No," she said, clenching her jaw, and calming the nonsensical urge she had to fire her right then and there. She didn't actually have that power, though. "You do not."

"Why not?" I mean, if he takes my number while he's here with you, he's no good for anything else, right?"

"Just... ugh." Cat sputtered. She hadn't expected that reply or the way the champagne and hors d'oeuvres started creeping back up her esophagus at the mental image of Josh and Kasey doing... that thing she'd just said. Maybe this was a bad idea.

"Fine. I'll do it." Kasey sighed. "Let me get another drink first." With that, she turned on her impossibly high heel and sashayed over to the bar.

Cat swallowed down the gross feeling that came over her, and the desire to chuck her champagne glass at the back of Kasey's head, and made her way back to where Josh was. She sidled up to him while he nodded and followed along with the story Cranshaw was still telling. Josh shot her a quick smile and wrapped an arm around her waist, then went right back to making the most boring man in the room feel like the host of a Ted Talk.

He'd been quite charming all evening, actually. He'd also turned a few heads. Kasey's bedroom eyes flashed in her brain, and she slid her hand further down his back, resting just low enough to claim her spot without being work-function inappropriate.

Cranshaw finally excused himself, doing a scan of the buffet table before heading off in that direction, and Cat wrapped her fingers around Josh's tie, pulling him to face her. She wanted to get another dose of those ocean-blue eyes before they became an unpleasant memory. "Snooze-fest, right?" she said, smoothing her hands over his shirt. "Sorry about him."

"It's cool. We both play golf, so we chatted about that for a while."

"You're a natural at small-talk. Sometimes I forget to look interested in situations like that."

Josh tipped his glass to his lips, and she watched his Adam's apple bob as he swallowed. "I have a lot of these things in my line of work. Client dinners, ground-breaking ceremonies. I like to let Dylan handle most of them, but sometimes we have to tag-team."

"What's it like running a business with your best friend?" she asked, nervously glancing around for Kasey or anyone else who might be looking at him like that.

"Truthfully?"

"Of course."

He laughed quietly, then finished his drink.

"It's awesome. Dylan's good at what he does. I'm good at what I do. It just works. Besides, we've been friends long enough that if we get on each other's nerves, we know how to hash it out."

"Oh yeah?" she said, smiling at the thought of him and Dylan bickering. "How's that?"

"Whenever he pisses me off, I usually invite him to play some basketball or go for a run. Two things that I'm better at than him. By the end of it, when he's wheezing like an old man or dragging the last mile of our run, I end up feeling sorry for him and forget about whatever he did."

A fit of genuine laughter surprised her. "How petty! I never would have guessed."

"I hide it well. You want another drink?"

"Sure," she said, taking the last sip of her champagne, then handing him her glass.

"I'm going to hit the restroom. I'll grab another round on my way back."

Cat turned over her shoulder, spotting Kasey perched on a bar stool like a bird of prey. She grabbed for his sleeve. "Josh, I can get—"

"Cat!" Her head swiveled again as Margo Fields, the executive director of her agency, appeared beside her with her arms outstretched. She gathered Cat into a boozy hug, launching straight into a conversation, and Josh flashed her one more grin before disappearing into the crowd.

Josh deposited their glasses on a tray as a black-tied waiter passed him, and he headed for the back of the room. He glanced around for a sign that would point him to the restrooms, and as he turned down the labeled corridor, he nearly collided with a red-headed woman in a short green dress. She was standing there like a toll collector, with her hands on her hips and head tipped up, eyeing him expectantly.

"Are the bathrooms this way?" he asked. It was rhetorical, he really just wanted to make it known that was his destination so she would step aside.

She shifted her weight, jutting one hip outward, and placed one perfectly manicured finger on her lower lip. "Do I know you?"

"Um, I don't think so," he replied, flicking his gaze past her toward the bathroom and hoping she would get the hint that he really had to take a leak.

"No? You look familiar." She stepped closer, and the scent of sandalwood and vanilla filled his space. "We must have met before."

"I don't live in the city," he said, searching his brain for her face. "Maybe we've worked together. Rideout Pierce Architecture?"

"No. This doesn't feel like a business thing."

He studied her again, coming up blank. Maybe she was one of Dylan's flings. They all sort of ran together. Though, she looked too young for him.

"Hmmm," she purred, reaching out to touch his sleeve. "Well, there's one way to get to the bottom of this."

"What's that?" He took his arm back, shoving his hands in his pockets. He really fucking had to pee.

"You could buy me a drink, and we could talk it through." She stepped closer still. "Let's figure out where we've seen each other before, and where we're going to see each other next."

Realization smacked him in the forehead, and he couldn't help the laugh that tumbled from his mouth. This woman was bold. "Sorry," he said, moving to step past her. "I'm here with someone."

The woman stopped him again, this time with a flat palm on his chest. "Are you sorry that you can't buy me a drink? Or sorry that you're here with someone? Because we could always do this another time."

Blood rushed to Josh's face, and he instinctively took a step back, glancing around the hallway. That was definitely his cue to end the conversation. The last thing he wanted was to give this girl the impression that he was going to entertain her request, or for one of Cat's co-workers to see him and come to the wrong conclusion.

"Sorry was the wrong word," he said, firmly. "I'm actually pretty damn happy about it. Listen, I'm gonna hit the head. It was nice to meet you."

Cat's boss finally spotted another target for her alcohol-induced affection, leaving Cat standing alone against a pillar with no one to talk to and no drink in her hand. All she had to occupy her was the sense of dread that had settled in her chest ever since Josh took off in the direction of the bathroom and Kasey disappeared from her spot at the bar.

The suspense of the whole thing had the bile churning in her stomach and she wished she'd eaten more from the buffet instead of staring at Josh all night, too nervous to finish the crackers and fruit she'd filled her plate with. She thought about standing in that bell tower, Josh smiling against her mouth, and how she'd wished for all of this to somehow be true. Now she'd set something in motion, and all she could do was wait it out.

Kasey was right, though. If Josh was going to fail this test, then at least she would know. It was only two dates—steamy, almost-sex on the beach notwithstanding. No harm, no foul. She'd win her bet, and Dani and Sonya would eat their words. Her heart wasn't even remotely on the line yet. Right? Then why did she feel so woozy and murderous at the same time? Like she wanted someone to give her a hug while she poked Kasey's eyes out.

She glanced toward the hallway again then sorted through all of the bodies at the bar, spotting neither of them. This was taking forever. Kasey was probably giving Josh that same pouty face she'd been flashing her phone in the bathroom, her tiny dress hiked up even higher on her thighs. Cat remembered what it was like to be twenty-one, a little buzzed and a lot sexy. Josh was probably eating it up, giving her that laser-beam stare of his, swiping his bottom lip with his tongue like he did. It probably wasn't every day a guy his age got hit on by a co-ed. Or maybe it was. Who knew? That thought didn't make her feel any better at all.

She glanced at the time, suddenly feeling like she needed a quick escape plan. Things would become extremely uncomfortable once Josh came back, and Kasey gave her all the disgusting details. She swiped her screen, pulling up her messages just as the phone vibrated in her hand.

Kasey: You're one lucky bitch

Cat: What happened?

Kasey: He is haaawwwttt

Cat: Kasey!!

Kasey: He totally blew me off. Now stop being a psycho.

Relief leaped around like a giddy child in her chest. She had the overwhelming urge to high-five someone. Instead, she stood there, bouncing on her toes and beaming at her screen while she read Kasey's message again and again.

"Hey," Josh whispered from behind her shoulder. She jumped, a shiver running down her spine as she rushed to lock her screen.

"Hi."

"Everything okay?"

"Everything is completely fine." She dropped her phone back into her purse, reaching for the back of his neck, and pulled him into a kiss that left a smear of red on the corner of his mouth. She wiped it with her thumb, then did it again. He had a drink in each hand, so his participation was limited to an enthusiastic tug on her bottom lip and a pleasantly surprised grin when she let him go. "Let's get out of here."

Josh glanced down at the two glasses of wine in his hands, then back at her. "You sure everything is fine?"

She nodded, taking her glass and swallowing one large sip. "I just want you to myself for a little bit."

Josh gave her a confused grin, clearly having no idea what he was being rewarded for, but he was obviously enjoying it.

"Do you want to come up?" Cat asked when their car had pulled away from the curb. They'd moved on from her work party to an upscale martini bar which Josh had very politely tolerated, then an all-night pizza place that served lukewarm slices and draft beers, where he'd seemed much more at home. After the Kasey test, she'd decided to give him the rest of the night off, and just enjoy his company. She had, more and more with each stop. Now they were back on her stoop, holding on to the last moments of whatever this night was going to be.

Josh leaned in, making a low growling noise into her neck before kissing his way down her shoulder. "I wish I could," he said, straightening. He dragged a hand over his face, stopping to massage the corners of his eyes. "I'm heading up to Ocean Beach tomorrow with Dylan to surf. We're leaving at six a.m. sharp."

"Josh! That's less than six hours from now, and you still have to drive home. You're going to be exhausted. You didn't have to come to this with me."

"I wanted to. I'm going to be gone for three days, and I wasn't giving up the chance to see you before I left."

Her heart flapped its wings inside her chest, sending a rush of blood to her cheeks. "Still," she said. "I feel bad keeping you out this late."

"I'll be back in the city on Wednesday. Can we meet for lunch?"

"I have court on Wednesday," she said, surprised by her disappointment. "But Dani and I always go out for drinks on Wednesday nights at the bar between our offices. You could meet us."

"I have dinner with a client that night." He scratched his brow. "Dylan is having a party Saturday. He has a pool... Shawn will be there. Will you come?"

Oddly enough, not a single excuse reared its head. "Sure."

"Good. I'll call you when I get home from my trip and give you the details. I wish it wasn't another week away."

Her smile pulled wider, and she laughed.

"What?"

"Nothing. It's just... me too."

Fourteen

"**I** LIKE THESE," DANI SAID, HOLDING up a pair of grey and white, leopard print shorts.

Sonya scrunched her nose from her spot, sprawled out on Cat's bed. "They're kinda short. Is that what she's going for?"

"Why wouldn't she be?"

They both turned to Cat. She'd been sitting cross-legged on the floor of her bedroom, letting the two discuss her outfit options for Dylan's pool party the next day while she scrolled through the thread of text messages between her and Josh for the hundredth time.

There was intention behind the outfit selecting appointment. She had a closet full of options, and what to wear had never really been something she dwelled on. What she did have was an entirely different problem that required a specific kind of help.

She'd been making herself insane all week wondering if Josh intended for this to be a sleepover date. *Probably.* And if she wanted it to be. *Yes*. This little game of hers was starting to feel more dangerous by the minute. The first two matches had landed squarely on Josh's board, given the way she'd been dreaming about him all week, and she didn't like the feeling that was starting to creep in.

She'd become more smitten with every text exchange and late-night phone call she and Josh shared. He'd yet to make a major misstep, and he also kept forgiving hers, watching her with a sort of amused adoration each time she made an ass of herself, as if it endeared her to him somehow. She needed to reshift the balance, which is why she needed Dani. She also needed to keep herself from backing out altogether, which was where Sonya came in. Emma was liable to turn this into a whole different discussion, so she'd purposely planned it on a night her friend with the perpetual rose-colored glasses was otherwise engaged.

"Cat," Dani said, dragging her back into the conversation. "Too short?"

Cat shook her head.

"That's my girl." Dani tossed the shorts into the keep pile and went back to the closet. "Should you even pack sleepwear? What's the point?"

"Of course she should," Sonya said. "She doesn't want to put her clothes from the night before back on as soon as she gets up. She needs something cute for coffee in the morning."

"Why are you guys assuming I'm sleeping there? And that I'll be waking up naked."

They both laughed, and Dani held a hand out to Sonya to take the explanation. "It's like this, Cat. The lunch date was the *I promise I'm not just in it for the sex* date," she explained, with Dani nodding in agreement. "Your co-worker's retirement thingy was the *see how hard I'm willing to work for it?* date. A party at his friend's house, an hour away and lasting into the night? That's the *but can we please have sex?* date."

"Very enlightening. Look, I have no idea if I even like him." That was a lie. What she meant was that she had no idea if she was willing to admit that she liked him. A lot. It wasn't just about the bet, admitting how Josh made her feel before she could rationally put a name to it was dangerous.

"So why did you agree to see him again for the third weekend in a row?" Dani asked, flipping through the catalog of blouses Cat had hanging in her closet.

Cat shrugged her shoulders. "To prove Emma wrong." More lies. She was pathological.

Sonya dropped the pile of bathing suits she was pawing through, her face turning hard. "Catia."

"Emma thinks I make my own problems—"

"We all think that," Dani interrupted.

"Okay, well, you'll all see then."

"You're playing games, Catia. Someone's going to get hurt."

"I'm not playing games. I'm just fast-forwarding to the inevitable. Why waste my time or his? Let's just get to the part where he ends up being a jerk, and I end up eating a couple pints of ice cream, and then I get over it."

Dani rolled her eyes. "So you've been seeing him every weekend just to speed up the time it takes to break up? That makes zero sense. Besides, it seems like things are going well, despite your ridiculous behavior."

They didn't even know the half of it. Specifically the Kasey half of it. "I don't know," she said. "Frankly, after the first date, I'm not sure why he even wanted to see me again. I think I accidentally brought up every sore subject imaginable, and that wasn't even the plan."

"Maybe he's a masochist who loves being tortured by your awkwardness," Dani suggested.

Sonya groaned. "You're not helping. Do you want to win this bet?"

"No," Cat said. "But maybe he's the type of guy who likes the chase. Every time I challenge him, he doubles down."

Sonya shook her head and mumbled under her breath, "Maybe he just really likes you."

"Well, he's put in this much effort," Dani said. "It's hard to see him not seeing it through to the reward."

Sonya scrunched her nose, and so did Cat.

Josh was going to disappoint her somehow, but even she didn't think he was a conquest type of guy. Still...

"Either way," she said, "you know how men are. Even if they tell themselves they're looking for a real thing, as soon as you start giving them girlfriend vibes too early, they freeze."

Dani agreed with a resounding "Mm-hmm."

"So, that's the new plan?" Sonya asked. "Be sweet instead of spicy?"

"I can't stop spicy, Sonya," Cat said, "but we're going to be at a party with all of his friends. I'll lay it on thick, see how he really feels about this relationship." And she'd see how she really felt about it because admit it or not, she knew there was no way she was getting out of this unscathed. She'd passed the point where disappointment was on the line. If Josh hurt her now, she was in for devastation.

"You're a mess," Sonya said, falling back into the pillow and leaving the packing to Dani.

Dani pulled out a red lace bra from Cat's top drawer and held it up. "So should we skip over the sexy underwear then, if you're already an old married couple?"

Cat shook her head, a little flutter going through her belly at the thought of Josh licking his lips when he saw her in that bra and the panties that matched it. "Keep that one out."

Josh heard Cat's car pull up and he rushed through the front door, and down the steps to meet her in the driveway. He'd been pacing around his house, making excuses to look out the window every five minutes. Now that she was there, it felt like he hadn't seen her in months.

He crossed the driveway to meet her, leaning an arm on her open door as she finished gathering her things. She twisted in her seat to grab a large tote bag from the back that he hoped was filled with overnight accessories, but he didn't want to be presumptuous.

"Hi," he said, offering her a hand. He helped her out of the car, then tugged her hand until she was pressed against him.

To his surprise, she grabbed his chin and immediately pulled him into a long, eager kiss. Her lips were cold from the air-conditioned car, and so were her fingers as they slipped up the back of his shirt.

This was new. He indulged in her newfound boldness, his hands traveling down to her ass and chancing a squeeze that had her sighing into his mouth. She finally released his mouth but kept her body pressed against his as she brushed her fingers through his hair.

"I missed you."

"I missed you too." He grinned, probably goofily so. "Let me take your bag." He slid the tote from her shoulder, resisting the urge to glance inside for any signs of sleepwear or a toothbrush.

Cat slipped her hand into his and followed him across the stone driveway to his front door. "Your house is beautiful," she said. Her head swiveled from wall to wall as he led her through the open-beamed living room, past the stone fireplace and leather couch, and into the granite and oak kitchen. Like most houses built in the little town on the bay, it had an inherent nautical flavor infused into the architecture, and he'd indulged it a bit with the decor. Her expression reflected her approval, and a beam of pride straightened his posture.

"Thanks." He set her bag down by the kitchen island. Taking it directly to his room might be pushing it. "Can I get you a drink?"

"Just water if you don't mind. What time are we leaving?"

He picked a glass from the cupboard and filled it from the dispenser on the fridge door. "Anytime," he said. "It's an all-day thing, and the weather is perfect to be by the pool."

She took a long sip of the water he gave her, and he used the opportunity to scan the rest of her outfit; sexy little short-shorts, a tank top that crisscrossed in the back. Her hair was up again like it had been the first night they met. It left her neck exposed, and he focused on the dip of it, thinking of pressing his tongue there.

"I shouldn't have parked behind you," she said. "Do you want to take my car?"

"Actually, I thought we could walk if that's okay with you. It's only a few streets over."

"Dylan lives a few streets away from you?"

"He used to live here with me, actually. This was my grandfather's house. The main portion, at least. When he passed, I took over the mortgage. After I finished school and moved back, I needed a roommate to afford it. Dylan lived here until Sarah and I got married." He hated thinking of this house as his and Sarah's. He'd lived there most of his life and he would always regret that he'd tainted it by starting a life there that didn't pan out. "Anyway, I guess he liked the neighborhood and the place he has happened to be for sale. After he left, I added the office over the garage, the master bedroom, and the sunroom." He turned to point in the direction of each of the additions.

"Wow. Guess it's true what they say that an architect's home is never finished."

He chuckled. "The expression is a builder's home, but same thing, I guess." He poured himself a quick glass of water, drinking it down in two gulps. "So, will you mind the walk? Driving is fine too."

"No, that sounds nice. You can show me the neighborhood."

"Sure."

After gathering her things, Cat followed him out of the house and waited while he locked up.

When he turned around, she pulled him into another kiss.

He suddenly regretted the rush. Maybe they could just show up late, after... *No. Slow down, Josh.*

They had all night, and he was going to take his time.

The water and the scent of beach roses perfumed the air as they walked down the quiet, tree-lined roads of the peninsula. Josh pointed out some of the more historic homes on the walk with an exuberance that Cat found infectious. Who knew architecture could be so interesting?

He told her that the shore was just past the rolling green lawns of the clapboard-sided estates that they passed, and she marveled alongside him at the stately mansions, all the while holding his hand. He seemed to be ready and willing to accept her increased affection. She glanced in his direction and was met with a happy smile. Of course, they were still alone and not in a group of his best guy friends, one of whom appeared to be a serial bachelor. She would see how things changed when they got to the party. For now, she would just enjoy the way he was stroking her hand with his thumb as they walked.

He looked extra handsome today. Not that he didn't always, but she'd seen him dressed for the beach and dressed for a date in the city, and until now she hadn't been able to decide which she liked better. Taking a discrete, sidelong look at him as they walked, and noticing the way his light grey t-shirt gave a shadowed hint at the definition of his lower abs, she decided casual Josh was a winner.

Dylan's house really was only a short walk away, and Josh slowed as they reached a bungalow-style home with cedar siding and bright white trim. It was smaller than Josh's, but she imagined it was similar to what Josh's might have looked like before he added on.

She pulled in a deep breath, nervousness beginning to stir in her belly as they approached. She'd already spent time with Dylan and Shawn, but this was different. Last time, they were doing shots and playing cards on neutral territory. This felt more like an official invitation into Josh's life, and she found herself wanting to make a good impression, despite her initial intentions. She reminded herself that worrying about his friends liking her was premature. Who knew how long this was going to last?

They walked through the front door without bothering to knock, and Josh led them through a much more cluttered living room than she'd found at his house. Josh's home had impressed her. It wasn't as if she was expecting some man-cave-esque flophouse, he was in his thirties after all, but she wondered if it was that clean all the time or he'd just made an extra effort for her. Additionally, her nosy self had noted that it had obviously been purged and redone since a woman had lived there, given the overtly masculine color scheme of greys and blues, and the vaguely utilitarian feel.

Dylan's house, on the other hand, with very little hanging on the walls and piles of mail and magazines littering the dining room table, looked more like a base camp than a home. Josh had a beautiful stone fireplace in his living room and an expensive-looking leather couch. Dylan had a giant screen television and a sofa that looked as though it might have once lived in a dorm room. It was colorful, though, and what the house lacked in decor, it made up for in unique amenities: a spiral staircase, beautiful granite countertops, and modern fixtures. It was sort of frat-boy chic if she had to give it a title.

They went straight through the house and out the sliding glass doors off the kitchen, landing in a fenced-in yard. A kidney-shaped pool, sparkling blue against the white concrete patio, took up most of the space, but there was also a grassy area, large enough that a few men were tossing a football back and forth on it with no danger of a Marcia Brady incident for any of the other guests milling around.

Dylan stood behind the kind of grill men dream about, with a beer in his hand and a towel slung over his shoulder. He was speaking to a boy around seven or eight years old. Josh wrapped an arm around her shoulders, kissing the top of her head as he led her over.

That was unexpected. But it was one thing to initiate it himself. She still didn't know how Josh would respond if the PDA were her idea.

"Hey, man," Dylan said, giving a slight smirk at the sight of them before putting on a full grin. "Hey, Cat. Really good to see you again."

"You too. Thanks for having me."

"Hey, Josh!" the little boy shouted, rushing to Josh's other side and hugging him around the waist. Cat let him go so he could receive the greeting.

"Mattie, this is Cat," he said, grinning. "Cat, this is Shawn's son, Matt."

"Hi, Matt." She smiled. "Nice to meet you."

Shawn appeared beside them with a petite woman with pale white skin and a bright smile. Matt's mother, quite obviously, given the round face and jet-black hair they shared. She'd have to take their word for it on Shawn's parentage since the boy didn't look a thing like him.

"You must be Cat," she said, offering a hand. "I'm Min-jung, but you can call me Minnie. I'm Shawn's wife."

"Hi, Minnie. It's nice to meet you. I actually saw your picture when I met these guys. Shawn passed it around first thing."

Minnie beamed at her husband, who puffed out his chest and wrapped an arm around her.

"Josh, have I mentioned how much I like Cat?" Shawn asked, with an appreciative smile. "Let's get her a drink."

Josh squeezed her hand. "Beer, wine, or cocktail?"

"It's a full bar, and I'm mixing," Shawn added. "Name your poison."

She thought about the bikini in her bag and the sugary bloat of a mixed drink, but the pool and the hot sun had her pining for something tropical. "Tequila?" she asked, to a trio of smiles from the men.

"Shot or margarita?"

"It's a little early for shots. A margarita sounds perfect."

"Good choice," Minnie said, holding up a blue plastic cup and indicating it had been hers as well.

"I'll be right back," Josh said to her.

Dylan and Shawn were both watching them, so she stood on her toes to give Josh a girlfriendy kiss goodbye, expecting to feel him cringe. The audience didn't seem to faze him in the least, though. He kissed her back as if he'd done it a hundred times, then took off for the bar with Shawn and Dylan, Mattie tagging along beside him.

"I like your earrings," Minnie said when they were left alone. "And you are as gorgeous as Josh said you were."

Cat flushed, fingering the silver teardrops hanging from her ears. "Thank you."

"So, you two met when Josh and Dylan were at their conference?" Minnie turned toward her, indicating she was going to keep Cat company, and she was grateful.

"We did. I was there for a pre-wedding celebration for a friend. She gets married next month."

As they chatted, a couple of guys came barreling out of the house, charging the pool and cannonballing into the deep end. Minnie rolled her eyes and turned back to Cat. "Did you bring a suit?"

"I did." Minnie wore hers under the black and white striped dress she had on.

"I told Josh inviting a girl to a party where she had to put on a bathing suit was a big ask, but he said I hadn't seen you in a bikini. Come on. I'll show you where you can change."

When Cat returned from Dylan's bathroom, Josh was waiting with her drink. He handed it to her, his eyes flicking to her outfit change as he touched the rim of his cup to hers. "How about we cool off?" he said, gesturing to the pool. "You wanna go in?"

"Sure." She was feeling a little exposed, and getting underwater sounded like a great idea. Josh pulled his t-shirt over his head, tossing it onto a lawn chair, and led her to the concrete stairs.

He paused before he stepped in. "Are you the type of girl who doesn't get her hair wet when she swims?" he asked.

She was. "Why do you ask that?"

"Just wondering."

He had a mischievous smile on, and she planted her feet. "Josh..." Before she could protest, he scooped her around the waist and placed her over his shoulder, carefully enough that she didn't spill her drink.

"I won't drop you," he said when she started kicking her feet, giggling despite herself. The two men who had dived in while she was talking to Minnie were still wading around, and he walked past them and set her down on a neon-green lounge float. She was side-saddle, so her weight dipped just enough so that her butt and thighs were in the water, but her top half stayed dry. She set her cup in the built-in cup holder, relieved at not having been tossed in.

"Thanks for the lift."

Josh settled his arms on the float beside her, causing it to dip further and the cool water to rise past her hips. He watched it rise, then pulled his eyes back to her face and took a sip of his drink.

"So tell me who everyone is."

Josh pointed around the yard, naming people he knew from work and a few college friends. A neighbor or two. As people came in and out of the pool, he introduced her, each one of them taking the first opportunity they got to tell her what a great guy Josh was. Everyone she met gushed about him, women and men. They had stories of favors Josh had done them or professional accolades he'd won that she knew instantly he never would have mentioned himself. It was like being at a meeting of the Josh Rideout Fan Club. Josh, for his part, was exceedingly humble, waving them all off.

By the time she'd met most of the guests, she realized she'd been holding his hand in her lap the entire time without even realizing she was doing it. Josh didn't seem to mind one bit.

Fifteen

A SALTY BREEZE RODE IN WITH the sunset, calming the temperature and purifying the thick summer air. The back of Cat's neck prickled with the wind, and it sent a shiver through her shoulders.

She'd changed out of her bathing suit and back into her clothes by then, adding a long-sleeved henley over her tank top, but goose-bumps still freckled her arms and legs.

Josh was still in his swim trunks, shirtless beside her and looking stunningly immune. He'd been sucked into some shop talk with Dylan and a couple of other men Cat guessed were contractors, given their contribution to the conversation. Cat sipped her drink, trying to follow along as they bounced around a current project. When Minnie approached her, however, and invited her to a picnic table where Mattie was coloring quietly, she was glad for the conversation she could participate in.

"You looked bored," Minnie said, as she

poured herself another drink from the bar cart behind her and took a seat.

"No," Cat replied, not wanting to seem rude. "Josh seems to enjoy his work."

"He does, but that doesn't mean you want to listen to them go on about it."

Cat laughed. She hadn't really been able to follow much. She'd been using the time to enjoy the view of Josh—the way his biceps flexed as he augmented the conversation with hand gestures and the way he would flick his eyes toward her or touch her every so often to remind her she hadn't been forgotten. She probably should have spent the time testing him like she planned, but she was enjoying watching him and hearing about him so much, it hadn't even occurred to her. She wondered what that meant.

"So," Minnie said, glancing at Mattie and seeing him occupied, "since you told me how sweet my husband was when he was off on vacation with the boys, I'll tell you a secret too. Josh has been on cloud nine since he met you."

Cat's mouth dropped into a little O, her eyelashes fluttering. She wasn't expecting a friend of Josh's, even a female one, to be so forthcoming.

"Don't tell me you couldn't tell." Minnie laughed, taking a sip of her drink and stretching her legs out beneath the table. "He's been smiling like a lunatic since the day they all got back from that beach."

"He seems like a pretty happy guy in general,"

Cat said. It was a nice thought, but she didn't want to cling to any wishful thinking from a happily married woman for her single friend.

"Oh, he is. Don't get me wrong. He's what you would call well-adjusted, given his past. He's just... cautious since Sarah. But it's clear he's enchanted by you." Cat paled, guilt over the games she'd been playing sucking the color from her cheeks. She stuttered for a response, and Minnie didn't miss it. "Maybe I'm speaking out of turn," Minnie said quickly, her lips pressing into a tight line.

"No, please," Cat said. "I'm just surprised. I really like him too." The confession tumbled from her mouth without her permission, and she nearly slapped her hand over her mouth.

It wasn't a lie. Being in a yard full of people who loved him had her realizing maybe she wasn't imagining things to be as good as they were. Maybe Josh really was worthy of all of the feelings she'd been battling with since the beach. He was so attentive, so genuine in his affection. Maybe this was real.

Minnie quirked an eyebrow at her, her mouth twitching with the need to smile. "You really couldn't tell?" Cat turned her head to see Josh watching her over the cup he was sipping from. He smiled, then turned back to his friends. "I feel like he's being a little obvious," Minnie said. "But Josh is the kind of person who doesn't argue with his heart. It's gotten him in trouble before."

Cat's eyes snapped back to Minnie to find her expression had hardened. Was she the one being tested now? She hadn't anticipated that. "I know how that is," she said, suddenly overcome with the need to convince Minnie that she wasn't looking to break Josh's heart. What a flip. *Well played, Minnie.* Emma would like this girl.

"Well, I think I've said enough. Except... Cat?"

"Yes?"

"You're being a little obvious too." Minnie laughed, then made a motion like zipping her lips together.

Josh had appeared beside Cat. He pressed his thumb and fingers into her shoulder in an affectionate squeeze, looking none-the-wiser about Minnie's breach of confidentiality.

"Can I steal her back?" he asked Minnie.

"Of course, Joshy." Minnie patted her hand. "Cat, find me later if you get sucked into a vortex of sports talk and testosterone. I'll be around."

"Thanks, Minnie," Cat said as Josh tugged her away.

"Sorry about that," he said as he led her to the edge of the pool and away from the larger group, most of whom had dried off and changed into regular clothes once the sun had set. "Off the clock is relative when we all get together."

"It's fine. I'm enjoying meeting your friends."

He smiled in response. A lazy, slow-building grin that indicated a deeper thought was stirring in his brain.

The backyard flickered under a row of lawn torches and music drifted from speakers set up in each corner of the fenced-in rectangle. She had a sudden vision of the balcony bar where Josh had pulled her away for that second drink. A cozy warmth spread through her chest at the memory.

"This feels familiar," Josh said, reading her mind. He wrapped his arms around her waist and buried his face in her neck. A few people were watching them curiously, but Josh didn't seem to notice or care. First, Minnie had pulled an Emma on Josh's behalf, and now he was beating her at her own game, already acting like they were a couple. This night was full of twists.

She could faintly smell tequila on his otherwise minty breath, and when he pulled back, his eyes were hooded, and he was openly gazing at her. She couldn't help the smile pulling at the corners of her mouth—Josh was drunk. He hadn't been either night they spent on the beach; she was sure of it now. She pressed a hand to her own cheeks, finding them on fire, and she swayed a little when he let her go. She was buzzed too.

"Let's sit." Cat plopped down to the ground and swung her legs over the edge of the pool into the water.

Josh followed, sitting with his legs crisscrossed. "Are you having a good time?"

"I am."

He leaned over, brushing the shell of her ear with his lips. "I told you we could have nights like this anytime we wanted. We're just missing the lightning."

"That's probably a good thing considering where we're sitting."

He huffed out a laugh, then turned serious. "That day in the water," he said, twirling a tendril of hair that had fallen from her ponytail between his fingers. "You mentioned your ex."

"Did I?" she asked, cheekily.

"Tell me about him."

"Why?"

"Because I want to know why you're so afraid of me."

Her mouth dropped into that O thing again. She was going to start catching flies. "I'm not afraid of you," she said with an awkward cackle of insincerity.

Josh tipped his head, his expression tenderly disbelieving. His eyes said, *bullshit, Cat.* His smile said *I can see that you're a terrified little girl who has no idea how to do this.* But he didn't say any of that out loud. Instead, he laced their fingers and looked out toward the pool, gently pulling her along, the way only he seemed to know how to do.

"His name was Micah," Cat answered cautiously. They were having such a nice time. Bringing up Micah seemed like inviting it to rain on a picnic—*or a make-out session on the beach*—but he'd asked. "We were together in college from my sophomore year on. He was a year ahead of me."

"Okay."

She sighed. "We had plans—the forever kind—but I had my own plans too. I wanted to go to Berkeley to study immigration law."

"California?"

"Yup. It was my dream. I got in, too. But Micah was already going to Georgetown for law school."

"Hometown guy."

"Right. He had a year in already. He asked me to wait until he was done, promised we would go together and…" She trailed off, not wanting to reveal how foolish she'd been.

It didn't matter. She was smarter now.

But Josh pressed. "And what?"

"And get married, buy a house… all that."

Josh nodded, settling back on his hands. "But, you didn't."

"Right before he graduated, after I'd wasted two years doing an internship instead of getting my own degree, he got offered a job here in D.C. He said it was too good of an opportunity to pass up."

Cat felt her skin heat in anger as she remembered Micah's face when he'd broken the news—rueful, embarrassed even, but in no way conflicted. He made his choice so easily. Cat and everything she ever wanted were collateral damage to a shrewd business decision. It was humiliating.

That was the thing with Micah. Not only had her dreams been smashed to pieces, but they'd been together since college. There was a huge web of friends and acquaintances who had witnessed her naivety. They probably still laughed about how easily she'd bought into that lie. *The girl who gave it all up for a guy.* It was something she'd watched her sisters do and vowed never to imitate.

Her oldest sister Maria had an MBA, and instead of using it to open the restaurant she'd always wanted to, she gave up that dream to do basic accounting for her husband's marina. Olivia had what you would call a face for the big screen. She'd modeled from the time she was a toddler, and everyone expected to see her name in lights one day. Instead, she got married as soon as she graduated high school, and she'd been popping out kids ever since. Goodbye, Sports Illustrated Swimsuit edition; hello, stretch marks. And after all of that, what had Cat done with the first guy she fell in love with? She'd happily skipped down the exact same path like Little Red Riding Hood to the wolf's house.

You can have love, or you can have your pride. You can't have both.

"So, no California?" Josh asked. He squeezed her hand and she wanted to sob.

"No California. I enrolled locally instead, and

here I am, twenty-seven and still not a lawyer yet."

"You're still doing it, though. You didn't give up. That's brave."

"Maybe." It hadn't felt brave. It felt like accepting a consolation prize. "The one light in all of it was that my internship was at the victim's advocacy firm where I work. After spending those two years there, I knew that's where I wanted to focus, so I stayed. When I pass the bar, I'll already have a position."

Josh was quiet again, and she listened to the pool water lap the concrete side, thinking. "I don't know the guy," he said after a moment, "so I can't speak for him… but I have a feeling if you asked me to go somewhere with you, anywhere, I would."

She swung her head around to look at him. His eyes were dark with sincerity. "Why?" she whispered.

"You can work anywhere. Having someone who wants to go through life with you? To be happy for your happiness, and you for theirs? I'd never let that go for a job. For anything, really."

It struck her that Josh must have felt the same way when his wife decided to renege on the plans the two of them had made together, and a sort of combined sadness settled over her. Some for him; some for her.

She took the last sip of her drink, setting the cup beside her, and leaned over to trail her fingers in the pool. The moonlight reflected off of the glassy surface, a sorrowfully-crooned country song drifting around them in surround sound. Josh moved closer to her, and instinctively she did the same until they were touching. Surprising herself, she leaned her head on his shoulder, feeling a little like being comforted.

He seemed to know as much. He wrapped an arm around her and pressed his mouth to the top of her head, breathing through her hair for a few moments. Cat's eyes began to prick with absurd tears, a vulnerability washing over her that she hadn't felt in a long time. It was probably just the tequila, she told herself, while snuggling closer to him, but she knew it was more than that. She felt open all of a sudden, and she needed to get back to something that made sense. Josh's hard chest and strong arms made sense. The physical reaction she was having to being pressed against him made sense. At the moment, it felt as simple as breathing. Physiology, biology. Tonight she was going to finish what she started on that beach.

She tipped her head up and let her lips graze his throat, feeling him swallow at the sensation. Pushing away the emotion bubbling up from years ago, she kissed him again, letting her tongue slip out on the next press. She took control of the moment, feigning the bravery he'd just accused her of. Call it liquid courage, or fake-it-till-you-make-it, either way, she wanted this, and she was going to take it.

Josh's hand moved from her shoulder to the back of her neck, and he rubbed tiny circles into her skin, feeling her while she tasted him. The voices from the other guests began to fade, and she had a vague recognition of someone directing people into the house for card games. "Do you want to go inside?" she asked.

"It's getting late." His voice sounded strangled. "Maybe we should start walking back."

She smiled against his skin, then pulled away, letting him stand to help her to her feet. "We should."

Sixteen

B Y THE TIME THEY GOT to Josh's front door, he was so painfully hard that he genuinely feared the string and Velcro closure on his shorts would fail him. The walk had taken twice as long as it should have, since they'd stopped numerous times along the way to kiss sloppily, touching as much as they could while standing upright. Cat had been touching him all night. He wasn't sure what had come over her, but he wasn't going to question it. Especially after she'd finally told him the story he'd known was hiding behind all of that fear in her eyes.

He wanted to touch her as much as she'd let him until she could feel his promise that he wasn't the next guy that was going to break her heart.

His hands were clumsy with anticipation when he put the key in the lock and opened the door for her. Cat trailed her fingers across his stomach as she brushed past him, and he had to bite down on his tongue to keep from moaning out loud. When the door shut behind them, he wrapped his arms around her, lifting her off of the ground so that they were face to face. He looked at his watch over her shoulder, seeing that it was past midnight. "It's late," he whispered against her lips. "You're not going to drive back to the city tonight, are you?"

"Do you want me to stay?" she asked breathily.

"More than anything."

She bit her lip, and he waited with bated breath while the options played out in her eyes. Finally, she gave him a little nod, and he led her to his bedroom.

Josh felt electric, like whatever happened next was going to be important. Maybe that was normal. It had been a long time since he'd slept with someone for the first time, or at all for that matter, and Cat wasn't just someone. There had been build up, lots of it. This was the culmination of all of that tension that started the night he'd met her and wondered if he would ever be the same. He was about to find out.

Cat emerged from his ensuite bathroom. The little makeup she'd been wearing was gone, and her face was still dewy from the water she'd splashed on it. He stood from the edge of the bed as she approached.

"I'm glad you're here," he said, brushing his fingers over her cheek.

"Me too."

"Do you, um, need something to sleep in?" He'd exchanged his bathing suit for a pair of cotton boxers, but she was still wearing her shorts and shirt. He didn't want to assume she'd be stripping too, even though he was practically salivating over the prospect.

"It's too hot for clothes," she said, crossing her arms at her waist and gracefully lifting her tank top and long-sleeve shirt over her head. They fell to the floor behind her, and he bit back a moan when he saw her perfect round breasts spilling out of the top of ruby-red lace cups. His attention was so seized that he didn't even see her pop open the button on her shorts, only noticing they had fallen away when a strip of matching red lace caught his eye from her hip.

"Fuck, Catia," he said, wishing his brain had thought of something better. She giggled though, seemingly unoffended.

"I'm beginning to think you think that's my name."

"Sorry," he said, stepping closer to massage her hip with his thumb. "Bad habit. I never learned the Southern Charm thing."

"I think you're very charming."

Cat's mouth twisted into a half pout, half smile. It was a challenge and an invitation wrapped into one, and he accepted both, scooping his hands underneath her and hoisting her into his arms. She squealed a delighted laugh that washed over him like the rain on a hot day. Her legs wrapped around his waist, and he took a few steps towards the bed, dropping her onto the mattress. The bun on top of her head loosened on impact, and he fingered the hair tie, pulling it all the way out and setting it on the bed beside her. A sea of caramel and chocolate waves fell around her head, and he licked his lips.

"You're so beautiful," he whispered as he connected the dots of her freckles with his eyes. One on the top of her lip, one on the side of her nose. Two on her left cheek, one on her right. She even had matching dark flecks floating in the honey-brown of her eyes.

"Come here." Cat reached for his hand and tugged, and he collapsed on top of her, breathing heavily. He dove into her neck, sighing at his first taste of salty skin, but something nagged just behind the anticipation—a vision of the sloppy, frantic sex that would come out a night like this. Fevered touching, a haze of inebriation smudging the details from his memory. He tried to ignore it, but his head was spinning from lust and tequila. Cat's eyes were glassy and her cheeks flushed. His plan to prove something to her started to feel like a plan to take something from her. It wasn't right.

"We shouldn't do this tonight," he heard himself say, then he buried his face in her hair to silence himself. *Shut up, Josh.* He was an idiot. Was he really going to stop this?

"What?" Cat huffed out her question in a desperate breath, clearly wondering the same thing.

They were finally here, alone in his bedroom, but his brain was battling his body, each making perfectly convincing arguments. He'd waited too long to stop now. But he'd waited too long for it not to be perfect. There was a reason they didn't sleep together that night in his hotel room. Sure, there was Dylan and Shawn's annoying appearance, but he liked to think even if they hadn't been there, he would have recognized that Cat wasn't a drunken hookup kind of girl.

He pulled up onto his hands, hovering above her. "We shouldn't do this tonight," he said again, hating himself. "We've had too much to drink."

Cat's face washed with surprise, then settled into something more mischievous. "Oh," she said, dropping her eyes down his front, an exaggerated look of pity taking over. "I understand."

His cheeks flamed. "Not because... I didn't mean..." She started giggling then, and the sound made him groan with regret. He grabbed her by the hips and pressed himself into the valley between her thigh and those little red panties, obliterating any confusion. Her giggling turned to a gasp. "I've waited too long," he said, kissing along the line of her jaw. "Since that night on the beach."

He ran his hands up her sides, and a trail of goosebumps appeared in their wake. His body seemed to want to make a liar out of him, so he forced himself to let her go, pulling up to his knees and straddling her warm thighs.

"You're right," she said shakily. They held each other's gaze, taking a moment to adjust to the decision they had made, then her eyes dropped to his mouth. "Can I still kiss you?"

He swore he could feel all the blood evacuating from his brain. "How about I kiss you?" he said, picking up her hand and bringing it to his mouth. He pressed his lips to the back of it, then turned her arm and kissed the inside of her wrist down to the bend of her elbow.

Her skin still smelled of sunscreen, and a vision of her in that little white bikini on the beach gave him another idea. He moved to the curve of her shoulder, nudging the red strap of her bra aside with his nose, and pulled in a full breath of her. Cat tipped her head back into the mattress while he worked his way to the peaks of her breasts then down to her stomach. Her muscles flexed beneath his lips as he moved around her belly button, his fingers toying with the waistband of her panties.

"Can I kiss you here?" he whispered. His eyes darted to hers for confirmation while his fingers grazed the inside of her thigh, waiting patiently until he had her answer.

He wasn't sure if it was a yes or a gasp, but

she said something, and her knees fell farther apart.

His hand was unsteady as he pulled her panties to the side, hooking the slick fabric over his thumb. Her sweet scent washed over him like a wave, crashing against his chest in a swirl of nerves. The build-up between them had gone from lightning fast to achingly slow, and it certainly left a lot of time to fantasize and wonder and imagine. This was a scene he'd played out in his mind more than once—making her squirm, making.her cry out, hooking her on him the way he was so pitifully hooked on her. With goals like that, it was hard not to be nervous.

Cat let out a sharp gasp at the first press of his tongue, her hips lifting against the gentle pressure of his palm. He pulled back, kissing her inner thigh until she settled into the mattress again. "Keep going?" His voice was raspy, breathless, and he wasn't sure which one of them he was asking.

She whimpered a simple "Please," and he was convinced enough for both of them.

Seventeen

*H*E WAS A SORCERER, SHE decided. Some sort of mind-melting Cat whisperer. That was the only explanation for the way he'd convinced her to grant him such intimate access to her. He'd barely had to ask. Maybe it was the fact that he *did* ask, politely at that, like she was doing him a favor. But still, this was the ultimate concession of control, and she'd just handed it over to him after a simple "can I?"

Josh was taking his time—pressing, exploring, devouring—and her nerves were responding to every movement. Her heels dug into the mattress, retreating self-consciously, but Josh increased the pressure of his hand on her hip, coaxing her to feel all of it: his warm breath, his soft lips, his steady tongue.

Jesus, he'd done this before. Of course, he had. He'd been married. He was a grown man. And she was a grown woman. She'd been here before too. Still, the sensation didn't feel altogether familiar. It had been a while, years, but she was quite sure this was a new thing for her.

The difference between experiencing something and experiencing something done well.

She tried again to pull back, embarrassed by the way she was bucking against him greedily. She murmured half-hearted requests for him to let her return the favor, to please not make her fall in front of him. He was greedy, too, though. She could feel his grip digging into her hip, hard enough that she knew there would be gorgeous little fingerprint-shaped marks on her skin. The flag of a conquering country.

"Please," she said louder. "Josh. I'm going to—"

"I want you to, Catia."

Her name breathed onto her skin sent a shiver through her limbs. She climbed, higher and higher until the steps began to disintegrate beneath her, and she tumbled in a free fall of sensation. Her fingers tightened in his hair, and her feet scrambled against the sheets. She wanted to push him away and hold him hostage at the same time. He seemingly had no intention of being anywhere else, though, still whispering to her as she crumbled against him.

Finally, all of the tension in her muscles released like the snap of a rubber band, and she relaxed into the mattress, her chest heaving. Josh pulled up so that his face rested on her stomach. He kissed the soft flesh around her belly button, while her body rode out the aftershocks still pulsing through her.

"I can't believe you just did that," she said, her fingers smoothing down the tufts of his hair that she'd been gripping.

He smiled into one of his kisses, then pressed his teeth against her playfully. "Why?"

"I haven't even touched you."

Josh adjusted himself in his boxers. "I've been thinking about doing that since that night on the beach."

"So that's where that was headed? I have a new hatred for rainstorms... and Dylan."

Josh's laughter vibrated against her hip, mixing with the warmth still flowing through her lower half. He pulled to his hands and knees and crawled up the bed, then lowered himself beside her, nuzzling his face into her neck, his arm slung over her belly.

She turned to look at the top of his head. "I'm not tired yet," she said. "Tell me something."

"You want a bedtime story?" He chuckled against her ear, his tongue flicking at the lobe as if it hadn't already put in a full day's work.

"I do. Something about you that no one knows."

"Something secret? I'm not that interesting." He snuggled closer and closed his eyes. Relaxation seeped into his words, making his accent rougher and more pronounced.

"What was it like moving here as a kid?" she asked. "Was it a big change?"

Josh didn't say anything for a moment, and

she was afraid he'd fallen asleep, or worse, she'd brought up something that was still painful. Finally, he let out a warm breath against her neck. "I lived on the Cape as a kid. Cape Cod. Beaches, tourists, fishing boats. The Bay's not that different. Water's warmer and the people talk weird—" Cat giggled. "But the atmosphere's the same."

"And your grandfather? Did you know him well before he took you in?"

"No. Mostly just from pictures. He and my father had a falling out. They weren't in touch the last few years of my parents' lives."

"So he was your father's father?"

"Yes. What about your parents?" he asked drowsily. "Are they happy?"

That was a strange question, one she'd never been asked before, and she wondered what it was that made him want to know. Nostalgia for his own parents, maybe. Or pessimism borne from his failed marriage. Did he assume the answer already? Maybe he was the type who didn't believe in true love. Maybe she was.

She pondered the question, digging through a lifetime of memories that she hoped would provide an answer. Were they happy? They'd been married for almost forty years. Something had to make them stay. But if she really thought about it, she'd never seen much affection between them. Nothing to make her say, "look at this. This is love." They were more like two business partners running a household. They were good at it, though; you'd have to be fond of each other to be good at it.

"I guess they're as happy as anyone else," she said, safely. How would she ever really know? How had she never wondered before?

Josh made a sound as if he were agreeing with the notion but shook his head. "Some people really are, though. My parents were happy. I was only a kid, but I remember that very clearly."

"Tell me," she whispered.

"My mother was beautiful," he said. "She had dark hair like yours, but the Italian kind—jet black instead of warm brown. She laughed all the time. Hysterically, like a hyena over the stupidest stuff, and my father would just shake his head and smile. Watching her."

"Was he tall and handsome like you?"

"He was English. Pale as the moon. He looked like a ghost compared to her and her Tuscan glow, as he called it. His hair was lighter too. When I was a kid, my hair would turn almost blonde in the summer. My mother would say it was my English genes coming out for some badly needed sun."

Cat laughed quietly, glancing at Josh's short dark hair and picturing the younger version. "And you got the perfect combination with this skin of yours," she said, stroking his cheek. "It's always wasted on the men—the prettiest DNA."

He snorted a laugh against her skin, then kissed her shoulder. "You've got some pretty nice

DNA yourself," he said. "Who do you look like? Your mother or your father?"

"They practically look like twins they've been together for so long, so who knows?" He laughed again, and the sound made her body warm and comfortable. She remembered the first time she heard that laugh and instantly craved more. It had a sort of child-like joy to it that she found intriguing, like maybe it was a stowaway from happy times. "My dad's skin is much darker than mine," she continued, to Josh's rapt attention. "My sister Maria got his features; curly hair, big eyes. Olivia is petite like my mother. I got a little bit from both, I guess. I have my grandmother's ass though. No doubt about that."

"She's a kind woman to share," he said, reaching between her and the mattress and squeezing.

"Who threw the baseball?" she asked.

"Huh?"

"Your scar. Who threw the baseball at you?" All this talk of how their features came to be had her thinking of the ones he'd earned instead of inherited.

Josh pulled his arm back and ran a thumb over the little white line.

"My father, actually."

She pulled in a startled breath. The picture she'd been drawing cracked and morphed into something else entirely. He must have felt it because he rushed to clarify. "It was an accident," he said. "The kid next door yelled to me just as he threw it, and I dropped my glove. I don't think I've ever seen a grown man cry like that."

"That's terrible," she said. She could hear his smile as he recounted it, and she smiled too, despite herself.

"There was so much blood, and I could tell he was terrified to bring me in to my mother. Rightly so, since she made his freak out look like a cool, professional assessment. Just like she laughed hard, she was also prone to hysterics when it came to crying."

"I can't say I blame her. It must have been scary to see her child like that."

"She lost her mind. She just kept crying 'his face, his face!'" Josh laughed. "She was on the phone to a plastic surgeon the next day. She was sure I was going to be deformed."

Cat joined in his laughter. Josh's face was quite possibly the most perfect one she'd ever seen, and that scar happened to be the most interesting part.

"So did he have to operate on you? The surgeon?"

Josh's laughing subsided, and he nuzzled into her shoulder again. "Nah, I canceled the appointment."

"Yourself?"

"Well, the social worker, Ms. Kocak, did. I asked her to. My parents died a couple of weeks after it happened, before I could get in to see him.

She said she would take me to the appointment herself before I moved in with my grandfather, but my busted mouth was the last big memory I had of my dad, and I guess I didn't want it erased. She wasn't sold on it. Like my mother, she thought I'd regret it, but she let me decide in the end. I appreciated that about her. Anyway, that's why it's all jagged like it is, instead of a neat little line."

Cat stroked her fingers along his arm, churning over Josh's tumultuous childhood in her mind. She'd only just heard the details, but it felt familiar at the same time—like maybe it was part of his whole being without him even realizing it. She supposed everyone was just a mosaic of the most important pieces of their lives. Scraps of experience twisted and turned until they fit a whole, then set in mortar to become our face in the world. She knew what had happened with Micah was suffused in her every expression, every decision. Including the way she'd been treating Josh.

She moved her fingers to his scalp, brushing through his hair, and he sighed heavily, peacefully. "I think it's perfect," she whispered. "Straight lines are boring. Your face wouldn't be the same without it."

"I think you're perfect," he said.

"How did your parents die?"

There was more silence, but this time she didn't worry. She was beginning to realize that

Josh simply thought through everything that came out of his mouth, so she waited patiently for him to decide the tone of his words.

"They were in a car accident," he said, matter-of-factly. "Late at night. I was at a friend's house."

"I'm sorry." She held him closer, but she could tell he was telling a version of the story that didn't require her support. Something he'd memorized to recite without actually reliving the moment. But then he sighed and kept going.

"They were never sure what caused it. They went out for dinner and a movie, then somehow their car ended up upside down in the marsh on a long stretch of road that led onto the peninsula. There was no long drawn out investigation, no sensational story of a drunk driver or an animal in the road. They were just alive, and then they weren't. There were three of us; then there was me. Then there were two of us—me and an old man I barely knew."

Cat's eyes began to well and she wished she could crane her neck enough to see Josh's expression, but it was dark, and he was resting comfortably, his cheek smooshed against her shoulder.

"He was a nice old man, though," he finally said, causing her to laugh plaintively.

"So, you got along?"

"He wasn't much for words," Josh explained. "He was kind of gruff and... different from my parents in a lot of ways. I figured that was why he and my dad didn't get along, but he tried his best."

"How so?"

"He didn't ask me about my day at school, or how baseball practice went, but he spent hours sitting out on a little rowboat with me, teaching me how to fish, then pretending not to notice when I spent the whole time wiping at my eyes. He just didn't know what to say is all."

She thought about that. Josh seemed older than his years. To have come to a conclusion like that at such a young age, he must have always been that way. When she was twelve, she was reading *Teen Beat* and worrying about what kind of milkshake to get after school. Certainly not trying to understand the emotional responses of the adults in her life.

Josh's head was getting heavier, his words crushed between his lips and her skin in a drowsy slur. His thumb stopped moving against her hip. Finally, his breathing turned to a faint snore that made her smile. The sound traveled from her brain down to her limbs, and soon she was cuddling into him, letting herself enjoy the heaviness of his arm on her waist and the warmth of his breath on her skin. She drifted off feeling spent and utterly content.

Eighteen

WHEN CAT'S EYES FLUTTERED OPEN again, it was in that milky half-light of early morning. She'd shifted sometime in the few hours she'd been asleep, her cheek now cradled in the crease between Josh's shoulder and bicep, her stomach pressed against his in a sticky sweat where the humidity of the room settled on their skin. His other arm draped over her shoulder, his heavy thigh resting between hers. It was a stifling tangle of limbs, and her neck was quirked at an awkward angle, but moving was the furthest thing from her mind.

They'd talked into the thickest part of the night, and she knew she'd be useless on such little sleep, but she found herself shunning another go at rest in favor of soaking Josh up through her pores. She listened to him breathe, trying to figure out when everything had changed. Minnie had flipped the entire script on her at the party, giving her a friendly but firm warning to be careful with him, and when she looked again, she saw exposure in Josh's eyes that she hadn't recognized before. She had this strange new need to be a good steward of it.

She slid even closer, until her nose was pressed into his neck, and took a deep breath, savoring the entirely masculine scent that emanated from him. She hoped she smelled as good, as hot as she was. She tried to lift her arm from under the weight of his and take a quick sniff, but he stirred, breathing in deeply, and tightened his grip, trapping her. Josh's eyes were still closed when the fingers he had tangled in her hair began to curl, pulling gently until her face was tipped toward his. He brushed his lips over hers, so softly, so lazily, that she thought he might still be asleep until his mouth curved into a wide grin.

"Hey," he whispered, against her lips, sending a flutter through her body.

"Hi."

"I thought maybe last night was a dream." He pressed again, this time finding her tongue. "But you really are in my bed."

Cat smiled into his kiss, opening wider. "It wasn't a dream."

With one hand still cradling her head, Josh ran his other from her back to her front, pausing every few inches to squeeze wherever it landed. His fingers splayed over her rib cage, then higher, palming the swell of her breast. She could feel him pressed into her tummy, solid and ready.

She peered up at him, taking in the way his

vivid features popped on his face in the dim light. His cobalt eyes, the dark day-old stubble peppering the rose-colored flush that painted his neck—the hues all seemed intensified, like she was suddenly seeing him in Technicolor.

"You're not going to stop again, are you?" she asked, only half in jest. "I couldn't take it."

Josh made a little growl sound and squeezed harder. "Not unless you tell me to."

Well, that wasn't happening.

As Josh marked her mouth and neck with his tongue, she wondered how things would change once they finally did this. Would he still look at her with that curious amusement once he knew her inside and out? She really liked that look. Was that what Minnie meant when she said he was enchanted? Would this be the thing that brought them back to reality where things were more complicated? Or was this the part where her safety rope finally snapped and she free-fell into whatever this was going to be?

There was only one way to find out.

She hooked her leg around his, sliding up his thigh like a fire pole until they were better aligned. The friction was enough to make her cry out, and Josh responded with a delightful press of his hips into hers. When she pressed back, his kisses became messier, almost desperate. It was the most unleashed she'd seen him: quickened breath, darting hands. She was dying to see him really lose control. What would it look like? Would he be loud? Rough? He was always so deliberate, she couldn't picture him like that, but his whole body was accelerating now, taking her with him.

He moved to her neck, nuzzling and biting, tipping her chin with his nose until all she could see was his rustic-looking, wooden headboard. Cat didn't even have a headboard. Her queen-sized bed sat on one of those old adjustable metal frames. This one was heavy and huge, and it wasn't even squeaking, even as the mattress rocked with their movement. Come to think of it, his sheets were amazing too. They were so soft, and if she remembered correctly, they matched the comforter—

"Catia," he said as if he could tell she was doing that nervous rambling thing inside her head. He purposely blew out the word over the moisture on her throat, making goosebumps flare over her skin, straight down to where she felt him brushing against the satin between her legs.

Josh's hands continued to roam, squeezing her waist, then along the curve of her hip, before he hooked his fingers on the waistband of her panties and slid them down her thighs. She grinned against his mouth as she squirmed her way out of them, kicking them off of her feet and into the twist of sheets.

"Your turn," she taunted, tugging at the boxers he still wore. When he took over, she clutched him tighter, forcing him to slither out of them with one hand, while maintaining their furious kiss. He laughed boyishly, his eyes sparking in the dark, and she thought maybe Minnie got it backward. Maybe Cat was the one who was enchanted.

When they were finally bare skin to bare skin, he slowed, cupping her jaw in his palm. Her pulse went wild as Josh broke their kiss and locked onto her with his gaze. His eyes were the black ocean of that night on the beach. His hips were the gentle ebb and flow of the tide. "You okay?" he breathed, just like he had then.

"I'm good."

He studied her expression so long that her cheeks flushed under his gaze, then, satisfied with whatever he saw there, he kissed her hard one time, and his heat was gone.

Cat whined out in protest, clenching her eyes shut to focus on the feel of their legs still tangled. The bed dipped beside her as he stretched and she heard a drawer open then close, then a tearing sound. The mattress rocked again, bouncing with the movement of his upper body, and then he was back.

"God, Cat… " he mumbled through a grin that was pressed against her breastbone. "From the moment I saw you, I wanted you underneath me. To put my mouth all over you… " He trailed off, snaking his arms under hers and tightening them around her back, then he shifted his weight, flipping them in one fluid motion so that she was on her back.

"You were very patient," she simpered.

"I'm done being patient."

She giggled, the noise sounding foreign in her mouth. She sounded like a schoolgirl, but she didn't care. She *felt* like giggling. She felt like screaming his name. She was screaming it right then in her head, but it was coming out as more of a whimper.

Josh kissed her again, every lick and nip like fire, then he nudged her thighs apart, slowly, inch by inch, until he was one pulse of his hips away. One moment from something she knew would change everything.

Nineteen

I
T WAS EXACTLY AS CAT imagined when he pushed into her. Josh was committed to every move he made, and this was no different. Where she was constantly measuring herself in his presence, he was always throwing himself whole-heartedly into the moment. She sucked in a hot breath, tremors shaking her body as he laced their fingers above her head and stayed perfectly still. "Cat," he whispered, though it almost seemed like he was speaking to himself now.

"Is this what you thought would happen when we met in that sleazy bar?" she asked against his temple.

He laughed. "I was just hoping for another slow dance. But I'm glad it is happening."

"Me too."

Josh curved his back, pressing his forehead to hers, and rolled his hips like a wave that built and broke in a crash of sensation inside her. Scooping a hand underneath her, he held their bodies together while he moved, skillfully hitting her pleasure on the inside and the outside.

Three gorgeously precise thrusts in, and he'd already put all of the jackhammer idiots she'd ever slept with to shame. Not that there were that many. She'd only slept with four other men: a few embarrassingly bad times in high school with her boyfriend in the back of his Chevy Caprice, an experiment in hook-up culture in college before she met Micah and gave him the remainder of those years, and one painfully impatient man whom she'd talked herself into dating over a year ago, to pop her post-Micah cherry. The rest of the men she'd dated she'd cut loose well before sleeping with them became an option. At twenty-seven, she had little experience in the grown-up version of sex, but Josh was giving her a crash course. Just like he had the night before.

He pressed his open mouth to her ear, alternating between kissing and whispering to her—how she felt, things he wanted to do. She knew if she tried to respond, it would be incoherent, so she let him keep going, delighting in the way he spoke to her. Perfect, polite Josh and his dirty mouth. It thrilled her a little to think that it was just a taste of what she would get once they were more comfortable with each other. *If we get that far.*

That thought, and all others, cleared her brain when he moved his hand to a particularly perfect spot between them. Her vision started to go white, her entire world shrinking to the mere sum of the synapses firing in her brain and the tremors building deep inside her core.

Josh said her name a few more times then some sort of an invocation followed by an expletive that changed the meaning completely. She was smiling at his strangled mutterings when it hit her. Every muscle in her body tightened, her back arched so high off the bed she must have looked like an acrobat performing some insane contortion.

"Josh," she spat out in time with the tremors that ripped through her body. She could feel him smiling against her cheek as he held her up, bracing himself on his elbow while she shuddered and shook in his arms. "Oh my God."

She sucked in a hard breath, and Josh clutched her to his chest like she was a prize he'd just won. Maybe she was because she suddenly wanted to live in this room forever. He could put her up on a shelf, and she could smile down at him and tell him how fucking amazing he was whenever he wanted.

When her muscles released, and she fell boneless against the pillow, Josh followed her. She watched him through the slits that were her eyes, his face glistening with sweat, his jaw tense as he continued to pump into her. The sensation was overwhelming as she hadn't yet recovered, and every stroke was an electric current that both pleased and shocked her.

He touched her cheek and kissed the tip of her nose, then her chin, beckoning her consciousness back to him. When she finally refocused on his face, he smiled a sweet self-satisfied grin, but she saw something else flickering in those pretty blue eyes. Something wolfish. She could tell that he was restraining a rougher touch, and she wanted it.

She lifted her hips to meet his, pressing into his side with her thigh and coaxing him to go faster. She wrapped her hands around his biceps, digging her nails into his skin as she used him for leverage to offer the resistance she knew he was craving.

Josh met her offer with a bruising grip on her thigh, pushing her bent leg toward her shoulder, and planting his other hand beside her on the pillow. Where his lips had been sucking at her skin, now his teeth scraped over her collarbone. His power surged, and his perfect stroke slipped and shook. She wanted nothing more than to see him come apart, to make him feel what she just had. It suddenly became more important than breathing.

She turned her head to see his fist twist the pillowcase, the veins in his forearms pulsing, and his muscles trembling from holding his weight. She whispered his name again on an exhale, and he made a noise like a growl that melted into a whimper. The sound of it, the dampness of his skin and the hair at his temples, the way his eyes lost focus and rolled before clenching shut, it all settled in her chest in this unfamiliar feeling of conjointment, like they were soldered together by some common goal that was bigger than either of them. Maybe that goal was just his physical release, but at that moment, it felt metaphorical, fucking philosophical.

It was furious when it happened, like a crack of thunder that catches you off guard even though the clouds have been building. Cat held the back of his neck and kissed his stubbled cheek as he gasped and cursed above her. She'd never been so intertwined with another person's pleasure. Each thrust of his hips and choked out profanity was a jolt of pride and shared gratification.

Josh's body finally relaxed, and she pushed her fingers into his hair, alternating between tugging and smoothing. After a moment of huffing short, raspy breaths into her neck, he peeled himself from her, flopping onto his back.

Cool air rushed her front, drying the fine mist of perspiration that had settled on her skin. Josh was silent, still breathing heavily beside her, and a sudden flush of modesty replaced the high Cat had been riding. She reached between them for the sheet to cover herself, but Josh snatched her wrist, bringing it up to his mouth and grazing the outside with his lips.

"Don't move," he said. "I'll be right back." He walked to the bathroom and disappeared inside.

The clock on Josh's bedside table glowed a disdainful six a.m., and as soon as Cat saw it, she yawned. A moment later, he dropped down beside her again, gathering her into his side. Exhaustion settled over her like a blanket as her breathing slowed to a crawl. She was just about to slip into a sated sleep when he whispered into her hair, "That was perfect."

When Cat woke again, Josh was gone, but the water was running in the bathroom off of his bedroom. Amazed that she hadn't woken up when he left the bed, she rolled over to see what time it was. Nine a.m. *Still early.* She closed her eyes again and snuggled back into the pillow with a yawn. That lasted for about thirty seconds. Then her brain exploded with a hundred different questions. What happened now? Was she supposed to leave? Was that the right way to handle this? *No, not this.* She got the impression that Josh might be offended if she hurried out. Besides, she knew deep down she didn't want to leave. She really should have asked Dani and Sonya when they were picking out her clothes. Morning-afters were not something she had much experience with.

While she was still convincing herself that she was reading Josh's signals correctly, the water turned off, and the shower curtain swung against the rod. Quickly, she found her hair tie and swept her hair up onto the top of her head. Then she reached down and arranged the sheets just so, making sure they were covering and exposing exactly the right spots for maximum flattery. She'd just adjusted her head on the pillow when the door opened, and Josh appeared wrapped in a towel from the waist down, a toothbrush hanging out of the corner of his smile, and... *oh my God...* a pair of sexy as hell, black-rimmed glasses. He looked absolutely delicious.

"Good morning again," he muttered around the brush. He stepped just out of sight, and the water turned on again. When he came back, his mouth was free, and he held onto the towel as he crossed the room.

Cat licked her lips, her eyes bouncing around his face.

"I slept in my contacts last night." He smiled and gestured to his eyes. "I had to take them out for a bit."

Was he seriously apologizing? "You... Josh, those are fucking hot."

Josh's grin grew from timid to confused until it finally broke into a laugh. "You're fucking hot," he said. He leaned down to kiss her, but she slapped her hand over her mouth.

"Let me brush too," she said through her fingers.

He laughed again, stepping back so that she could get out of bed and go to the bathroom, but she suddenly remembered that her clothing was in various spots around the room. He'd already been there seen that, but she wasn't a walk-to-the-bathroom-naked-in-broad-daylight-the-first-morning type of girl.

Josh saw her hesitation and reached down and tugged the sheet free from the mattress, tucking it around her like a toga. "You look like a goddess. You need one of those crowns of leaves."

"Too bad I didn't think to pack mine." She felt more like a kid dressed as a ghost for Halloween than a goddess, but it was sweet of him to say.

"I'll meet you in the kitchen," he said, tapping her butt as she shuffled by him like he did it all the time.

After brushing her teeth and doing the same staging with her outfit that she had when she'd woken up in his hotel room, she made her way out to the kitchen. She'd put on a new pair of underwear that she'd packed just in case and her henley from the night before, the buttons left open with nothing underneath.

Josh turned from the sink in just his boxers, giving her a discreet head to toe, and smiled a smile that was far more shy than she would have expected after what had just transpired between them. After staring for a moment, he snapped to and pulled out one of the leather stools at the breakfast bar, offering it to her.

When she hopped up onto it, he leaned in

and claimed the kiss she'd denied him earlier. He tasted like peppermint, the same as the toothpaste she'd just borrowed in his bathroom, and his stubble felt as good as it looked as it brushed against her chin.

"Do you want coffee?" he asked, with a final peck on her cheek.

"Please."

"How's your head this morning after Shawn's famous margaritas?"

"I can handle my tequila," she said, rolling the L off of the roof of her mouth.

"I think I believe you."

He moved toward the coffee maker on his countertop. It was a simple, two setting machine, nothing like the one she'd invested half a paycheck in when she first found her condo. She supposed she could get used to it. Or maybe she could convince him to upgrade once he tasted the Americano from her Delonghi...

Okay, she was getting way ahead of herself. Maybe he had no intention of this being a new habit.

He offered her cream and sugar, then picked up the mug he was already drinking from. They each took a sip, their eyes locked over their cups. "I have something for you," he said after a moment. He turned back toward the counter and reached for a white cardboard box, opening it as he approached.

Cat stretched to peek inside, her eyes going

wide when she saw an assortment of pastries arranged neatly on a white and blue striped tissue. "Croissants?"

"That's how you roll, right?"

"Always." She was grinning so hard, she could feel all her teeth showing, and her cheeks burned from the stretch. *Get it together, Cat. It's just pastry.* But it was no use—she was straight up beaming. She reached in and chose a perfectly iced, raspberry-filled croissant, and tore off a piece with her fingers while Josh watched.

"I hope you don't think I was being presumptuous, assuming you'd be here for breakfast."

"Not at all," she said, savoring the sugary fruit. "I'm glad you picked up on my 'better get croissants' signals when we planned this."

Josh laughed, looking pleased with her reaction.

"Are you going to have one? Don't make me eat by myself."

"I was just going to have some stale crackers and beer."

She laughed around her mouthful of sugar. "Not on my watch," she said when she'd finished her bite. "This is the only way to live." She pushed the box toward him, and he looked inside, studying his options before selecting a plain one with no fruit and tearing it in two. He left one half sitting in the box and took a bite of the other.

"Are you on a new diet since I last saw you?" she asked, popping another piece in her mouth.

"Me? No. I'm just a bacon and eggs guy. I'm going to get a sugar rush from this thing. I won't be able to sleep tonight."

Her giggling turned to belly laughing, with a hand over her mouth to keep from spitting out her food. Josh didn't seem to mind her lack of table manners, though, as he watched her with a wide grin. She finally finished her bite and grinned back. "You're sweet. You know that?"

"You say that like we just met. We've been doing this thing for a little while now."

"I suppose we have. But I knew that right away."

"I knew a lot of things about you right away," he said with a cocky grin that she decided he'd earned.

"Like what?" She was intrigued to hear him verbalize his first impressions, though Minnie was right. He hadn't put any effort into hiding them that night or any other time since.

He turned away to refill his coffee. "I knew how good it was going to be when we finally did this," he said, obviously hiding a grin.

"Oh, really?" She laughed again. "You got that from one drink and a slow dance?"

"I did. Those hips. The way you moved with the music... " He pulled his lower lip between his teeth and made a little hissing noise.

"Okay," she said, not willing to let him off with a joke. "What else?"

"I don't know." His demeanor shifted back to reticent, and she decided she liked how easily he embraced both sides of himself, confident and vulnerable. "I guess I knew you were a force. Someone who knew what she wanted from this world and took it." He shrugged, the tips of his ears turning a light shade of pink. "And I wanted to be what you wanted."

The compliment rushed her bloodstream, making her skin burn. Sometimes it seemed like her life was in a constant battle with her strong personality. The one time she'd tried to want what everyone else wanted her to want, she'd fallen flat on her face. To hear Josh flatter her for being—as her sister put it—unyielding, was quite possibly the nicest thing anyone had ever said to her.

"You are what I want," she said quietly, almost to herself. She did want him. She wanted him to be real—to be as good as he seemed. And if he wasn't, she didn't want to find out just yet.

Josh came around to her side of the breakfast bar and cupped her cheek, kissing her gently on the lips, then on the tip of her nose. Her heart slammed in her chest, and her belly flipped. God, was she really going to be that girl who sleeps with a guy and immediately falls in love? She squirmed in her seat, desperate to change the subject, or make a joke, anything to stop that free-fall feeling that had just come over her. But Josh wasn't done.

"Good," he said. "Because I'm not seeing anybody else. Maybe that's obvious, since we've been together every weekend since that trip, but I wanted you to know."

She nodded, feeling like a pupil in Josh's course on emotional honesty. Was this how mature adults handled relationships? She certainly hadn't been one the last time she was in a relationship. Maybe she wasn't even one now, considering how she'd been acting. Josh was older than her. He'd been married before; he owned a house and a business. She wasn't young and silly like Kasey, but she'd known most of her friends since she was eighteen, Dani even longer, and sometimes being around them made her still feel that way. And as far as her post-Micah dating life went, she was like a solitary animal that only emerged from her den to feed and prepare for the long winter alone. She'd also been known to bite the heads off of the opposite sex, just to show them who's in charge. Though, she was getting the distinct feeling she wasn't anymore.

"Oh," she said when she realized she hadn't responded yet. "I'm not seeing anybody else either."

Josh smiled, two parts amusement at her awkwardness and one part relief, then he dipped his head and peered up at her with the sweetest pair of nervous eyes she'd ever seen. "What would you think about keeping it that way?"

"Are you asking me to go steady?" she asked. *That's it, Cat, flirt, act like your heart isn't about to punch a hole through your sternum.*

"That's exactly what I'm doing."

Her stomach flipped all the way over and back again. After the whole Kasey fiasco, keeping it that way was exactly what she wanted. Besides, she was the youngest of three sisters; she wasn't good at sharing. But what did that mean for the bet? Did she lose already? Did she care? Because this felt really, really right.

"Okay," she said.

Josh's face split into a grin, rivaled only by her own when he'd handed her that box of croissants. "Yeah?"

"Yeah," she said. "I'd like that."

Twenty

J OSH WAS ALWAYS HAPPIEST IN the summer. Most of his hobbies revolved around the ocean, and he paid for the terrible gas mileage of his Jeep all year round just for the few months he got to drive around with the top down. Sunshine and salt were the cure to pretty much anything that ever ailed him, but the second half of this particular summer had been his best one yet.

He and Cat fell into an easy routine, splitting weekends between the island and the city. When she was in his bed, they'd get up early and walk on the beach. When he was at her place, they'd stay out later than he had in years, then sleep until noon. Josh had to be at the Abbott Building more often as the job picked up, and being so close to Cat's office, they occasionally got to meet for lunch during the week too.

When fall came, and he found himself standing in a single stall bathroom at the fancy-as-hell bed and breakfast where Emma was getting married, watching Cat fix her hair, it occurred to him that this might be the happiest he'd ever been.

"How do I look?" Cat smoothed her hands over her plum-colored bridesmaid dress, and his mouth began to water again. "Everything in place?"

"You're good." He tucked his shirt back into his pants and zipped his fly. "You're a bad influence," he said, pressing his lips to her bare shoulder then running a hand through his own tousled hair.

His complaint was pure jest. He couldn't make it in time for the rehearsal the night before because of an out of town job, so this was the first time he'd seen her in a week. After sitting in a wooden pew next to a handful of old ladies, watching Cat go through the ceremony in that sexy halter-style gown, he was more than ready to hike that thing up around her hips and show her just how much he'd missed her wherever they could find a place.

"Me?" She turned to face him and ran a finger along the lapels of his jacket. "What about you, showing up here looking like this?"

"We do have a room upstairs."

Cat lowered her voice to a whisper as if the public nature of their location had just occurred to her. "There was no time for that. I'm already supposed to be out there. Will you be okay until I get done with pictures?"

"I'll be fine. I'm gonna get a drink. I need to

start now if you're gonna make me dance at this thing."

"Oh, you know I am."

"Okay. Go get your picture taken." He kissed her forehead, letting his hands stray one more time. "I'll see you soon."

Emma's wedding day was exactly what one would expect from a girl who used to walk around her house with a lace curtain for a veil and a bouquet of dandelions, the family cat decked out in a tiny bow tie. Sonya had wrangled that story from Emma's older sister, and they hadn't let her live it down. Today though, even the weather had bowed to her daydream. Cobalt September sky, a warm breeze leftover from the summer, birds sang, butterflies flitted—it was a postcard from nuptial heaven. Interestingly enough, Cat hadn't felt the urge to roll her eyes once. Not even at the harpist in the baby-pink gown playing on the front lawn.

She stood in a circle with Dani and Sonya on the rolling green lawn of the vintage bed and breakfast Emma had chosen for the big day, pretending to laugh at something hilarious as the camera captured the joyous tableau.

"Josh looks handsome in his suit," Sonya said through an exaggerated grin for the camera. "What's he in for today?"

"What do you mean?" Cat held her bouquet up higher at the photographer's request and pretended to smell it.

"The bet. Your ridiculous games."

"Oh." Cat's picture-perfect pose slumped. She'd been having so much fun with Josh that she hadn't had any desire to intentionally ruin her time with him. She didn't get very much of it with the long-distance mostly limiting them to weekends together, and it seemed a shame to spend it playing games instead of playing under the covers.

Her neck heated as she remembered pulling him into that bathroom, how she'd missed him so desperately that she couldn't wait another minute to touch him. It wasn't just the sex either, though there was plenty of that. It was all of it. Ever since she'd invited him to be her date for this wedding, she'd been practically giddy with excitement over it. When was the last time she was giddy? She was finding Josh's company had that effect on all the events in her life.

"I'm calling the bet off for the day," Cat decided as she said it.

"Oh, really?" Dani flashed a confident wink at Sonya. "Why's that?"

"It's Emma's day, and she doesn't like the idea of it."

Sonya laughed for real this time, and the camera clicked rapidly. "So just for Emma? That's sweet."

"I'm a sweet girl."

"Please, Catia," Dani said. "'You guys win' was written all over your face when he showed up."

"She was practically swooning when Josh kissed her hello before she jumped in the limo," Sonya added.

"I didn't swoon." *She was totally swooning.*

The photographer shouted across the grass to them. "Can you three pretend to be whispering a secret? Maybe something about the bride and groom."

Sonya rolled her eyes but did as he asked and leaned into the circle. "Cat, I'm gonna do you a favor and let you off the hook with this bet."

"What?" Dani exclaimed. The photographer huffed as she pulled out of the shot. She leaned back in and plastered on a grin. "You're just going to let her out of it, right when we're about to win?"

"Who said you've won?" Cat whispered through her own forced smile.

"How long is this supposed to last, Cat? Until *your* wedding night?"

Cat huffed out a laugh. "That's dramatic."

"We barely saw you all summer," Sonya said. "You were either on the island or you two were holed up in your condo. Call it what you want, Cat, but you two are together and—" She covered her mouth in a fake gasp. "—dare I say... you look happy?"

It was true. She was stupid happy, which was just the kind of happy that got your heart broken. On the one hand, she was glad to relinquish the bet. She wanted to admit she'd been wrong about Josh. So far, his biggest flaws were his shitty coffee maker and the fact that he celebrated baseball season like it was second Christmas. But on the other hand, maybe the writing on the wall just hadn't appeared yet.

Even as the thought occurred to her, it felt old and heavy. She was tired of pinning her fear like an addendum to the end of every happy moment. It was like something about Josh had changed her DNA—for the first time in a long time, she didn't feel like stomping on the little embers of hope she felt. She wanted to see what would happen if she breathed just a little of herself onto them and let them flare. She wanted to give in to what felt good and trust that it wouldn't hurt later. That *he* wouldn't hurt.

"Okay." She sighed. "Yes, I'm happy."

Dani did a little victory dance, to the photographer's delight, but Sonya shook her head. "You're the only person I know who could sound disappointed that you found a good guy."

"I'm not disappointed," she said, standing taller. She pushed her chin out and confessed. "Things are great. He passed all of my tests, and I really, really like him. Okay?"

"You really, really like him?" Dani's mouth twisted from holding back a triumphant grin.

"Yes." Cat gave a firm nod. She more than liked him, but she wasn't going to explore that any further, other than to admit that she'd lost that bet when she started keeping a toothbrush at his place. "The bet's over," she said. "You win."

Dinner was nothing short of fabulous. Knowing the amount of planning that went into this event, Cat had been looking forward to it all day. She'd shoveled cake into her mouth, despite the zipper on her dress begging her to stop, and she'd convinced Josh to work off some of the calories out on the dance floor.

When the music slowed, he took her hand, letting his other fall to the small of her back.

"I'm so glad you're here," she said. "I missed you this week."

"I missed you too."

"How was your trip?"

"Too long, considering I should have been with you last night."

"You really should have," she flirted. "You would have liked my dress for the rehearsal."

"Don't tease me, Catia. I'll take you right back to that bathroom stall."

"You wouldn't dare."

Josh lifted her off the floor, and she squealed, attracting the attention of Emma's mother, who looked at her curiously. "You look beautiful," he said into her ear as he set her back on her toes. "I've been watching you all day waiting for this part."

"Looks like you were well taken care of." The knot of his tie was loosened in a comfortable, sexy way, and a lopsided grin hung on his face.

"Let's go to the bar after this so you can catch up," he said. "I liked the way that champagne was affecting you earlier." His hand crept lower, sliding down the smooth satin of her dress to rest scandalously on her ass.

She laughed at him, feeling a bit like they were at a middle school dance, but loving every minute of it. Her heart swelled, remembering the first time they'd danced like this—when they were strangers. Now he'd been hers for months, and the effect hadn't worn off. She dropped his hand so that she could drape both arms around his neck and ran her fingers through his short hair as they swayed. "You said I was a bad influence."

"I didn't say I didn't like it."

His accent was getting thicker, and she smiled at the tell. "You know, we spend a lot of our time together tipsy," she offered, feeling her own words start to swim.

Josh shrugged, lazily. "Guess that's what happens when you only see each other on weekends."

"True," she agreed, thinking back to the dive bar they met at, and dinners out, and work parties, and barbeques they had been accompanying each other to week after week since.

"Does that bother you?"

"No. It just seems like we're still on vacation sometimes."

Josh nodded, his brow creasing as if he were searching for a solution in his head. He was always doing that: taking her seriously, putting in the work he'd said he wasn't afraid of. She settled her head on his chest, feeling her affection for him surge.

"Next weekend, we'll stay in," he decided. "I'll help you study, and then we can argue about what to watch on television like a Tuesday night couple."

"That actually sounds like a very enjoyable day."

He leaned in to kiss her, offering a chaste peck that was suffused with promise. "I think so too."

"Hands on hips, Josh." Sonya's boyfriend twirled her over toward them, and she gestured to the lack of space between them. "Make some room for Jesus."

"She went to parochial school," Cat explained. "And she thinks she's funny."

"Sorry, Ma'am. Won't happen again."

"That's right. Good to see you again."

"You too. Been a while."

"Cat likes to keep you to herself when you're

in town. She doesn't like it when we see her all smiley and giggly. Hurts her image."

She shot Sonya a look, but Josh was quick as usual. "I'm the one with the smile tonight," he said. "Look at her. She's beautiful."

The blood rushed to Cat's cheeks. She wished Sonya and Marcus would find another spot on the floor, but they were quickly joined by the bride herself and her new husband.

"Hey, Josh!" Emma's cumulus cloud of a dress rustled as she wrapped her arms around Josh's shoulders.

Josh paused their dance to hug her back. "Emma, Adam, congratulations. It's a beautiful wedding."

"Thanks," Adam replied. "We're really glad you could come."

Adam and Josh had hit it off immediately the day they'd been introduced. Their budding bromance was on full display as she watched them fist-bump their hellos. If there was a part of her life that Josh didn't fit perfectly into, she hadn't found it yet.

Cat held her high heels in her hand, the gaudy but plush hotel carpet squishing like a cloud under her tired feet. Josh had his arm slung around her waist, initially to help with her wobbly legs, but now it was serving as more of a distraction with his hand roaming up and down her belly, dipping lower and lower as they approached the door to their room. She tilted her head up, nipping at his jaw, and he let out a low growl.

"Here we are again," she simpered. "Stumbling toward a hotel room in the middle of the night."

"Dylan better not be in there." He dipped his head to catch her attempt at another bite and turn it into a kiss. "And you're the only one stumbling."

That might be true. You couldn't ask for a better wedding date than Josh Rideout. He danced, made small talk with a hundred people he didn't know, gave her half his cake. She had every intention of rewarding him as soon as her head stopped spinning.

When he opened the door to their room, Cat made a beeline for the bed, tossing her shoes aside, and fell face-first onto the mattress. "I drank too much."

Josh pulled his shoes off too, discarding his suit jacket on the back of a chair, and came to sit beside her. "You feel okay?"

"I do right now. It's tomorrow I'm worried about."

He leaned over her, found the little hook that kept her dress closed, and flicked it open, then he ran the zipper down, pausing to leave small kisses on her back as he exposed it. "Cat, this is working between us, right?" He stood to tug the short dress out from under her and down her legs.

"Yes, of course." She smiled, resting her head on the crook of her arm, and watched over her shoulder as he ditched his tie.

"I know it's a lot of driving, but I'm happy." He rid himself of the rest of his suit, stripping down to a pair of tight black boxer briefs that captured all of her attention as he climbed onto the bed beside her.

"I'm happy too." Maybe it was the alcohol, or the day, or the fact that she'd admitted it to Sonya and Dani, but she felt like screaming it: *I'm so happy!*

Except screaming was a little too much effort at the moment. She crawled toward him on all fours, flopping on top of him like a starfish, and began pulling pins out of her hair. Curls tumbled one by one onto his bare chest, and he lifted each one, weighing it before swapping it for the next. "This was fun," he said. "Thanks for inviting me."

She giggled a little drunkenly. "As if there was any question. You're actually required to go to things like this with me now, so it's good that you enjoyed it."

"I can deal with being your permanent plus one, and I definitely enjoyed it. Weddings are always a good time."

"What was your wedding like?"

Josh froze, his hand falling away from her

head as the question dropped like a hammer. She immediately regretted it. Why on earth would she ask him something like that while they were lying half-naked in a hotel room?

"Um, it was not as nice as this one."

Cat's throat tightened. "I don't know why I asked that."

"It's fine." He adjusted his position beneath her, running a hand through his hair. "It was small. We were really young. We couldn't afford much because I had just bought my grandfather's house. Anyway, we got married in a stuffy church I had no connection to and had a small reception at a restaurant that a friend of her family owned. Dylan was there, Shawn and Minnie, though they weren't married yet. A few other friends and some family of hers."

"Were you happy?"

"I was. For a short time." He took a deep breath and wrapped his arms around her tighter as he blew it out. "I was old enough when my parents died to remember what it was like to have a family. I guess I sort of always told myself I'd have one again someday. When Sarah and I had been together for a while, and things were... comfortable, it just felt like my chance to make that happen. I didn't understand that my parents had something special. You can't force that."

Cat nuzzled into his neck, wanting to take

away the melancholy in his voice. "I'm sorry I brought that up."

"You say that a lot, like you think I don't want to do the hard stuff with you." He ran a thumb over her cheek, then went back to exploring her hair. "Do you wanna do the hard stuff with me, Catia? Cause you were just saying this was feeling a little too easy."

"I didn't say that," she said quietly. "This feels perfect."

Josh kissed the top of her head, and his energy shifted.

"All right then, tell me what your wedding would be like. Who knows, maybe I'll be there."

She laughed out loud at his nonchalance. It was as impressive as it was terrifying. She pushed up on her arms to look him in the eye, and she was met with a cocky smile that had her stomach teeming with butterflies. "You're drunk."

"So are you," he said, massaging her hip just above her panties. "But if I asked you if you wanted more wedding cake right now, would you say yes?"

"Of course I would." A small part of her brain started to wonder if she could finagle that.

"So, you still know what you want."

"I know exactly what I want," she said, kissing him to avoid the rest of the conversation. Thinking about the future with him was tempting, but she certainly wasn't going to daydream about white dresses and flowers out loud.

Thankfully, his buzz had him easily distracted. He reached around her, flicking the hooks on her strapless bra one by one until it fell away. She pressed her hips into his, drawing a sound from his lips she was sure was that of all coherent thought draining from his brain. Because he was exhausted, and more inebriated than he was admitting, he let her stay on top, manipulating him in a way that she didn't normally get to. She traced his pecs with her manicured nails, curling her back to kiss his stomach.

"Now I'm thinking about the honeymoon," he joked through quickening breaths. He flipped her onto her back, and when she'd stopped giggling, he tucked a piece of her hair behind her ear. "I know exactly what I want too. Finding you on that beach feels like the first twist of fate that's ever been in my favor." He let his tongue graze her lobe, sucking in a tight breath before letting it out in a soft whisper. "I love you, Catia. I'm in love with you."

Cat tried to pull in a breath, but the air in the room felt like it could spontaneously combust. A prickly warmth bloomed through her body, pooling in her chest and burning behind her eyes. She loved him too. She'd known it for a while now, but she'd locked it up like you would a loaded gun. If she admitted it, what then? There would be nothing to hide behind if her feelings got hurt, nothing to say, *well, at least I didn't...*

Josh worked his way down her stomach with his mouth, showing no signs of being concerned with her response, or lack thereof. *Did he already know?*

"Josh, I..." She chanced a glance down to where he'd landed, only the top of his head visible, his hair sticking up in all directions from her fingers pulling at it. Her attempt at a reply melted into pleasured gasps.

"You what?" He smiled against her lace panties.

He did already know. He had to. He'd seen through every lie she told herself since the moment they met.

Josh's hands were warm against the back of her thighs. His mouth was soft and comforting, and she focused on the feel of him until her heartbeat began to settle into a more sustainable rhythm. She let her muscles relax and thought of all of the happiness he'd brought to her life over the past few months. His quiet intelligence and playful energy—the way one minute he looked at her like a man who had so much to teach her, and the next like a boy with a crush. It made her feel safe and hopeful, and nothing like the angry person she was before. He was being honest with her now, vulnerable. He always was. She could do it too. She leaned on her elbows to look at him. "I love you too, Josh."

"But you're also afraid," he said, his lips on the inside of her knee. "You don't have to be."

"It feels dangerous to love you like this so quickly."

Against her wishes, he paused, picking up his head up to look at her. "I was with Sarah for years and look what happened. Maybe it doesn't make sense on paper, how quickly I knew what you were going to be to me, but it feels more right than anything ever has." She settled her head back into the pillow and closed her eyes, letting him convince her. "We'll go at whatever pace you want, Cat. I know where we're heading. We'll get there when you say."

Twenty-one

ANI FLAGGED DOWN THE BARTENDER as she and Cat took a seat at the bar at Bruno's, a little pub halfway between their office buildings. They'd been coming there on Wednesday nights for the last three years—ever since Dani got a job in the same neighborhood as Cat—and the smell of slightly-burnt nachos and hoppy beer always relieved Cat's mid-week slump. But tonight it was the end of a short work week, and she was looking forward to an extra drink to celebrate. It was also the eve of an important milestone for her and Josh and not a single hair on her neck stood up in warning. *Cheers to that.*

"So, Prince Charming is going to the Roday Family Thanksgiving Extravaganza, huh?" Dani asked while she waited for service.

"Don't call him that anymore," Cat said. "The game is over."

"Fine. Does *Josh* know what he's getting into?"

"My parents are going to adore him. You

know all he has to do is not be Micah and he gets a gold star."

"I'm not talking about Carlos and Cynthia. I'm talking about the wall to wall people and the kids screaming from every room in the house."

Dani had spent two of four Thanksgivings at Cat's parents' house during college when finances had made it necessary for her to choose between turkey or Christmas with her own parents who'd moved to Florida. She knew it could be overwhelming at times.

The bartender set two margaritas down in front of them, and Dani's lips were wrapped around the straw before she could thank him.

"Ladies." He greeted them both, leaning his elbows on the bar like a man who intended to stay awhile. "How's the drink, Dani?"

"Perfection as always, Jay."

"Cat?"

She took a long pull from her straw and let her eyes roll back in her head. "Exactly what I needed today."

"You're always coming in here stressed, Catia," Jay said. "You work too hard."

"No such thing."

"Well, I hope you have someone who can work all that stress out of you at the end of a long day."

"Do you hope she does, Jay?" Dani asked.

"Pretty girl like that shouldn't be sitting next to you every night, Dani."

Dani flashed him a supermodel grin. "You love me."

"I love Cat more."

"You're breaking my heart, baby."

Jay blew a kiss to her as he walked away, and Dani turned back to Cat.

"He wants that kitty, Cat."

"Shut up. He does not, and you're crass."

"Yeah, all right, Catia Patron Saint of bathroom quickies."

"Shhh!" Cat glanced nervously around the bar, though she didn't know anyone there. "I told you that in confidence."

"Okay, fine. So, you prepared Josh then? For Thanksgiving."

"Josh can handle them. He's good at that stuff. Probably better than me, and they're my family."

"Are you worried about Maria?"

"What about her?"

"That she'll have something judgmental to say."

"To Josh? She's too proper to risk offending a dinner guest. Besides, Prince Charming, right? What could she say?"

"I meant to you. Every time you see her, you leave feeling bad about some new thing. Remember when she told you your highlights made you look like a stripper? Or when she saw that picture of you in the paper for work, and she said you had too much Roday in your ass to wear pencil skirts? Or—"

"Okay! Yes, Maria thinks I'm a perpetual loser, I get it."

"You're not a loser, and I don't like how she makes you feel like one. You should tell Josh you two have a messy relationship so he won't be surprised when you turn into a fire-breathing dragon by dessert."

"I'm not going to complain about a stupid sibling rivalry to Josh of all people."

"Why not?"

Cat stared at Dani for a few beats until her furrowed brow shot up in recognition. "Oh, because of the fact that he has no family, and you have an army?" Dani bit down on her straw and pouted. "You think it's going to be weird for him?"

"I don't know. He's probably used to it."

"You should ask him."

"Wow, we're really racking up the heart-to-hearts before this one dinner. Can't we just go eat turkey and watch football and not make it weird?"

"Being in a relationship is about the weird stuff, Cat. That's what makes it different from hooking up. If it were the other way around, would he ask you about it?"

"Probably. He's like that. I'm not."

"Like what?"

"Open. Nothing scares him; he's like this

bombproof horse galloping into the middle of tough conversations."

"Well, maybe it would be nice if you did that for him for once in a while. Love is a two-way street."

"Listen to you with the relationship advice. Did Emma leave you her file on me when she and Adam went home for the holiday?"

"I'm just saying."

Cat rolled her eyes and took a big gulp of her drink, but something niggled at her. "He knows I love him," she said. "I tell him."

"Yeah, but 'Oh my God, Josh! Don't stop! I love you!' is different than 'I love you. Let's talk about holidays as an orphan'."

"He's thirty-three. Can we really call him an orphan?"

"Fine. Next topic. What are you wearing?"

"To Thanksgiving?"

"To your first Thanksgiving as a couple."

"God. Emma really did put you on her pay-roll."

The November wind whipped around Josh's face as he stepped out of Cat's car and met her on the sidewalk. Cars were crammed side by side in the driveway, more lining the little side street where her parents lived in a bright red, oversized colonial. Cat wasn't exaggerating when she said holidays at the Rodays' were a really big deal.

Sarah didn't have a big family. Often times it was just the two of them for holidays, or occasionally they would travel to North Carolina to spend Christmas with her sister's family. The first few years he enjoyed it—the family atmosphere, the table full of food and laughter—but after a while, when he and Sarah began the slow, steady descent into the end of their relationship, the entire affair felt forced and uncomfortable. It was like there was a buzzer clock counting down the time they had left as a family, and they all knew it.

Before that, in the years following his grandfather's death, he would sometimes accompany Dylan home for holidays. Dylan's mother was a fantastic cook, like Josh's own mother had been, and she would greet him as enthusiastically as she would her own son and daughter. Eventually, though, Dylan's sister began taking over hosting holidays when she had her own husband and kids. She always made sure to extend an invitation to Josh, but he'd never felt right about accepting. Dylan's mother genuinely enjoyed having another honorary child to dote on, but his sister was just being kind.

Last year, two months after his divorce was final and six months after he'd been living alone in his house, he'd made himself a turkey sandwich and spent the day watching football in his pajamas. Now he was wearing a shirt and tie, standing next to a beautiful woman who he was completely head over heels for, preparing to meet her extended family. He never could have predicted it.

Cat looped her arm through his, leading them down a paver path and up a set of stone steps where she paused in front of a frosted glass front door to fluff her hair. Cat's father opened the door before they even had a chance to knock, pulling Cat into a hug immediately. When he released her, Josh shifted the bottle of wine he'd brought into his left hand and accepted a hearty handshake from him.

"Josh, it's so nice to meet you," he said, his eyes sparkling with genuineness. "We're very pleased you were able to come."

"Thank you for inviting me, sir." Cat took his arm again as they stepped into the house, and he was more grateful for the support than he'd anticipated. He wasn't nervous exactly. He had plenty of experience mingling with people he didn't know, but he was struck by the feeling that maybe this was a place he wanted to be more than just a guest someday.

As soon as they closed the door behind them, they were rushed by Cat's mother Cynthia, a finely aged version of Cat with a crown of grey hair pinned up around her head and a frilly, holiday-themed apron tied around her middle. Cynthia greeted Josh with a hug, and when she pulled away, she brushed the lapels of his coat in that way only mothers do. He couldn't deny the touch and the smell of nutmeg and sage that wafted from her warmed a place in his chest he hadn't felt in a long time.

A woman whom he assumed was one of Cat's sisters rounded the corner next. He recognized the honey-brown eyes that seemed to be a Roday family trait, as well as their shared smattering of dark freckles. This woman's skin was a few shades darker than Cat's, making the marks less noticeable, but they were there.

Cat's probable sister offered her hand. "You must be Josh."

"This is my sister, Maria," Cat said, letting her arm slide down his until their fingers were intertwined. Maria stole a glance at the gesture.

A strange energy radiated from Cat as soon as Maria spoke. Her shoulders straightened, and her lips pursed—she began obsessively smoothing her skirt with her free hand. There was definitely some tension between the two.

"Nice to meet you, Maria." She had a firm handshake that reminded him of the women he knew professionally. It was all power suits and pumps, and he wondered what Maria did for a living, assuming it was something corporate. Maybe the two were competitive in their careers. Though, Cat was certainly no disappointment on that front.

"It's nice to meet you too. Olivia is in the

kitchen, pulling pies out of the oven. Cat, bring him in." Maria turned on her heel and waved them along behind her.

Cat squeezed his hand, and with a roll of her eyes, they followed into the kitchen, finding Olivia where Maria had said she was.

"You must be Josh," Olivia said, pulling him in for a hug. He couldn't remember the last time he'd been hugged this much. "Cat has told us so much about you. It's so good to finally meet you."

Olivia was obviously much closer in age to Maria than Cat, but she had a big smile and warm eyes, that were more reminiscent of her younger sister. She also had a very large pregnant belly that was completely undetectable from the back. It surprised him when she'd turned to greet him, and given their similarities it was impossible for him not to picture the way Cat might look someday.

"It's good to meet you too," he said, pushing aside the daydreams. "Thank you for having me."

The three older Roday women stood in a semicircle in almost matching posture, taking him in until Cat interrupted them. "Josh, would you like something to drink? I'm sure my mother was just about to ask you."

Cynthia seemed to snap back to attention at that, shaking her head and rushing to the refrigerator. "What can I get you, sweetheart?" she said. "Coffee? Iced tea?"

"Are you driving, son?"

Carlos appeared then, and Josh spun around to face him. "No, sir. Catia drove."

"In that case, skip the tea and come have a drink with me."

Josh didn't get the impression he was asking, so he squeezed Cat's hand then followed her father out of the room and down a dim hallway with rich, antique-looking wallpaper.

"Beer or whiskey?" Carlos asked when he'd led them into a parlor with leather furniture and an enormous, polished-wood bar. It was a retirement hobby for Carlos, Cat had told him. He'd built it himself and was learning how to make exotic cocktails from around the world to impress his friends and family.

There were a few other men gathered on the couches watching the Cowboys game, and they looked at him with mild interest as he passed. Josh quickly scanned their drink choices, noting an array of glass tumblers and amber liquid.

"Whiskey is good. Thank you."

"Boys, this is Josh," Carlos called to the group of men as he set about selecting a bottle from the top shelf. "He's Catia's boyfriend. That's Antonio, Rick, Daniel, and Eddie." He went down the row on the couch, and each man nodded in response. "The little one in the chair is Jaime."

Jaime waved sheepishly, then glanced at Antonio, who Josh assumed was his father.

"Nice to meet you all," he said, holding up the glass Carlos had pushed in front of him.

"Woohee," Rick said. "Would you listen to that accent? Cat found herself a Yankee."

Josh chuckled, used to the reaction after spending more than half of his life hearing it. Rick didn't seem to mean any harm, but Antonio sent a hard elbow his way anyway. "This from the only other gringo in the room," he said. Rick didn't seem offended by that either, and Josh took a moment to try to discern their relationship. Rick was a blond-haired, chisel-jawed cowboy with a thick drawl and what was probably his fanciest pearl-buttoned shirt tucked into a pair of jeans. Antonio and the other men all clearly shared the same heritage as the Rodays. Antonio wore a tie like Josh, along with khakis and a pair of loafers, and looked as though he just stepped off of one of the sailboats on the island. Josh made the guess that he belonged to Maria. The other two, Daniel and Eddie, were younger than all of them. Probably mid-twenties. He wasn't sure where they fit in, but process of elimination led him to believe Rick was probably Olivia's husband. He found out he was correct a moment later when she popped her head in and asked him to grab something from their car.

Apparently, the gaggle of children playing in the front yard belonged to Olivia and Rick, and Daniel and Eddie were cousins. Carlos explained all of this while Josh sipped at the hard liquor and tried to keep all of the names straight. Beyond them, through the archway that led to a larger, more casual family room, Josh could see even more family members: another couple sharing a drink, and a woman in a floral dress and heels attempting to chase after a toddler. He was going to have to make flashcards for the next holiday.

"So, Josh," Carlos said, coming around the bar and taking the seat Rick had just vacated. He gestured for Josh to take the matching chair to Jaime. "Cat says you own your own business."

"Yes, sir. I'm an architect. I own a small firm with a good friend of mine."

"Ambitious."

"I was the lead there when it happened to come up for sale. I had a little money tucked away. I got lucky." He'd never been sure how lucky it actually was, given that spending his inheritance from his grandfather on buying a small business had been nail number one in the coffin of his marriage. All the dominoes that fell after that had put him on that beach, though, where he met Cat. Now it seemed like he could chalk it up as a win.

"And you live on the island?"

"I do. I own a house out there." He thought the mention of his homeownership might earn him some points in her father's eyes. Carlos seemed like the type who would value the responsibility that came with it. He hadn't anticipated the line of questioning that would follow, though.

"Single man owning his own house. Don't find that much nowadays," Carlos mused, leaning back into the couch and searching Josh's face. "What made you want to buy a house for just you?"

"It was the house I grew up in. My grandfather's house. He passed, and I couldn't let it go." He hesitated on the next part, unsure whether Cat had mentioned it, but he wasn't going to lie, even by omission. "I was also engaged at the time, and it seemed like the right step."

Carlos seemed displeased to hear that information. Josh could have guessed he would be. The Rodays seemed like a traditional family.

"Married, huh?" he asked, looking as if he'd just discovered the thread that would unravel the whole thing. "Divorced or widowed?"

"Divorced."

"How long?"

"Little over a year."

"What happened?"

Antonio laughed from his spot where he'd been pretending not to listen. "Jesus, Carlos."

"Seems like a valid question for a man who wants to date my daughter."

Maria's husband gave Josh a reassuring wink. "Looks to me like he already is."

Josh glanced back and forth between Cat's father and the man who had seemingly already passed these tests and lived to tell about it. He still wasn't sure if he was supposed to answer the question. Though it wasn't his favorite subject, he decided to just lay his cards on the table before his lack of answer caused any undue speculation.

"She left," he stated, bringing all the eyes in the room back to him. "We got married young, grew apart, and she found someone else who was better suited for the woman she'd become. I didn't intend for my marriage to fall apart, and I made my own mistakes, but I like to think I learned from them. It was nothing scandalous, it just... happened."

Antonio looked at Carlos, who seemed to be searching his brain for a response, blinking rapidly and scratching his fingers along his thick jowls.

"No kids?" he finally asked.

"No, sir."

"And she let you keep the house?"

Josh allowed a grin to spread across his face. He recognized the look of a man who was ready to lay down his arms. He shrugged, offering a resolute look. "She moved into his, so it only seemed fair."

Carlos steepled his fingers, taking a long moment to let Josh's statement hang in the air. Finally, he stood and stepped back to his bar. Antonio grinned, then turned back to the television.

"It's my job," Carlos said, retrieving the bottle of whiskey and nodding for Josh to come back for a top off. "You understand?"

"I do."

They were out of earshot of the others now, due to the blaring football game, but Carlos leaned in conspiratorially anyway. "I like to weed them out early, you see. Cat is tough, self-reliant. Anyone who can handle me is well-suited to handle... to attempt to handle her." Josh nodded knowingly, though he was pretty sure Cat would not approve of that explanation. He'd been drawn to Cat's independence from the beginning. It was important to him to know she was with him because she wanted to be, not out of some need that she could outgrow. "She seems happy," Carlos said.

"I'd like to keep it that way, sir. She makes me happy too."

It was Carlos's turn to nod, as he tapped his glass to Josh's and took a sip. "Well then, I think you and I will get along just fine, Josh."

"I'm glad to hear that." He brought his glass to his lips, allowing the fire from the whiskey to burn in his throat as he breathed a sigh of relief.

"You're looking awfully sophisticated today, Catia." Maria was perched at the breakfast bar in the kitchen, scanning Cat from head to toe over her glass of wine. "That top is a little low-cut, but I like the pearls."

"Thank you, Maria." Cat's blood pressure was beginning to rise already and dinner hadn't even begun. She wanted to escape this 1950's holiday card and go and hang out with Josh, but her father hadn't invited her for a reason. Hopefully, he was ingratiating him to the men in the other room while they shared that drink. Those who married into the Roday family were a tight-knit clan of their own, and the introduction wouldn't go by without a little hazing.

"And it's nice to see you with such a hand-some, successful man beside you," Maria contin-ued. "So when are we getting babies?"

"You know I'm about to take the bar exam right, Maria? I'm not thinking about babies."

"Yes, of course, I know that. We are all very proud of you." Maria crossed her legs and set her glass on the counter so she could gesture with her hand as she spoke. "I'm just hoping that maybe you're finally starting to think about your life in the long term. Emma just got married, and Sonya is not far behind. You're not getting any younger."

Olivia waddled toward them from her spot by the oven, wrapping an arm around Cat's waist as she joined the conversation. "How was the wedding?" she asked. "Was Emma as beautiful as ever?"

"Of course." Cat turned her attention to her

kinder sister, wrapping her arms around Olivia's baby bump and leaning her head on her shoulder. "She and Adam both looked great."

"Emma has always had a good head on her shoulders," Maria said. "Now see, she has a good career and now a husband and soon a family. She didn't let her job get in the way of settling down."

"She wanted to settle down."

"And you don't?"

Cat gulped her wine. She still hadn't really thought about what all the happiness she'd found with Josh meant in future terms. She'd been busting her ass trying to get back what Micah took from her. She had other goals at the moment, and she sure as hell wasn't looking to put them on the line again. "I like my life the way it is, Maria."

"Does Josh know this? Because with the way he looks at you, I'm surprised he hasn't gotten down on one knee already."

Here we go. "It hasn't even been six months." Cat sighed.

"Yes, but he's older, right?"

"Five years. It's not like we're from different generations."

Maria continued on as if Cat hadn't spoken. "Men have a longer window, but still, if he wants kids, a family of his own, he's at an age where he is going to be thinking of these things."

Josh's easy suggestion about their future after Emma's wedding played like a movie in Cat's mind. He was being cheeky, goofing around. *Right?* "You don't even know him," she said, feeling her cheeks begin to warm under Maria's gaze. "How could you possibly know what he wants?"

"I know men, Catia. You're not dealing with a little boy like you were with Micah. Let me guess, he opens doors and picks up the tab everywhere you go? He calls you instead of firing off a text. You're dating a grown-up. Grown-ups want grown-up things."

She had to admit, Josh did seem decidedly more adult than the men she'd dated in the past, but he didn't seem to have a problem with the way things were. They both had busy lives, and it made the time they did have together all the more special. And by special, she meant filled with amazing sex and laughing more than she could ever remember. It had probably been years since either of her sisters had gotten laid like that. She straightened her posture, taking another sip of her wine to hide the smirk on her face at the thought.

"Oh, Cat," Olivia said, squeezing her waist. "He does seem to adore you. This is a good thing for you."

"And you're quite smitten too," Maria added. "It's all over your face. You'll see, soon you're going to realize you've outgrown these long hours and your tiny little apartment in the city, and you'll want more. There are worse things than letting a man take care of you, Cat."

Cat bit the inside of her lip to keep from snarling. She didn't need anyone to take care of her, and Micah was the one who wanted her to make a choice for him. Josh hadn't asked her to give up anything. Yet.

Laughter erupted from the room where Josh had disappeared to. At least he was having a good time. Cat fingered the neckline of her blouse, her skin prickling with the urge to escape. "You don't know what you're talking about, Maria," she said. "Just because that's the choice you and Olivia and mom made, doesn't mean I have to follow in your footsteps." She hated to lump Olivia in her rebuttal, but sacrifices had to be made. She would understand. "Everything I have, I gave myself. My life is just fine."

"All right, Cat. There's no need to get upset." Maria took a sip of her wine and hopped off the stool, crossing the room. "I only want you to be happy. You know that, right?"

"*Si*, Maria."

Maria joined the hug Cat and Olivia were sharing, and just like that Cat was back in the ten-year-old version of herself, awkwardly caught between wanting to impress her big sisters and being a source of amusement to them. Her life had always seemed trite in the wake of whatever phase they were living through. Silly and naive Cat. A perpetual little girl. She was an adult now; she didn't need them to tell her what to do or judge her choices.

"I'm going to find Josh," she said, extricating herself from their embrace. "Dad is probably torturing him with bad jokes."

Olivia squeezed her once more, then let her go. "*Te amamos*, Kit Cat."

"I love you guys too."

Cat followed the sound of the football game, wandering into the parlor to find Josh seated in one of her father's chairs with a drink balanced on his knee. Her father beamed proudly at her from the couch. Josh had clearly already won him over, but she hadn't expected any less.

Josh stood when she crossed the threshold, holding an arm out to receive her, and she curled into his side.

"Hey," he said, wrapping an arm around her waist. "You okay?"

"Yeah. Just came to check the score." She snuggled under his arm and hugged him back, feeling shaky from the conversation with Maria. When he kissed the top of her head, it struck her that her first instinct had been to come running to him for a safe place to hide.

Maybe she was already letting him take care of her without even realizing it.

Cat rubbed her hands together, waiting for the

heat in her car to reach an acceptable temperature before she put it in drive. "I can't find my gloves," she said, turning in her seat to scan the back of her car.

Josh sat beside her, watching her with a curious look as she dug through the center console again. He held a stack of Pyrex filled with everything from turkey to pie, to the spicy-as-hell chipotle chorizo stuffing he'd politely suffered through and was now stuck with. Her mother had insisted on sending him with enough leftovers to eat until Christmas.

He reached a hand out around the food and rubbed her bouncing bare knee. "You seem upset about something."

"Is this blouse too low cut?"

"What?"

"Nothing. Nevermind."

Josh grabbed ahold of her hand and brought it to his mouth, blowing warm air on her fingers and massaging them. "What's wrong, Cat?"

"I'm fine," she said. She was, for the most part. Dinner had been pleasant, and once her cousins had started to fill the house, she had less opportunity to brood over the constant friction between her and Maria. Josh had been a dream, impressing everyone he met. Whenever she wasn't standing beside him, she was getting winks and encouraging elbow nudges from her relatives.

"Josh is so handsome, Catia," they gushed.

"A new boyfriend?" they asked with wide eyes and pearls clutched.

Apparently, she wasn't the only one who noticed it had been a long time since she'd introduced anyone to them.

She shifted in her seat to tell him how impressed she was, but found him looking at her with an expression she couldn't quite read. "What?"

"I just want to make sure that was okay for you. Me being there, meeting your whole family."

Her heart sank. "Oh, baby," she said. "It was more than okay." In fact, Josh being there had been the best part of the day. She would unpack that later, now she just wanted to wipe that look off of his face. She reached out to touch his cheek. "It was just my sister. We have a tense relationship sometimes."

"Do you want to tell me about it?"

She shook her head and put the car in gear. She'd had enough of Maria for the day. "It's old stuff. Nothing to worry about. You being there today made me very happy."

"It made me happy too."

She agreed with a nod to herself. They were both perfectly happy. Maria couldn't be more wrong.

Twenty-two

C AT READ THROUGH HER SHOPPING list, wandering through the produce aisle while Josh leaned on the cart behind her. "Why are there so many different kinds of onions?" she despaired, scanning the rows for the third time.

Josh shrugged, his eyelids drooping. It was almost eight o'clock by the time he'd arrived at her condo, changed, and got back in her car to go to the grocery store. She knew he just wanted to be done with this errand and back on her couch, scrolling through the options on her Netflix subscription. "I'm sure it'll taste good with any of them," he said through a yawn.

She blew him a kiss and grabbed a few of the red ones, moving down her list. "Almost done."

Twenty minutes and nine ingredients later, they were ready to check out. Emma and Adam were having everyone over to watch the UVA football game at their house the next day, and she'd promised to make something potluck. However, her motivation the past Monday afternoon when she'd decided on her contribution was much stronger than it was so late on Friday evening. Why didn't she just volunteer to bring cookies?

She glanced once more at her list to make sure she hadn't forgotten anything, then headed to the checkout. Josh helped her load all of the items onto the counter and a perky redhead, whom he'd been having a friendly conversation with all the while, informed them that the total came to $38.16.

Josh reached for his wallet in his back pocket, his body squared off in front of the card reader.

Cat dug through her purse. "I've got it, Josh."

"It's fine," he replied, retrieving his card from its sleeve. "You're gonna do the cooking. I'll get the ingredients."

"You don't have to do that. I volunteered to make something."

He smiled at her, his lip twitching in amusement as he dismissed her with a wave of his hand.

"Babe..."

He ignored her and swiped his card.

"Josh!"

Everyone around them froze, staring at her—except the cashier who turned away and pretended to organize some pens. Her face heated. She took a deep breath and lowered her voice. "I said, I can get it."

Josh regarded her face as if he didn't recognize it. He took a step back, putting his hands up in surrender, and went to help the grey-haired man at the end of the line put the bags into their cart.

After an uncomfortable walk to the parking lot, Josh loaded the groceries into the back seat of Cat's car while she warmed the engine. He climbed in beside her, switching off the radio. "You wanna tell me what that was about?" he asked, calmly but oh so seriously.

Cat kept her eyes trained on the windshield, counting down from ten to let her anger ebb away. She'd over-reacted, she knew that, but that didn't mean it shouldn't be said.

"Josh, I have a good job that I work very hard at. I take care of myself all week when you aren't here. You don't have to pay for everything all the time."

He was quiet, gazing out the side window with his cheeks sucked in and his thumb tapping on his knee. Cat's skin prickled with discomfort. She'd hurt his feelings. Or maybe he was pissed, and they were about to have their first fight. She wished she hadn't said anything.

That was a first.

After a few excruciating moments, Josh nodded his head in the dark, turning toward her seat to catch her eye in the light from the dashboard. "Okay," he said. "I'm sorry. I didn't know it bothered you."

He said it so matter-of-factly, her cheeks burned over her outburst. All she could manage was a quiet, "thank you."

The rest of the ride was comfortable, status quo—flirty even. They rehashed their long workdays and joked about being late to Emma's because the recipe Cat had chosen was going to take all day to make. Neither one of them was interested in letting that awkward blip interfere with the rest of their night.

After putting away all of the groceries, Cat offered him a shower while she changed out of her work clothes and picked a movie to put on.

Josh met her on the couch, not long after. His bare chest was still damp, and his hair was tousled from being towel dried. He wore his glasses and the same pajama pants she'd borrowed in his hotel room. He looked refreshed, even as he fell hard into the cushions with a sigh.

"What's this?" he asked, gesturing to the television. He didn't wait for an answer, though. He hooked her arm and pulled her onto his lap.

Cat laughed then pressed her nose into his neck, taking a deep pull. He smelled like the soap he'd started keeping in her shower. Plain. Not scented with any botanicals or musk or herbs like all of her products, just clean. It was the sexiest scent she'd ever inhaled, and she thought they should bottle him up and sell it to all those boys who liked to spray themselves with faux masculinity.

"I missed you," she said, her words coming out a little bit strangled.

"I missed you too."

"I know it's late, and you're exhausted, but I'm glad you didn't wait until tomorrow to drive up."

"That wasn't even an option, Cat." He slid his hands up her sides and underneath her shirt, looking pleasantly surprised that she'd already removed her bra when she'd changed out of her work clothes.

Cat tossed her head back, letting him re-acquaint himself with every part of her body, his familiar touch pulling a sigh from deep inside her chest. Sometimes, when she was without him with only his voice on the telephone and her own memories, she would try to recreate the feeling of him, but her body knew the difference.

Whatever television station she'd been stuck on suddenly switched to a commercial, and the volume change startled them both.

"Are you watching this?" he asked, his eyes glinting with building intent.

She shook her head.

"Good. Let's go to bed."

"Fuck, I needed to do that." Josh groaned as he slid off of her and flopped face down in the pillow.

Cat laughed at his confession. He'd given up on trying to be more eloquent when he realized she liked reducing him to a caveman. She scooted closer to drape an arm over his back, and he turned his head to look at her. Her skin was rosy from the warm light of the lamp and the way he'd just made her come. She stroked her fingers up and down his back tenderly, giving him a self-satisfied smirk. She always seemed to know when he'd had a particularly long day that needed to end with being buried inside her. Unfortunately, besides the occasional mid-week sleepover when he had a meeting in the city, they were still getting by on weekends.

He reached out to toy with her hair, lifting the heavy waves and letting them cascade off of his fingers and pool onto the pillow. He'd been waiting all week to be here, surrounded by everything Catia.

"There was no way I wasn't coming here tonight, Cat." His eyelids were demanding to close, but his sated state left him flooded with the desire to tell her how much his body missed her on the nights they slept apart, how he wasn't sure he could make it another week when he got in his car to go home on Sunday. "I don't care how exhausted I am. If it's a choice between sleeping alone or sleeping next to you, I'm gonna make the drive."

Her eyes had fallen shut, and her fingers had moved to a slow crawl. A slight hum of agreement slipped from her lazy smile, urging him on.

"I know it's only an hour, and I'd drive any distance to get to you, but maybe we should think about skipping all that." He pushed off of the pillow and propped his head on his hand. His thoughts were flowing unchecked from his brain to his mouth now, but it was something he'd been thinking about for a while. Since Emma's wedding, when he'd told her time meant nothing. Two months, five months, a year. Who was to say what was right? He'd spent ten years with Sarah all told, and he'd never felt the kind of passion he felt for Cat. The need to be around her, to soak her up. The way she made him feel nervous and confident all at once. The way she lit up a room and warmed him from the inside out when she smiled at him. Things were good, but he was greedy. He was hung up on her and needed more. "We could have nights like this every night, Cat. Instead of missing each other for five out of the seven." He pressed his mouth to her shoulder and breathed. "You should move in with me."

Cat's eyes blinked open, her brow knitting as if she wasn't sure if she'd dreamed his question. The seconds got more and more uncomfortable as she parted her lips then clamped them shut, once, twice, before pulling her bottom between her teeth and looking at him pitifully. "Josh," she whispered after a few moments, offering him a weak smile. "Baby, let's get some sleep."

She kissed him with a finality that landed in his gut like a punch, then she rolled away to switch off the light. The sudden darkness forced his eyes to close, but the prospect of sleep had completely disappeared.

A dull ache of self-pity, the kind he didn't usually allow himself, bucked at him from the pit of his stomach. He should have known. He *did* know. He'd just run headlong into a wall he was fully aware existed. He'd felt it from the beginning, that gentle counterpressure that she always applied whenever he pulled them forward. At first, it was cute, the way she eyed him with suspicion when he professed with utter certainty that this thing with her was it for him, or the bashfulness that overtook her willful demeanor whenever her friends called her out for the way she looked at him. Those looks were what kept him content to let her stroll along behind him, knowing she would meet him where they were headed. But this time, he saw something different. This was the first time her pushback had been strong enough to knock him down; the first time she'd pulled away from him, and he wasn't entirely sure she wanted to catch up.

Twenty-three

CAT WAS ALREADY SHOWERED AND dressed by the time Josh got up the next morning. She was used to rising early every day for work and couldn't break the habit. She'd discovered early on that, depending on what kind of night they'd had, Josh could just as easily wake at sunrise or sleep well past breakfast. It was one of the perks of working for himself.

That morning he'd split the difference, wandering into her kitchen at eight a.m. He'd put on a pair of jeans, but he still held his t-shirt in his hand as he padded toward her. She took in his puffy eyes and sleep-tossed hair and almost had a complete change of heart at the first sight of him. The man wore mornings well.

She needed to be stronger than that, though. Being taken by him in this way is what landed her here, teetering on the edge of who she promised she wouldn't become again.

"Want some breakfast?" she asked casually, holding up a small frying pan filled with egg whites and pico de gallo.

"Sure." A small smile played on his face as he acknowledged she was teasing him. "If you make it right," he said.

She smiled back. Maybe the heavy conversation that was simmering could somehow just evaporate into their normal easy banter. He would apologize for talking crazy, and she would laugh it off. They could go back to the same page and set up camp, try to stay there for a few more months, years.

"This one is mine." She pointed to a block of cheddar cheese she'd set aside. "I'll make yours the way you like it."

"Thank you." He dropped a kiss on her cheek before taking a seat at the breakfast nook nestled in front of a tall window that looked out over the heart of the city. She watched him gazing out at the tall buildings stabbing the horizon, hard steel slicing through the soft blue winter sky, and he suddenly looked oddly out of place in this world she'd built for herself.

Maybe he felt it too. Despite his smile, his lips were tentative against her skin, distant. Her punishment for not just answering his question the night before, letting it simmer.

She'd spent the night dancing with the idea in her head, Josh's words and Maria's taking turns cutting in to lead a sort of angry Tango with her thoughts. If there were a cartoon animation of her reaction, it would be her eyes popping out of her head, little heart bubbles floating up to the sky. She'd look up at them dreamily, and a huge anvil would fall, crushing her for being so stupid. She was finally living the life she'd put on hold for Micah after clawing her way here alone, two years later than she should have arrived. Moving in with Josh would mean scrapping all of that for him. It was too familiar.

"Josh," she said, interrupting what looked like his own rumination on the matter. "Last night... you weren't serious, right? About me moving in with you." She kept her back to him, afraid to watch his reaction. She knew he was serious. He didn't make off-the-cuff remarks. But she wanted to give him an out, an opportunity to agree to the absurdity of trying to tie their worlds together so soon.

He wouldn't take the easy way out, though. That wasn't him either. "I was serious," he said simply. "But I guess you feel differently about it."

Cat flipped her omelet out onto a plate and got to work assembling his. She could feel him staring, but now was not the time to get lost in that intense gaze of his. "It just seems a bit illogical."

"Illogical? You sound like you're talking about a math problem, Cat." He gave her a small chuckle, and she found herself bristling at the sound. His confidence turned her on when he was using it to charm her, but this was the first time they had been at odds. All of a sudden, it wasn't so endearing.

"Yes, illogical," she repeated. "That's a giant leap of faith after five months."

"We've already talked about this, Cat. Look, we're both old enough and experienced enough to know when something's right. I love you. You know this is more than a weekend thing."

"Josh," she sighed. "You know I love you too, and I miss you when we're apart, but I have a whole life here."

"I have a life, too, and I want it to include you." He leaned back in his chair, gesturing casually with his hand as if he was explaining something as simple as the rainfall in the spring. "This is going somewhere. Why should we wait to have it?"

"You think everything is so easy," she muttered, half to herself.

"It was easy until right now." He pulled his t-shirt over his head. His eyes had turned into an icy blue, looking jaded and impatient, and she felt the conversation slipping somewhere they had yet to travel together.

She abandoned his breakfast. "Okay," she said, trying to sound rational, open to a counter-argument. Maybe he could enlighten her. "So I'll just give up my condo, my life here, and move into yours, and then what? You're asking me to put a lot on the line. What if it doesn't work out?"

"And what if this is exactly what we think it is?" He pushed his chair out and came to stand across from her, dipping his head to force her to meet his eyes. "If anyone should have any doubts, it should be me. I've done this before. I know how it could turn out, but I told you I'm not scared. Why are you so afraid?"

Cat's cheeks glowed with irritation. They'd been over this; he knew exactly what she was scared of. He'd made her explain it to him, tell him the whole sorry story. "Just because I didn't have a ring on my finger doesn't make my experiences any less valid, Josh. I have reasons for the way I feel too. Micah—"

"I'm not him," he said, cutting her off before she could finish the argument he obviously knew was coming. "I think I've proven that."

"No, you're not." She came around the island that separated them, tipping her chin up toward his face. "You're the opposite, Josh. He dragged his feet, and you dive in headfirst. Whatever happened to just making a plan and seeing it through? Looking before you leap? Because if we do this thing, and we don't land where you think we will, I'm the one who loses. Again."

"Okay then, Cat, what's the plan? I told you we could go at your pace, but you gotta tell me what that pace is. Throw me a bone here. Are we heading where I think we are, or am I wasting my time?"

"Why is figuring that out wasting time?" Her exasperation rang in her heightened pitch, but she couldn't seem to cap it. "You have somewhere else you need to be? You can't wait and see what happens?"

"So, that's what we're doing here? Just seeing what happens?"

"That's not all we're doing, but I'm not like you, Josh. You let your gut guide you. You jump into things because you feel a certain way, and maybe that's what I should be worried about. You let your heart make all your decisions, but you've been wrong before."

The impact of her words appeared on his face instantly, and she winced. She hadn't meant it—not that part.

Josh's lip curled up ever so slightly, and he nodded, turning his head to refocus his gaze over her shoulder. "I have been wrong before," he said, sounding as if she'd sucked the air out of his lungs. "That was a big one, and I paid for it. I guess I'm still paying for it if that's what you want to use as your excuse."

"Josh," she whispered, her stomach churning with remorse.

"No, Cat, look, I say this is right for us, that I know beyond a doubt that this is different than anything I've felt before, but maybe I am wrong. *Again.*" He stepped past her into the living room, and she followed him, her heartbeat ringing in her ears.

"Wait..."

"Wait for what? Wait for you to decide if we have a right to what we have? Wait to see if there's another way I can prove myself to you? If you don't want to move in together, that's okay. Really, it is, but you need to tell me what we're doing here." He walked to the front door where his shoes were set on the floor, and he yanked them on.

"What are you doing?"

"I should go." He picked up his overnight bag from where he'd dropped it the night before and slung it over his shoulder.

"We're supposed to go to Emma's," she said, her throat tightening around the words. Hot tears burned the corners of her eyes, and she turned her head away to keep them from materializing.

"Tell them I'm sorry, all right?" He grabbed his keys from the hook next to hers, his knuckles white as he clutched them. "You know, at least when Sarah left me, she was choosing someone else who made her happy. You? You're trying to choose between being with me and being alone as if that might be better."

Her heart took off in a sprint. "I'm not leaving you, Josh. That's never what I was saying."

He pulled in a long breath, letting it out through his nose before speaking. "I'm not leaving you either," he said, crossing the few steps between them and dropping a stiff kiss on her cheek. "I'm just going home. I'll call you later."

Twenty-four

"**W**HERE'S JOSH?" ADAM ASKED, IMMEDIATELY upon opening the door.

"Good to see you too."

Adam folded his arms across his chest as Cat pushed past him. She placed the bowl she was carrying on his kitchen counter and shrugged off her coat.

"Are you not answering on purpose?"

"He had to go home. Do you have a serving spoon for this?"

"In that drawer," he answered, pointing across the room.

"Hey, Cat!" Emma chirped as she came into the room to greet her. "Where's Josh?"

Adam's eyes were burning a hole into the back of Cat's head as she dug through their kitchen utensils and pretended not to hear Emma's question. She finally found a large slotted spoon and turned back around to see her friends wearing matching expressions.

"You know, it wasn't that long ago you two used to be excited to see *me* when I showed up."

"That's not an answer," Emma said.

"We had a... disagreement."

"Shoulda known it was too good to be true," Adam said, shaking his head.

"We didn't break up." Cat sighed, wishing she'd just made up an excuse not to come. "You still have your new best friend."

"I'm saying this because I'm *your* friend, Cat. Don't fuck this one up."

"Why are you assuming it was my fault?" She sounded more incredulous than she actually was, given the fact that it was completely her fault.

"Because that's what you do," Adam said, his face reddening. Adam, the guy who still played Hacky Sack and designed kids educational websites for a living was raising his voice. Cat froze like a child being scolded. "You always duck out of the way when something goods about to hit, Cat. I really thought this was different. I thought you were gonna let him stick around a while, but nah, it's starting. I can already see you making up problems."

"Adam," Emma said softly, "give us a minute."

"Yeah, all right." He took the bowl Cat brought and headed back into the living room. "Sorry, Cat. I really hope you two fix this."

Cat watched Adam's back as he retreated out of the room, then she went to the refrigerator to help herself to a beer, hoping to dodge Emma's eyes. "I should just go home," she said, once she was left alone with Emma.

"Don't be silly. There's no need for that."

"I don't feel like going in there and repeating this conversation with everyone else." She gestured to the next room where the rest of the group was laughing and enjoying themselves.

"So don't." Emma threw an arm around her shoulders and dragged her into the living room. "Hey guys," she said. "Cat's here. She brought food. She didn't bring Josh. Don't ask."

The room went quiet, save for the zealous announcers chattering on the TV. Sonya looked back and forth between the two. Sonya's boyfriend kept his eyes mercifully on the television, trying his best to ignore the situation. "We're talking about this later, Cat," Sonya said, eyeing her in that watchdog way of hers.

Adam's expression had softened by then, and he pretended to punch Cat's arm. "God damned soap opera around here. I thought y'all came to watch football?"

"Go, Virginia." Cat pumped a fist in the air listlessly as she found a spot in Adam's armchair to begin her Academy Award performance of an exuberant Cavs fan. In reality, she wasn't seeing a thing that was happening on the screen. All her current headspace was being used to analyze the fact that Josh's absence was already dulling an event she'd been looking forward to all week long.

Josh pulled out the last bottle of beer from his fridge, forcefully popping the cap on the edge of his counter, then he sunk into his couch and flipped on the television. The football game he was supposed to be watching with Cat blared through the room, but his stomach rumbled even louder. He never did get breakfast, and since he was supposed to be at Cat's for the whole weekend, he hadn't bothered stocking his refrigerator with any food before he left. Now he was out of beer, too.

Unfortunately, going to the supermarket wasn't in the cards, since his liquid diet for the day had left him too buzzed to drive. He grabbed a pillow from the end of the couch and wedged it behind his head, hoping the ache in his stomach could at least edge out the ache in his chest. That old expression "feeling no pain" was such a crock. He was well past the point of inebriation, and he still felt every ounce of misery that came from fighting with Cat.

From the first moment he'd laid eyes on her, he knew Cat would either be his salvation or his undoing. He'd taken the chance anyway, without regard for the consequences. He thought she was taking it with him, but the doubts she had when they first met had suddenly snuck back in, like the bitterness that snuck up on the fall air and turned it to winter.

He tried to lose his thoughts in the game, focusing on the satisfying, angry crack of the helmets and the cheers from the crowd of people who still found some part of this day to enjoy. He could tell by the first quarter that it was shaping up to be a blow out, though, and his attention strayed. Had Cat still gone to Emma's house? Was she was laughing and enjoying her friends, while he sat there applying an alcohol compress to the bruise her words left?

Figuring things out, seeing what happens— he never would have described what they were doing in such tentative terms, but she'd used them, right before she suggested he might be prone to the type of emotional naivety that could bring them both down. Did she really think that he was being careless with her? He'd never been careless with anything in his life. But he supposed walking out wasn't the best way to convince her of that.

He picked up his phone, contemplating calling her and apologizing for the way he'd reacted, ending the whole argument right then and there. The problem was, if she was dealing with it better than he was, just going on with her day, he really didn't want to know about it.

He changed his mind and dialed Dylan's number instead.

"Hey," Dylan said after one ring. Josh could

hear the sound of the same game he was watching in the background. "What's up? I thought you were at Cat's for the weekend."

"I was, but now I'm not."

"Okay...You wanna swing by and watch the game?"

"I can't. I've had too much to drink. Why don't you come over here? Bring some food or something."

"Not like you to be half in the bag by four-thirty," Dylan said. "Why'd you leave Cat's?"

"Not like you to ask so many questions," he fired back. "You coming or what?"

"I'll call in a couple of burgers at the place down the street, and I'll be over by halftime, okay?"

"All right, I'll see you then."

As promised, Dylan came bearing a full meal just as the marching band took the field on Josh's television screen.

"You didn't tell me you drank *all* the beer," Dylan grumbled as he rummaged through Josh's near-empty fridge, settling for a soda he found in one of the drawers. "Better off anyway. I don't wanna end up walking home tonight."

Josh nodded, biting into his burger with the zeal of a man who hadn't eaten in almost twenty-four hours.

Dylan took the seat opposite and eyed him over the can of Coke he was sipping from. "So, why are we here, man? What's going on with Cat?"

"We didn't have a good day," Josh answered, keeping his eyes on the screen.

"What's that mean?"

"It means we had an argument, and I came home."

"You gonna tell me what it was about?"

Josh continued chewing, watching the men on the screen smash into each other, and ignored Dylan's question.

"Mmm," Dylan hummed. He looked Josh up and down, lingering on his wrinkled t-shirt and bloodshot eyes. "And you been sitting on your ass draining your fridge of alcohol since you been back?"

"Something like that."

"Storming off has always kinda been my thing, Josh. Gotta say I'm a bit surprised."

"I didn't storm off," he replied, finishing the rest of his burger and moving onto his fries. "I just thought it better if she did her thing without me this weekend."

"I see... you still feeling like that's best?"

Josh set his food down and leaned back into the couch with a sigh. "Maybe not."

"Well, it's still early. Why don't you sober up some and go see if you can salvage the rest of your Saturday night?"

"Drive back there?"

"Or you could just sit here and wallow all night, but it looks like you've done enough of that." He gave Josh another once over, gesturing to his disheveled appearance. "Go take a shower, brew some coffee, and by the time this game is done, you'll feel a lot better."

"I don't know if that's a good idea." Considering all he'd already put on the line in the last twenty-four hours, if he was going to find out he didn't have what he thought he had, he didn't need to go rushing toward that realization.

"Josh, you're shit company right now, and I don't know how much of this I can take. Go fix it so I can get back to being astounded that you pulled a girl like that in the first place."

Josh rubbed at his stinging eyes. Listening to Dylan wasn't something he made a habit of, but he had to admit he'd been trying to put an end to his misery all day, and his way had been unsuccessful.

He pushed off of the couch, taking an inventory of the state of his motor skills, and went to start a pot of coffee. He was the one who left. At the very least, he should make up for that.

No one seemed ready to leave the party, even after the game had ended in an easy win. Cat glanced around at her friends, still chatting and drinking in Emma's living room, and finished her now-warm bottle of beer. She was ready to be done with the tragedy that was her day, but the thought of going home to her empty house didn't appeal to her. Instead, she pulled her phone out, deciding to text Dani, the only one of them who hadn't made it to Emma's.

Cat: Are you home? Can I come over?

Dani: My date is dropping me off in fifteen minutes. Meet me there.

Cat: Are you sure? I don't want to intrude.

Dani: No, it's fine. It'll give me a reason not to invite him up.

Cat: You know that's always an option, right?

Dani: Yeah, yeah. I'll see you in a few.

"I think I'm going to head out," Cat announced to a chorus of groans and boos.

"Come on, Cat," Sonya whined. "You don't have to leave. Stay and at least try to have fun."

"I'm not really up for it tonight," she said. "It's been a long day, and I just want it to be over."

They all gave her varying versions of sympathetic looks and said their goodbyes. Except for

Adam. He stood to follow her, grabbing a couple of empty beer bottles on his way.

"Thanks for hosting," Cat said when they reached the front door. "I'm sorry I wasn't much fun."

"You were never that much fun."

"Cute," she said with a sad smile. Her face was too tired from pouting to fake another happy one.

"Nah, you know I love you." He punched her in the arm before wrapping her in one of those big brother hugs that kinda hurt. "But listen, I'm not kidding around. I don't want to see this going the way it always goes with you. You're too good to make yourself miserable."

"Thanks, Adam."

"You're welcome." He gave her a kiss on the top of her head, then pushed her out the door. "Bring my boy back next time, you hear me?"

"I'm starting to worry about you two."

"Tell Josh, I miss him," he yelled, as she got in her car.

It had only been a few hours since he left, but she missed him too. She'd spent the entire afternoon feeling utterly alone in a room full of her closest friends because the other half of her was somewhere else. She wondered where that somewhere was, if he'd just gone home or made some other plans to replace their ruined ones.

Cat glanced at her phone one more time before putting her car in drive, hoping that it was close to later, the ambiguous time Josh said he would call. Unless maybe later was more of a broad expression, and she'd be forced to float around on this unfamiliar plane of existence indefinitely. It took her by surprise how clashing with Josh threw off her equilibrium, made her feel unsteady on her own two feet. She was going to be a lawyer; she didn't shy away from a fight. She was good at it. Good at standing her ground, making her point heard. She didn't want to fight with Josh, though. She didn't want to win. She just wanted him back beside her.

Twenty-five

BEFORE CAT HAD A CHANCE to ring the bell, Dani swung the door open and waved her in. She wore tight jeans and a low cut top, but her feet were bare, and her hair was hanging in crazy curls as if she'd just pulled it down from a more elaborate style.

"Hey. What kind of date ends at seven p.m. on a Saturday night?" Cat shrugged off her vest and scarf and trudged into Dani's kitchen, making herself at home with a sparkling water from the fridge while Dani headed down the hall to her bedroom.

"We were watching the game."

"So, you ditched us to watch it with some guy?"

"I did," Dani called from the next room. "But I shouldn't have. He was kind of a dud. That's why I'm home." She came back to the kitchen wearing a sweatshirt and shorts and pulled a bottle of wine down from the shelf above her fridge. Pushing a stack of mail around to make room on the counter, she opened a cupboard to find no clean glasses and decided to wash a couple while they talked.

"Aren't you a well-paid marketing consultant?" Cat asked, watching her shuffle more items out of the way so she could set down her newly clean glass.

"I am. Thank you for remembering."

"Why don't you hire someone to come clean this place once in a while?"

Dani ran a dish towel over the glasses and set about pouring two drinks. "Oh, I see," she said unfazed. "It's going to be one of those nights. Why am I subjected to this on a Saturday night? I thought Josh had custody of you on weekends."

"He left."

Dani tilted her head, slowly pushing Cat's wine across the counter. "Like *left,* left?"

"No. At least I don't think so. Not yet." Cat took a sip and leaned back in her stool. "Let me ask you something, can you picture me being a housewife like Maria and Olivia?"

Dani laughed, clamping her lips shut to keep from spitting out her wine. "Come on, Cat. You can barely cook an egg, and you pay someone to do your laundry."

Cat laughed too, making her eyes water. Before she knew it, her laughter had turned into quiet sobs.

Dani gaped at her, her mouth wide open and her wine glass hovering underneath her bottom lip. "Are you crying?"

Cat wiped frantically at her eyes with the back of her hand. She was crying. She hadn't let anyone see her cry over a man since high school. Not even Micah. All the tears she shed for him were in private; she wouldn't give him that embarrassment on top of everything else. Yet here she was, sobbing like a melodramatic teenager over Josh. It was fitting, though. She hadn't giggled, or played, or felt as light as Josh made her feel since she was a kid either.

"I've never seen you cry."

"That's not true," Cat muttered, sniffing loudly. "I cried when I broke my wrist in fifth-grade playing volleyball."

"No, you whimpered. I cried." Dani walked around the island and took a seat next to her. "What happened, Cat?"

Dani's soft expression hit her right in the gut, and her confession rushed out through her trembling lips. "Josh asked me to move in with him, and I brought up his ex-wife and told him he has a history of making bad decisions."

Dani looked aghast. She should—it was awful. "Oh my God, Cat," she exclaimed. "His ex-wife who cheated on him?"

Cat nodded, feeling the fresh slap of guilt on her cheeks.

"You really don't know how to let someone love you, do you?" Dani leaned back on her own stool, crossing her arms around her chest and shaking her head.

"I thought I did. I was. Things were different this time."

"You were doing really well. Even Emma was impressed."

"It was just that Maria started talking about how it was time for me to think about settling down, let a man take care of me, and then Josh tried to pay for my groceries—"

"Wow. What an ass."

Cat shot her a sharp look and continued. "Okay, but then Josh asked me to move in with him after five months! And he didn't even consider it the other way around. He just assumed I should give up my place, change *my* whole life trajectory to be with him. It was Micah all over again." Cat sighed at her own retelling of the story. Hearing herself compare Josh to Micah sounded ludicrous, but she'd done it. "Adam was right. It was too good to be true."

"First of all," Dani countered, "Adam is never right. Second, I love your sisters, but they don't know you, Cat. You grew up after they were already wives and mothers. If advice doesn't come from me or Sonya or sometimes Emma, then it doesn't count." She smiled at Cat, but her amusement went unreturned. "So, what's the real issue here? The timing, or the fact that you'd have to give up your place? If Josh had asked to move in with you, give up his house and move to the city, would you have done it?"

"I don't know." She was still swimming in the

shallow end of this whole dilemma. The length of their relationship, his house or hers, those were excuses, black and white solutions to a grey problem. "It probably doesn't matter anyway. I doubt that it's a possibility anymore. I shot him down pretty hard."

"Oh, Cat," Dani sighed. "This can't be what you want."

"It's not," she said, finishing her glass of wine, and helping herself to more. She definitely knew that much. "I didn't handle it well."

"So, what did you think was going to happen?"

"I thought he would get it. He would understand that it wasn't that easy. Or maybe I thought he would somehow convince me like he always does." Her chest tightened as she replayed the conversation over in her head, how quickly it had slipped out of her control. She posed the tough questions, and Josh gave her the perfect answer. That's how it was with them. But this time, she had questioned Josh himself—his judgment, his heart. She had no right to do that, but he hadn't even given her a chance to take it back. She let out a short sigh of frustration, turning back to Dani with a frown. "I certainly didn't think he was going to leave," she said. "But that's exactly what happened. After convincing me to trust him, he still walked right out the door."

"No way," Dani said, shaking her head at the suggestion. "It's not the same, and you know it.

He's coming back. But maybe Cat, did you ever think that you always know how things are going to go because you're the one writing the ending? I mean, one guy asks you for a mile, now you won't even give an inch."

Cat was quiet for a few minutes, accepting the admonishment. Micah had held her back from being her best self; that was a fact. But once she'd cut that tether and started running, she never stopped. She was running toward her own dreams, but also away from something. She wasn't even sure what that something was anymore, but every man since Micah had somehow been incapable of matching her stride. They were weaker than her and threatened by it, or they were just as strong, but their interests collided with hers. Until Josh. He was strong, confident, and he made it clear her interests were his interests. Falling in love with Josh was like putting on a cozy winter coat after shivering in her own cold detachment for so long.

Maybe she just didn't know how to be this happy. Maybe she had some deep character flaw that wouldn't allow her to maintain that type of connection. She'd spent the last few years determined to move mountains to get what she wanted, but in doing so, she'd become one, and now she stood squarely in her own way.

"Cat," Dani continued, "I know you don't want to hear this, but there were two sides to what happened with Micah. Sure, he changed his mind after you had held up your end of the deal, and that was shitty. But he didn't break up with you. That was your choice."

"I couldn't stay with him after he asked me to give up my dreams for his. That's not the kind of person you tie yourself to forever."

"Maybe. But you wanted the other part too, to be with him and have a life together."

"So?"

"So, I'm just saying sometimes you can compromise. Do you want this thing with Josh?"

"Yes. You know that I do."

Dani shrugged. "Then you have to give a little of yourself too. Do the thing you wished Micah had done for you. I'm not saying you have to move in with him, but you've got to do something."

Cat swirled her wine around in her glass. Any indignation she'd been claiming was replaced by a sinking feeling of remorse as she pictured Josh's face when he walked out the door. He looked defeated, finally, by her constant challenge. All she wanted was to forfeit this win and just be on his side for good.

"I know you're right," she said quietly. "I just hope I still have that chance."

"I know you do," Dani promised, giving her a confident smile. "And you do too. This one is different."

She looked down at her phone again, hoping that despite the fact that she'd it in her hand all night, she'd somehow missed a call or text from Josh. Instead of the blinking light she hoped to find, all she saw was a drained battery indicator taunting her from the corner of her screen. "Can I use your charger?" she asked Dani, hopping down from her stool and heading in the direction of the outlet where she knew it would be.

"You can try, but I don't think it will fit. I got a new phone; work finally switched us all over to iPhones."

Cat fiddled with the cord, trying her hardest to will the tiny end to fit into the wider port on her work-issued Droid. "Damn it," she cursed. The waning block of energy displayed on her phone was a perfect metaphor for her current stamina for continuing the day. "I should go." She moved to the stool to retrieve her coat.

"Uh-uh," Dani said. "I'm not letting you drive across town with no cellphone after a bottle of wine. Sleep here. We'll order a movie and hang out like our dorm days."

"We couldn't afford to order movies in college," Cat said. "We had to steal your boyfriend's Netflix password."

"Well, we've finally made it, Cat. Come on. We'll even spring for HD."

The ride to Cat's was shorter and lonelier at this time of night. Josh made it to the city limit in record time, and his blood began to pump faster as he flipped his signal switch to get off the highway and head downtown.

He wasn't sure exactly what he was going to say when he got there. He would apologize for leaving, he knew that much, but the rest of the conversation still sat in a lump in his throat. He wanted to forget about what she'd said, chalk it up to a weak moment, but he wasn't convinced Cat experienced weakness. He'd never seen it, and he'd certainly never heard that tone of voice from her before. She was angry, and even though he was more hurt, he was angry too. The combination unnerved him, and that's why he figured he shouldn't try to have this conversation over the phone. It was too easy to say things you didn't mean when you didn't have to look into the other person's eyes. He only wanted to hear the truth from her right now, whatever it might be.

Josh glanced down at the clock again, hoping that showing up unannounced wouldn't piss her off, but when he finally turned into the parking lot of her building, bad manners became the least of his worries. Cat's assigned parking spot was empty. She wasn't even there.

He pulled his Jeep over to the side, scanning the other spaces. Maybe she'd just parked somewhere else, he thought, trying to soothe his emerging panic by making up a reason. *She wanted the extra steps. Someone had parked in her spot inadvertently.* But when he didn't see her little Jetta anywhere in the parking lot, his stomach sank.

He'd convinced himself, with Dylan's help, that Cat was just as upset about their argument as he was, and she was likely home stewing over it the same as him. She wasn't a big partier. At this hour on a Saturday night, when he wasn't there, he truly expected her to be home, whether she was upset or not.

She was probably still at Emma's. That was his attempt at hopefulness. The game had been over for hours, but they could still be together. Giving up on his previous aversion to handling this over the phone, he picked up his cell from the dash and dialed her number before he'd even fully made the decision. Her voicemail chimed in immediately, though, and he hung up, tossing the phone back at the passenger seat with the full force of his disappointment. It bounced to a lonely spot on the floor.

A headache was knocking on his temples, and he pressed his fingers into them. It was still early by most people's standards. He pulled his car into his usual spot and turned off the engine, the winter air rushing the cabin as soon as the heat stopped blowing.

He would wait.

Twenty-six

SOMETIMES, THE LONGER YOU SIT with a version of events, the more the edges blur between what you've imagined and what you actually know. Josh knew by the latest hour to tick by on his dashboard clock that Cat wasn't sleeping at home. The rest was left to his imagination, and it wasn't treating him kindly.

He held his fingers against his lips to warm them, blowing out an exasperated breath that materialized before him. Leaving now somehow felt like another retreat, but he'd been there all night, and he was ready to end this exercise in futility. Leaning over the center console, he reached around in the dark for his phone and found it still sitting on the floor where he'd thrown it. Did he have any more of his pride to put on the line? He knew he didn't, but something in him couldn't leave until he'd at least tried.

"Hey, Cat," he rasped when her voicemail picked up. His voice was raw from cold and lack of sleep, and he cleared his throat of any weakness before he continued. "Um. It's about one a.m. I've been here more than a few hours now, and I guess you aren't coming home tonight." He paused, crushing his eyes shut as he ran through all of the various reasons for her to be out all night, trying to pick the one he wanted to believe in when he chose his next words.

"I was hoping to see you... so we could talk about everything, but your phone is off, and you're not here. Look, Cat, I'm sorry I left. I shouldn't have. Just... call me tomorrow, please. Let me know you're safe. I love you."

He started his Jeep, still stuck between staying and going, being scared and being angry. Maybe he should bear the cold and wait it out a few more hours, make sure she was safe. Maybe he should go inside and sit by her door until she walked back in, so he could see for himself where she'd been. He was adamant that he wanted to see the truth in her eyes when they spoke again, but now her absence had him wondering if whatever she had to say might be too much up close. He knew the face of a woman who had changed her mind; he'd already seen it once in his life. He didn't need to see it on her.

Maybe he shouldn't have come at all.

It was barely dawn when Cat pushed through the door of her condo. It was the time of year when she had to put the heat on when she woke up to take the chill out of the early morning air, and the house was frigid and dreary in its greeting. Or maybe it was just Josh's marked absence that suddenly had her feeling like she was walking into a void instead of her own home. The irony of that wasn't lost on her.

She was desperate for some coffee after a long, sleepless night, but first things first. She dug her phone out of her purse and connected it to the white cord sticking out of the wall near her laptop. Josh probably wouldn't be up yet, but she wanted a fully charged battery when he finally called. A night of teary contemplation, staring at the ceiling from Dani's couch, had convinced her that he would call like he said he would, and she would fix this.

She started her coffee machine and opened her fridge to look for her breakfast options while her phone powered on. She was pulling out some Greek yogurt and fruit when the familiar double beep of a voicemail sounded from the table.

Maybe he *was* up already. Maybe he was feeling the same about their night apart, and they could deal with this right then and there.

She pressed the voicemail icon, and her eyes rolled shut in relief as soon she heard Josh's voice. Then the relief hardened like a stone in the pit of her stomach. While she'd been crying herself to sleep on Dani's couch, Josh had been sitting in his Jeep, waiting for her and wondering where she was. He'd come back—apologized for leaving even after she said what she said. Defeat and exhaustion wound their way through his voice as he spoke, but he ended his message with an earnest "I love you", proving yet again that he wasn't going to let her ruin this for them. She wasn't sure whether to curse or cry.

Her finger swept to the return call button before the last syllable of his message was finished, and it took four excruciating rings before his thick voice offered a sleep-slurred hello.

"It's me," she said, though modern calling technology had rendered that bit superfluous. "I got your message."

"Just now?"

"My phone was dead." He didn't reply and the realization that he might not believe her twisted in her gut. "Can I come over?"

Josh's outward breath crackled on the phone. "It's a long drive, Cat. Why don't you just tell me what you want to say over the phone?"

What she wanted to say? What did that mean? "Josh. I want to see you."

There was a long pause before he answered. "Yeah. Okay. I'll be here."

It wasn't the enthusiastic invitation she'd hoped for, but she would take it. "I'll see you in an hour."

Josh's Jeep was parked crooked in the gravel driveway as if he'd given little care to where it landed when he'd arrived there in the dark. A fresh layer of frost shimmered on the dying grass of his lawn. He must have been cold the night before, sitting in her parking lot, waiting for her to come home. He would have been worried, probably frustrated, and cold. The thought made fresh tears spring, but Cat wiped them away. She couldn't go in there a blubbering mess. She had an apology to make.

She knocked on Josh's front door, and it opened almost immediately as if he'd been waiting by it. Though he certainly didn't look eager.

Josh hovered in the doorway, his hands hanging restlessly at his sides. He didn't reach for her. He didn't smile. He was wearing the same clothes as the day before: jeans, a long-sleeved t-shirt, the same color as his eyes. His eyes were puffy, his hair a mess—the sight of him made her want to crumble.

"Hi," she whispered, feeling like her voice would crack if she gave it any more volume.

"Hey."

She stepped closer, standing on her tiptoes to kiss him, but fear started to claw at her belly when her mouth bounced off of the corner of his. "Josh..."

He dropped his eyes to the ground. *What is happening?*

Despite his coldness, Cat threw her arms

around his waist and buried her face in his chest. It felt like an eternity, crying into his shirt while he stood wooden, tense, but finally, he wrapped his arms around her back and shoulders and whispered a tiny *shhh* into the top of her head. She clung to it like a security blanket.

"You came back to my house last night," she said.

"Yes."

She dabbed at her eyes with the sleeve of her shirt. "You were there all night?"

"Most of it."

"I'm so sorry for what I said, Josh." When she'd heard his message, she was sure she was rushing over here to put this all behind them, but it wasn't going at all how she planned. She needed to fix this, get him to look at her the way she was used to. She put a hand on his chest and tipped her head to meet his eyes, but instead he ran a thumb along his lip, his gaze dropping to the ground between them.

"Where'd you sleep, Cat?"

It hit her then, as she watched him square his jaw, every awful thing he must have been imagining flashing in his eyes. Guilt burned at the back of her throat like a match. Did he really think...

"I went to Dani's," she said, desperate to erase the thought forever. "Hey... " She touched his cheek, prickly with a second day's worth of stubble, and forced his eyes to hers. "Josh, I was at Dani's. I drank a bottle of wine and my phone was dead. We watched movies and I slept on her couch."

She watched him watching her as the story tumbled from her mouth, bating her breath as she searched for some sign of where they stood. Finally, he let the weight of his cheek rest in her palm, his eyes closing with what she hoped was relief.

"I left because I was afraid you'd come back and I'd see something I didn't want to see," he said.

"No, Josh." Tears rushed her eyes again. "Can we go inside?" Her fingers ached from the cold, and her muscles were stiff from shivering.

Josh stepped aside, closing the door behind her, then walked straight to the couch and dropped onto it in a boneless heap. "I'm sorry I left, Cat. I shouldn't have walked out like that. That's not how I want things to be between us."

"I'm sorry, too," she said, allowing herself the indulgence of touching his arm. He was looking at her with a sort of exhausted misery that made her gut hurt, and she had to fight the urge to crawl into a ball on his lap and hold him until all of this weird tension melted away.

"It's just that for the first time, this is starting to feel like you and I aren't doing the same thing."

"I didn't mean what I said, Josh. I had no right to hold your past over your head while I'm still sorting through mine. I love you. We are absolutely doing the same thing."

Josh sighed heavily, dropping his face into his hands. "Look, you were right about some of it," he offered like the grown-up that he was. "I was rushing you after I said I wouldn't."

"You weren't rushing me." This was her chance. Dani was right. She needed to meet him halfway. She hadn't put an ounce of skin in the game yet, and that was about to change. This was what he wanted, and it only took one night for her to realize that losing him was not an option. "Josh, I don't want to hold us back anymore," she said, lacing their fingers and squeezing. "I want this. I want all of it. Ask me again."

Twenty-seven

THEY SAY THAT SOMETIMES SILENCE can be louder than words. This was one of those times.

Josh's lips parted then snapped shut, his gaze dropped from her face and landed like a stone in the empty space between them. She heard her answer loud and clear.

"Cat..." His voice was full of pity, and she wasn't sure if it was for her or for himself.

"It's okay. I understand. I—"

"I will ask you again, Cat." He reached out to cup her cheek and kissed her forehead. "But not today. I can't wake up one morning and find you changed your mind too. That's the thing that scares me. So I'm gonna give you more time."

Cat swallowed hard, nodding against his palm. She deserved that. She didn't want more time. She knew that now, but what could she say? *Please? You can trust me. Let me move into your house so you can pin all of your hopes on me. I promise never to hurt you again.* Who would believe her after this? She wouldn't believe herself.

"I love you, Josh," she said. No matter what happened next, she knew that for sure.

Josh wrapped his arm around her waist, tugging her onto his lap. "I love you too. I don't want to fight with you. I don't want to do this again."

"I don't either."

He brushed his nose against hers, then his lips in the kind of slow kiss that made all of her limbs feel loose and liquid.

"It's still so early," she whispered, nodding toward his bedroom.

Josh laughed, a full and genuine laugh against the hollow of her throat, and relief started to bloom inside her chest.

"You wanna go back to bed?" He scooped his hands under her thighs and stood. Cat laughed too, and the uncertainty in his eyes disappeared, his pupils going black with the kind of intensity she was used to. She used to fidget nervously whenever he would trap her in it. There was so much feeling there, so much emotion right at the surface, that her heart would race, and her skin would flush under his stare. Now, though, she reveled in it, setting herself firmly in his sights and waiting to be beamed into him.

Josh carried her down the hallway to his bedroom, dropping her in the middle of his mattress. He lowered himself above her, hovering just shy of pressing with all of his weight.

"I missed you last night," she said as she reached between them to unbuckle his belt.

He helped her, then reached for her shirt. They both tugged until she was free of it, then he moved to her jeans, helping her kick them off. All of the anger and fear from the night before was simmering into something else, and her skin was prickling with the electricity of it.

"I missed you too."

"Show me."

His hand fell between them, fitting perfectly between her thighs, and she almost burst into tears at the sensation of having him back. Being with Josh wasn't like being with other men. He made an impression, one she was sure was permanently part of her now. Like a scar but happier, something there wasn't a word for. Whatever it was, she was never walking away from it again.

She clung to him a little desperately, fingertips and thighs squeezing around him until he could barely move. He stopped kissing her neck and looked into her eyes. "You okay?"

It had been a long time since he'd asked her that, and the whole of how they got to this place flashed before her eyes. "Yeah, baby," she whispered. "I'm okay."

She wanted to ask him if he was okay. If they were okay, but the shake in his voice when he spoke again told her the answer was "not yet."

"Tell me you're still mine, Cat," he said. His

eyes were begging for a promise that he could believe in. He needed to hear it now when she was open and exposed beneath him, and their bodies were so close that a lie could never fit between them. She wished like hell she'd never made him question it.

"I'm yours, Josh." She slipped her fingers into his hair, pulling lightly, and looked at him with all of the devotion and love she felt pulsing through her blood. "I'm right here."

Josh kissed her temple, blowing a relieved breath into her ear. "Me too," he said. "I'm right here too."

Twenty-eight

THE THING WAS, THOUGH, HE wasn't.

Cat sat at the breakfast bar, watching Josh's back muscles flex as he moved around the kitchen, making himself a cup of coffee. They'd stayed in bed until almost one in the afternoon, lounging, touching, hovering in that place between *I should get up* and *I'm still dreaming*. Even when he was asleep, she could feel it—something between them had shifted. Now his smile was restrained, his words clipped to no more than necessary. He'd made love to her, held her like everything was fine, but his face told a different story. She recognized that wariness. The old Cat had it trademarked. *I don't trust you* had been practically tattooed in big letters on her forehead. She wondered how many times she'd looked at Josh like that in the beginning.

"Josh?" she said, pulling him out of his quiet contemplation. "I just wanted to say that wherever you are right now, I'm there too. You're not pulling me along anymore."

"Good." A glance, a forced smile, then right back to his coffee.

She opened her mouth then shut it, resisting the urge to ramble. Instead, she changed the subject. "Do you want to go to dinner in the city Friday night? Emma invited us. Adam will be there. Dani, Sonya. We could get some Christmas shopping done beforehand. Make a night of it."

"Sure." He finally poured himself a cup as she took the last sip of hers. "I'll be in town for the Abbott Building anyway, so I can meet you somewhere right after work."

"Pick me up," she urged. "Park in the lot for my building, and we can walk from there. We'll eat across the street at Bruno's."

"All right." Josh finally looked at her, rubbing absently at the scar on his lip.

Cat glanced at the clock on the stove. She hated to leave now when things still felt off between them, but she hadn't done a single thing to prepare for her workday, and the pile of test prep books she'd planned to tackle that weekend still sat on her dining room table, untouched.

"Back to normal then, right?" she asked, hopefully. "We'll have the whole weekend?"

"I'm all yours." It was the first real smile he'd given her all morning, and her lungs finally filled.

When they had both dressed, Josh walked her out to her car. She hadn't come with anything but her keys, so when she went to hug him goodbye, her hands felt empty and awkward without her usual armful of overnight supplies. Josh held her, burying his nose in her hair, and she wanted to hold him hostage there, find a way to live the rest of her days with him wrapped around her.

But she'd lost that chance.

"I'll see you next weekend then," he said, before reaching around her to open the car door.

"Next weekend." She stood on her tiptoes and kissed him. "I'll call you tonight before bed."

He nodded. "I love you, Catia."

"I love you too."

The following week was normal. Better than normal, actually. Cat had spoken to Josh every night—long lingering conversations that felt more like the early days of their relationship than anything that had been warped by this moment between them. That's what she was considering it. Just a minor hiccup in their otherwise happy existence, and he hadn't given her any more reason to doubt it. At least not over the phone. She'd even talked him into a Skype session on Tuesday night when she'd returned home from dinner with Sonya, a little buzzed and missing him like crazy. He'd answered the late evening video call shirtless and wearing his glasses, and it had devolved from there.

She told herself all was well on the Josh front. Emma had agreed when she'd relayed the whole fight and subsequent make up to her over coffee the previous day.

"I think you're projecting your guilt over your initial mistrust onto Josh," she'd explained from the rolling leather chair of her office, a pen between her teeth and her brow furrowed. Cat had wanted to roll her eyes when the psychoanalysis started, but she couldn't deny Emma was good at this stuff, and Cat was a classic basket case. They made a good pair.

Still, when Josh rapped his knuckles on the open door to her office at six o'clock on Friday evening, he looked... different.

"Hey," Cat whispered, holding one hand over the receiver of her phone as she waved him in.

He slipped inside, closing the door behind him, and took a seat in the chair across from her while she tried desperately to finish the conversation that was eating into her evening. He'd come straight from his own workday, looking handsome in jeans and a dress shirt under a dark fleece. His nose and cheeks were pink from the December air, and she glanced over her shoulder out the window to see that with the setting sun, the sky had begun to spit.

"Yes, I understand," she said into the phone. "I'll have it ready for her review Monday."

Josh's eyes slipped closed, his head tipped back against the back of the chair, and she made a mental note to check in with him before they rushed out the door. When she finally finagled her way off of the phone, she pushed out of her chair, stopping to kiss his cheek before closing the blinds to her office. "I'm just going to change my clothes," she said, hoping that might perk him up.

She went to the standing coat closet in the corner of her office and pulled out a tote bag that she'd stuffed some casual clothes in.

"Can you unzip me?" She backed her way over to him, and he set the zipper of her dress free without any attempt to let his hands stray. Her Spidey-senses flared again. "You okay, baby?"

Josh ran the back of his hand over his brow. "I think I'm coming down with something," he said. "Probably shouldn't get too close to me."

She leaned into him despite the warning, brushing his hair with her fingers. It was somewhat relieving to hear, given what she was imagining, but she still didn't like the sound of it. "You want to skip tonight?"

"No. I can make it."

She'd never heard Josh complain about anything physical before, but if he said he was okay, she would believe him. She'd never hear the end of it if they didn't show up to dinner with everyone after she'd promised. They had bailed on more than a few of these get-togethers in the good old days when there was no tension between them, and they'd ditch any plans to spend time alone.

After stepping into her jeans, she pulled a shirt from her bag, tugging the elastic from her hair and letting it fall around her shoulders. Socks and knee-high boots, and she was done. This time when she looked back at him, Josh was gathering her coat from the chair where she'd tossed it, looking slightly more alive.

She closed the door to her office behind her and hooked her arm through his, heading down the hall. As they passed the last office before they got to the lobby, Kasey poked her head of the door and waved.

"Hey, Cat. You leaving?"

Cat's heart did a little skip. She peeked at Josh to see him staring at Kasey, and not the way most men stared at Kasey. He squinted at her, his brow knitted in a *you look very familiar* way.

Cat tugged him ahead and called over her shoulder. "Yup. Headed out. I'll see you Monday. Bye!" Luckily, Kasey retreated back into the office, and Josh seemed to have moved on without giving it any more thought.

"Where do you want to go?" he asked, squeezing her arm as they stepped onto the sidewalk outside of her building.

"I need to pick out a Christmas gift for my father, and I need your help."

"My help?"

"Yes. I wanted to get him something nice for his bar—you know he thinks he is a mixologist now—and I had my eye on this really nice crystal highball set by Martha Stewart, but now I'm thinking I should find something more masculine."

"Martha Stewart, huh? You do need my help." A smile crossed his face, the kind where one side of his mouth pushed upward, and his nose crinkled. It was his *you're adorable, Cat* smile, and she ate it up as usual.

"Rachel Ray?" she asked, fluttering her eyelashes innocently. Josh shook his head and smiled at the ground.

They spent an hour browsing the shopping center a few blocks from her office. When she'd selected a set of copper mugs and an old-timey looking bartender's encyclopedia, Josh helped her pick out a bottle of whiskey to go with it. With everything checked off the list, they headed to Bruno's.

"You're going to be there to see him open this, right?" Cat asked. "So you can tell him what the liquor guy said about the whiskey?"

"If you want me there, I'll be there."

"Of course I do."

"If it's anything like Thanksgiving with your family, I'd better start dieting now. I had to use a different notch on my belt."

"I don't think it's done you any harm," she flirted.

Josh laughed, kissing her on her forehead, and the last bubble of tension in her chest popped.

He was fine. Everything was fine. The whole world was fine.

Twenty-nine

JOSH SUCKED THE WARM AIR from the bar into his lungs as they wove through the crowd. He'd woken up that morning feeling like he was swallowing glass, his head pounding. By noon, he'd thought he all but willed it away, but after spending the day outside on a job site, his throat had started to sting again, and the wet snow accumulating on the collar of his jacket had his teeth chattering.

"We have time for a drink at the bar before dinner," Cat said, glancing at her phone. "The rest of them aren't here yet."

He held out his hand to help her climb up onto a barstool before taking a seat beside her. Her pretty face glowed as she studied the drink menu adorably like she wasn't just going to order a gin and tonic.

Sometimes when he looked at her, adoration squeezed his chest so tight that he found it hard to breathe. There was an opposition mounting in his head now, though, warning him not to let himself look at her like that after that day in her condo. He'd been playing way too dangerously with the way he loved her. It was compulsive, all-encompassing, but Cat was right, letting his gut lead had only ever caused him pain. He'd felt it in the way his stomach bottomed out when she'd pulled him back to reality. It was a warning. If he didn't listen, he only had himself to blame. Still—her hand on his knee, her brow furrowed in concentration over the cocktail options like it was Sophie's Choice—it was impossible not to look at her like that.

"I'm going to get a gin and tonic." Cat sighed, tossing the menu on the bar and blowing a little breath out of her pink lips that made her hair flutter upward.

He pushed her hair off her shoulder, holding in a laugh. "Good choice, babe."

Dani arrived a few moments later, floating in on a rush of cold air that wove its way inside his jacket and made him shiver. "Josh!" she squealed, throwing her arms around his shoulders. "I haven't seen you in ages. Just your spirit in that afterglow Cat wears on Monday mornings."

Cat leveled a look at her friend that made him smile, but he couldn't help thinking Dani sounded just a little too surprised to see him. He wondered what Cat had said to her about their fight. He hugged her hello, trying not to share any of his germs, then hopped down and offered her his stool.

"Kit Cat!" Someone called from behind Cat's shoulder. It was a masculine voice, and Josh's ears perked at the endearment. He turned to see the bartender heading their way with an eager grin on his face.

"Hi, Jay." Cat smiled back, spinning her stool in his direction.

With jet-black hair and a golden, island-vacation complexion, Jay looked like he should be wearing a Hawaiian shirt and juggling bottles of booze for tips. Josh watched the conversation, trying to think if he'd ever heard the name Jay before.

"It's been a while since you've been here on a Friday night." Jay leaned over the bar and planted his lips squarely on Cat's cheek.

Josh's stomach tightened, but he figured Cat would introduce him any second now, and Jay would keep his lips to himself. There was no need to overreact.

"You look good," Jay said, his eyes combing over her.

Or not. Josh forced himself to stand up a little straighter despite the fact that his body was willing him to find a corner to lie down in. This was all wrong. Cat hated guys like this. Jay was Snake Guy but taller, tanner. Better looking.

"Yeah, she's adorable," Dani snarked. "Can I get a shot, please? Tequila. Double."

Jay's attention bounced over to Dani. She had a way of directing the flow of conversation her way, and it was suddenly Josh's favorite thing about her.

"Gin and tonic," Cat added, looking expectantly toward him.

"Whiskey neat," he said. Maybe he could burn away this cold with some hard alcohol therapy. He handed over his card, circling his finger to let Jay know that both women belonged on his tab. "Keep it open, will you?"

"Josh is in Friday night mode," Dani said with a little wiggle in her seat. "Thanks. You're a doll."

"He is," Cat said, kissing him on the cheek. "I'm going to use the ladies' room."

"So, Josh," Dani said, slipping off her coat and getting comfortable on the stool. "Cat said you're working on the Abbott Building."

"I was there today."

"My grandmother is moving in there when it's done. Think I can get the architect to give her some nice skylights? Maybe a rooftop deck?"

"Well, the plans have already been submitted, but I'll see what I can do."

"That's my boy."

"Hey, what's his deal?" he asked, jutting his chin in Jay's direction.

Dani laughed, waving away the suspicious tone Josh had let slip. "Jay? He's just good at his job."

Josh looked again while Jay poured their drinks a few feet away. He supposed Jay looked professional enough, smiling and making conversation with the other patrons. He'd almost convinced himself he was blowing it all out of proportion until Jay set their glasses in a row on the bar, and the first thing out of his mouth was: "Where's Cat?"

"Bathroom," Dani answered, sipping her shot.

"Cool, cool. I almost forgot, she left her gloves here last time you ladies were in." Jay pulled Cat's favorite grey knit gloves out of the pocket of his apron with a wink.

"Thanks, man," Josh chimed in, using the opportunity to stake his claim. "I can take them for her." He reached a hand across the bar with a tight-lipped grin he hoped said *back off.* But Jay just peered at Josh's open palm with his own loaded look.

"I'll wait."

Josh's pulse drummed angrily in his ears, and he could feel Dani's eyes on the side of his face. He shook off the urge to fire back at him. Cat would set this guy straight when she got back. "Suit yourself," he said, wrapping his arm around the back of Cat's empty stool, possessively. He'd be damned if he was going to let some asshole who poured her booze make him feel like the third wheel when it came to Cat. He took a sip of his whiskey and waited.

When Cat returned, Josh pulled out her stool, making sure Jay saw his hand settle on her back.

"Oh, extra lime!" she said, plucking one from

the rim of her glass and squeezing it into her drink. "Thanks, Jay." She tossed her hair behind her shoulder adorably, and Josh's jaw twitched.

"Extra gin, too," Jay replied. "Just enough to get those cheeks nice and pink like I like."

That was it. There was no way Cat was going to let this guy hit on her like that. Even if he wasn't standing right there, Catia hated smarmy lines. She'd put him in his place.

Before she had a chance to spit out a spunky retort, Jay pulled the gloves out from behind his back, displaying them before her like a dozen long-stemmed roses.

Cat gasped, bringing a hand to her mouth in surprise. "I was heartbroken. You're the best!"

Now Josh's whole body was burning with the urge to tell this guy off. Or maybe it was a low-grade fever. He couldn't tell. He swallowed painfully and moved his hand to a more conspicuous spot on Cat's shoulder.

Dani's head bobbed back and forth in his peripheral vision, tossing between Jay's brilliant smile and Josh's clenched jaw. She cleared her throat loudly, stealing Cat's attention back.

Cat suddenly remembered his existence and decided to introduce them. "Jay, this is my boyfriend Josh," she said, completely oblivious to the slight downturn in the corner of Jay's mouth as the title left her tongue. Josh didn't miss it, though, and his lips curled in the opposite direction when he reached across the bar for the second time. "Jay bartends here on Wednesday nights when Dani and I have our Happy Hour date."

They exchanged a bruising handshake, and Josh could practically see the steam pouring from Jay's ears. He wasn't ashamed to admit he liked it.

Jay wasn't giving up yet, though. "You've missed a few lately, Cat," he said, his gaze back on her the second Josh released his hand. "I was getting kinda used to seeing that pretty smile every week."

"That would be my fault," Josh said. He pulled Cat closer and kissed her hair.

Now Cat's eyes were on the two of them, her mouth in a tight line.

"That right?" Jay asked with just enough amusement in his tone to set Josh's jaw to stone.

"It is."

Jay tugged at the rag that was slung over his shoulder and began wiping at some moisture that had pooled on the bar. "That must be why I haven't met you yet," he said. "Or even heard of you."

"Josh lives out of town," Cat said, reaching for his wrist. She wrapped her fingers around him and squeezed in a gesture that he wasn't quite sure was meant to be comforting or threatening. He didn't care much for either at the moment.

"That's right," Josh said, lowering his voice and firing a look across the bar. "I'm not in the city all that often, but if you want, we can step outside and I can introduce myself."

Cat's mouth dropped open, her eyes pure fire. Dani nearly choked on her tequila.

He didn't know why he said it. He'd never been in a fight in his life. He was the exact opposite of a hothead, but something about Jay had his blood pumping with testosterone.

"Okay!" Dani chimed in. "Another shot? Should we get a table? I wonder where Sonya is."

Jay stared at him, sucking his teeth while sizing up how much of Josh's threat was going to be a promise. "I should get back to the bar," he finally said.

Josh watched Jay retreat before daring to look back at Cat. Her nostrils flared, her face tipped up at him and plastered with a scowl that could freeze the Sahara. She didn't have time to say whatever was on her tongue, though, because Emma and Adam showed up, filling in around them at the bar.

When Sonya finally arrived, the group started filing toward the main dining area, but Cat planted her feet and wrapped an arm around Josh's bicep, holding him in place. She held a finger up to Dani to let her know they would be a minute, and he sucked in a calming breath, ready to take his punishment.

"What was that about?" Cat hissed when her friends were out of hearing range.

"What do you mean?"

"Your little standoff with Jay." She crossed her arms over her chest. "Was that supposed to impress me?"

"That depends," he said. "Was the hair flipping and giggling supposed to impress him?"

Her mouth fell open, her eyebrows jumping to her hairline. "Why are you acting like a jealous jerk?" she whispered sharply. "This isn't like you."

"Sure it is," he said. "Gut decisions, right?" That was a shit thing to say. He regretted it almost immediately, but he knew even though they had said their "I'm sorrys" he hadn't let it go yet. Was this what figuring things out meant to Cat? Keeping her options open by flirting with guys like Jay?

Cat was fuming now. She looked fully prepared to give him a piece of her mind in the middle of the restaurant until the anger on her face slid into concern. "Are you sure you're okay?"

"I'm fine," he lied for no particular reason. He wasn't exactly. Every breath he took hurt, and the whiskey had only served to weigh down his eyelids even more.

"He's never been that forward before." She stood on her toes and pressed a hand to his forehead. Her fingers felt like ice, and he couldn't help but lean in. "It was disrespectful, and I'm sorry he made you uncomfortable."

"He's right, though. I'm not with you most of the time. Why wouldn't he think he had a shot?"

She didn't like that either. "Look," she said, obviously being gracious with him, "you're not feeling well. Let's just drop it."

"Fine."

"Fine."

Thirty

ROPPING IT WASN'T THAT EASY, it turned out. Clearly missing the daggers Cat was staring at her, Dani had just finished embellishing the story of Josh's moment for a captive audience over dinner.

"Jay from behind the bar?" Adam laughed around a mouthful of cheeseburger.

Josh set down the fork he was using to push food around his plate and stared at him. "You know him too?"

"Yeah, he's the guy that's been drooling over Cat for years now."

"What the hell, Adam?" Cat said, unimpressed.

"What? It some secret?"

"You really don't see this?" Josh asked.

She could see him getting testy again, and she wanted to put an end to it before that side of him appeared again. Josh's pettiness was only amusing when it was directed at Dylan.

"There's nothing to see," Cat said. "He works for tips; it's his job to flirt."

Adam shook his head. "Cat's never been good at reading signs right."

Sonya hummed a co-sign. "If they're too forward, they're creeps. If they're too casual, she misses it altogether."

"What'd you do right?" Emma smiled, nudging Josh with her arm.

"Pretty much everything, remember?" Dani laughed. "But even then, she was so focused on that stupid bet that she almost missed out."

Josh paused with his drink halfway to his lips. "What bet?"

Heat rushed up the back of Cat's neck when he turned his eyes on her. "Nothing," she said nervously, glaring at Dani for some sort of retraction. It was a hopeless effort, really. Josh wasn't going to let that go. She wouldn't have.

He set his glass down and looked at her until she was forced to speak again.

"It was just something I said to them after you and I first met."

His eyes didn't budge. This was not going to go well. Josh was already in a mood she hadn't seen from him before.

"You made a bet about me?"

Cat shifted in her seat, stalling. It wouldn't sound that bad now that they were what they were, right? Or at least what they were a week ago, and she hoped they still were. Shit. Dani had horrible timing. Maybe Josh would see the humor in it. He had to.

"I just bet them that you were too good to be true," she explained, keeping her voice light.

"Christ, Cat," Adam muttered, shaking his head at the table.

"What do you mean?" Josh asked. "Like I was lying to you?"

"No. Of course not. Just that there had to be some catch or something because you seemed so perfect." She reached a hand out to touch his cheek, but he jerked his head away. *Definitely not going well.*

"Did you think I was feeding you lines like your friend Jay? Just trying to get you into bed?"

"Josh!"

Josh shoved his hand in his hair and sniffed loudly, then he looked up at the ceiling. Dani looked at her, guilt-stricken; Sonya looked at her plate. Adam and Emma looked... disappointed.

"I'm going to get some air," he said, his chair scratching along the floor as he pushed away from the table.

"Nice job, Dani," Adam said.

Dani held her hand over her mouth as she watched Josh push out the front door. "Cat, I'm so sorry. I don't know why I said that."

"It's not your fault." If she hadn't said what she'd said the other day, maybe they would all be laughing about this right now, instead of staring down at their plates awkwardly. She looked at Emma across the empty chair Josh had left, praying she would see one of her soothing *every-*

thing is going to be fine, Cat smiles, but she was sharing a look with Sonya that seemed like the opposite.

"You gonna go after him?" Adam asked, snapping her thoughts back.

"Of course." She would just go talk to him. Josh just needed a minute to cool down. He was always rational. This was a glitch, a fluke. She pushed her chair out and stood, praying this wasn't as bad as it felt.

The snow that had drifted dreamily from the sky while they shopped had turned to icy little pinpricks, stinging Cat's skin when she stepped out of the restaurant. She spotted Josh leaning on his Jeep in the parking lot across the street, his back turned to her. The holiday lights strung around the lamp posts cast a festive rainbow over his dark jacket and damp hair, but there was a heaviness in the way his shoulders hung that made her breath unsteady. She waited for a break in the traffic, then crossed the street.

"Josh," she said when her boots hit the crunchy gravel of the parking lot.

"It's okay, Catia. I just needed some air."

"No. It's not okay."

"Just give me a minute."

She touched his arm. "Please look at me."

She regretted that when he did turn, and

she saw his eyes narrowed into angry slits. "You know what, Cat? You're right. It's not okay. It was incredibly selfish and immature."

She took a step back, startled. "Josh... I—"

"Was this all a game to you?"

"No. Of course not."

"All this time, Cat..." His voice trailed off, and he caught it with a cough that came from deep in his chest. She wanted to reach out to him, but his eyes told her not to. "All this time I was falling in love with you, and you had one foot out the door. You wanted this to fail from the beginning."

"It wasn't like that." But as soon as she said it, she knew it was. That was exactly what she'd wanted, only it was her who had failed. She failed gloriously, spectacularly. She'd fallen flat on her face, and Josh pulled her up, brushed her off, and gave her this amazing thing that she treasured. He'd beat her at her own game, and she'd never been more happy to lose. "It was a long time ago, Josh," she said, her voice beginning to crack.

He brought his hands to his temples, suddenly exasperated. "It was the foundation that we built *everything* on, Cat!"

"No—"

"This is why you didn't want to move in."

"I did!" she reminded him. "You said no."

With one withering look, he projected the entire conversation onto his face, and she stopped her tired, useless defense.

"Josh, I didn't know what you and I were going to be when I made that stupid bet. You're right, I didn't want to fall in love with you, but I did anyway, and I'm so glad I did. Please. You're taking this all wrong."

The wind picked up, tossing the ice around their faces, and Josh squinted against the onslaught making his face look even angrier. "What have I ever done to make you think I was going to hurt you, Cat? What has ever happened between us that made you so sure it couldn't be me?"

"Nothing," she cried. "Nothing at all. You've never been anything but... perfect."

"Well," he said, "you win, Catia. Cause I'm not." He pulled his key fob out of his pocket and unlocked his car door.

"Wait," she said, grabbing at the sleeve of his jacket. "Josh, you said you didn't want to do this—that you were sorry for leaving last time."

Hesitation flashed across his expression, but he kept going, opening the door.

"Josh, please." This felt too final. She couldn't let him leave. "You're not feeling well," she said, grasping. Her voice became frantic, heightening in pitch as she rambled. "Don't drive home. Just come back to my place and get some sleep. We can talk this all out tomorrow when you're feeling better. You'll see how this was just a big misunderstanding. I love you, Josh. We can talk this out. I didn't mean for any of this to happen. Please."

He reached for her hand, slowly uncurling her fingers from the fabric of his jacket, then slid behind the wheel. "I love you too, Catia." His brow pinched as if saying it was suddenly too much to bear. "I love you more than I should have let myself, but this isn't what I thought it was."

"No," she cried, tears spilling freely now, blurring all of the lights into a weeping watercolor. *How the hell did we get here?* "Don't say that, Josh. It's not true."

"Go back to the restaurant, Cat," he said as he pushed the ignition, and his Jeep rumbled to life. "I need to go. I want to see that you're back inside first."

"No," she said, digging her boots into the gravel like a child. "Josh. Please."

"Cat... " His face fell to a neutral, exhausted expression, and he pressed his fingers into his eyes. "Please go back inside."

"I'm not going. If you're going to leave me, then you'll have to leave me here."

"Please?"

"No. Josh—"

"Catia!" He slammed his palm against the steering wheel, and her whole body flinched. He'd never raised his voice before, definitely not at her. She stood frozen, gaping at this new version of him, the one she'd created.

Josh pulled his phone out of his pocket and

started typing furiously. A second later, his phone lit up in reply, and he shut the door and backed his Jeep out of the spot. His brake lights glowed an angry red as he idled in place.

She held her breath waiting for him to put the car in park and get out. He would pull her into his arms, and they would apologize to each other and end this whole ridiculous misunderstanding. But a moment later, Adam appeared across the street, waving with his phone in his hand. Josh's brake lights dimmed, and he pulled away.

Thirty-one

*J*OSH TURNED THE SHOWER OFF and leaned against the tile, letting the steam that lingered in the stall fill his lungs. His head pounded as he swallowed, thick and painful. Standing outside in an ice storm fighting with Catia was probably a shit idea when he knew he was coming down with something.

He was full of shit ideas lately. Like letting himself do this again, falling for someone who couldn't love him back. His stomach contracted painfully as he thought of the tears streaming down her face, mixing with the sleet and ice as he drove away from what he'd thought was his future.

So he was wrong. There were no guarantees in life. He understood that better than most people. He'd gone from a normal, happy childhood with two parents who loved him, to living with a man who barely knew he existed. Then, he'd bet his future on a woman who took a vow with him but would later tell him she'd never been sure in the first place. Fine. Things change, people leave.

He thought he knew how to handle it by now. But damn it if he couldn't just build one thing on concrete instead of sand. If for nothing else other than to keep from being blindsided again.

He ran a hand through his hair, gathering up the strength to get himself dried off and back into bed. The window in his bathroom was open because he'd been in a full flop sweat when he'd decided he needed a shower. Now he shivered violently, but he needed another minute before he could cross the room to close it.

A gust of snowy, salty air rattled the blinds, and the scent of the estuaries on the peninsula hit him in the chest. He had a sudden, fever-blurred vision of that rowboat. The one he'd told Cat about where he'd spent hours silently drowning while sitting on top of the water. He could feel his grandfather's stoic presence behind him, waiting for him to pull himself out his self-pity. He could hear the intermittent throat-clearing meant to remind him that the old man was there, but he wasn't going to give him anything.

It was because of those fishing trips that he had pulled himself together. He'd learned how to be with people but not need anything from them. Not to ask too much. He'd momentarily forgotten that lesson. He'd needed something from Cat. He'd wanted her too much. He'd learned the lesson his grandfather was trying to teach him, but he still had a little too much of his parents in him. He could still never resist when his gut and that lonely place in his chest conspired and told him to do something. He was a fucking dog who couldn't stop dreaming about catching cars, and he'd finally ended up under the front tires of one.

Now he was shivering so hard his teeth were chattering. He wrapped the towel around his hips and went to slam the window shut, then he walked back to his bedroom and crawled under his duvet. He immediately regretted getting his sheets wet, knowing he didn't have the strength to put new ones on. He dragged himself back out of bed, tossing the wet towel on a chair in the corner of his room, and dug through his dresser drawers for a pair of pajama pants and a hooded sweatshirt. He bundled up and dragged the top blanket behind him into the living room, settling for the couch. Maybe if he was lucky, whatever he'd caught would give him the punch in the face he needed to pass out and forget about Cat for a while. He curled up into a ball beneath the blanket and tried to think warm thoughts. Hot soup. The desert. The beach. The way the summer sweat made Cat's skin glow the first night they'd met, holding her after they'd made love, sticky and sweltering but unable to stop touching.

He threw the blanket off and let himself shiver. He didn't want to think about summer nights right now. It was December, and it was cold, and all of that was gone.

Josh dozed off after a while, his body finally

accepting defeat, and it was mid-day when a faint buzzing sound pulled him out of his fever sleep. Without opening his eyes, he reached around under the blanket for his phone, coming up short. The buzzing continued while he rolled to his side and parted his lids just enough to scan the coffee table. His phone was traveling toward the edge on the wave of vibration, and he grabbed it just before it plunged over the side.

Shawn. He hadn't had a chance to fill him or Dylan in on the previous night and the thought of doing it now, when his throat was on fire, and his tongue was parched from breathing through his mouth, exhausted him. He let it go to voicemail, then pressed the little mail icon and listened. Shawn said something about Christmas day dinner, (a tradition he shared with them last Christmas after his divorce), an offer to come with him and Minnie to Midnight Mass, (the same offer he always declined), then a tacked-on addendum from Mattie's voice reminding him that Uncle Josh had promised him a transforming car with chrome wheels, (Cat had wrapped it last week and put it in his closet). He ended the message and ran a hand over his face. His skin was hot even to his own fingers, and he groaned as he tossed the phone back on the table.

He was supposed to go to Cat's family's house for Christmas. He probably would have ended up at Mass after all, sitting in the pew next to a hundred of her family members. He hadn't told

Minnie that yet, so he guessed he'd found his backup plan. He was thankful to have one, even though he'd been looking forward to not being a third wheel this year. Minnie and Shawn never made him feel that way, though. Minnie had moved to a different country for Shawn, and she knew what it was like being a singular member of your family. Ever since he and Sarah had split up, Minnie had gone out of her way to make sure he didn't feel that way on the important days. She was going to hate to hear about him and Cat. It would break her heart.

Thirty-two

CHRISTMAS EVE WAS A BLURRY, red and white streaked dream. At least that's the way Cat remembered it. She'd floated through the formal, candle-lit dinner, then Midnight Mass, faking just enough cheer to keep from breaking down in front of her sisters, though she doubted her thin smile and festive attire was fooling anyone. Now she was putting the finishing touches on her costume for act two: a cozy red sweater and leggings, Ugg boots, and pearl earrings. The goal was to look like her heart was still beating, and she'd pulled it off by the skin of her teeth. It was a Christmas miracle.

She'd just finished her makeup when her phone buzzed on the bathroom counter beside her.

"Merry Christmas!" Emma's voice filled the little bathroom when Cat answered the call on speaker.

"You too."

She could practically hear Emma's face fall from across the line. "Still no word from Josh?"

"No."

"I had hoped maybe he would call last night. Are you going to call him?"

"You didn't see his face, Em. I doubt he would answer if I did."

"Where do you think he's spending the holiday?"

Cat let out a sigh. She'd been wondering, no worrying about that for the last two weeks. "I hope with Minnie and Shawn," she said, her voice shaking. "I can't believe I was so cruel, Emma."

"You weren't meaning to be."

"He really was perfect, you know. Until I came along and broke him."

"No one is perfect, Cat, and people aren't made of glass. You didn't break him. You just stumbled upon a trigger."

"I think I stumbled on a few of them." She sighed. "And I pulled them all."

"We all have them, but Josh loves you, Cat. Anyone can see that."

"I want him to love me from here. I just want him back."

"I know, sweetheart. Just try to have a good day today, okay?"

Cat held back a sardonic laugh. All she was really hoping for was to get through it, but she knew Emma wouldn't let her get away with that. "I'll try," she promised.

Christmas Day brunch at her parents' was,

as ceremony goes, comparable to a state dinner for a foreign dignitary. Her mother hated to make a fuss.

The food was delicious as always, and the chaos that every large-scale gathering of her family dissolved into was in full swing. But even between sleep-deprived children and eggnog-indulging adults, the noise still wasn't enough to drown out her incessant thoughts. They looped like a miniature train underneath the tree: *Josh. Where was he spending the day? He was supposed to be here. Was he alone? Josh. Josh. Josh—*

"Where's Josh?" her cousin Rose asked, plopping down in the chair beside her, where Olivia had sat during the meal. Her sister was helping with the dishes now, leaving Cat's flank exposed to a surprise assault such as this.

She'd spent the previous evening stuttering like a fool at each repeat of that question from a different family member. Today she simply turned her head and let her lips part, the answer tumbling out. "He's not coming." Her voice was so flat she almost stopped to check her own pulse.

Rose quirked an eyebrow at her, probably wondering if she was on some sort of narcotic. She didn't push, though, instead she launched into a story about her job as a dental hygienist that sounded like a string of *blah-blah-blah* with no particular conversational cadence and threatened to have Cat dozing over her dessert. Where was Rose last night when she was sobbing into her pillow, begging for sleep to grant her a reprieve?

"Catia," her father called, poking his head into the dining room. A last minute stay to her impending execution by boredom. "Come with me."

Cat rose slowly from her chair, waving a half-hearted goodbye to Rose, and followed her father into the parlor where the shimmer of his bar gave her mother's eight-foot-tall, silver and gold Christmas tree a run for its money. Colorful bottles and fancy new tools decked the space like ornaments. It seemed there had been a theme for his gifts this year.

Her father walked behind the polished wooden surface, gesturing for her to take a seat on one of the leather stools. She glanced over her shoulder to see the rest of the family split like atoms into smaller groups around the tree and in the living room. They were alone over in this corner, and she suddenly got the impression she'd been lured into a stern talking to with the promise of alcohol.

Carlos grabbed two of the copper Moscow Mule mugs Josh had helped her pick out from the hooks he'd already assigned them, then set his hands on his hips, inspecting the array of pain-relieving options. She hoped he picked the strongest one.

He settled on something dark, and after a few other ingredients were gathered, he began pouring. "We were all sorry to hear Josh wouldn't be coming last night or today," he said, his eyes on the measuring jigger.

She didn't respond. They couldn't be any more sorry than she was, so what could she say?

"You know, Catia, your mother and your sisters are traditional in their choices. It's served them all well. Maria and Olivia have beautiful families. There is no doubt about that. But you? You always danced a different step."

"Not always," she whispered, thinking of the white picket fence around her and Micah's college dreams.

"Always." He looked up for some stern eye contact before dropping back to his work. "You've tried in the past to go that route, but somewhere along the way, you swung so hard in the other direction that you lost your balance. You've been wobbling ever since."

Cat bit back a sigh, wondering how much longer this drink took to mix. Did becoming a hobby mixologist turn you into one of those hybrid bartender-therapists from television?

He must have felt her brushing him off, though, because he forced her to meet his eyes again as he slid the copper mug across the bar. "Your mother makes me feel the way Josh looks when he looks at you. I'm not as good at showing it, but I recognize it in him."

That got her attention. She knew her face was betraying her surprise, but she couldn't help it. Carlos Roday waxing poetic was an absolute first. Maybe he'd been sampling his gifts.

He laughed quietly at her astonishment. "What, Catia?" he asked. "You think an old man can't feel these things?"

"It's not that." She thought of Josh's question that night they'd stayed up until morning, talking and touching until she was sure she'd revealed every thought she'd ever had to him. He'd asked her that night if her parents were happy and the question had set off a wildfire of new ones, about them, about her, about how any of that was supposed to look.

"You think then that we don't show it." He shook his head. "That has never been my style, or hers. Josh is brave; he shows all his cards. I saw that from the start, and I saw the way it caught you off guard. Maybe that is our fault, the example I set. I've always had a harder time baring my soul, but I worked hard for your mother and you girls. I was there for everything that has ever happened to that woman, standing beside her, and her me. Things maybe you don't even know about. There are different ways to give love, Catia. Even for those of us who are afraid. You'll find yours."

She hung her head in deference to her father's knowing eyes. There was no sense in trying to deny it this time. She was afraid. He knew it just like Josh had. She was afraid to let someone else hold her whole heart, and she was afraid to look away, even for a moment, and lose sight of who she wanted to be. The problem was lately, without Josh, she didn't recognize who that was anymore. "Maybe I'm not cut out for it," she said. She traced the cold metal mug with her fingers as she considered that possibility and what it really meant. Not a silly bet with her friends, or proving something to the world after Micah. What it really meant was heartache. Permanent loneliness.

Carlos leaned on the bar on his forearms, his looming proximity giving her that familiar feeling of shrinking back in time whenever she was in this house. "You are so much like your grandmother, Catia," he said. "When she wanted something, nothing could stop her. Some people thought she was stubborn, but she wasn't. She was tenacious. The difference between the two is being able to understand that the journey unfolds as you go. You need to be willing to change course when the path emerges and it looks different than you expected. You'll remember a very important time when she made that choice. Your sisters have done the same at times."

"Maria gave up everything she ever wanted for her husband's dream." Even as the judgment came out of her mouth, she knew between the last time she'd made it and now, her own desires had shifted exponentially.

"Catia, you tell your grandmother's story to people like it is a badge of honor on your name, but you question your sisters for their similar paths. Tell me why."

"It's different."

"How?

"Aba didn't give up anything. She accomplished way more as Grampy's wife than she could have with her vows of poverty."

"Maybe it was more in your eyes, Cat, but you know how important her faith was to her."

Cat pressed the heel of her hand to her eyes. The lack of sleep and the constant threat of a deluge of tears made them burn.

"Maria and Olivia are happy, no?"

"Yes."

"Sometimes, our journey changes along the way. But know this, it doesn't mean you were wrong. It just means you haven't come far enough yet to see the next turn. You're so afraid of being somebody's fool, Catia, that you forget you get nowhere in this world alone." He settled back on his heels, his expression softening. "I think that's a lesson Josh has already learned."

Cat turned away, sipping from her drink to hide her reaction. She was sure her father had meant for that to be a pep-talk of sorts. They all thought this was one of Catia's silly little moments. That she'd put Josh out over something trite and that she had the ability to fix it by being a little more reasonable. This was what they thought of her, and she couldn't decide whether it was better or worse than what she'd actually done. Instead of pushing Josh away like everyone expected, she'd kept him close and hurt him. They had no idea that he was the one who left her, or that she deserved it. The truth was, whether she learned the lesson or not, she'd already lost Josh in the process.

Thirty-three

THE DAY AFTER CHRISTMAS WAS a terrible time to hold a ground-breaking ceremony. In fact, the entire month of December would have been off of Josh's list if he'd been in charge. It was cold, there had been a threat of a snowstorm that had to be monitored up until it went out to sea just in time, and everyone was fresh off of celebrating with their families, their minds still sipping eggnog and relaxing. Everyone except him.

His holiday with Shawn's family had been over by lunch, and he'd spent the rest of it in bed. Christmas Eve had been even more pathetic: a movie and a microwave lasagna that was meant to be a tribute to the Italian feast his mother made when he was a kid, but ended up being more of a mockery. And as if he needed another reminder of how he should have spent the holiday, the cold he caught the night he and Cat broke up was still hanging around his neck like a cheap souvenir.

A stiff wind whipped down the corridor streets

making his eyes sting, and the pain in his chest when he coughed was like ice shattering. Somehow, despite his windpipe frosting over with each breath, his forehead and cheeks were on fire. He could even feel a fine sheen of sweat forming on the nape of his neck behind the turned-up collar of his jacket.

"Jim!" Josh called to a group of contractors huddled around the coffee station that had been set up for the guests. Jim trotted over to where Josh was leaning over a podium, flipping through the final version of the plans he'd drawn.

"You look like absolute shit," Jim said, as he looked down at the drawing Josh was pressing his index finger into.

"Hey, thanks." Josh wiped at his brow, and his vision tunneled as he tried to focus on the sheets of paper. "What happened to the front doors? Why are they back to steel? I specified restoring the originals."

Jim pulled out his phone and started scrolling. "Looks like the client didn't want to pay for it," he said, reading from an email. "Steel saves a few hundred bucks."

"Take it out of my contract fee."

"Seriously, man?"

Dylan would probably say the same thing, but he would deal with that later. "Yeah, seriously. Clear it with the client, then adjust the invoice. Be persuasive."

"All right, Josh. Whatever you say."

Satisfied, Josh closed the packet and looked at his watch. Ten minutes to start. "Let's grab our seats. The quicker we get this over with, the quicker you can get back to your kids, and I can get back to bed."

"No complaints here." Jim gestured to the row of folding chairs behind the ones ribboned off for the politicians. The congressmen and senators were all on break—another testament to the shit timing—so the seats would be filled with city councilors and the mayor. It's not like they had been working on this for over a year, Josh thought with a sneer he wasn't sure he hid from his face. The least the city could do was give it a proper ground-breaking. He guessed not everyone could get excited about the local history of an old convent in a city full of national treasures.

Cat had been excited, though. He glanced at the empty chair beside him. She would have been there if things had turned out differently. Wearing some pretty dress, looking at him with pride, and bouncing in her seat excitedly.

Great. So much for focusing on work to keep from thinking about her.

The mayor's speech was long and held little regard for the arctic climate in which it was being delivered. The sweat on Josh's neck began to bead and roll down into his collar. His tie was a noose, and the loud, throaty cough that he couldn't seem to quiet became too embarrassing after a while, so he slipped out of his chair and made his way around the corner. He was leaned against one of the builder's trailers, trying to keep his eyes open, when applause sounded from the stage area. The ceremony was over, and now it was time to mingle. He just needed to stay upright for a little longer.

Jim appeared a moment later, and Josh watched him look left then right before finally spotting him slumped between the metal wall and the railing that led inside. "Josh, you gotta go home. You're not going to be able to shmooze these guys while you're hacking up a lung."

"There's no one here but me," he explained. "Dylan is out of town for the holiday, and the project manager has the week off."

"Listen, man, I got you covered. I know the design inside and out. I can speak on it."

"I can't leave you here by yourself."

"You pulled me into this project, Josh. I appreciate it. Let me do this for you. I won't let you down."

"You're sure?" The exertion it took to push the subject had him light-headed again. He had no choice. He trusted Jim. "All right. Thanks." He reached a hand out to shake Jim's, but his friend took a step back and shook his head.

"I don't need that plague, bro. You get some rest."

He tried to laugh, but it came out as another

cough. He settled for a wave over his shoulder as he set off to try and make it to his Jeep.

The turnout hadn't been huge, but they'd insisted on keeping the spots out front for the guests of honor. The satellite construction lot a block away was the closest he could get. He could have been walking to the center of the earth the way his skin burned. He definitely had a fever, and the extra breaths it took to propel him down the street were razor-sharp knives poking at his lungs. When he spotted his Jeep, he pushed himself to make the last few feet, then fell against it, sucking in air like a diver resurfacing.

After he caught his breath, it occurred to him that his hood was sloped at an awkward angle. He pried himself away to get a better look and saw the front right tire was low. No, strike that, it was completely flat.

Shit. Just what he needed. At the risk of not having the strength to get back up, he lowered himself to his knee to get a better look and found a three-inch framing nail jammed in the tread, air hissing out around it. He glanced at the spare on the hatch from his crouched position. There was no way he was changing that tire. He had half a mind to lower himself the rest of the way to the ground and fall asleep where he was.

"God damn it," he muttered, wiping at his brow again. He managed to get up from the ground and hoist himself into the car, starting the engine for the heat while he devised a plan.

Maybe he could just sleep here for a little while, wake up rested enough to change the tire himself. He'd probably run out of gas or freeze, though. He glanced at the clock. Shawn was still at work on the other side of the Bay, which meant two hours until he could get there. He could call Minnie, but she was home with Matt, probably still in Christmas pajamas and enjoying leftovers from the holiday. He couldn't ask her to pack her kid up and haul him into the city, exposing him to these germs in the process.

Maybe he could call Adam. Would that be weird? He ran a hand down his clammy face. He'd traveled so far around the obvious answer, but there it was, staring him in the face. Cat was the only one he knew in the city. He was a mile from her office, but he hadn't spoken to her since that night in the parking lot.

He closed his eyes again, willing his head to stop throbbing, but it was no use. Now he was starting to shake from the cold sweat forming on his body. Cat would give him a ride home. She'd never turn him down, but seeing her was the last thing he needed right now. He didn't have the strength to look at her pretty brown eyes and let her fuss over him the way he was sure she would.

He had no other choice though, unless he wanted to start calling hired cars to see about the hour-long trip. The hemming and hawing was exhausting him even more, so he picked up the phone and with one quick keystroke, it was done. The line was ringing.

Cat had been halfway out the door for her lunch break when her phone rang from the depths of her purse. She almost didn't answer it. She almost silenced it without even looking at the caller ID. But she had looked at it, and her heart had leaped into her throat when she saw Josh's name on the screen. It only sank a fraction when he'd told her about his flat tire, and asked if she could give him a ride home. Maybe it was pathetic, but an hour in the car with him was worth the whole night crying into her pillow after she dropped him off.

She didn't have the proper credentials to pull into the construction lot, so she'd parked just outside of it on the street. When she glanced up at the bell tower of the Abbott Building as she got out of her car, she thought how ironic it was that the second time she and Josh would be here together would be under such painfully different circumstances.

Josh's Jeep was parked in a row of pickup trucks and marked SUVs, and her blood began to pump harder as she approached it. She had no idea how it would be to see him again—if she could handle having him look at her with that flat, exhausted expression he'd given her when she'd watched him drive away.

But anything was better than missing him like this.

She knocked on the passenger side window, then opened the door and slid in beside him with her heart racing. It only took one glance to see Josh looked like absolute hell. His eyes looked like he'd been on a week-long bender, bloodshot and rimmed in purple. His skin was pale, except for angry strokes of pink on his cheeks and nose.

"Josh, are you still sick?" It had been weeks—surely he should be better by now. She instinctively pressed a hand onto his forehead and he didn't resist, his head falling limp against the headrest.

"I'm not feeling great," he said blandly. "I appreciate you giving me a ride home."

Her hopefulness for a chance to clear the air faded into worry. "You need to see a doctor, Josh." His skin burned, even against her numb fingertips. He didn't respond, and in the silence every breath he took crackled like an open flame. "There's an urgent care a few miles from here. I parked on the street. Can you make it to my car?"

He nodded affirmatively, then huffed in a few shallow breaths and pushed himself out into the cold air.

Cat pulled into the circular drive of the urgent care, snagging the last spot reserved for patients just as a red pickup truck reversed out of it. The fluorescent lights gleamed from the automatic glass doors, bright and clinical against the smudged grey sky. It had only taken ten minutes to get there, but Josh had fallen asleep in half that time.

"Hey," Cat said, feathering her fingers over his cheek to keep from startling him into a painful gasp. "We're here."

Josh rolled to his right, unfastening his seatbelt without opening his eyes. She rushed to meet him as he opened the door, offering her arm to lean on. To her mild surprise, he took it, letting her walk him into the building and to one of three empty chairs in the waiting room. Naturally, with the holidays being the least convenient time for a medical emergency, the room was full.

When she came back from the check-in desk with a clipboard and stack of paperwork, he straightened in his seat like he'd suddenly come back to life. "You don't have to stay," he said. "I'm sure this will take a while, and by the time I'm done, Shawn will be out of work and he can come pick me up."

Cat's stomach twisted at being dismissed.

She'd had her heart set on an hour of his time, and she couldn't settle for any less. "I'll stay," she said. His eyes closed again, and she wasn't sure if it was from exhaustion or exasperation. "Please, Josh. I want to stay."

"Okay," he said, his voice barely louder than a breath. "Thank you."

The wait was shorter than they expected. A nurse came to gather them, leading them down a hallway and into an exam area separated by curtains. Josh hoisted himself up onto the cot with noticeable effort, and the nurse quickly took his vital signs, typing furiously on a little portable computer as she inquired about his symptoms.

"When did the cough start?" she asked, without looking up from the screen.

Josh glanced in Cat's direction, and she was sure his mind was revisiting that night outside the restaurant, just like hers was. "A little over two weeks ago."

Two weeks. It felt like an eternity since she'd last kissed him, last heard him laugh. Had it really only been two weeks?

"Other symptoms?"

"Chest pain," he replied with an audible wheeze. "Headache."

"Fever," Cat jumped in. "Loss of appetite." She remembered him barely touching his meal at the restaurant that night and looking at him now, his face looked thin.

"I'll check his temp in a moment," the nurse

said, clearly uninterested in the help. She typed a few more notes then turned to gather supplies from the small rolling cart beside her. By this time, Josh was shivering hard enough that Cat could see the tremors in his body.

"Can we get him a blanket or something?" Cat asked, fighting the urge to wrap her arms around him.

"I'll have someone bring one in. Open up." After she'd stuck a thermometer in his mouth and clamped the plastic O2 meter on his finger, she busied herself watching the second hand of her watch. "Mmm," she said, plucking it out with the same lack of tenderness "I don't like that fever, and I can hear your breathing from here. The doctor will probably want to run some tests. Settle in. It will be a while."

"Blanket," Cat called after her as she wrenched the curtain shut and disappeared.

"She was pleasant," Josh muttered when she was out of earshot.

"They've got a full house." Though Cat had to agree, the woman's bedside manner needed some work. He was obviously feeling miserable. "Go ahead and lie down. I'm sure you have time to kill."

"I'm all right."

"Josh. You need to rest. I'll wake you up when the doctor comes in."

A painful-sounding cough took over his emerging stubbornness, and he gave up. He stretched out on the bed then tossed onto his side, bringing his knees up toward his stomach. He flipped the pillow over, then rolled to his other side. Cat stood at the foot of the bed, wishing she could help somehow. Finally, he seemed to settle on a position, and his eyes slipped closed.

"You cut your hair," he said, his face smooshed against the stiff, white pillow.

Cat reached up to finger the strands that now brushed just above her shoulder, watching him breathe in shallow little spurts. She'd gone right before Christmas, and despite Sonya telling her not to do anything rash, she'd chopped five inches off in a fit of self-pity. Josh loved her hair.

"Just a little." Her voice came out a whisper, a shaky, fragile thing. Now that they were together in an enclosed space, with nothing to do but wait, the distance between them felt like another presence in the room. She'd wanted to come. When he called her that afternoon, her hopeful heart sang, but being here with him now was harder than she thought it would be. It had been weeks since she'd rested in his arms, or felt his warmth curled behind her in bed, and she missed him with her entire body. Being a foot away and not being able to touch him was excruciating. She wanted to crawl up beside him and hold him, stroke her fingers through his hair. That always soothed him. She could make him fall asleep in two minutes by scratching her nails along his scalp.

She stole a glance at his wristwatch, finding that only a few minutes had passed since they'd been told to settle in. There had to be something she could do. She had no idea what to say, or even what to feel, but doing was easier. She'd always been a doer.

He still had his tie on from the ground-breaking ceremony, and she came around to the side of the bed, leaning in to loosen it for him. He grunted his approval, so she moved on to his collar, unbuttoning the top few buttons. The sensuality of the gesture caused her heart to lurch again. She'd done it so many times before under different circumstances.

His neck and chest were damp from his fever, his cheeks lit up like a Christmas tree. The nurse still hadn't come back with a blanket, so she unwrapped the big scarf she wore and draped it over his shoulder, fighting the urge to run her hand over his hair. Instead, she dropped into the plastic chair in the corner of their tiny space and watched him.

"It's like eating your mom's ghost pepper enchiladas," he mumbled without looking at her. "My whole body is on fire."

She managed a laugh, though the thought made her want to cry. "She made them for Christmas Eve," she said. "You wouldn't have been able to stand them."

"Probably not."

Chancing rejection, she pulled the chair closer to the side of the cot and touched his sleeve, fingering the button at his wrist. "Where did you go?"

"I stayed in," he said like it was any other night. "Shawn asked me to go to Mass with them, but that's not really my thing. And I felt like shit."

"So you wouldn't have gone with me?" she asked quietly. "If things had been different."

"I didn't say that."

She wasn't sure which answer she'd been hoping for, but that one hurt.

Thirty-four

WHEN THEY WALKED OUT OF the doors of the urgent care into the dark, the parking lot had turned completely white. It had been snowing for days, just enough to coat the ground and cars and make slushy puddles on all of the walkways. During the day, it would melt, then collect all over again when the sun went down.

After chest x-rays and blood tests, more breathing monitors, and a round of fever-reducing drugs, Josh had finally been diagnosed with pneumonia—the kind that required antibiotics and a case the doctor deemed fairly severe. The only reason he wasn't admitted overnight was his relatively young age and good health, and the fact that the doctor had probably assumed Cat being by his side meant he had some supervision. With a prescription in hand, they were finally allowed to leave.

The Tylenol they'd given him had dropped his fever enough that his teeth weren't chattering anymore. Even so, the cold night air hit him like a punch to the chest.

"I'll go get the car," Cat said when the first breath he took launched him into a coughing fit. "You can wait inside."

"I can make it." She looked at him like she wanted to put her foot down. In another lifetime, she certainly would have, but she simply sighed and started walking. "I really feel okay to," he said, so she wouldn't think he was being intentionally defiant. It was the last thing he wanted to do, but he also didn't know how he was supposed to act. Seeing her was as hard as he thought it would be. At first, he'd been preoccupied with the pain and the fever. He barely remembered the ride there, but once they were left alone in that room, and he saw the sadness in her eyes while she cared for him like she was still his, he wasn't sure he could take it on top of how shitty he felt. Now he just wanted to be home in his bed, asleep and unaware for as long as he could manage.

They drove a few blocks in silence, and Cat left the car running as she ran into the pharmacy to fill his prescription for him. Another thing he'd told her she didn't have to do. Somehow, telling her that seemed to hurt her more than just letting her do it, so he stopped protesting.

They finally arrived at his house after a long ride where he'd been in and out of sleep.

She carried a couple of bags she'd ferried over from his car, standing so close he could feel her body heat as he unlocked the door and flipped on the porch light. He turned to take the things from her, but she shook her head, nodding for him to lead the way into his house.

The cold and the car ride had exhausted him, and he walked straight to the couch and flopped onto it, kicking off his dress shoes. He threw an arm over his eyes, but not before glancing around the room and noting the evidence of the depressing last couple of weeks still littering his house. Half-empty mugs of water and ginger-ale were on the end tables. His recycling bin was overflowing with the remnants of microwavable groceries. There were sweatshirts and socks on the floor where he'd gone through cycles of bundling and stripping, depending on his fickle temperature.

Cat took a seat in the chair across from him, sitting silently for a few moments while he rested his eyes. Finally, she stood and walked to the kitchen. "I'm going to stay," she said over her shoulder as she began opening cabinet doors.

"Cat..."

"You need to rest, and you need to eat and drink enough to keep your strength up. You can't do both of those things if you're here by yourself." She pulled down a mug and walked to the stove where the kettle sat on the burner, turning it on.

"I can't ask you to do that," he said once she was back in front of him. Getting through the holiday was hard enough; he couldn't go back-ward in this.

"You didn't ask. I offered."

"It's not... we're not..." He sighed, running a hand through his hair and pulling himself up to sit. "I'm not your responsibility," he said, forcing himself to look in her eyes.

"Look, I'm not going to get the wrong idea," she said. She was forcing her voice to sound neu-tral, but he heard the shake. "I understand what this is. And afterward, if we can't be friends, well then I'll accept it, but right now you need some-one and I'm already here. I haven't stopped car-ing about you, Josh. Let me do it for one more night."

The fever was still lapping at his brain as he considered it. An almost dream-like vision filled the dark behind his eyelids: waking up in the morning and finding her there making coffee in the kitchen, her laying on the couch with her legs slung over the arm, watching some ridicu-lous reality show. He forced the picture from his mind before he got used to it.

"It's too hard, Catia."

"Then go to bed," she said matter-of-factly. "Just pretend I'm not here." She turned away then, hiding her quivering bottom lip with a fake yawn.

Josh pulled in a breath to respond, but it stabbed at his ribs. He was too tired to argue, too weak to look out for either one of them. "Fine," he said, pushing off of the couch and standing with some difficulty. "Do what you want, Cat. I can't stop you."

She nodded. "Is the guest room okay? I'll find the stuff."

"It's all yours." He turned toward his bedroom, the darkness of the hallway calling to him as he tried to ignore the image of Cat sleeping in the double bed in his spare room upstairs, alone. It was the same room he'd moved into as a kid when his parents died, then moved back into when he and Sarah had done this: played house even though they both knew it was over. He should board up that room—let it rot. He should tell Cat to sleep on the couch, keep her memory from mixing with the other ones that lived there. But he couldn't tell her that without explaining how much it hurt, and that was the last thing he wanted to do.

The t-shirt Josh had worn to bed was stuck to his chest with sweat. He'd been asleep for hours, and it had been at least a couple before that since he'd taken any Tylenol. He knew he must be due to take another dose by the way the pain in his chest had returned, clawing at him from the bottom of each breath. He kicked the sheets off of his legs and pulled in as much air as he could muster.

Cat was still up. The sound of the television floated in from the living room as he stood from his bed. He wasn't surprised. She was a bit of a night owl, always keeping up the pillow talk well after his eyes had closed, and his answers became monosyllabic. He hadn't gotten around to deleting the multiple shows she'd added to his DVR, so at least she wouldn't be bored.

He used the bathroom and was just crawling back into his bed when the floorboards outside of his door creaked. Then there was a quiet knock. *She fucking knocked.* Being reduced to these formalities after all of the moments they'd shared in that room, all the ways they knew each other, was salt in a gaping wound. It was exactly why he didn't want her to stay.

"Come in," he rasped, his stomach sour.

Cat opened the door, the light from the hallway shadowing her face as she hovered hesitantly in the threshold. "I brought you more pain meds," she said, holding out the bottle. In her other hand, she held a glass of water.

He used the advantage of the dark to take her in inconspicuously, now that she wasn't bundled in winter gear. She had on a tight pair of jeans and a red and white striped sweater that hung off one shoulder. Her feet were bare, and without her heels, she looked tiny—like a little Christmas elf bearing narcotics. Maybe he was just high from his fever.

Her hair was up on top of her head now, and

he was glad to see she could still tie it in that wild-looking knot he liked, even though she'd cut it.

Christ, he needed to stop. What did it matter to him anymore what she did with her hair?

Cat handed him two pills, and he took them, finishing the glass of water in two gulps.

"Do you want something to eat?" she asked. "It's been a long time since you've had anything."

"I'm fine."

"You should eat."

He didn't answer. The thought didn't appeal to him in the least, but even if it had, he wasn't going to let her wait on him.

She seemed intent on it, though, taking a few more steps in as he settled into bed. *Their bed.* She picked up his dress pants and shirt that he'd tossed on the floor and laid them on his chair. "Josh, I'm here so I can help you. You need to eat something to get your energy—"

"I said, I'm fine, Cat," he snapped. "I've been taking care of myself for twenty years for Christ's sake." She froze, her shoulders slumping, and he dropped his face into his hands, rubbing at his pounding temples with his thumbs. "I'm sorry. I'm just... I'm really not hungry. What about you?" He knew he'd stolen her lunch break, and they hadn't exactly been in the mood to stop for dinner.

"I made a sandwich," she admitted. "I hope you don't mind."

"Of course not." Again the way she spoke to him like a stranger burned in his chest. As if he'd ever care about her eating his food. It was only a few weeks ago that he'd asked her to share this house with him and everything in it. And she'd turned him down.

It was all wrong, this new reality between them. It was awkward and painful. They weren't strangers or polite acquaintances—he missed her. That was why he couldn't be this close to her. He rolled to his side, pulling the heavy blanket up to his neck. "I should probably go back to sleep."

"Well, just let me know if you get hungry."

"Cat." She stopped in the doorway, looking back at him over her shoulder. "You probably don't have any clothes."

She shook her head.

"You can borrow something to sleep in," he said, turning onto his side and adjusting his pillow. "Help yourself. You know where everything is."

He heard her shuffling around in the dark, opening his drawers and closing them. Then she went into the bathroom, probably looking for her toothbrush. It was still there next to his. He was simultaneously embarrassed that he hadn't tossed it and glad she'd have it tonight.

"Thank you," she whispered. Then the door shut, and he was alone again.

Thirty-five

C AT TOSSED TO HER SIDE on the stiff mattress in Josh's guest room, using the extra pillow to cover her eyes from the morning sun. She'd barely slept, instead replaying their conversation over and over while she stared at the glow-in-the-dark planet stickers on his ceiling. The rest of the room had been redecorated, but the little solar system was still there to remind her that twelve-year-old Josh had once slept in this bed.

I've been taking care of myself for twenty years.

There was something in his voice when he'd told her that the night before that she couldn't get out of her head. It was a sort of a resigned sadness, maybe even bitterness. It didn't mesh with the generally happy guy she knew. *What was it Minnie had called him? Well-adjusted.* Josh was well-adjusted. He didn't carry around secret emotional baggage. He talked about things; he showed all his cards. She was the one who shoved things down and let them fester, like a decade-long grudge with her sister, and every single thing that had ever transpired between her and Micah. She didn't think Josh held onto that stuff. It wasn't like him to let things hide until they burst out in a moment of weakness. Or maybe it was like him, and she just didn't know him like she thought she did.

Had Josh felt uncared for as a kid? Did he still feel that way? Guilt wiggled inside her belly. Maybe Josh wasn't as well-adjusted as everyone thought he was. Maybe he'd shown her that, but she just hadn't listened. She cared about him more than she'd believed she was capable of, and she hadn't let him know.

She tossed off the blankets and let the chilly air hit her legs. The snow was falling heavier than the day before, and there was still the issue of Josh's Jeep being stranded in the city. He definitely wasn't going out in this weather as sick as he was. Maybe Dylan would take a ride with her to get it. Though, she was quickly reminded that she would have no reason to come back if he did. Dylan could take over helping Josh, and there would be nothing left for her to do, no excuse to be there. As much as she'd wanted to deny it, Josh was acting like this was done and over with. Maybe that would be the last time she'd ever see him. The thought snaked through her, tightening around her already wounded heart.

She didn't have much time to dwell on it, though. As soon as the worst-case scenarios began forming in her brain, she heard the click of his bedroom door opening. Despite her fears about an awkward *good morning*, she still rushed down the stairs to check on him.

When she saw him in the kitchen, standing back to her and looking through the refrigerator, her stomach fell. Maybe this was a bad idea, after all. How could she think she would be okay with waking up to him, his hair damp and messy, a pair of sweatpants slung low on his hips and a plain white t-shirt clinging to his back muscles? Even like this, he was so beautiful and he used to be hers. Now she was sleeping in his guest bed.

She cleared her throat and rubbed her arms nervously. "Hey. How are you feeling?"

He turned in her direction, and his eyes traveled the length of her, quickly as if it were a habit his brain had forgotten to quit with all of the rest. Like loving her, touching her, looking her in the eye.

"I think my fever's down."

"That's good. Hopefully, it will keep going down. Did you take your medication?"

He held out the hand that had been by his side, opening his fist to reveal two oblong tablets. Cat crossed the room to get a glass for him. She tipped her head toward the breakfast bar, and he padded over to it, taking a seat on the stool and leaned his elbows on the counter. She poured him a glass of orange juice and another of water and set them both in front of him. He used the O.J. to take the pills.

"Please let me make you some food," she tried again. He was in a little bit of a better mood than he was the night before. "You need some energy."

"I can't really think of anything that sounds appealing right now."

"Still..."

"All right. I'll have some toast." He started to get up, but she rolled her eyes at him as she moved to the toaster, and he sat back down.

"Is Dylan around to go get your car?" She hadn't thought of a way around that yet. At the very least, she could feel out how eager he was to get rid of her.

"He's out of town until tomorrow."

That news made her happier than it should have. He didn't seem well enough for her to leave yet, and maybe it wasn't the smartest decision emotionally, but she wanted to stay. She'd promised him she wouldn't get the wrong idea about what she was doing there, but not-so-deep down she was hoping for a second chance. A way to prove to him how much she loved him despite her failure. Her father had told her there were different ways to show love, and maybe this was hers.

This had been a learning curve for her from the start, a lesson in taking things as they come and letting her heart tell her how to act and what to do. She'd failed miserably, but now she had a specific action plan for how to show him how much she cared, and she loved a good to-do list.

The toast popped up, and she spread a thick layer of butter on it just like he liked, plating it and sliding it across the breakfast bar.

"You don't have a lot of food here," she said. She'd gone through and taken inventory after he'd gone to bed the night before. "I'll go to the store and get some soup. Maybe some stuff to make dinner if you feel like eating by then."

Josh kept his eyes on his plate as he took a small bite, and she couldn't tell if he was pleased with her offer. She could hear him wheezing from across the kitchen, though, so she wasn't taking no for an answer.

They talked for a short time while he ate—stilted, overly formal conversation that made her feel even more awkward than the silence. Except when she'd made another dig at his coffee maker. "I couldn't live like this," she'd said before she'd realized how that sounded, what she would give to live like this.

He'd laughed though, light enough to not cause himself any pain, but it had been a laugh. She scooped up the sound and put it in her pocket for safekeeping, not knowing if it would be the last time she would hear it.

When he'd finished his toast and headed back to his room, she made a grocery list of all of the things she thought he might need, whether she was there or not. An hour later, Josh still behind his bedroom door, she wrote a quick note explaining where she'd gone and headed to the local grocery store. It was a short drive, but it gave her time to call Dani through her Bluetooth and tell her where she was. It was Saturday, and she'd made a loose promise to spend the evening with her and Sonya. She'd never intended to follow through with it, but she still needed to break the news.

"So, you stayed the night?" Dani asked after she'd relayed the story of Josh's hospital visit.

"I slept in the guest room."

"Oh." She was silent for a moment. "But how was it this morning? Did you guys talk?"

"We... chatted. I wouldn't say we talked."

"Oh, Cat. Are you sure you're up for putting yourself through this?"

"He needs me."

"He needs someone. It doesn't have to be you."

"I want it to be me."

"I know." Dani's voice turned soft, tentative. "I'm just worried it's too much. It might not go the way you want it to."

"I love him, Dani, and he's sick. No matter how it works out, I want to be there."

"You can't just stay at his house and not talk about things between you two. You'll drive yourself crazy."

"I don't know what else there is to say." Cat caught the choke that was trying to worm its way into her voice, and cast it aside. She'd already made her decision. She was staying, no matter the price.

"I just don't want to see you get hurt again."

"He's hurt too," Cat said. "I did this."

"Well, maybe this is your chance to make it right, Cat. To show him that you really were all in. I mean, exposing yourself to a communicable disease is the definition of for better or worse, right?"

Cat laughed through the tears that were forming in her vision. "Yeah, I guess it is. All right, I have to go. I'm almost there, and I have to call my mother for her *Estrellita Sopita* recipe."

"You're cooking?" Dani said with a gasp. "Now that's love."

"Ha. Ha."

"Good luck, Kit Cat. I'll talk to you soon."

Cat's mom gave her a list of ingredients, but not without a flurry of worried questions about Josh's condition and a list of home remedies she swore by. None of them would substitute for the drugs he was already taking, so she didn't bother writing them down.

When she arrived back at Josh's with an armful of groceries, she set about making the stock. It would take all day for the soup to be ready, but it didn't look like Josh would be up for lunch anyway. She adjusted the burner to let it simmer, and went upstairs to change back into the pajama pants and t-shirt she'd borrowed from him. She'd just settled onto his couch with a basket of his laundry to fold when there was a knock at the door. It swung open before she could get up, and there was Dylan cleaning snow off of his boots on the mat outside the door.

He stopped mid-scuff when he saw her. "Cat?" His forehead wrinkled in confusion. "Where's Josh's Jeep?"

"It's still in the city," she replied, hugging her arms against the rush of cold air he carried in. "I thought you were out of town."

"Came home a day early. I've been calling Josh since last night."

"He's sick," she explained, assuming Josh's phone must be dead in the pocket of his coat. "He has pneumonia."

"Pneumonia?" Dylan closed the door behind him. "When did this happen?"

"He's probably had it a while, given how sick he is. He called me from the ground-breaking ceremony. He had a flat and needed a ride. We went to the urgent care center instead."

"The Abbott Building ground-breaking? You've been here since yesterday? He let you stay the night?" Dylan fired off all of his questions at once.

"I'm staying in the guest room."

His face softened, obviously picking up on

the sting of his disbelief. "Sorry. I didn't mean it like that."

Dylan glanced down the hallway toward Josh's bedroom, then back at her. She was silly to think this was anything more than what it was. Dylan was looking at her like she was an apparition that couldn't possibly be sitting there after what had happened between her and Josh. "He's really sick," she said, feeling the need to justify her presence. "He didn't have a choice."

He eyed her again, then plopped down in the chair across from her. "There's always a choice."

A rush of heat hit her cheeks, and she changed the subject. "We'll have to go get his car. He can't go out in this weather. I can drive us there. I came right from work, so I don't have any of my things. That's why I have his clothes on." She was starting to ramble. She'd been dreading this moment. Dylan was here now. Josh wouldn't need her to stay, and once she left, she knew it would be for the final time.

Dylan seemed less affected. He leaned back casually in his chair, regarding her with equal parts pity and suspicion. "We go get his car, and then what?"

"I can fill you in on what the doctor said. He'll still need some help. I'll write down his medication schedule. I made a soup..."

"Cat." He shook his head. "You don't want to leave, do you?"

"No. I don't want any of this. I love him,

Dylan." She wiped at the tears threatening to spill from the corners of her eyes. She wasn't going to lose it in front of Dylan of all people.

Dylan chewed his lip, looking again toward the closed door at the end of the hall. "The thing with Josh is," he started, lowering his voice as if he were telling her a secret, "sometimes he's too quick to cut his losses."

She sniffed and met his gaze. "How do you mean?"

"See, Josh woke up one morning and everything was gone, you know? Now, once he sees a crack forming, a hint he might be losing something, he just tears the whole thing down. That way, it ends on his terms. I've seen him do it before. When things went bad with Sarah, he just gave up."

"But, she left him."

"Sure, she did. After he completely closed himself off. Look, I'm not saying it was all his fault. He gave up because he thought he saw the end, then she proved him right."

Cat swallowed hard. She had a sense of this by the way he'd shut down in that parking lot, seemingly accepting that their time was over, and there was nothing either of them could do to change it.

"What I'm saying is, Cat, if you really love him, I think it might be good for you to stay. Don't let him be right this time."

"He's not right."

"Good. His ego doesn't need it." He laughed, but it quickly petered out into a sad little shake of his head. "You should hear the way he talks about you. Like you're this amazing gift someone left on his doorstep. I've known him for a long time, and I've never seen him like that."

"He was a few firsts for me too," Cat choked out. She wasn't trying to hold it in anymore. Her tears fell freely down her face, and the sight seemed to steal all of the confidence that Dylan usually carried around, leaving him squirming in his chair.

He took a deep breath, letting it out as he leaned over his knees. "You know, we don't have to go get his car today," he said with a tone of conspiracy. Cat looked up at him to see a smirk on his lips, his eyes empathetic. "In fact, I just remembered I have a pretty full day."

Cat opened her mouth to reply, but the lump in her throat wouldn't let her. She simply blinked away a few more tears, then nodded silently.

Dylan stood. "I should go," he said, squeezing her shoulder as he passed. "You don't have to tell him I came by. I'll catch up with him. And Cat?"

"Yeah?" She turned over her shoulder to watch him from her spot on the couch.

"The other thing about Josh is he doesn't do anything he doesn't want to. He might say he doesn't want to, like going on that trip to the beach. He might even put up a fuss, but if he's letting you take care of him, it's because he wants you here."

She smiled through her tears. That was all she needed to hear.

Thirty-six

JOSH COULDN'T KEEP TRACK OF the hours passing. One minute it was daylight, and the next, he woke up in a pitch-dark room, wondering when he'd fallen asleep again. Cat was beside him last he remembered. She'd come in at some point to hand him some pills and run a cold washcloth over his head. Unless that was some sort of cruel fever hallucination.

No. The cloth was still there on the pillow beside him.

He had a splitting headache, probably from dehydration, he assumed, since his sheets were marked with sweat like a chalk outline at a crime scene. He turned over his shoulder and looked at the clock. Eight p.m. His body was beginning to run on six-hour cycles now, stirring him back to life when it was time for another dose of medicine, and like clockwork, his chest began to ache along with his head.

Also like clockwork, Cat appeared where his door was left ajar, a silhouette against the light of the hallway.

"Are you awake?" she asked, her voice just loud enough to reach him over the silent, dark ocean of space between them.

"Yeah. Come in."

"I brought your medicine." She set the pills on his nightstand, along with a glass of water, and began untwisting the sheets from his legs.

"What smells so good?" he asked when he'd dragged himself up to a half-sitting position and reached for the pills. The scent of spices and garlic wafted through his door, and his stomach responded with a painful growl.

"A Mexican soup. It's for colds and flu, so it should help your chest feel better and give you some energy."

"Is it going to set my stomach on fire?" he asked, wiping at his damp brow.

"No. It's very mild."

She looked up at him once she'd straightened the sheet and tucked it back into the foot of the mattress. God, she was pretty. Even in his t-shirt, two sizes too big for her, her hair wild from air drying. He'd looked at her a thousand times, but her face still set something aflight inside of him. He lassoed it down with a picture of the bartender's face instead, his lips pressed against her temple. Then her friends' faces when Dani had spilled her secret, their pitied expressions, though none looked entirely surprised.

Cat picked up the washcloth and brought it into the bathroom, running it under the faucet.

When she returned, she folded the cloth and pressed it to his forehead, then the back of his neck. Despite himself, he let her.

"The soup is ready. Do you want me to bring it in here or do you feel like a change of scenery?"

She wasn't asking anymore, but for the first time since he'd been home, he did actually feel like eating. "I could stretch my legs," he said, then remembering he'd stripped down to his boxer briefs, he paused. "Just... give me a minute."

The television was on when he finally emerged from his cave, dressed in sweatpants and a thick henley. "Baby It's Cold Outside" serenaded him from the screen on his way into the kitchen.

"What are you watching?"

Cat stood at his stove, stirring a large pot, and she answered with a smile that hit him right in the chest. "*Elf.*"

He swallowed, bobbing his head in response. "Christmas is over, you know."

"Technically, the Christmas season doesn't end until the twelfth day. My grandmother used to keep the tree up and let us do all of the Christmasy stuff until January sixth—the Epiphany holiday." She spooned some soup into a bowl while she spoke and slid it across the counter to him.

The way her eyes danced merrily while she spoke reminded him that it was the first year in a long time he'd been looking forward to the holidays, until their ill-timed breakup.

"Can I come watch it with you?"

Her lips quirked into an amused smile at the request, given he was asking to come out into his own living room. "Yeah," she said. "Of course."

They both took a seat on the couch, squished into opposite corners, and Josh took a big gulp of his soup. Another time he might have waited until it cooled, but now he needed the heat in his body as much as he needed those pain pills, even if it burned his tongue as he took it.

"The soup is good. Thank you."

"I'm glad you like it. It's better when my mother makes it."

"I think you did a great job."

She dropped her gaze to her bowl, slurping from her spoon as she was prone to do. "She gave me the recipe this morning. She was really worried about you. I had to convince her not to make it herself and bring it here."

Josh wasn't sure if the idea of Cynthia driving over an hour to bring him soup felt comforting or like the twist of a knife. "Your family has been very kind to me," he said quietly.

Cat looked at him with an expression that spread like a thorny vine around his heart and squeezed. "They love you, Josh."

The closing credits of the movie scrolled across the screen, and Cat peeked at Josh out of the corner of her eye. He looked stationary enough— his head cradled by the arm of the couch, his legs tucked up beside him—like he might keep her company for a little while longer.

"What do you want to watch now?" she asked with a hint of hope in her voice that she couldn't hide.

Josh's shoulders jolted, and she immediately regretted it.

Of course. He'd fallen asleep; that's why he was still there. Was he going to retreat back to his room now that she'd woken him? Or worse, suggest she head home? Neither one of them had mentioned her staying again, but judging by the raspiness of his breathing and the slight sheen on his forehead, he was still in no condition to care for himself. Besides, it was dark and the weather was a tentative mixture of half snow, half rain. Even in his state of hating her, he wouldn't want her to drive the hour back to the city.

Disappointment clattered through her when he pulled himself up to sitting and ran a hand through his hair. But then he gave her the tiniest hint of a smile. "Might as well pick another Christmas movie," he said. "Since we have twelve days and all."

Cat swallowed the acid that had begun to burn the back of her throat, and her face burst into a smile bigger than she'd intended. "Okay. Any suggestions?"

"Whatever you want."

His indifference didn't dampen her. It was typical of his demeanor: easy-going, congenial. Normal Josh—the one who saved any forcefulness for the things that mattered in life. His uncomplaining nature was why she'd been so taken aback by his reaction to Jay that night. But to him, it looked as though *she* were indifferent to what they had, and that definitely mattered. She thought of Dylan's assessment, of all the cracks she'd put in this thing between them, and how in that parking lot, Josh had tried to tear it all down.

Don't let him be right.

"Cat." His voice startled her despite the near-whisper of it. When he'd adjusted his position, he'd moved ever so slightly toward the middle of the couch, and she turned toward him, doing the same. "I just wanted to say I really appreciate you being here. I know it's hard. It's hard for me too. And you were right. I wouldn't have been able to cook for myself or do any of the other stuff you're doing. So, thank you."

She swallowed, fighting the urge to touch him. She wasn't sure how he managed to look so handsome in baggy sweatpants with dark circles under his eyes, his pale cheeks looking hollow, but manage it he did. The vulnerability in his eyes and the sandpaper scratch of his voice made the room feel like its edges were folding in on themselves, curling around them until Josh's couch was the only place that existed in the world.

This was the kind of night he'd been talking about when he'd asked her to move in. The two of them in their pajamas, watching television with the light from the gas fireplace flickering across his face. Quiet, intimate, home. It took breaking up for her to realize how much she wanted it too.

"I couldn't not be here, Josh." She gave in and touched his face, pressing her fingers against his hot cheek, and when he rested the weight of his head in her palm, she grew bolder, stroking her fingers upward into his hair. There was a force occupying the small space between them, like the invisible pull that exists when you hold two magnets just close enough that they start to rebel against the little bit of distance. He had to feel it too, the way his laser-beam gaze was set on her.

Before she knew it, their foreheads were pressed together, his eyes closed.

"Please don't," he whispered, but he didn't move, even as she cupped his other cheek.

"Can we just talk about what happened? Please?"

"What's there to talk about, Catia?"

"Us."

His shoulders fell, and he pulled out of her hands. "This was a bad idea."

"No. You just said you needed help—"

"I know what I said. I mean this." He gestured at the lack of space between them with a pained expression. "Hanging out on the couch, touching. We're acting like it's the same. It's not."

"But it can be."

"No, Catia. It can't."

The tight line of his mouth was a dagger hovering over her chest. She braced herself for the plunge, but she had to say something. Dani was right. It was killing her to be in the same house with him and not talk about it. "I'm so sorry, Josh. I never meant to hurt you."

"Stop." All the emotion drained from his face then. She could see it in the square of his shoulders and the way his cheeks sucked in as he bit his tongue—a switch had flipped.

His resignation began to worm its way through her fragile resistance. She believed in what Dylan had said, but she couldn't sit there with him and hope for something he wasn't willing to give. Not if what he was saying was true, that this wasn't an option anymore.

"I'm going to go to bed," she said. Her words sounded like they were tumbling over rocks as she held back a sob. She stood and turned away quickly before he could see her lose control. "Dylan's home. He can go with you tomorrow to get your car."

Josh's chest felt tight, his heart and lungs calcifying into something brittle and ready to shatter. When he watched Cat walk up the stairs, the room felt instantly cold—like the chill that creeps into an old house when the hearth is put out.

He'd tried to keep things safe for both of them, but it was getting harder to deny how much he wanted her there. When she'd touched his cheek and stroked his hair, it was all he could do not to pull her into his arms and hold her like he was used to.

If someone had asked him right then why he was denying himself that type of love, why he'd ever walked away from her, he might not have been able to explain it. She didn't understand. Maybe he didn't either, but she thought his distance was punitive, and that was the furthest thing from the truth. There was an unsteadiness that came with the way he loved her. It was that kind of all-in infatuation you have when you're a kid and you don't know how gruesome the fall can be. But he did know. He'd known falling in love with Cat was going to be more dangerous from the start, and he did it anyway. Leaving that night hadn't changed that, but now every time he felt that pull in his chest or flutter in his gut, a warning tempered it: *She's not really yours.*

Still, he couldn't help but hold on to the fact that he should be alone right now, yet here she was taking care of him. He'd told her he'd been taking care of himself for twenty years, but what he didn't say was how good it felt not to have to.

For some reason, maybe that very same one, he pulled his aching body off of the couch and headed toward the stairs where she'd disappeared. As he approached the door to his guest room, he saw her standing at the foot of the bed, back to him, and bathed in the soft light of the table lamp. His pajama pants were rolled low on her hips like they were in his hotel room that night when he'd let himself imagine what having her would feel like.

He watched as she pulled her sweater up over her head, her ponytail swinging from the breeze, and his body stirred at the sight. Not a sexual stirring. He was far too exhausted for that. Though if he wasn't, that lacy bra would have been impossible to resist. But no, this was a different kind of warmth washing over him—the warmth of comfortability, the feeling of knowing someone inside and out. He knew about that tiny birthmark so high up on the inside of her thigh that he was innately jealous of anyone else who'd ever seen it. He knew the exact curve of that little bit of extra flesh just above the waistband of her jeans that she hated, but he loved to squeeze. He knew the way soft tendrils of hair always fell out of the back of her ponytail, gracing the nape of her neck and causing her to pin and repin them up throughout the day. He didn't even have to look at her to know the vignette of her body. He'd memorized it a long time ago, and he'd called upon it night after night while he lie in bed, miserable and alone since he'd broken things off. Now she was back within his reach, and he was standing there like a thirsty man at a river, refusing to drink on principle.

"Cat."

She jumped at the sound of his voice, pulling in a shaky breath. When she turned, he saw the tears running down her cheeks. She reached up to wipe at her eyes, but he stepped toward her, grabbing her wrist, and pulled her against him. "Please don't cry," he said, catching her tears with his thumb.

"I'm sorry, Josh. I thought I could do this." She pushed against him with her forearms, trying to take a step back, but even though he was weaker than usual, he still easily held her in place. She relaxed in his arms and sniffed. "I thought I could be your friend with no agenda, but you were right. It's too hard. I miss you so much."

"I miss you too." His heart was already bleeding from the exposure, but he couldn't deny it. He'd been miserable since he watched her disappear in his rearview mirror. She was the spark that had been lighting his life for months now. Without her, the days felt longer, the nights darker, the air too thick to breathe. Missing her was an understatement.

"I'm so sorry," she said again. Her face twisted from holding in a sob, and he tucked her head under his chin, shushing her with his lips in her hair.

"You can't keep apologizing to me."

"Then, you have to forgive me!" Her voice was desperate, and he squeezed her tighter. "Even if we can't fix it. Please. Just say you forgive me."

"It's not like that, Cat. I do forgive you. I know you didn't mean anything by that stupid bet. I just... I can't settle for loving you more than you love me. I can't look at you every day knowing that. Not you."

He dropped his hold on her, startling himself with the truth of what he'd said. Ever since he was a kid, living in this very bedroom, that was his reality. What he'd said about his grandfather wasn't true—he hadn't tried his best. He could have done more, could have made him feel more wanted, like less of a stranger that he had an obligation to. He was all the family he had until Dylan and Shawn.

He wasn't exaggerating when he called his two best friends his family, but he'd always been acutely aware that they both had people in their lives that fit that label more appropriately.

And Sarah? She was never the type of woman who wanted what she had. She'd changed her major three times in four years, her job a few more times after that. He'd wanted a life with her, but he'd just been one of her growing pains, a stop on the way to something better. He was tired of never actually having what he thought he had, of wanting more from people than they could give.

When he met Cat, though, he knew. If she picked him, he could damn well bet she'd already thought of all the reasons she shouldn't. When Cat set her heart on something, she wasn't giving it up for anything. Having a woman like that love him? He could live off of that for a hundred years.

"Josh," she said, pulling him back to her, "please don't say that. I know I fought it in the beginning, and I screwed it up more than once, but I *do* love you." She gripped his shirt, forcing him to hold her gaze. "The truth is, I don't think I even knew what that meant until you showed me. I used to think loving someone was a weakness I had to fight off. But you always knew better than that. Don't change because I had to catch up. I'm here with you now."

Her tears were falling faster than he could catch them now, running in little rivers down her pretty pink cheeks. God, he wanted her back. He'd earned his wariness, just like her, but the fact of the matter was that she *was* there. She'd fed him, washed his face, made sure he woke up to take his medicine. It was the first time in his life that he truly couldn't rely on himself, and she'd been there without any obligation or charity. No questioning if he was worth it. She wanted to be there, and he hadn't made it easy, but she'd stayed anyway. He'd been looking for something solid to build on; maybe this was it.

"I love you too, Cat," he said. He pressed a kiss to her temple, then her cheek, then she tipped her chin and he caught her lips, sighing as he savored the familiar feel. "I never stopped."

A long breath of relief escaped her, and she trembled against his chest. When she'd caught her breath, she ran the back of her hand over her eyes. "So, now what?"

"I guess we try to go back to where we were." He pushed her hair out of her eyes, kissing her forehead.

"Can we do that? After all of this?"

"We have to. It's been hell without you. Let's just go back to being happy and take the rest step by step."

"Okay," she said, nodding and wiping at her eyes, then kissing him again. "Yes. We'll go back."

He didn't want to let go, but his muscles were screaming from the exertion. "I need to lie down," he said. "Come on. You're not sleeping up here tonight."

"Yeah," she said, finally cracking a smile. "I'm not."

The next morning, Josh woke to the familiar

scent of coconut on his pillowcase. He closed his eyes and opened them a few more times to make sure he wasn't dreaming. He wasn't, though. Cat was still asleep behind him, her arm around his stomach and her knees pressed into the back of his.

His sheets were still damp with sweat, but instead of slick and clammy, his skin was finally dry and what felt like a normal temperature. His fever must have broken.

He rolled over in her arms, carefully untangling himself, and stood. He stretched his muscles, each one groaning from disuse, then headed to the bathroom. After brushing the taste of sleep and medicine out of his mouth, he cupped his hands under the cold water, gulping it like a crash survivor who'd stumbled upon a creek.

Cat was awake when he returned. Her hair had fallen halfway out of its ponytail, and she was still wearing just his pajama pants and her bra. He crawled back in and pressed himself against her, kissing her neck. He was definitely feeling better.

"You feel cooler," she said when he let her go.

"Fever's gone."

A smile lit up her face at that. "Do you feel like eating?"

As if on cue, his stomach growled its disapproval at being forced to survive on broth and toast. "I'm starving."

"I'll make you breakfast, but I need more clothes."

"You don't really." He ran his hands over her bare skin, relishing in her warmth now that he wasn't sweating. "I like you just like this."

She stopped him, pulling his fingers to her lips instead. "I'm cold, baby."

Hearing her call him baby made him want to do things he knew he wasn't up for yet. She was still being level-headed, though. He nipped at her shoulder as she wiggled away from him, and he followed her out of bed, just a little slower. "Take whatever you want," he relented.

"Maybe I should leave a bag here," she said. She tossed her head upside down, gathering her hair into a ball and tying it. "In case I'm ever here unexpectedly again. I can't walk around all day in just your t-shirts."

"I don't mind if you do." She laughed, but he could tell she wanted a real answer. "You can just take a drawer. Leave whatever you want." *Step by step, right? This was a step.*

"Yeah?"

"I should be able to spare it," he joked. "I don't have a big wardrobe." He wandered over to where she stood and wrapped his arms around her waist. Now that he'd given himself permission to touch her again, he couldn't seem to stop. He stroked his fingers along her belly, nuzzling his face into her neck and breathing her in. This was right. She was back, and it seemed as though they could slip back into the comfortable way they fit together. Sure, they still had stuff to work through, but right then, it did feel like he had all of her. He could be happy wherever she was, now that he knew the alternative was unbearable.

She pulled a shirt over her head, then turned in his embrace and ran her fingers through his emerging beard. "Come on," she said. "Let's get you some food."

For the rest of the day, Cat was beside him. They lounged on the couch, kissed, made up until the sun went down again. He could close his eyes and imagine that she'd said yes when he'd first asked her to move in, and this was life—a quiet Sunday evening at home, together. But all too soon, he was reminded that wasn't real.

Cat's legs stirred underneath his cheek as he lie in her lap in the darkened living room. Her fingers left his hair and reached toward the ceiling in a reluctant stretch.

"I should head back," she said, sounding exhausted by the thought.

He peeled himself from her warmth, pressing his thumb and index finger into his eyes to break them out of their near-sleep state. "Yeah, I figured that time was coming." He stood, lifting their empty bowls that had been sitting on the coffee table since lunch.

They made their way to his bedroom after he dropped the dirty dishes off in the kitchen, and she picked up her clothes.

"You can keep the shirt," he said, as she was about to pull it over her head. "You need something warmer?"

"No. My jacket is here somewhere." She tossed his pajamas into his hamper and pulled on the jeans and underwear she'd put on two days ago, with a little crinkle of her nose.

It was their typical Sunday night routine, but watching her leave this time was harder. He didn't know exactly what place they had settled on to move forward from. They'd agreed to go back, but nothing felt the way it was before.

"Bring back some stuff for that drawer," he said, nodding behind him.

She smiled mischievously at him. "Be careful what you wish for."

"Guess I should." He was actually hoping to see her show up with armfuls of her stuff next time she came, but it was too soon to start that conversation again.

He pulled on socks and shoes so he could walk her out, keeping one eye on her form as she gathered her things from around the room. "I have a meeting in the city on Wednesday," he said, standing to meet her in the doorway. "I could come up the night before."

"Good."

He propped an arm on the wall above her, and let out a small groan when she wrapped her hands around him, slipping into the waistband of his sweatpants. Saying goodbye had him questioning whether moving backward was good judgment or sheer stubbornness, but it was done and he needed to see it through.

He dropped a kiss to her cheek and ushered her out into the twilight. The brisk air hit him in the face as he followed. He reached around her when they got to her car, opening the driver's side door for her, and she turned around to kiss him goodbye. "Get some rest. I'll see you in a few days."

A few days, he thought, as he kissed her back. It was better than a week, but not better than her not leaving at all. "I'll call you tomorrow," he said.

"Good night, Josh."

"Good night, Catia."

Thirty-seven

THE AIR IN CAT'S APARTMENT was cold and unwelcoming when she finally pushed through her front door. The room felt empty and lifeless. There was none of that *ahh, it's good to be home* feeling.

This is right. Right? She dropped her purse on the table beside the door with a thud that echoed in the quiet room and kicked her shoes off. They were back together, so why did she still feel so sad?

The floor was ice beneath her feet, and she padded on her toes to the bathroom to splash some water on her face. Two days without her blow-dryer or hair products, and a few teary, sleepless nights, and she looked like a survivor of some natural disaster. She fixed her bun and went to her closet. With nothing else to do, she figured she could prep an outfit for work before bed and earn herself a couple of extra snooze minutes on her alarm.

Ugh. Her alarm. She didn't want to wake up alone to a blaring electronic greeting. She wanted to wake up to Josh, his body curled around hers, his hand on her belly as he slept, then creeping lower as he started to wake up. She wanted to make a subpar cup of coffee in his stupid coffee maker. Well, maybe not that. But she did want to get ready with him in his luxurious walk-in shower and eat breakfast beside him before she had to go to work.

Stop, Cat. He said he wanted to go back, and she was going to give him that. This was back—her sleeping here, him sleeping there. She'd hoped when she'd asked him what came next, that he would tell her not to leave, that they could just keep building in the place they'd found themselves. But Josh wanted to go back to the time when their lives were still separate, when neither of them had everything on the line. She supposed it was safe after all that had transpired.

She kicked a pair of shoes out of the way to shuffle between the wall and her unmade bed and fell backward onto the mattress. Why did her room suddenly seem so small? How did Josh even fit in this bed? He never complained, though, even when he had to fight the city traffic to get there after a long day of work, or set his laptop up at her dining room table instead of his home office. He just wanted to be with her.

Josh was complicated in that he loved harder than anyone she'd ever known, but he was simple in that all he asked in return was to be loved back. He'd told her once that she was a force, that he wanted to be what she wanted, and she knew now that she'd never wanted anything more.

She turned on her side, staring into her disaster of a closet, and willed herself to focus on preparing for the next day. It was no use. All she could think about was how out of place she felt. Everything was upside down and crisscrossed. Josh was being safe now, and she was the one itching to do something scary and completely heart-driven.

Maybe that was what he needed—to see her go just a little mad over him. After almost losing him, she knew she really was.

Standing on her tiptoes, she grabbed the strap of a duffle bag, yanking until she freed it from the top of her closet. When it landed on the floor, she unzipped it and plucked a few dresses down, still attached to their hangers, and shoved them carelessly inside. Josh had one of those really expensive irons. They'd be fine. A pair of black heels, a pair of nude ones—she'd be good for a few days. She dragged the bag behind her down the hall and into the bathroom, tossing in a few essentials. Blow-dryer, makeup, her own toothpaste—she was a spearmint girl, that was non-negotiable—she dropped her deodorant and hairspray in the top and zipped it shut.

She slid her feet into boots and bundled up her winter coat. The snow had turned to rain, and the drive there had been smooth sailing. She'd be back to the island in under an hour at this time of night. She was halfway out the door before she remembered one last thing. Something that would prove to him she was there to stay.

Josh lie on his couch, drifting in and out of consciousness while the television droned on in the background. Some ridiculous show about meerkats that Cat was watching before she left had ended, but he didn't have the energy to change the channel. Besides, the one that came on after was just as silly, and letting it play made him feel like she was still there. He already missed her, but at least he was back to the kind of missing her that would be remedied on a weekly basis.

He was trying to decide if he had the energy to heat up a bowl of leftover soup for dinner, when he heard the doorknob on his front door turn.

That jolted him upright. He slung an arm over the back of the couch and craned his neck, expecting to see Dylan. He hadn't heard from him all weekend, and who else would just walk in like they lived there? Those boots didn't sound like Dylan's, though, and whoever it was clearly had their hands full as he heard a scuffle behind the half-open door.

He went to the foyer and pulled the door the rest of the way.

"Cat?" She had a bag as big as her slung over her shoulder and her arms wrapped around her oversized, barista-style cappuccino machine. "What are you doing?"

"I don't want to go backward."

"What?" He reached for the coffee maker, but she shook her head. The bag slipped off onto the snowy stoop.

"I don't want to go back to before all of this, Josh. I'm not the same. We're not the same." She shifted the machine into the crook of one arm, balancing it on her hip, and reached up with her gloved hand to grab his shirt. "My clothes are in that bag. Enough for at least a few days until I can get the rest. I'm not going anywhere, so ask me again."

"Cat..."

"Don't say no. I can't take it."

He couldn't either. Even if he had any inclination left to fight this, he definitely didn't have the heart to. Everything he wanted was literally knocking on his door. "I'm not going to say no, Cat." He leaned over her armful and kissed her forehead, then her lips. "But are you sure? You have to be sure."

"I'm so sure. I've spent years being afraid, Josh. Afraid of looking foolish for believing in something that might turn out to not be real. Afraid of getting attached. Well, it doesn't get much more foolish than standing in the sleet, holding my DeLonghi, and asking to move into your house, and I'm already hopelessly attached. So take my heart or break it, Josh, but do it now because I'm freezing."

He laughed, causing his chest to throb, but it was worth it. This time he wrestled the machine out of her arms and pulled her against his chest, kissing her freezing cold lips. "Come on," he said, tugging the sleeve of her coat.

"Wait! You didn't ask."

"I thought you were freezing. I have pneumonia, you know? Can we do this inside?"

"No. Ask me."

He shook his head, but stepped closer, cupping her face with his free hand. "Move in with me, Cat. All our nights could be like this."

"It's going to be hard to make it work," she said. Her eyes started to water, and her voice trailed. "With our jobs, real-world stuff..."

"Everything's harder than being on vacation."

She nodded, the motion spilling the tears that had gathered in the corners of her eyes. "Not everything."

Cat stood beside him at the sink, brushing her teeth and wearing his pajama pants again. She'd packed enough dresses for the week, but somehow sleepwear had slipped her mind—not that he was complaining.

"I can't believe you brought your own toothpaste," he said around his mouthful.

"Spearmint, Josh. Your peppermint would have been a dealbreaker, just like the coffee maker."

He laughed, nudging her with his hip before rinsing. "Noted."

"So, how are we going to do this?" she asked. "The logistics, I mean." He quirked an eyebrow at her. "Like... finances, closet space. I haven't even filled my drawer yet. I have a lot of stuff."

She finished her own brushing and followed him into the bedroom, where he started pulling the sheets off of his bed. She went around the other side to help.

"Well, you should probably get the groceries," he said. "I don't want to get yelled at for buying your food again."

"Okay, smartass. Where are the clean sheets?"

"Top shelf of the closet. We'll figure all of that out, Cat."

Cat crossed the room and climbed up on the chair beside the closet to reach the top shelf. As she tugged a set of sheets free, a little black box came tumbling down onto the floor. He froze, watching as she hopped down and picked up the velvet container, flipping it around in her fingers.

She looked at him with saucer-sized eyes,

and it was as though someone had lassoed him off of the cloud he'd woken up on and dropped him back onto the hard ground. If anything would make her freeze up again, it was that.

"Josh, when you asked me to move in, were you going to—"

"No," he said, but the quickness of his answer felt like a lie. He had no plan, but it wasn't like he hadn't thought about it. If she'd found that ring a few weeks ago, he might have put it on her finger right then and there. He was glad it hadn't happened that way, though. When he finally did give her that ring, he wanted to be sure he would never have to watch her take it off.

"That was my mother's ring," he explained as she opened the box, revealing the princess cut diamond wrapped in a platinum, filigree setting. He hadn't looked at it in a long time, and a myriad of memories, tangled with the emotion of seeing it in Cat's hand, rushed him.

"Was it Sarah's too?"

"No. Sarah tried to give me hers back after the divorce, but I didn't want it. I told her to keep it, pawn it. Whatever she wanted." He took the box from her, running his thumb over the band. "She didn't want this one."

Cat raised a suspicious-looking eyebrow at him. "Why do you say that?"

"She knew I had it. When we started talking about getting married, she made a point of letting me know she wanted something that was only hers."

"You're kidding." Cat studied him as she took in the story, looking as if she was waiting for a punchline.

"I wish I was. First time I ever went into debt for something. I was twenty-four; I had no business buying a diamond ring, or this house for that matter, but at least I'm getting better use out of the house."

Cat nodded, tracing the band of the ring, and then his hand. "I think it's gorgeous."

"Yeah?" he asked. "It's something you'd wear?" It still felt risky to ask the question, but he wanted to know.

"I'd wear anything you gave me."

His mind went tumbling from that image to a lifetime of complimenting ones before he could stop it. He dared to fantasize a little bit further, picturing her in a long white gown, her hair swept away from her neck. He handed the box back to her and cupped her cheek. "I want that one day," he said. "Does that scare you?"

"No. Not at all."

"Good. There is something in that closet for you, actually."

"Oh, yeah?"

"Your Christmas present."

"Oh! I actually have yours too. It's in my car." She jumped up and ran to the door, slipping her winter coat over her pajamas.

When she returned, she was holding a red envelope, and he handed her a box wrapped in silver paper. She took it and sat down on the sheetless bed, tearing through the wrapping. When she got to the sturdy cardboard box filled with tissue paper, she waded through the crinkly mess until her eyes flew open wide. "Josh! How on earth?"

"I tried to get the buyer to keep them intact," he said, "but they had their mind made up about ripping them all out. I figured this was the next best thing. Jim cut it down for me."

She reached into the box and pulled out the wooden angel statue that had hung on the wall at the Abbott Building for a century. He'd taken it to one of the carpenters he worked with and had it affixed to a wooden base with a little gold plaque that listed the date it was built.

"This is—" Her sentence caught in her throat. "Thank you."

He kissed the top of her head, taking the seat beside her. "You're welcome."

She handed him the envelope. "They're baseball tickets. Right behind home plate. Your team is playing my dad's team. He wants to go with you, and I thought you might like that. The game's in June." Her eyes were still on the statue, and she was tracing the wooden details with her thumb. She didn't see the way he had to press his thumbs into his eyes to keep them from watering. A game with her dad, six months into the future—had she even realized what that meant when she bought them?

"Cat." She finally looked up at him, grinning. "Thank you."

"You're welcome." She laughed when he pulled her into him and squeezed hard.

Thirty-eight

6 months later

"CONGRATULATIONS!" MINNIE SET A TRAY of brownies on the kitchen island and gave Cat a hug. "I'm so happy for you. How's it feel?"

"Um, not so different yet." Cat laughed. It had only been a few weeks since she found out she passed the bar exam, and it was all still sinking in. She'd insisted on waiting until she was actually promoted at work before letting Josh throw this party, still somewhat leery of jinxing anything. Somehow, though, even if it was years late according to her original plan, she still had the overwhelming feeling that she needed to become the person she was now before any of her success would mean this much.

"Well, thanks for letting us celebrate with you. The house looks amazing, by the way. You really put your mark on it."

"Just a little. Josh always had good taste."

"Still, it needed some color. It looks happier."

She handed Minnie a glass of wine and gestured for her to head out to the yard. They passed through the sunroom—the only place where Cat had made any real changes. Josh had given her carte blanche on decorating when she moved in, but she wasn't just being kind, she loved his house from the minute she saw it. This room, though, she liked to think she'd rescued from neglect. She'd replaced the old wooden patio set that Josh had furnished it with with the couch from her condo, and keeping with the understated boat-house thing he had going on in the rest of the house, she'd added some nautical lanterns for mood lighting and a pallet and glass coffee table that was currently covered with her laptop and case files. She hadn't taken him up on sharing his office space, preferring the bright, natural light the sunroom offered. The wooden statue from the Abbott Building sat on a bookshelf, along with a few other mementos. It was her favorite spot, and if the night hadn't have been so warm, she might have crammed everyone in there for dinner.

Josh liked being outside, though, so they kept walking through the screen door and down the concrete steps to the backyard. Josh, Dylan, and Adam were standing around the grill, while Shawn and Mattie tossed a football in the grass. Josh caught her eye as she crossed the small patio to the fire pit, smiling at her.

"Minnie!" Emma squealed, jumping up from

her seat to give her a hug. Just like Cat had predicted, the two got along like gangbusters. Since Emma had found out she was pregnant with a little boy, they'd even begun spending time with each other outside of these little group gatherings.

"Hey, Emma," Minnie replied, hugging her back. "And Dani. Where's Sonya?"

Dani stood to greet Minnie as well, clinking their wine glasses together. "She's on vacation with her man. We're hoping she's coming back with a ring."

Minnie turned to Cat. "Wow," Minnie said, pulling up a seat. "Well, I hope it happens. Weddings are the best."

Cat dropped into one of the wooden Adirondack chairs, pulling her knees up to her chest. She looked over at Josh again, smiling when she saw he'd joined the football game. He snatched the ball out of the air, pretending to fall to a fit of laughter from Mattie.

"Maybe Cat and Josh will give us one," Emma said, sharing a mischievous look with Minnie.

"God, this again?" Dani rolled her eyes. "Didn't Maria teach you anything? Don't push Cat. She's emotionally unstable; she's liable to fall."

Cat frowned. "Says the last single one in the group. Dani's putting my legacy to shame with all the guys she turns down."

"Like Dylan," Minnie said.

Cat oohed annoyingly. Dani and Dylan had been especially celebratory last New Year's Eve, and Cat had been using the incident to get Dani back for years of torment.

Dani kicked her foot. "Just because we're stuck in this group of love birds doesn't mean we have to hook up too."

Emma smirked over her glass of wine. "I give it the summer until they're hooking up."

"What would you like to bet?"

"No," Cat said. "No more bets."

"The fish is great, guys," Emma said, digging into her grilled haddock.

"Catia prepared it," Josh said. "We just threw it on the fire." He nudged her knee with his under the table and watched her blush in the light of the citronella candles flickering down the length of the picnic table.

Dani took a bite and shook her head. "Josh, if you even knew how much Ramen this girl ate in college. Now she's making her mother's Soupa and preparing haddock. You put her in a house with a real kitchen, and all of a sudden she's Barefoot Contessa."

Josh laughed but watched Cat carefully out of the corner of his eye. So far, she'd seemed just as confident as she said she was in their new life together, and now was not the time for her to be spooked by an offhand comment. She was smiling though, a look of self-satisfaction on her face as the rest of the table chimed in with their compliments to the chef.

When dinner was finished, everyone moved to the firepit. The breeze off the water that was keeping the temperature comfortable made the flames flit and dance almost in time to the soft music pumping from the kitchen window.

Cat was perched on his knee. He set the beer he'd been drinking down in the grass beside him and clasped his hands around her stomach. The hot summer night and the whole group together had him feeling nostalgic. Or maybe it was the weekend they had planned. He and Cat were leaving the next morning for four days in Virginia Beach. That trip a year ago had changed his life, and he was hoping this one would too.

"It's a beautiful night to be by the water," Dani said, taking a deep breath of the salt-tinged air through her nose. "You really do live in paradise."

"You thinking of making the move?" Dylan asked, flopping down beside her. Josh shared a look with Cat. Dylan had been trying to close that deal for a year now to no avail. Cat shook her head discreetly and leaned her head on his shoulder. Just like the first time she'd done it, everyone else disappeared.

"Babe," Cat called from the bathroom, ribbons of impatience threading through the honey of her voice. The shower had been running for ten minutes now, and the fruity scent of her shampoo was already wafting throughout the room. She'd clearly started without him.

After another hour or so of celebrating, Josh had not-so-smoothly suggested it was time to end the portion of the night where he had to share her. They'd seen everyone out, done a quick clean up, and now he had one more thing to do before he could finish his night the way he wanted to.

"I'm coming." He pulled his t-shirt over his head with one hand, still tossing last-minute items into the suitcase that lay open on their bed—sunglasses, deodorant, Cat's overflowing bag of toiletries that wouldn't fit in her own case. When he'd filled it beyond reasonable capacity, he peeked around the open bathroom door to make sure she was still behind the curtain.

Satisfied by the sound of Cat's humming, Josh moved stealthily over to his closet and reached around under the linens. With one more glance over his shoulder, he pulled out the last thing he needed to pack.

The little velvet box snapped open with a push of his thumb, and he inspected his mother's ring. He'd asked Cat's father for his blessing when they'd spent the day at the baseball game, and Carlos had agreed without hesitation. Josh had it polished and re-sized right after, and the platinum and diamonds flashed as he turned it beneath the soft light of their bedroom. A reassuring wink.

The next day he would pack it into his Jeep, and they would head off to the tiny little patch of sand where it all started. There'd been a moment since then when he'd thought this wasn't going to happen. A moment where he'd questioned why he was meant to find this woman just to see her slip away, but they'd come back stronger than ever. Having Cat full time was better than he imagined and he needed to tie that up with a promise

"You're not going to have any hot water," she sang.

Josh smiled, closing the box and tucking it into the inside pocket of his luggage. He stepped out of his shorts, leaving them in a puddle on the floor, and followed the sound of her humming. He swung open the curtain, startling her, and she screamed, then giggled, slapping her wet palm against his chest.

"So impatient," he joked.

She whipped her wet hair over her shoulder and moved aside so he could step under the stream. "I've been waiting for you forever."

"Me too."

Acknowledgments

Some of my favorite things to do include reading, writing, and fangirling over t.v. shows. It was the combination of those things that brought me to a group of women who changed the course of my life.

As the dedication in the front of this book hints, I have a writing group chat—or should I say, multiple chats. But they're not like every chat. This chat is full of the most amazing women you'll ever meet. They're badass friends who will cheer for you, fight for you, and be that voice in the darkest times of self-doubt, whispering: "Shut up and finish your book before I kick your ass." None of this—NONE OF THIS—would be possible without them. I wouldn't have written this book, let alone had the balls to publish it if it wasn't for them. So to Sophia, Nat, Cici, Jordyn, Nattah, and Demi—thank you for being bright shining lanterns of hope on the dark and sometimes scary path to pursuing my dreams.

Twin, thanks for a hundred Instas, and a thousand collages, and a million character development discussions. The Twinbox is where a lot of this came about and I'll never forget that.

To my Village, there was a very distinctive moment when 'I want to be a writer' me became 'I want to be an author' me, and it was time to confess this scary dream to a group of women who have known many versions of me over the years. It was on our trip to Portsmouth, at a dark pizza place, with lots of cocktails when I told you about this dream I had. Even then, a little voice inside my head said: "you don't have it in you".

But the five of you said, much louder and much more emphatically, "I see this in you". That meant the absolute world. To Suna, Laurie, Pam, Haley, and Rachel—you are my family. Your families are my family. This Village is my happy place.

To my husband and boys, the time it took me to write this book came directly from you and I can't express how grateful I am for that generosity. TJ, from the minute I said I wanted to do this, you were fully on board. Whether you were not-so-jokingly asking me why I was in my chat and not writing, or supporting without question every decision I made along the way, your belief in me means more than you'll ever know. Anytime I've had to do a hard thing in life, you just believed that I could and that made me believe that I could. By the way, bearing you two children is now only the second hardest thing I've ever done.

To my Aunt Gail who brought me champagne and a card when I published my first paid article—thank you for celebrating my successes even when they felt small. It got me to the big ones.

To my amazing illustrator, Leni Kauffman, thank you for bringing my characters to life. This cover is my dream in color. To Matthew Hanover, my indie author mentor (check out his book: Not Famous) thank you for all of your help. To Streetlight Graphics for their awesome formatting and many emails.

And to all the readers who know me as Tigerwalk, you are the reason I wanted to do this. This book is for you.

Coming Soon

The Rules

Don't miss book two in the
Summer Nights Series: The Rules!

Featuring a bonus epilogue to The Catch.

Pre-order Summer 2020

Follow me on Twitter, Facebook, and Instagram, or subscribe to my website for
updates, release info, and cover reveals.
www.laurenhmae.com

Made in the USA
Middletown, DE
25 May 2021